Born in County Wexford, Andrew Hughes was educated at Trinity College, Dublin. A qualified archivist, he worked for RTE before going freelance. He lives in Dublin.

You can discover more about the author at http://andrewhughesbooks.com

THE CORONER'S DAUGHTER

1816: A rare climatic event has brought frost to July in Dublin — a city stirred by zealotry and civil unrest, torn between evangelical and rationalist dogma. Amid the disquiet, a young nursemaid in a pious household conceals a pregnancy and then murders her newborn. Rumours swirl about the identity of the child's father, but before an inquest can be held, the maid is found dead. When Abigail Lawless, the eighteen-year-old daughter of Dublin's coroner, by chance discovers a message from the maid's seducer, she is drawn into a world of hidden meanings and deceit. Pushing against the restrictions society places on a girl her age, she pursues an increasingly dangerous investigation. And watching from the shadows is a sinister figure who she believes has killed twice already, and is waiting to kill again . . .

ANDREW HUGHES

THE CORONER'S DAUGHTER

Complete and Unabridged

CHARNWOOD
Leicester

First published in Great Britain in 2017 by
Doubleday Ireland
an imprint of Transworld Publishers
Dublin

First Charnwood Edition
published 2018
by arrangement with
Transworld Publishers
Penguin Random House
London

The moral right of the author has been asserted

A catalogue record for this book is available
from the British Library.

ISBN 978–1–4448–3644–8

Published by
F. A. Thorpe (Publishing)
Anstey, Leicestershire

Set by Words & Graphics Ltd.
Anstey, Leicestershire
Printed and bound in Great Britain by
T. J. International Ltd., Padstow, Cornwall

This book is printed on acid-free paper

For Trish

1

For my eighteenth birthday, Father promised me the hand of a handsome young man, which he duly delivered mounted in a glass bell-jar. The gift-box had been waiting for me in the parlour, neatly tied with a single black ribbon. Firelight danced along the curve of the glass as I held it up. The bones, blackened at their joints, were closed over in a loose grip. The index finger and thumb curled upwards, like a figure pointing in some old Italian painting.

Father said, 'Can you believe they were going to throw that away from the storage room in York Street?'

I tilted the jar so the forefinger moved ever so slightly, as if it wanted to tap against the glass. 'How old is it?'

'No one was sure, though I seem to remember it being there when I was a student.'

'I thought you said that he was young and handsome.'

'Ah, well, I can tell these things.'

I glanced at him. 'Is that so?'

'It's the ratio of the distal and middle phalanges,' he said, flexing his own fingers. 'A dead certainty.'

I spent the morning finding it a home. Mrs Perrin wouldn't allow it in the parlour, and the bookcases in the study were full, so I placed the jar on a shelf in my bedroom, nudging it between framed portraits of John Hunter and Edward Jenner. Both had been frontispiece etchings, which I'd removed with the aid of a ruler and one of Father's scalpels. On my desk, a raven's quill lay across an unsigned letter. I'd meant to show that to Father earlier, so I fetched my shawl, hoping to catch him before he became ensconced in his work. I glanced out of my window. Frost still lingered on the lawn, and his footprints were visible leading to the mews at the bottom of the garden.

We called it Father's little charnel house, but from the outside it looked quite cheery — almost a house in its own right, with grey slates and red bricks and ivy crowding the sash windows. The stables took up the ground floor. Newton and Boyle lifted their heads above the half-doors as I passed by the carriage and cadaver cart. The rooms upstairs had once been home for the coachman and his family, and even now whenever a new case arrived, Father liked to direct the pall-bearers up to 'the living quarters'.

Its front office was sparse, just a few desks and shuttered cabinets, and a long worktable in the middle of the room. Ewan was there, seated in the corner and writing in a ledger. His pen stilled. We both waited for the other to speak, then began to greet each other at once, then stopped and fell silent. I said, 'I was just looking . . . '

'He is in the dissecting room.'

'Oh.' The only room that I was not allowed to enter.

Ewan noticed the letter in my hand. 'But I can

deliver that to him if you wish.'

'Do you mind if I wait instead?'

'No,' he said. 'Not at all.' He seemed ready to find me a chair, but I hoisted myself up to sit on the edge of the examination table. Ewan cast his eyes over the work surface, before returning his attention to the ledger.

Father's assistant was a young man from the Scottish Lowlands who had come to Dublin to study medicine at Trinity. His second year would begin in the autumn, but for several months he had worked alongside Father for practical experience. Ewan was tall, a few inches taller than me, with slim fingers, a thicket of chestnut hair, and eyes with a downward, wistful slant. He would often work late into the evening, and from my room I'd see candlelight flickering in the windows at the foot of the garden.

Father emerged from the dissecting room bearing a tray covered in white cloth. He smiled when he saw me, pushed the door closed with his heel and placed the tray on a side table.

I slipped from the bench and held my letter out. 'Can you sign this?'

'What is it?' he said, reaching for his spectacles.

'A letter to the editor of the Royal Society.'

'Your observations on the sunspots?'

'Among other things.'

Once the glasses were perched on his nose, he took the page and held it close to his face. 'Abigail, did I not forbid you from writing to the Royal Society?' His lower lip protruded as he tilted the page towards the light. 'After last time.'

'No, you only forbade me from forging your name.'

'Oh, yes. That was it.'

I went to the table where the covered tray had been set down. Ewan stood next to it, filling a glass bowl with water from a pewter jug.

I said, 'What's this?'

'I'm not sure I should — '

'A very sad case. Came in yesterday.' Father spoke while continuing to read, the corners of his mouth downturned. He frowned at the letter. 'Are you sure this figure is correct?'

'I checked it twice. May I take a look?'

Ewan gripped the side of the tray between his thumb and forefinger. 'Really, I am not at all — '

'You may.'

The edge of the cloth was thick because of the double-fold of the hem. I waited for Ewan to remove his hand and then drew the fabric aside.

Two small organs sat in the middle of the tray lying perpendicular to one another. They were squat with a slight tapering, appeared dry to the touch, and were coloured a strange blend of pallid brown and red, with tinges of green and blue.

'Lungs,' I said. 'The lungs of an infant.'

Father dipped a pen in ink and signed his name to the letter. 'A new-born boy.'

'Brought from the Rotunda?'

'No. There was an incident in the home of Mr Nesham in number forty-four.'

I knew of the man — a middle-aged barrister who lived across the square with his young wife and toddler daughter. The family would take

4

strolls together in the sheltered paths of Rutland Gardens, the girl swaddled against the unseasonable cold.

I looked down at the tray. 'Was this . . . his son?'

'Oh no, no.' Father paused and pursed his lips. 'Well, I presume not.'

He said that the child belonged to a young servant first employed by the Neshams as a nursemaid. 'In the past few weeks, Mr Nesham came to suspect that the maid was in the family way, though the girl denied it. On Sunday she took to her bed complaining of sickness, with symptoms so severe that a doctor was called, and he found that she had given birth within the previous twenty-four hours.'

Father placed his pen nib-first in its upright holder. 'The girl said the child fell from her, early in the morning while she happened to be out of bed. He was already dead, or died when he struck the ground, and she was so distraught, and felt so forlorn, that she bundled him up and dropped him in the Blessington Street Basin.'

The basin was a city reservoir not far from here. Father paused in his account and came to the table. 'Mr Weir, put some more water into that beaker. Up to the gallon.'

Ewan poured until the level reached a small marker etched in the glass.

'Did they find the child in the reservoir?' I said.

'No, there is more to it.' He straightened his shoulders and cleared his throat. 'But first, you may have noticed, Mr Weir, that the lungs are not displayed in their true position. They are back-to-front and top-to-bottom. So,' he said, raising an index finger, 'how can we tell the left from the right?'

Ewan blinked twice, and bent lower to peer at the tray. 'Yes,' he said quietly, 'the way to distinguish the lungs.' He folded his arms across his chest. 'The distinct features of the left and right . . .'

I began tapping my thumb against the corner of the table. 'Where did they find the baby if not the reservoir?'

'Come now, Ewan,' said Father, eager for his pupil to get the answer. 'We went over this just a few weeks ago.'

After more of his humming, I pointed into the tray. 'That one was on the left. It contains the cardiac notch and has no middle lobe.'

'Abigail, the question was for Mr Weir.'

'But I want to hear the rest of the Nesham story.'

'Ah, yes. Well, before he asked the authorities to trawl the city basin, Mr Nesham decided it best to search the maid's room. The child was discovered wrapped in a rug and concealed beneath the bed. As Mr Nesham unfolded the bundle, he said to the girl that he hoped she had done no violence to the child, and she replied, 'Oh sir, you will soon see.' He found the boy with his throat cut, and a penknife lying on his breast.'

I glanced again at the two tiny lungs, stark against the metal tray. 'She murdered her own baby?'

'That is the assumption. Though the maid

insists the child was dead-born; that she had taken the blade to cut the navel string, and at that moment, when she saw the consequences of her sin and shame, such was her state of mind that she did not know her actions.'

Ewan's face was solemn. 'That is hardly a credible claim.'

'No,' said my father. 'But since it could spare her being charged with murder, it is one that deserves to be tested.'

He drew the glass bowl towards him and placed an oil-lamp beside it. The water was a bit cloudy, with tiny particles swirling this way and that as if they'd been startled by the light.

Father picked up each lung in turn and slipped them into the water, as Mrs Perrin would drop fillets of meat into a pan. The organs drifted down; tiny bubbles formed and clung to their sides. They slowed as they neared the bottom, bumped against the base of the bowl and each other, before beginning to climb again. They rotated upwards, breached the water's surface and remained afloat, their tops bobbing and glistening in the lamplight.

Ewan and I had leaned down to look closer so our heads almost touched. He said, 'The lungs are buoyant.'

'What does that mean?'

'The baby must have taken a breath.'

Father prodded one so it submerged, and he watched it float to the surface again. 'I would say several. In fact, he may have cried for a few moments. I am surprised that it did not alert the household.'

There had been a hailstorm that night. I'd lain awake listening to the incessant tattoo — the strongest gusts had sounded like boots crunching through gravel.

'She did murder him,' I said.

'Abigail, what have I told you about jumping to conclusions? This only confirms that the child *was* murdered.' He picked up a large perforated spoon, like those used to remove poached eggs, and the lungs drained as he fished them out. 'Though I admit she is by far the most likely culprit.'

'Why would you doubt it?'

Father handed the spoon to Ewan. 'Mr Weir, will you return this to the kitchen, preferably without Mrs Perrin seeing you, then use the water on the orchids in the greenhouse?'

'Yes, sir.'

'I promised Nesham that I would visit his home in the afternoon to tell him what I had found. Then I have a lecture to give.' Father began to look around his office while patting the sides of his pockets. 'Abigail, we also have an appointment in town, so you'd best come with me.'

I thought he'd forgotten — had *hoped* he'd forgotten. An afternoon undisturbed in the library had beckoned. 'Perhaps we should postpone that. Your meeting with Mr Nesham is too important.'

'We cannot. Mrs Meekins is our only remaining option. And when we speak to her, you are not to question her methods.'

'Even if they make no sense?'

8

'Especially if they make no sense.'

Ewan had been watching our exchange, but when I glanced at him, he took up the spoon and withdrew. Father said, 'You know your mother wished for you to develop pastimes that were more . . . typical for a young lady.'

'But — '

'So I want you to be good.'

My letter remained on his desk, and I gently brushed a finger over his signature. The ink didn't smudge, at least not very much, so I folded the sheet into my pocket and said, 'Yes, Father.'

★ ★ ★

My bedroom was on the second floor of our house in Rutland Square, bought by my father just before I was born, reflecting his intention then to have a large and sprawling family. But that was not to be. Since there was no shortage of space, I had been given my own room from an early age: a wide chamber with two tall windows and a high ceiling, which I grew into like a hand-me-down dress. I lay reading on my bed for much of the morning, though occasionally I had to leaf back a page or two when my mind would wander to the infant in Father's workrooms.

Clarissa called on me before noon and suggested we while away an hour at the art exhibition in Hawkins Street. By the time we set off, a fog had settled over the city, lending each shop window a candlelit glow. The mist drifted over the Liffey and swallowed up the masts moored outside the Customs House.

Clarissa and I had been friends since childhood, ever since the day I whispered an answer in her ear as she floundered in Sunday school. We were the same age, give or take a few months, and though she was the daughter of our pastor, Rev Egan, Mrs Perrin was rather wary of her influence. Clarissa suffered from anaemia, and had been prescribed iron-rich stout by her physician. Early on, she began saving up the bottles in order to share them with me. She would smuggle the stout beneath bundles of cotton in her embroidery basket, and we would sip and chat and giggle at our boldness. At first I told her not to, since they were intended to make her feel better, but she said not to be silly; after all, she liked having a pale complexion.

In the carriage, she sat huddled in her fur-lined pelisse, and looked at the sky with displeasure. 'If the summer continues like this, Abby, I am resolved to move to East India, or the Carolinas.'

'You would soon complain of the heat,' I said.

'Never.'

I followed her gaze. Back in the spring, almost overnight, a dry fog had crept over the city, and had lingered ever since despite the buffeting of wind and rain. Electrical storms had become frequent, discharging so much forked lightning that people thought the skies must clear, that the atmosphere would be diffused and spent like the inside of a Leyden jar. But each time, we rose to discover the arid mist still in place, dimming and reddening the sun, and making the black dots scattered about its disc quite clear to the naked eye.

I turned back to Clarissa. 'What about all the suitors you would leave broken-hearted?'

'I would be sure to remember them with great fondness.'

The carriage slowed as we neared the Society of Arts, a handsome building on a narrow side street. A queue had formed at the entrance, but another group of people were standing nearby, men and women all dressed in black. The men wore coats fastened with metal hooks instead of buttons, and a white cravat tucked beneath the collar.

Clarissa said, 'The Brethren.'

I had seen their members quite often of late, standing outside church railings, or handing out leaflets beneath Nelson's Pillar. They were led by a preacher named Mr Darby, who had arrived in the city the year before, and as the weather became ever worse, their numbers seemed to grow. They conducted strange rites in public — dark processions that wound through the streets, and baptisms by immersion in the sea.

Clarissa said, 'My father has come to dislike these evangelicals. Though I think he is mostly saddened at losing members of his own congregation. The Bowens, the Neshams, the Walkers, they have all been seduced away.'

'The Neshams?'

'Yes,' she said. 'They were among the first.'

We alighted from the carriage and joined the queue. The Brethren remained silent, casting cold stares in our direction until we paid for our tickets and entered the hall.

The exhibition room was warm and brightly lit by tall, arched windows. Every inch of wall from floor to ceiling was covered in paintings, huge pastorals and battle scenes in gilded frames, small portraits of dogs and children, all fitting together like the pieces of a puzzle. Men and women wandered the floor, pausing beneath a particular canvas, or talking together on sofas in the middle of the room. Smaller galleries were attached to the main hall, dedicated to the sciences, geology and engineering. One contained pillars taken from the Giant's Causeway, and a polished white opal enclosing a drop of water. Another displayed pieces of fossil, all neatly arranged and labelled, and antlers from a giant elk found in a Kilkenny bog.

Clarissa preferred new paintings to old relics, and so we stayed in the main hall, pointing out pictures that caught our fancy. One showed a young woman reclining in a woodland. She wore nothing except for some diaphanous material that covered her legs, and she rested her head in the crook of her arm. Her skin was pale, and the trees in the background were dark and forbidding.

We regarded it for a few moments, and I said, 'She must be freezing.'

Clarissa smiled and tilted her head. 'I wonder what Mrs Hone would make of it.'

When we were younger, we had attended drawing lessons together at a house in Merrion Square. An old master portraitist taught local

12

boys in the use of oils, while his wife, Mrs Hone, gave lessons in watercolours to three girls: myself, Clarissa, and Edith Gould from Fitzwilliam Square. Mrs Hone referred to us as her Three Graces, and we spent many warm afternoons wandering the paths in Merrion Park picking flowers for our still lifes. Edith was by far the most talented, and we had remained friends for several years, but neither Clarissa nor I had spoken to her in months. The Goulds had been another family to join Mr Darby's church, and now our paths rarely met.

The final gallery was the hall of statuary, a semicircular room lined with busts and pieces of cast bronze, dominated by three life-size sculptures of Greek gods: Poseidon and Zeus, all twisting torsos and taut muscles, and Aphrodite, partially draped, her head downcast with blank, staring eyes. Each statue stood on its own plinth, and people walked between them. There was some commotion behind us, and I turned to see two members of the Brethren marching through the hall, an older man and a girl of no more than sixteen. They must have barged in without paying, for a curator followed behind them, remonstrating loudly.

The man reached the hall of statues and gazed up at them, his face a mixture of horror and anger. 'We may as well be in the temple of Belial,' he said almost in a whisper, and he faced the crowd. 'Look at you all, revering these devils, these vices of the heathen made manifest. For such things God poured his fire on the Cities of the Plain.'

The curator had caught up, and he said, 'Sir, you must leave. You cannot — '

'And you are the worst of them, sir, to peddle such filth, to allow such wanton and indecent displays, and to young ladies in particular,' he said, pointing in our direction. Clarissa glanced at me, and I saw her mask a smile.

The curator had to catch his breath. He said, 'Decency or indecency, sir, depends entirely on the prurient imagination of the observer. Perhaps that is your cross to bear.'

Other wardens and patrons surrounded the man and, despite his spluttered warnings of God's retribution, they began to escort him towards the door. No one noticed when the girl, most likely his daughter, climbed on to the plinth of Aphrodite. The statue was freestanding, and with the first push it rocked back and forth. People began to yell and point, but too late. With a final shove, the statue lurched and tilted forward, until it toppled over.

It fell to the flagstones with a resounding boom, and was dashed to pieces; luckily, it was not an original, just a plaster cast. Fragments skittered across the floor — a section of her face showing the corner of her lips, and a hand gripping a fold of cloth.

Everyone in the hall looked upon the wreckage in silence, and then at the girl standing in the place of Aphrodite, her hands by her sides, her black dress and white bonnet, and the expression on her face — no fear or guilt or contrition. She gazed back at us, her eyes wide, a smile on her lips, almost in a state of rapture.

The hall was cleared, the girl and her father taken to a local magistrate, and Clarissa and I returned home. I told my father of what had happened over lunch. He pursed his lips and shook his head at the vandalism.

'What a pity,' he said, 'that anyone should have so little regard for the history and art of such an object.'

'If you had only seen her. She seemed so sure of her own righteousness.'

'She is young, Abigail, and may yet look back on her actions with remorse. You must have faith in people's good nature.'

He returned to his workrooms for a while, but by mid-afternoon was ready to see Mr Nesham. Liam was already waiting at the bottom of the steps. He took my hand to help me into the carriage. Father gathered his coat beneath his chin and slid the window shut to keep out a whistling breeze. After a few moments, he said, 'I shall only be speaking to Nesham for ten minutes, if that.'

I watched him sitting with his shoulders hunched, one hand clasping the top of his collar. 'Do you not have your scarf?'

'I may have misplaced it.'

'Mrs Perrin spent a week knitting it.'

'A week? I daresay it'll turn up.'

The carriage turned into Palace Row: the north side of the square, and the most fashionable, since its height gave the houses a view over the city and central gardens. A small

Tuscan temple stood just inside the railings, where porters used to keep sedan chairs back when the Sunday evening promenade was considered the most elegant amusement in the city. Now the doors to the grand granite shelter were padlocked shut.

I removed my own scarf and looped it over Father's shoulders. He told me not to fuss, but still stuffed it beneath the lapels of his coat. 'What about you?' he said. 'You'll catch your death.'

'I don't feel the cold.'

'I was saying, that when we get to Mr — '

'I know. Ten minutes.'

The Lying-In Hospital took up the south side of the square in its entirety, and the gardens were used to provide for its upkeep, for the gentry would pay fivepence for open-air concerts, with tea rooms and card assemblies in the Rotunda. I used to look out each Sunday evening at the gaily dressed couples strolling the paths. Hundreds of coloured lamps festooned the branches, and I'd hear the strains of an army band and snatches of bright laughter. But then my eye would wander to the windows of the hospital overlooking the scene, and I'd imagine the women within, many from the poorer parts of the city, packed in squalid wards with unclean sheets and no ventilation, and mothers cradling those children — one in six — who would not live past their tenth day.

The promenades no longer took place, and not just because of the peculiar weather. A group calling itself the Association for the Discountenancing of Vice had petitioned the hospital to halt the weekly entertainments since they took place on the Sabbath, and the governors complied. Clarissa had said that it was typical: the finest amusement available in the city, shut down just as we were old enough to attend.

When we reached the house, a maid answered the door and brought us up to the front drawing room. It wasn't long before Mr Nesham entered. He stood on the threshold, and said, 'Lawless,' in greeting while holding out his hand. Nesham had a thin, lined face, and a blood-red cravat spilled from the collar of his shirt. He was about to speak again, but then noticed me standing near the window.

Father said, 'My daughter and I have business in town. You do not mind if she waits while we speak in your study?'

'Of course not.' Nesham looked at me squarely. 'I shall have Martha bring you some tea. It's Alice, isn't it?'

'Abigail, sir.'

His eye lingered a moment longer, and I thought of how his wife was only four or five years my senior.

Both men withdrew, and I was left alone to drift about the room, listening to the muted sounds of an unfamiliar house. I looked out over the central garden, and towards the terrace away in the distance, counting the chimneys over the treetops until I fixed on a pair of windows with tendrils of ivy curling about the sills. That used to be my mother's room. On the wall, there hung an oil painting of a man in powdered wig and fur-lined robe. He reminded me of Mr Nesham; something about the eyes. He stood with his

17

shoulders back, a gavel clutched in one hand and a Bible in the other, his finger inserted at a certain page. I looked closer, but there was no verse or passage visible in the gap.

The door of the drawing room opened and the maid, Martha, backed in bearing a tea-set on a silver tray. She was followed a moment later by the mistress of the house. Mrs Nesham was dressed in the garb of the Brethren, a black dress with white lace around the neck, and she carried three letters fanned in her right hand, their stamped red seals unbroken.

She stopped when she saw me. 'Who is this?'

The maid said, 'The coroner's daughter, ma'am.'

I straightened my shoulders and clasped my hands demurely in front, as my mother had taught me.

'Martha, if anyone calls, I shall be busy until four. Have you checked on Lucia?'

'She's still napping.'

'And where is Mr Darby?'

'He is taking some air in the back garden. Shall I fetch him?'

'No, I shall look for him there.' Without further comment, Mrs Nesham left the room. Martha placed the tea on a nest of tables and went to follow her mistress. She pointed to a pull cord, saying, 'If you need anything else, miss, just ring,' with a demeanour that suggested such an action would not be looked upon kindly.

The minutes passed and there was no sign of Father. We would miss our appointment if he did not come soon. Martha had left the door ajar, and I pulled it wider. Nothing stirred in the landing. Across the hall, just at the edge of hearing, Father and Mr Nesham were speaking in the study.

Nesham was saying, 'Emilie had always been a fine servant. Meek and conscientious. It has been a dreadful shock. Especially for my wife — to know that Lucia had been nursed by a . . .' There was a pause then, and the clink of a decanter. 'When I questioned her, she told me of an intimacy with a fisherman in Gorey while visiting her family last year. I wrote to Mr Casey on Monday. I tell you it wasn't easy; such a thing for a man to discover about his daughter.'

A door opened and banged shut in the ground floor, causing my heart to leap, but there was no other movement in the stairwell.

'They confined her in the Rotunda, though considering what you found, it won't be long before they take her to Newgate.'

After another pause, Nesham asked about the proceedings at inquest. He said, 'There are some who may be concerned at what might be aired at a public hearing.' His voice became muffled, as if he'd turned and moved to another part of the room, or perhaps he just spoke more quietly. No matter how I listened, I could hear no more of the conversation.

The carpet on the stairs was dappled with colour from a stained-glass window at the top of the return: four panels depicting each of the seasons as classical figures. I went to look closer. Spring was a fair-haired maiden in a flowing blue robe; Winter an old man with a bundle of sticks

19

gathered against his shoulder. A line of poetry in a garland of holly read, *See, Winter comes to rule the varied year.*

The window looked out over the back yard, where a man in a dark morning coat was wandering along the path, his starched collar turned up against his chin. He stopped beneath a tree and reached towards a low-hanging leaf, holding it for a moment as if feeling its texture. Then he tugged on it, bending the bough until the leaf was plucked away.

Before now, my glimpses of Mr Darby had been fleeting. He was younger than I had thought, with little or no grey in his dark hair, and his shoulders were square.

Mrs Nesham came into view, and Darby watched her approach without offering a greeting. She had left the house without a shawl, and she gripped both her elbows. They spoke for a few moments, standing close to one another like dancers at the beginning of a set. She gestured towards the house, and he swept his eyes up and over the windows. I took a step back in case he saw me. When I peeked again, they had turned to walk away, and I watched until the path became hidden by a trellis of creeping vines.

I should have returned to the drawing room, but didn't relish the prospect of sitting alone beneath the gaze of Nesham's ancestor. In the floor above, one of the doors was half open, and I glimpsed Martha next to a crib holding the Neshams' daughter, Lucia. The child was tired and ill-tempered, attempting to pull her

20

sleeping-cap away while Martha hummed strains from a lullaby.

At the end of the hall, another open door revealed the foot of a bed, its thin mattress undressed and stained, and I knew that this had to be the room of the nursemaid, Miss Casey. I went to look closer. A simple locker stood between the bed and a cast-iron fireplace, with a large closet in one corner. The room was tranquil and still, and I held my breath to listen. How different it would have been a few nights before: a storm blowing outside; the lonely, frantic labour; the violence done to the child and the grim purpose in concealing his body.

The bedside locker was empty except for a small King James Bible bound in black leather. I leafed through the pages, and was about to return it when I noticed an inscription in ink on the title page:

My Dearest Emilie, To light the way . . .

There was an elaborate monogram of three initials, embellished with swashes and ribbons and wide figure eights. One of the letters was an R, but I couldn't tell if that denoted a Christian, middle or surname. The handwriting belonged to a man, but a close relative wouldn't have signed off so formally, and I didn't think the sentiment or penmanship belonged to a fisherman from Gorey. I held the cover open with my palm to grip the thin sheet by its corner, but then I paused. Wouldn't tearing a page from a Bible be deemed a desecration?

The binding in the book was rather loose so the page ripped out easily. I folded it twice, placed it in the pocket of my dress, and surveyed the room more closely. There were dull brown stains in the knots and gaps of the floorboards. Inside the wardrobe, the maid's clothes hung from a rail and her undergarments were stacked on shelves. The corner of a wicker basket peeked from behind a bundle of petticoats.

It held knitting materials: balls of wool and needles, newly made articles of baby clothes, as well as flannels and calico. A tiny cardigan of light grey wool was unfinished; the needle inserted in the looped stitches; a trail of yarn attached to the ball, still unsnipped. I looked over to the bed and imagined the maid working by candlelight during the cold evenings, hastily concealing the basket whenever anyone entered the room. I delved through some of the completed items: stockings and mittens, coats and hoods — hours and hours of labour. How could the girl's intentions towards her child have changed so drastically?

I'd lingered too long. Footsteps approached in the hallway, and, with the door wide open, I was sure to be spotted. What could I say, except that I'd come up out of curiosity, but my intrusion would reflect badly on Father. Perhaps he would forgive me when I told him what I'd found.

Then Lucia let out a piercing cry. Martha muttered and walked back towards the nursery. I replaced the basket and crept to the door, watched as the maid entered the child's room, then darted silently to the main staircase of the house, heedless now of running into anyone else.

The drawing room was as I'd left it. I sank

into one of the sofas to catch my breath, just as Nesham and my father entered the corridor. I sat up to compose myself. Then I saw that my cup was untouched, still full to the brim. I poured the tea into a potted houseplant beside the armrest, and held the empty cup in my lap as the gentlemen walked in.

Nesham was first through the door, and I thought his face betrayed a hint of displeasure or irritation, but the look was fleeting. Father followed after, and he said, 'My dear, we're sorry to have kept you.'

I placed the cup on a side table, smiled sweetly and said, 'I was hardly conscious of the time.'

2

Father was in a rush to get to his lecture. He quickly introduced himself to Mrs Meekins before heading off, and I was left in the old widow's clutches for well over an hour. The lesson wasn't all that taxing. We sat beside her six-octave piano while she described her style of tuition, as well as exercises to master phrasing and musical expression. At one point she said, 'Show me your hands, my dear.'

Her skin was cold and dry to the touch. She noted that my fingers were slender enough to fit between the black keys to play the tail ends of the ivories, but then she tutted. 'A shame that they're so bereft of muscle.'

I was about to mention that the muscles controlling the fingers were in the palms and forearms, but thought better of it.

'Your mother's were the very same,' she said.

'You taught my mother?'

'Oh, yes. When she was just a girl. Not much older than you are now.'

I looked around and imagined my mother in her youth entering the room, sitting here just like me, perhaps at this very piano. I ran my fingers along the grain of the key slip.

Mrs Meekins said, 'She played with great tenderness, and learned many tunes by ear, but she was too impatient to master proper technique. I hope you do not take after her.'

I had never heard my mother play, even though we always had a piano in the parlour. 'People say that I am more like my father.'

By the time the lesson had finished, the air outside had grown colder and a heavy rain was turning to sleet. Liam was waiting with the carriage, a welcome haven from the chill wind. People on Sackville Street hurried to take shelter, some looking for refuge under the granite plinth of Nelson's Pillar. The gate porter kept them at bay. It cost tenpence to climb the internal staircase and look upon the city from the viewing platform, and he was determined that none should sneak up without paying.

I was eleven when that monument was completed. Father and I had joined the crowds to watch the statue hoisted into place. There was bunting on the GPO, and the union flag billowed overhead. Nelson had listed as he was lifted up. Even then I'd imagined the consternation if he slipped from his ropes at so great a height to be dashed against the pavement. I was a little disappointed when he was set securely atop the column, as those around us cheered.

We arrived at the College of Surgeons, a grey building of arched windows overlooking St Stephen's Green. I peered through the railings into the park. This time of year, there should have been a promenade of ladies in light muslin dresses and opened parasols, but today the paths were empty. I settled back in the seat-cushions and waited for Father to emerge.

He had been giving demonstrations in the college for years — to prepare new surgeons for what they would face in the law courts if ever called to testify. Father had been elected coroner for Dublin's north wards at a time when it was more common to appoint a solicitor or barrister. When he was a young surgeon, he had given evidence at several inquests and was often troubled by their failure to identify cases of murder.

He explained it to me once, how coroners from the legal tradition were quick to side with their brother lawyers during the examination of doctors, so that the significance of medical testimony was routinely undermined. And those doctors, my father excluded, were often cautious in their evidence, fearful that a frank opinion later dismissed at trial could lead to a loss of reputation.

After he was elected, he did all he could to remind lawyers that they were permitted in his court as a courtesy — they had no right to be there, though he never refused a suspect the proper representation. His forthrightness raised the hackles of the legal profession, a sensitive body to begin with, he said. 'They question my grasp of jurisprudence. As if any man or woman of moderate intelligence could not master the laws dealing with my duties in the course of an afternoon. The real problem lies with coroners who have no understanding of forensic science.'

Father would compose his lectures in the parlour at night, and would often ask me to retrieve books from the library, to track down some obscure reference or case study, so much so that I came to know the location of every volume, and at least some of their contents.

A gust of wind caused the sleet to swirl, and grey flecks alighted on the oily surface of a puddle like ash from a bonfire. Father was late, as usual, and poor Liam was sitting out in the weather. If I invited him into the carriage, he would refuse, so I got out instead.

He looked down at me. 'What is it, miss?'

'Father has probably become lost in conversation with a student or some old professor,' I said, the side of my bonnet fluttering against my cheek. 'I shall fetch him.'

I turned and leaped over the puddle, climbed the steps and pushed open the heavy wooden door.

The noise of the wind and clatter of hooves was replaced by a cool, shadowy hush. Trainee surgeons walked through the corridors, satchels and books clasped beneath their arms. Some turned their heads to look at me, for not many girls my age would have been seen in those halls; not many girls at all, except for those carried in lifeless on stretchers.

I followed a passageway that led to a set of double doors. A young man approached, opened them and slipped inside, giving me a brief glimpse of tiered benches rising into the gloom, and the corner of a table in a bright pool of light. I also caught a snatch of my father's voice before it was shut out again. I climbed some stairs in the hallway that led to the upper tiers, pushed one of the doors ajar, and crept through.

Several students sat in the benches before me, but none looked back to see my entrance. Others were dotted about in shadowy rows that filled the circular hall. There were large windows just below the ceiling, the shutters opened in such a way that grey light fell upon the dais at the front of the hall, where oil-lamps and candles illuminated a narrow worktable.

Father stood behind it, his coat removed and shirtsleeves rolled up. A man lay on the table, naked except for a piece of sack-cloth covering his face, and with a gaping hole in his torso, the skin folded back on each side like white linen. I had often seen bodies brought to Father's workrooms, but none like this, none so exposed and undone. I was ready to back out of the room, return to the shelter of the carriage, but I stayed to hear what Father would say.

He referred to the man as 'this poor fellow', and described how he had mistaken mercurial salts for a powder to cure persistent headaches. 'No foul play was suspected,' Father said, 'but if any of you are faced with a similar case, there is a test to establish the presence of poison, in this instance mercury.'

He lifted a glass tube containing a muddy liquid and swirled the contents about as if it were a glass of claret. 'A sample of bile, blood and mucus taken from the man's stomach.'

With metal tongs, he placed the tube over a spirit lamp, allowing the pale yellow flame to lick against the glass. A pungent smell of garlic filled the hall. After a few moments, the fumes began to coat the inside of the tube in a white substance, and when Father held a copper strip above the vapours, it acquired a silvery hue.

28

'If we just look hard enough, gentlemen, if we use the proper techniques, then the truth can be found. Not only that, it is indisputable, and no cleverly formed questions can possibly cast doubt upon it.'

The tip of the copper glinted in the lamplight. It was so pleasing to think that such tiny particles of mercury, dredged up from the dregs of a man's life, could leave such an elegant indicator. I looked around the theatre, expecting the students to be enthralled by the demonstration, but they slouched in their seats, drowsy and indifferent. Father hadn't spoken for a few moments, and I noticed him peering upwards towards the back of the hall where I was standing. He frowned and straightened his lips, but then looked down, perhaps conscious of others following his gaze. He replaced the tongs and the copper, and took a piece of cloth to drape over the body. But then he hesitated, for the cloth wasn't large enough to hide both the internal and external organs. Before he could choose which was the more indecent, I slipped out and made my way back to the carriage.

The rain had let up a little. Liam clambered down and opened the door, and I told him that Father would be a while yet. After a few minutes, students began to emerge from the college in ones and twos, lifting their lapels against the breeze. Father was among the last to leave. He walked towards the carriage slowly, spoke with Liam, then opened the door and climbed in to sit beside me.

He didn't say anything as we set off, just rifled

29

in his satchel to arrange some papers. He closed the buckle and propped the bag on the seat opposite, while I looked at the passing houses.

I heard him take a breath, and say, 'Abigail —'

'I had no idea that the test for mercury could produce such a clear result.'

'Abigail, what were you doing up there?'

'Father, I only went looking for you. I didn't know that you would be working with a cadaver.'

'But why would you stay for so long? You know that you cannot come to places where such things are displayed. It is just not —'

'Fair?'

'Proper.' He still wore the scarf I had given him that morning, and he loosened it around his neck. 'What if others had seen you?'

'I'm sure they could have coped.'

'You know what people are like. Why risk having them say that you are fixated by such morbid subjects?'

'If I were a young man they would say I was fascinated by them.'

A stray dog ran alongside the carriage for a while, snapping at Newton's legs, and I heard Liam yell at it.

Father said, 'You know that I have always been proud of your curiosity.' He removed his hat and placed it on his lap, then tossed it on to the seat next to the satchel. 'It is a great consolation to be able to share my interests with you, but there are other, more important things that I must consider. Especially now that your mother is gone. Your reputation, your future, even matrimony.'

'Father, please —'

He held up his hand. 'I am just mentioning it, for you to be aware. There is no need to discuss it today.'

We remained silent for the remainder of the journey. The rain turned mizzling, then stopped altogether, though the road was still muddy as we approached the house.

I said, 'Father?' and he looked at me. 'Are there other tests like the one you carried out today — tests to detect the presence of poison?'

He said that there were. Though they varied, depending on whether the poison was mineral or vegetable.

'Will you show them to me?'

'If it stops you from sneaking into the anatomical theatre, then yes. After all,' he said, reaching for his hat, 'all the tools we need are here.'

★ ★ ★

The long grey hours of the afternoon slipped by, and the fire dwindled in my room. I took the page from Miss Casey's Bible and laid it flat on my desk, examining the message and signature once again. I thought of showing it to Father, but after our last conversation I did not think he'd appreciate the means by which I'd found it. Besides, what could I say? That because Miss Casey was knitting clothes for her child, she couldn't have murdered him? What did it matter if some gentleman inscribed her Bible? It could have been anyone. For all I knew, it may have been sitting in her drawer gathering dust for years.

From my window I could see the weathervane on the steeple of St George's Church. It had been bent in the storm last week, stuck facing south-west as if mutely pointing towards some unseen threat. At the bottom of the yard, Liam and Mrs Perrin's son Jimmy were rolling a wheel into the stables to make a repair to the cadaver cart. Father and Ewan were still in their workrooms, and would likely remain until evening. That just left Mrs Perrin and Kathy — a parlourmaid who had been part of the household for three years — but they were both hard at work in the kitchen and would leave me undisturbed until the call for supper.

I donned my kid-leather half-boots and the navy pelisse that I usually wore to church, and descended the stairs, listening for any sound of movement. After a final check of the house, I slipped into the street. The sun was still up, visible only as a glare in the clouds above the trees in the park. The curved wall of the Rotunda faced our side of the square, its entrance only a few hundred yards away.

Usually if I was out of the house beyond this hour, it was in a carriage with Father by my side and Liam riding in front. If I walked the streets it was only to accompany my family to church, or Mrs Perrin to the Moore Street markets. Now I felt as if people were regarding me, taking stock of my age and the cut of my coat. In the distance, a man came shambling forwards, stooped and seemingly bound in chains. It was a seller of dog collars, the circular bands all linked together, strapped around his torso and hanging from his belt. A terrier scampered along behind him, untethered and seemingly the happier for it. As he passed, the man raised his hat to me, revealing a freckled, bald pate.

I stopped to wait for a carriage to trundle by. Someone took hold of my wrist, and I twisted about.

Ewan's face was full of concern. 'Miss Lawless, where on earth are you going?'

My relief was fleeting, tempered by an irritation that I'd been followed and that my plan was being jeopardized. I took a breath and disengaged my arm. 'Why were you skulking behind me?'

'I was on my way home for the evening. My rooms are in Great Britain Street.'

'Well, you should continue there.'

'Does your father know that you are out of the house?'

I straightened my mouth and remained silent.

'I must escort you home.'

'No,' I said. 'I'm going to the Rotunda.'

Ewan looked over my shoulder towards the hospital and frowned. 'Are you unwell?'

I held his eye a little longer, and told him that I wished to speak with Miss Casey.

'But . . . that is not your responsibility,' he said. 'It's not your place.' He lowered his voice in an attempt to be authoritative. 'We must return immediately.'

'I am certain she didn't kill her baby on a whim, Ewan. Something or someone induced her to do it.'

He paused, perhaps because his name was

spoken so earnestly. 'Miss Lawless, you must know that this is impossible.'

'I am going to the hospital. Unless you intend to lead me back by the arm.'

'Then I shall have to inform your father.'

'Do as you wish.' And with that, I checked that the road was clear and hurried across.

The wide foyer of the Rotunda echoed with the footsteps of midwives and orderlies. Tall windows cast scant light upon the mosaic floor, and the timber rafters above were lost in shadow. Expectant mothers walked to and fro, or waited in chairs that lined the walls, a few attended by older women, others surrounded by gaggles of young children. I went to a counter situated in the corner and waited for a clerk to glance up. His wide forehead tapered to a narrow chin, and there was a hairline crack in the lens of his spectacles.

'I wish to visit Miss Emilie Casey,' I said, then wondered if my use of the honorific had been indelicate. The man opened a ledger and scanned a list of names beginning with C.

'There is no mention of her,' he said. 'When was she admitted?'

'In the past few days.'

He turned to the back of the book, where there was a jumble of shorter lists for the surgical and infectious wards. One in particular had only two names, which I could see from my side of the counter: Mrs Longsworth and Miss Casey.

'There,' I said, pointing to them.

The clerk looked up. 'That patient is not allowed visitors.'

'It's very important.'

The spine of the ledger creaked as he closed it over, but he said nothing.

'I would not keep her long.'

'There is nothing I can do,' he said. 'Why do you wish to see her?' His eyes narrowed, as if a thought had just occurred. 'How did you even know she was here?'

A voice over my shoulder said, 'Well, which room is she in?'

Ewan had spoken in a distracted manner while looking down at a pocket watch held open at his side.

'I am trying to find out,' I said, 'but this gentleman will not tell me.'

Ewan frowned and stepped up to the counter. 'And what is your name, sir?'

'Gray.' The man let his eyes drift over Ewan's clean-shaven cheeks and willowy neck. 'May I ask yours?'

'I am Mr Weir, the assistant coroner for north Dublin. I need to see a patient on a matter of some importance for a forthcoming inquest.'

'Yes,' the clerk said. 'So this lady said. But that particular patient is — '

'I know who she is, Mr Gray. Emilie Casey from County Wexford; suspected of the murder of her son in the home of Mr Nesham last Sunday evening, and confined here due to postpartum haemorrhage and infection.' He placed his satchel on the counter.

'I was about to say, that the patient is not — '

'We don't have time for this. Is Dr Labatt here?'

The clerk glanced over the rim of his glasses. 'He is on his rounds.'

'Send for him.'

'He's too busy.'

'Of course. But I shall carefully explain the reason for the imposition.'

They regarded each other, and I hoped Ewan would not be the first to look away. Behind us, a hungry infant began to cry, the noise echoing in the vaulted ceiling. The clerk opened a notebook and began to write. 'Mr Weir, was it?' He waved the top of his quill towards me. 'And who is this?'

'My assistant.'

Both the clerk and I raised an eyebrow.

'This girl?'

'Would it have been more appropriate to bring a young man?'

Gray considered this, shook his head and made a further note. He said, 'Miss Casey is in recovery ward B, on the third floor in the western colonnade.'

I fell into step beside Ewan as we climbed the staircase. He kept his eyes straight ahead, but a colour had crept into his cheeks.

'Thank you for coming back, Ewan.'

He said, 'Your father will send me home when he finds out.'

I was about to reassure him, but then a nurse passed on the stairs and we fell silent. Once she got beyond earshot, I said, 'Who is Dr Labatt?'

'The assistant master here. He'll be teaching a class in Trinity when my new term begins in the autumn.' Ewan glanced at me. 'If I am allowed to attend. I knew the clerk wouldn't want to deal with him. He has a severe reputation.'

We reached the third floor and Ewan began to move off to the right. I stopped him by touching his elbow, pointed and said, 'It is this way, I think.' An arched corridor stretched before us, with wards on both sides. The air was stifling, filled with the smells of unwashed bodies and unemptied bedpans.

Each room contained about a dozen beds, with simple wooden cribs at the foot of each. Some of the women appeared sickly and cold and were swaddled in blankets; others were flushed and feverish with the covers drawn down; and a few sat propped up nursing their new-borns. The corridor was busy, and though one or two mid-wives glanced at us, none bothered to stop.

We reached Ward B. Ewan waited at the door and told me not to be long. The room was dimly lit, with patches of damp on the whitewashed walls. Only two of the beds were occupied, but I could tell Emilie Casey at once, for she was the one manacled to the bed frame. She lay with her hand resting on the pillow due to the short span of the chain. Her pretty face was tear-streaked, with sandy hair brushed back on both sides, and her eyes were pressed closed as if in prayer.

I had never been this close to someone accused of murder, and wasn't sure what to expect. Some mark of guilt perhaps. All I saw was a sickly young woman in a tangle of sheets. She could have been any grieving mother.

I spoke her name and she opened her eyes. My light bonnet was similar to those worn by the nurses, though the dark pelisse would have appeared unusual. Emilie squinted and shifted back on to her elbows.

I pulled a chair to the bedside; the harsh sound of its legs scraping on the tiled floor made her flinch. 'Are you feeling all right?' I said. 'Would you like anything?'

She glanced around the room, and then at the bedside table. 'Some water.' Her voice was hushed, the soft *t* barely audible.

I poured her a cup, and the water spilled from the corner of her mouth as she drank, running from her chin on to the bed-clothes. She panted, then placed the cup on the edge of the table beside the glass jug.

She said, 'Who are you?'

I was about to tell her my name, but thought better of it. 'We have never met,' I said. 'But Martha asked me to check on you.'

'You know Martha?'

'I was speaking with her this morning.'

She still regarded me with wary and weary eyes.

'Did you see the child?' she asked.

For a moment, I thought she meant her own, but she was talking about Lucia. 'Yes,' I said, and then remembered something. 'Martha despaired because she wouldn't go down for her nap.'

A half-smile crept over Emilie's lip, but then she covered her face and wept quietly into the crook of her elbow. Just as I was about to lean forward to offer comfort, she whispered, 'Lucia was the only one I told.'

I imagined her playing with the girl in the

Neshams' nursery, and, amidst the baby talk and prattle, confiding in the toddler that she would soon have a child of her own. Did she really believe that the Neshams would allow her baby to be raised in their household; that Lucia might have looked upon the new-born as a half-brother, or at least a playing companion?

'What were you going to name him?'

This time Emilie remained silent, and I thought that I'd said the wrong thing. With her manacled hand, she began to scratch at a loose flake of whitewash on the wall. Crumbs of grey mortar sifted to the floor.

'When I was a girl in Gorey,' she said, 'I had a smaller brother. His hair was almost white, and whenever the wind blew in the thatch he'd cling to me in the dark. He died when he was only three. He was called Morgan.' She brushed some of the dust that had collected at the side of her bed, and then lay still. She no longer seemed able to cry.

'Martha wanted to know who gave you the Bible that was in your room.'

The red marks on her face became more vivid, but she remained silent.

'She saw the inscription, Emilie.'

'It wasn't anyone she knew.'

'Was it — '

'She didn't know him.'

Emilie rolled on to her side and pulled at the blankets. Her manacle scraped along the bed frame.

I spoke her name a few more times, but she didn't stir. The other patient in the ward, Mrs

Longsworth, had woken up. Strands of hair covered her face as she peered at me from her pillow. I stood and replaced the chair by the wall, taking care to lift it this time.

To Emilie, I said, 'I shall try to have Morgan's grave marked. For his name to be put on the cross.'

My bonnet had become loose, and I undid the string to tie it again. When I looked down, she had turned about to face me.

'You can do that?'

'Yes.'

We regarded each other. Perhaps I should have said something more, but nothing seemed appropriate. In a matter of weeks, Miss Casey would be sent to gaol probably for the remainder of her life, or possibly to the gallows. I bent my head and began walking towards the door.

'He was one of the congregation.'

I paused in the middle of the ward. 'Mr Darby's congregation?'

'Every week he would arrive early for their meetings, and we would speak when I brought him tea. No one like him had ever shown interest in me before.'

I wanted to ask his name, but thought she would become quiet again. In the hallway, I could hear Ewan's voice.

'I would go to his home whenever he knew it would be empty. My cousin lived around the corner on Clare Street, so I pretended to be visiting her.'

'Did Martha ever meet him?'

Emilie didn't seem to hear. She pulled against

the manacle so the edge bit into her wrist. 'At first he was happy when I told him. He said that he would talk to his father; arrange everything.' She hadn't blinked for some time, and her eyes had begun to glisten. 'But then he wanted rid of it, and when I refused, he stopped speaking to me. He only sent letters, saying that I had tricked him, led him astray, that nothing grew in me except the consequence of sin and shame. I couldn't even show the letters to anyone. All I could do was read them and burn them.'

There were more voices in the hallway, Mr Gray's among them.

'He said that he was going to take the baby away, place him with the foundlings in Fleet Street.' She wrapped her fingers around the chain, and began twisting her wrist in the cuff, causing the skin to chafe and tear. 'He said he would not allow his child to be raised by someone like me.'

'What was his name, Emilie?'

'What does it matter?'

I reached over to stop the maid from harming herself, but she roughly knocked my hand away.

'How will you be able to mark Morgan's grave?' she said. 'You're just a girl.'

'Because of my father.'

'What about him?'

'He is the coroner.'

Emilie's eyes widened. '*He* sent you here.'

'No.'

'He sent you to ask these questions.' Her voice had become shrill, and she sat up in the bed. 'You lied to me.'

'I didn't mean to.'

'You've lied to me like the others.'

She leaned over to pick up the water jug with her free hand, which she threw with a wide sweep of her arm. The water splashed over my face and the front of my dress, and the jug smashed against the wall, sending shards of lead glass across the room. She shouted, 'You're just like the others.'

Two nurses and a male orderly ran into the ward, bumping against me as they passed. They advanced on Emilie, and the maid cried out as they clasped her arms and pushed her down. The orderly covered her face with his thick hand, but Emilie forced open her mouth and bit down on his fingers. He cursed, and struck her head with his fist, while the nurses pulled at her ears until she released her hold.

I yelled for them to stop, but they didn't listen. Ewan touched my elbow and spoke my name. I turned to see the clerk, Mr Gray, on the threshold of the ward. He stood beside another man who wore a light-blue frock coat. Though Emilie continued to struggle, with her legs exposed and thrashing about, and with a nurse attempting to cover her face with a laudanum-soaked rag, the men in the doorway looked only towards me.

Mr Gray's superior approached. I lowered my eyes and said, 'Please, sir, get them to stop.'

'It's Miss Lawless, is it not?'

I nodded. 'I didn't intend for — '

'My name is Dr Labatt.' Another orderly entered the ward carrying large leather straps to secure Emilie fully to the bed.

Labatt said, 'We have met before, Abigail.'

I looked up and met his eye.

'Though you were quite young.' He surveyed the room again, scraping a fragment of glass over the tiled floor with the toe of his boot. 'I think the time has come to have a word with your father.'

★ ★ ★

It was a sombre procession back to the house. Dr Labatt and I walked in front, my hand in his elbow. He'd insisted I take it, in quite a gentlemanly manner, but I felt uncomfortable doing so, as in any situation where one hasn't the option to refuse. Kathy stared when she opened the door to the three of us. Labatt asked her to fetch my father, and we waited for him in the parlour. I felt like a visitor to my own home. Ewan stood by the fire, his hands behind his back, his chin held upright as if braced by the high knot of his cravat. The doctor examined glazed figurines on the mantelpiece — a series of ladies with wide-brimmed hats and flowing skirts.

'Was your mother a collector, Miss Lawless?'

I said the figures belonged to our housekeeper, Mrs Perrin.

'And she's allowed to place them here?'

The answer to that seemed self-evident, so I remained silent.

My father entered the room carrying an oil-lamp, his brow already creased as if he could not believe the reason for his summons. He looked from me to Ewan, and then greeted Dr

43

Labatt, inviting him to explain what had happened.

The doctor did so, saying that he would have dismissed the affair as youthful high spirits, except there had been several grave breaches of medical and professional practice, not to mention distress caused to a vulnerable young woman. He gestured towards Ewan. 'I can only assume that your assistant took it upon himself to question Emilie Casey, and that he used your daughter for that purpose.'

His assumption was unjust to Ewan of course, but I was stung more by the personal slight. 'That's untrue.'

Father said, 'Abigail, please.'

Ewan had been standing in the same position throughout. 'Mr Lawless, I take full responsibility. There is no excuse. I can only apologize and consent to any punishment you deem — '

'Father, I was the one who wished to speak with Miss Casey. Mr Weir made every effort to dissuade me.'

The doctor said, 'That is not how Mr Gray described it.'

Father held up both hands to appeal for quiet, then closed them together with his fingers in a steeple. He looked at me and said that it didn't matter who had instigated the affair; it had been up to Ewan to call a halt.

I began to protest again, and when I saw his intention to speak over me, I said, 'Do you think me incapable of taking responsibility?'

The corners of his mouth turned down for a moment, and I knew his answer. For how could I be held accountable? What could be *my* punishment except some trifling and temporary loss of favour: denied access to the library, or a trip to the theatre, or a visit from Clarissa?

'Why did you wish to talk to this girl, Abigail?'

With all three men looking at me, my earlier resolve seemed feeble. 'Because I couldn't believe a mother would act with such cruelty to her new-born unless forced by another, and the only way to find that out was to ask her.'

Dr Labatt's legs were crossed at the shins, his hands perched on the head of his cane. He spoke in a tone so disdainful that I knew he couldn't have had daughters. 'Miss Lawless, if you only saw the babies that are brought to my care, those found in sewer pipes and animal pens and frozen ditches, you would know that women of a certain character are capable of anything.'

But my father had been regarding me more closely. 'Did Miss Casey answer your questions when you put them to her?' He saw me pause and said, 'Abigail, this is a moment to be completely frank.'

'The baby's father is one of the congregation that meet in the home of Mr Nesham.'

'The Brethren?'

'Yes. She told me that he threatened to — '

'Impossible.' Dr Labatt's eyes had hardened, and he looked at me from beneath his brow. 'The character of Mr Darby's church is founded on the strictest principles of good conduct.'

'That may be,' Father said, 'but every flock has its black sheep.'

'Their name cannot be tainted because of

rumour. Why, the nursemaid changes her story at every turn. She told her employer something quite different, and I suspect she may have no idea who the father was.'

Ewan had been quiet for some time, but this suggestion of Emilie's easy virtue made him raise his head. 'Doctor, such speculation is hardly proper in this company.'

'I shall not be guided on appropriate behaviour by you, Mr Weir. If Miss Lawless did not wish to hear such things discussed then she shouldn't have interfered.' He turned to my father. 'I have found that Miss Casey has displayed several signs of *furor uterinus*.'

He may have thought that I wouldn't recognize the term; my father knew that I would, and he briefly closed his eyes. How anyone could be offended by a medical condition . . . Though I doubted whether Emilie could have presented such symptoms during the days of her confinement, especially following such trauma.

'It is one thing for your daughter to sneak into my hospital and interfere with my patient. It is quite another for her to disseminate the girl's lies.'

Father's face darkened, which always made him appear older. 'I believe that is an unfair characterization.'

A log shifted in the fire, and an ember rolled on to the hearthstone where it dwindled and died.

'Dr Labatt.' I waited for him to look at me. 'I feel I have always been adept at spotting when someone is not telling the truth.'

46

The doctor stood and clasped his cane beneath his arm. He said, 'I have nothing more to add. The board of the hospital will consider this, and we shall decide if any other authority should be notified.' Father rose as Labatt bid us all a curt good night. Kathy had lingered in the hallway, ready with Labatt's hat and coat. We heard her open the front door and warn the doctor that a shower had made the steps slippery.

Father remained standing by his chair for a moment. He lowered his head as if wearied, noticed the middle button of his waistcoat undone, but let it be. As he went to place a guard in front of the fire, his foot brushed the edge of the hearthrug, making the tasselled fringe dishevelled. 'Mr Weir,' he said, 'will you join me in my study?'

I was about to speak, but Father held up a hand. 'Perhaps it's best if you retire early, Abigail.' He said that he would deal with me in the morning.

I lay alone atop the covers of my bed like a monk in his beehive hut, or a felon in her cell, and listened for sounds of movement. Those tiptoed treads ascending the stairs belonged to Kathy going to her quarters in the loft. Mrs Perrin moved with a heavier step as she went from room to room, shutting doors and snuffing candles. I heard a scratching, and rose to let Kepler into my chamber. Our house-cat had a thick coat of black and grey with stripes forming an M on his forehead, as if he had eyebrows that were always arched. The tip of his tongue extruded because of an old injury — the result of an encounter with a love-rival, or possibly a love-interest. He padded over to the bed and curled up on the blanket, which was warm from where I had lain.

The study door creaked open in the floor below. Ewan must have walked with particular care, for there was no other sound until the front door was pulled shut, making the lid of the letter box rattle. I opened one shutter and saw him set off towards Sackville Street. He paused in the dim glow of a lamp to look up and over his shoulder. I was about to step back from the window, but I waited, and when he continued to gaze upwards, I raised my hand in greeting. The single candle in my room would have made me a shadowy figure.

But Ewan had only looked skywards because a cold rain had started to fall. He fastened the top button of his coat with one hand, pulled the brim of his hat lower and moved off into the darkened street. I closed the shutter and slipped the hooked latch into place, feeling tired and pensive and disappointed.

★ ★ ★

The most convivial part of our home had always been the basement kitchen, a haven of warmth and hard work overseen by Mrs Perrin. We called her the housekeeper mainly so Father could pay her that level of salary, but she assumed many lesser duties. She cooked and cleaned and had been a lady's maid for my mother. We were a small household, despite our large home, and so there was little need for a steward or more than one parlourmaid or hall boy. Mrs Perrin was approaching fifty. She was thin and wiry, with a strong constitution, and had been the wife of the previous coachman, Raymond. Two of their daughters still worked as maids in separate houses in the countryside. Ray Perrin had died of a punctured lung when he was kicked by a mare at the Smithfield market; the tragedy all the more cruel because it came during his wife's final and no doubt unexpected pregnancy.

Jimmy arrived so late that it almost killed both mother and child, but once they were out of danger, Father assured Mrs Perrin that she would have a home and job for life if she wished it, and that Jimmy could be raised here. He was a beautiful dark-haired infant and, for a seven-year-old girl, a delightful distraction and playmate. One of the first words he uttered was 'Abby', and he had called me that ever since, despite his mother's half-hearted appeals for him to say 'Miss Abigail'. As my own mother withdrew into herself and her chamber, I developed a closer relationship with Mrs Perrin and her son.

I did chores alongside them as well. Father wished for me to be able to take care of myself; to know how to pump water, build a fire or cook a meal. This was partly due to principle. It was difficult, he said, to work with the dead on a daily basis and not develop some egalitarian beliefs. But it was also true that we lived in uncertain times. I had been born in the midst of rebellion at home, and there had been wars in

Europe all my life. An uneasy mood persisted among our neighbours that at any moment the social order could be overturned, and all our fortunes reversed.

I was just pleased to have an unaffected bond with everyone in the household; with Liam the coachman and the young maids who came and went. I could join in their discussions and occasionally sit with them for meals, though I noticed from an early age that conversations without me were more unguarded and the laughter brighter.

When I came down the following morning, two unplucked pheasants lay on the kitchen table, their wrung necks lolling over the side. Mrs Perrin was kneading dough, the sleeves of her housedress rolled up and her forearms dusted with flour. She kept a close eye on Kepler in the corner. I bid her good morning, and she beckoned me to the table by cocking her head. She showed me her dough-covered hands, leaned her face towards me and said, 'Can you scratch the front of my nose?'

I did so with the tip of my index finger and she smiled back.

She began kneading again in earnest. 'What have you done now to vex your father?'

'Why, what did he say?'

'Nothing, but I can tell by him. He wants to see you in his study before breakfast.'

Father was writing at his desk when I entered. I sat across from him without speaking. He sprinkled his sheet with a pounce-pot, set it aside, and then placed his glasses on the desk with the temples still raised.

I'd intended to let him speak first, but in the silence I said, 'What did you decide for Mr Weir?'

'We agreed that it might be best if he continue his studies at home for a week or two.'

'I feared you had sent him away for good.'

Father picked up another sheet of paper, its edges weighed down by a broken seal, and seemed ready to hand it to me, but then changed his mind. 'A note came from the Rotunda before dawn,' he said. 'Emilie Casey killed herself in the small hours.'

He folded the sheet again as if he'd been reciting from it. The pieces of the wax seal fitted together like a black horn button, made shiny and lacquered by the morning light.

'How?'

'She cut her wrist with a piece of broken glass.'

It had only been twelve hours since I'd spoken with her, and I recalled her distress, the exhaustion that I'd roused into anguish. Had I thought to help by going to see her; to somehow uncover the truth? All I had done was add to her torment.

Father looked at me directly, for how long I wasn't sure, because I lowered my gaze. He spoke for several minutes. In gentle but firm tones, he said that medical and legal systems had been developed over generations to deal with cases like that of Miss Casey, precisely because rash and unthinking interference like mine could have such tragic consequences. He paused, perhaps expecting me to defend my actions, but

I remained silent. He said that I had to understand that people were fragile things, not to be easily analysed or explained, especially in their capacity for pain.

He picked up his spectacles and told me that I could go.

When I was halfway to the door he said, 'Abigail,' and I looked back at him. 'You asked me last night if I thought you were capable of taking responsibility.' He held my eye for a moment. 'That is something you will have to decide yourself.'

3

My mother hardly left her chamber in the years before she died. On most days she would rise and dress and take her meals at a small table. The shutters remained closed, and though candle-lit, the room was always gloomy. She relied on a few precious links to the outside world: conversations with my father and Mrs Perrin; her correspondence — though she always received far fewer letters than she sent; and the daily papers, which I would read with her each morning, perched at the foot of her bed. She would go through all the broadsheets no matter their politics or religious slant, and kept them stacked in leaning, dog-eared piles.

Once, when we'd settled down at the start of another morning, I heard her read aloud for a moment, under her breath. She recited the paper's date, its title and motto, the price and page number, and I realized that Mother had a compulsion to read every word. I felt embarrassed, as if I'd overheard a delicate conversation. I considered telling my father, but he probably knew already.

It was difficult now to recall Mother as she was before. I could remember little things: flyaway strands of hair about her cap as she wrote a letter in slanting afternoon light; a plume on her headdress bent beneath the ceiling of the carriage; her wedding-band stark against her fingers, which had turned white because of her grip on a black iron railing. My clearest memory, the only one in which I could still see her face and remember how she spoke, was in Rutland Gardens when I was no more than four or five. We sat beneath a tree by the gate nearest the house, and she plucked a buttercup from the grass. The light glowed yellow against my chin, which meant, she said, that I was fond of butter. I protested that she'd known that already, and she smiled and touched the flower against my nose and said, 'Well, this confirms it.' Later on, I picked another buttercup in the back garden and ate some of the petals, thinking they would taste as good as the name suggested. The sap had stung my mouth, and made me ill, and Father sat me down to explain the poisons of common plants.

By the time I was old enough to notice, Mother no longer left our home. Occasionally she would dress herself to go out, don her gloves and coat, but she'd only make it to the front hall before deciding she could go no further. I remember my father trying to coax her through the door, doing his best to remain patient, but if ever his voice hardened, even for a moment, Mother would retreat up the stairs and that would be the end of it.

She began to skip meals, would avoid unshuttered windows in the parlour, and disliked it when the folding doors between the drawing rooms were left open. One day in the kitchen, I found her slumped on the flagstones before the cooking range, her skirts spread about in a circle.

She was hunched and panting with her eyes closed tight, her hands over her shoulders trying to loosen the laces of her dress. I knelt beside her, asking what had happened, looking about the room for sign of danger. I took her hands, and kept repeating, 'Mama,' until she quietened and her breathing returned to normal. She didn't get up. She just leaned her head against my shoulder and began to weep.

As the years passed, we talked less and less. She couldn't understand the interest I had in natural philosophy and Father's work — though she never discouraged me. And I didn't know the people she spoke about in the society pages, or much care for their alliances and intrigues. I would often look with regret at Clarissa chatting or bickering with Mrs Egan, though it was hard to pine for something I had never possessed. A year after my own mother's death, the saddest thing was that the house didn't seem all that different without her.

Even now, Jimmy's first task each morning was to fetch the early editions. I would take them to her cold, empty room and read at the foot of the bed, with all the other furniture covered in dust sheets. When finished, I left the papers on the kitchen table and they were picked off one by one: Father took the *Morning Post*; Liam the *Freeman's Journal*; Mrs Perrin the *Dublin Gazette*.

All summer long, the lead articles had dealt with the curious weather, concentrating on the effects for farming and trade. But today, the *Gazette* told of a prophecy by an astronomer in

Bologna who predicted the world's end. The spots visible on the sun were the calderas of huge solar volcanoes, whose emissions would engulf the earth, by his calculations, in a fortnight's time a little after lunch hour. The prediction had instilled dread in the minds of some. In Ghent, a storm happened to be blowing over the city when a regiment of cavalry had sounded their trumpets.

Suddenly cries, groans and lamentations were heard on every side. Three-fourths of the inhabitants rushed from their houses and threw themselves on their knees in the streets and public places, believing they had heard the Seventh Trumpet of the Last Judgement.

On another day I would have clipped that out to show Father over supper, so we could laugh at its silliness, but not today. Father had been at work all morning, summoning a jury, and accompanying them to the Rotunda so they could observe Miss Casey as she lay in her hospital bed. Father's examination would come next, while the inquest itself would be held the following morning in the parish hall of St Thomas's.

At around noon, Liam drove the cadaver cart through the back gate and into the wide entrance of the coach house. The bed of the cart had been covered in tarpaulin, hiding its cargo. Liam emerged soon after, and he closed the double doors. He must have left Emilie in the cart. Of course, Ewan wasn't there to help him, and Father was away at the parish hall making arrangements for the hearing. Emilie would have to be taken to the dissection room later. Liam walked out into the stable lane, and he locked the gates behind him.

I hurried downstairs and through the kitchen, where Jimmy was cleaning a candelabra with a tin of polish, and out into the garden. The clouds had become low and heavy, and a sudden breeze whipped up the leaves on the path. There was no lock on the coach house, just a slide-bolt which I drew back, allowing me to slip inside.

Newton shuffled and nickered in his stall, but otherwise everything was still. Weak light filtered through the grubby, opaque windows, casting the clutter on the floor in a gloom. The carriage sat unhitched in the corner, and beside it the cadaver cart was propped on some wooden stocks so it stayed horizontal. I peeked beneath the tarpaulin. Emilie's body lay beneath a white sheet that was tucked around the edges of a stretcher. I drew the tarpaulin aside, and gingerly pulled the sheet back to reveal her face.

Even in this light, she was ashen, her hair untied and lank. One of the eyelids had opened slightly, but all I could see was a sliver of dull white. It took me a moment to recognize her. When we had spoken, her expression had shifted between fear, suspicion and anger. Now it was blank and drawn. The sheet that covered her was spotless, but how her bedclothes must have been soaked and scarlet when they found her. I uncovered her left arm, steeling myself for how it would look, but the wrist was untouched and intact. I moved to the other side of the cart, plucked at the sheet and folded it back.

Two deep gashes had been carved on the inside of her right arm, one across the wrist, the other down the forearm to the heel of her hand, intersecting to form an upturned cross like that of St Peter. I reached out to touch her elbow, but couldn't bring myself to do it, and had to turn away to take a breath. I waited for the constriction in my chest to ease, and then forced myself to look again.

The flesh was parted, bloodless and raw. Someone had cleaned her arm — not very thoroughly, and streaks of red remained. Where the cuts met, the four corners of skin were raised and puckered like the petals of a flower.

I tried to recall how she lay in the ward. This was the hand that had been restrained; I could see the broken skin and chafing from her manacle, and felt sure that she couldn't have made these wounds if her wrist was bound in metal. Perhaps a nurse had removed the cuffs. But Emilie was a prisoner — she could not have been left unfettered for long. The cuts themselves were clinical, like incisions from a knife instead of a ragged shard of glass, no matter how razor-sharp it may have been.

I tried to picture her in the dead of night, hunched in the bed, scoring these marks into herself. I ran my thumb over the sleeve of my dress. In what order had she done them? And after the first, would she have been able for the second?

Outside in the yard, Jimmy was calling my name. I hurriedly replaced the sheet and tarpaulin, and left the coach house before he could come in. He stopped on the path when he saw me, and said, 'What were you doing?'

'Looking for Kepler. I can't find him anywhere.'

Jimmy pointed his thumb over his shoulder. 'He's in the parlour by the fire, like always.'

'Oh.'

'Mam asked me to fetch you for lunch.'

I felt my stomach turn. How did Father muster an appetite every day? I nodded and thanked him, and we both returned to the house.

When Father came back from the parish hall he went straight to his workrooms. All the shutters in the top floor of the coach house were opened — Father said that a body was best examined in natural light — but the clouds continued to gather, with odd flecks of yellow and brown, and when the rain began to fall, I could see the flicker of oil-lamps in the windows. I knew that he would see the peculiar features of Emilie's wounds. He would decipher them as well. For my father, the dead rarely kept their secrets. I curled up on a chair as a chill draught entered the room, keeping a shawl closed with one hand, and my book open with the other.

Father remained at work for much of the day. He skipped supper to retire to his study, which wasn't unusual on the eve of an inquest, for he could record his observations, prepare his remarks, and issue any final summonses.

It was late when the front doorbell rang.

Darkness had fallen, and I stepped outside my room to where I could see down below. Kathy opened the door, and after an exchange of words four men passed into the hallway. They were dressed in the garb of the Brethren, jackets with hooks fastened up to the collar, the black cloth lost in the shadows. Kathy offered to take their coats, but one man flatly said, 'No.' As they filed into the parlour, the flicker of a candle shone its yellow light on the face of Mr Darby.

Kathy brought a message to my father, and he emerged from his study looking tired and irritated, spectacles still perched on his head. As he passed on the stairs, I said, 'Why has Mr Darby come?'

It was the first I had spoken to him since that morning. 'I do not know,' he said, about to move on. Then he smiled briefly. 'Perhaps they wish to convert me.' He touched my forearm, continued on down the stairs and into the parlour.

Their meeting began without a call for refreshment, no request for Mrs Perrin to stoke the fire or trim the candles. I lingered in the hall, but could hear nothing of their discussion except a low murmur. One voice led the conversation, a soft drone that would be broken by quiet interludes. I placed my ear against the door frame. Father was speaking now, and I heard him say, 'Gentlemen,' in a terse, impatient tone. His armchair creaked, and footsteps strode across the wooden floor. I moved towards the basement stairs, pretending to be passing that way, just as the doorknob of the parlour twisted.

However, the door didn't open. The knob

remained turned for a few seconds, as if someone still held on to it, and then released slowly, small dents in the brass rotating in the candlelight. There was silence in the room. The voices resumed, soft and dull as before, and I went down to the kitchen.

Kathy and Jimmy waited for a while before going to bed. Mrs Perrin remained up, scouring plates in a washbasin. She told me that I should retire as well. 'I'll see the gentlemen out when they're ready.'

'I want to ask Father what they are speaking about.'

'Perhaps it's not meant for your ears,' she said, letting murky water trickle from an upturned cup.

I bade her good night, and slipped through the darkened house again, pausing at the bottom of the stairs. The conversation continued. I listened for a moment longer, then knocked on the parlour door and entered.

Father sat in his usual place by the fire, both hands on the armrests. The flames had become low and red, and did little to dispel the cold. Three of the Brethren men stood in the middle of the room, all facing Father and looking down on him. They were known to me: Mr Nesham from across the square, Dr Labatt, and Judge Gould, who was the father of Edith, my former friend. Mr Darby stood separately by one of the bookcases, a volume opened in his hand, its ribbon dangling from the top of the spine.

Judge Gould was tall and stout, his Brethren coat well tailored. I could tell by his expression that he was the one who had been speaking. With a furrowed brow, he made his way to the window, hands held behind his back, and he gazed outside, though all he could see in the inky blackness was a pale reflection of the room.

Father shifted forward in his seat. 'Was there something you wanted, Abigail?' he said, a slight rasp in his voice.

'Just to tell you that I am retiring for the night.'

Darby had not looked up since I'd entered. He touched his middle finger to the tip of his tongue, leaving it there for a second or two, before sweeping over a page of the book.

Father said, 'Very well. I shall see you in the morning.'

He was ill at ease, meeting my eye only briefly. It could not have been through talk of religion. Father would have looked upon attempts to proselytize him with amusement; the more zealous the argument, the easier it would be to bat away.

None of the men said a word to me, as if my presence were an intrusion, when in fact the opposite was true.

'Good evening, Judge Gould,' I said. 'I hope that Edith is well.'

He looked over his shoulder, his eyes cast down on the floor as though my friendship with his daughter belonged to a different time, or a different life. Darby lifted his head at the mention of Edith's name. He took the ribbon to mark the page, and slipped the book back onto its shelf. 'You must excuse us, Miss Lawless,' he said. I thought he was apologizing for their aloofness, but rather he was asking me to leave. 'We are not yet finished with your father.'

I looked towards Father in his chair, his shoulders sloping down. He nodded to me once, and I backed out of the parlour. Mr Darby's eyes were upon me as I drew the door shut.

I waited ten or twenty minutes in my room before they departed and the front door rattled shut. Not long after, Mrs Perrin's bright voice wished my father good night. I lay for another hour in the dark, waiting to hear him trudge to his chamber in the floor above. But he did not stir. A half-moon shone in my window, wispy and beige in the static haze. I watched it creep towards the window frame, and then rose to go downstairs.

The door to the parlour was ajar, and the only light inside came from a low candle. Father was still in his chair. At first I thought his head had dipped in slumber, but he was looking at something in his hands: a golden locket on a simple chain, which held a tress of my mother's auburn hair curled up in a spiral. He rubbed his thumb over the oval disc, and placed it back into his fob pocket.

'It's late, Father,' I said.

He looked up, and roused himself slightly in the chair. 'I must have dozed off.'

He remained seated, and I moved towards him to kneel by the armrest. 'What did those gentlemen want?'

Father patted his waistcoat to ensure the chain was secure. 'It was as I feared,' he said, forcing some humour into his voice. 'They bored me to death with their canons and dogmas.' He smiled at me, but it was half-hearted.

'Was it because of what I did in the Rotunda?'

He reached out to take my hand. 'No, Abigail. There is nothing for you to concern yourself with.'

Before I could speak again, he said, 'I really must get to bed. There is work to be done in the morning.' He seemed weary as he rose to place the guard before a fire that was spent and cold. He cupped his hand behind the candle, and blew it out.

★　★　★

When Father returned from St Thomas's the following afternoon, I asked him about the inquest. He said that it had gone as expected. The jury found that Miss Casey's son had been born alive and murdered by his mother, while her own death was declared suicide, or rather *felo de se*: a crime against herself.

I wanted to ask him about the wounds on Emilie's arm, but he would no longer speak of the subject. Besides, how could I admit to knowing about them if I had not sneaked into the coach house, and I feared he would consider that a transgression too far. I told myself that it was the jury that came to the decision. They saw all the evidence, and I could only assume their verdict was deliberate and correct.

Father and I began to take our meals together again. For a week, we tried to avoid mention of

64

Ewan's absence, or the death of Miss Casey, but there had been one thing that I could not put off. I approached him in his study, and when I mentioned the nursemaid's name he placed his pen flat on the desk. I handed him a thin length of wood, planed and varnished. Letters had been etched and painted black, spelling out the name 'Morgan Casey'. Liam had fashioned it using his tools in the coach house.

'In the Rotunda,' I said, 'I promised Emilie that I would mark her son's grave. But I don't know where it is.'

Father frowned at the nameplate, but when he looked at me his eyes softened. 'He is in the still-born plot of St George's,' he said. 'I shall make the arrangements.'

★ ★ ★

It had been a forlorn few days, so I was pleased when Clarissa sent a note saying she could accompany Mrs Perrin and me to the oyster sheds in Clontarf. We left on an overcast afternoon, the carriage rather crowded since Jimmy came as well. He sat beside his mother, reading from an alphabet chapbook: woodcut pictures of objects with their names printed and first letters underlined. The C was a crown; the H a harp; the W a whip. Clarissa sat beside me, resting her head on the window frame as the streets became narrow and the houses low. When we turned into Summer Hill, she had to lift her head as the carriage rattled over the uneven cobbles.

There was plenty to talk about. Gossip

surrounding events in the Nesham household had turned the tragedy into a scandal. The tale of the fallen servant in a pious family spread quickly, and many people, even the irreligious, had become aware of the Brethren and its leader, Mr Darby. It was said that he was unmarried, and had been living with the Neshams for several months, at least as long as Emilie had been pregnant, but any direct suggestion of impropriety was left unspoken. Emilie's story of the Gorey fisherman had been the one told at the inquest, but that did not stop the speculation.

Eventually, Mrs Perrin said that we shouldn't discuss these things in front of Jimmy, though the topic was already exhausted. The conversation turned to other subjects. Clarissa had arrived with news of a ball to be hosted in Charlemont House at the start of August. She relished these occasions: the anticipation and spectacle, the music and dancing. She enjoyed them because she fitted in so well. She was beautiful and carried herself gracefully; she could talk with anyone, and never seemed ill at ease.

I was less enthusiastic. 'The season was supposed to end in late spring. I thought these gatherings were done with for another year.'

'Usually they would be, but there's nothing to do in the countryside in weather like this,' she said. 'Everyone is returning to the city.'

I'd once spent a winter with cousins in Meath so I knew she was right. Estate houses could be bleak and draughty places, especially when cut off by muddy roads and swollen rivers.

'It'll be amusing, Abby. Anything for some diversion.'

'I'm just not looking forward to practising dance-steps in my room with an invisible partner.'

'Jimmy can help,' she said.

He looked at me and smiled uncertainly, but his mother said, 'Miss Egan is teasing, Jimmy. Pay her no mind.'

The sounds of a crowd could be heard up ahead, and the carriage slowed. There were shouts, as well as the high keening voices of women. Smoke came rolling from two tall chimneys on a building adjacent to Clarke's Bridge. There was only one gated entrance, where a line of soldiers kept a shifting mass of men and women at bay.

Barefooted youngsters clung to their mothers' frayed skirts. I saw one infant with his head lolling over his father's elbow. The men pushed forward against raised muskets and bayonets, and the red coats of the soldiers stood out against the tattered rags of the crowd.

Jimmy said, 'What do they want?'

I raised the window and secured the latch. 'It's a soup kitchen, Jimmy. They want something to eat.'

The carriage had almost come to a halt, and we could hear Liam shouting for people to make way. Others wandered past our windows on both sides. Mrs Perrin put her knitting into the bag, but she kept one needle on the seat next to her. The road was too narrow for us to turn, and the further we went towards the canal, the closer the

67

press of people seemed to be.

A young woman in a black dress pushed her way to the front and began remonstrating with one of the soldiers. She reached out to grasp his coat and the baldric that ran diagonally over his chest. He stepped away, then in one quick movement swung the butt of his rifle into the woman's jaw. Her head snapped back, and she crumpled out of sight.

The people near the front surged forward, incensed by the strike, and the soldiers re-formed their line, elbowing and shoving against the advance. An officer with silver epaulettes disengaged from the others to stand behind them. He loaded his musket, withdrew the slim ramrod to compress a bullet into the barrel, then replaced the rammer calmly despite the turmoil all around. He raised the musket at an angle that would barely clear the heads of the people, and fired.

The muzzle flashed with a loud bang and cloud of smoke, and everyone in the front line ducked. Others in the crowd, especially mothers with young children, hurried from the building. The soldiers used the moment's respite to retreat behind the wall and shut the gate.

Mrs Perrin struck her fist against the ceiling and called for Liam to drive ahead. He attempted to do so, but after a few jerking movements, we came to a standstill.

The people had settled, aware that the shot had been a distraction. For a few moments they wandered around the carriage, as if oblivious to its presence. Then, one by one, they approached and began to peer through the glass. An old man with a gaunt face and chapped lips squinted at me. I slipped my fingers through the door handle, ready to resist should he attempt to open it. A woman appeared beside Mrs Perrin's window. She carried a toddler in her arms, a freckled boy with blond curls and serious eyes. He placed a slender hand against the glass and drew his fingers across, leaving a long curving streak.

Other faces crowded the window. Mrs Perrin told Jimmy to stay still. She said that everything would be all right. I couldn't fathom why Liam wasn't acting, but then realized that if he made a rash move — the flick of a lash, or a voiced urging of the horses — it could spell disaster. For the first time in my life, I was scared of my own countrymen. I didn't know whether to sit upright and defiant, or to shrink back in my seat.

A woman only a few years my senior, with straight black hair swept behind her ears, surveyed the inside of the carriage, and then looked at me directly. I returned her gaze, without raising my chin or bowing my head. Finally, she gestured to the front of the carriage and called out, 'Clear a path.'

After a moment, a male voice said the same thing, and then several others. The people on the roadway moved aside and regarded us silently as we passed. The horses crested the hump of Clarke's Bridge and, as the road widened, Liam urged them to gather pace.

We neared the city limits. The houses became scarce, and after a few minutes Liam pulled in by the fields of Loves-charity. He clambered down and opened the door beside Mrs Perrin. 'Is everyone all right?'

I said that we were. 'I think the greater danger was posed by the musketeer.'

Mrs Perrin said, 'Nonsense. It's not right that people can't travel through the streets unmolested.'

'They did not molest us.'

She was going to reply, but then turned to Liam. 'And why didn't you drive on?'

'There were children in the way. But if they had attempted to do anything . . .'

Jimmy said quietly, 'What would they have attempted?'

'Nothing, Jimmy,' I said. 'They were hungry, that is all.'

Mrs Perrin and Liam discussed whether they should return home, and by which route. I said it would be best to continue to the coast as planned. The crowd would disperse in time, and on the way back we could choose our path with care.

There was no more conversation as we journeyed on. A smell of sulphur hung in the air near the vitriol works in Ballybough. Beyond that lay a small Jewish burial ground, with listing headstones bearing letters in Hebrew. Finally, we reached the coast road. The tide was partially out. A large expanse of mudflats and sandbars lay before us, with creeks and rivulets winding through the strand. We disembarked at the oyster sheds. Tendrils of smoke escaped from slats in the curing-houses. Liam took the carriage into the stables of an inn to refresh the horses. Jimmy and his mother went off to buy supplies, while Clarissa and I wandered towards the North Bull Wall: a tide breaker that extended straight into the bay. Mrs Perrin told us to remain on the drier gravel beds, and not to venture too far out.

With our mantles tied and hoods raised, we began to ramble over the shingle. Occasionally I'd bend down to inspect a smooth pebble or scallop shell. We went out on to the sea wall, though the water's edge was still in the distance, dull grey and indistinct against the sky's hazy pall. The breeze grew stronger, whipping our cloaks about our legs, and it was uncanny to see the dry fog remain static despite the buffeting.

A few people could be seen among the oyster beds in the middle distance, hunched beside wicker baskets. Some oyster-catchers were pecking and winkling morsels from the eelgrass. They all took flight at once, and I saw a fox padding over the rippled sand, his white paws caked in mud. A heron remained standing poised and erect, its long bill turned towards the interloper. The fox came quite near to it, and raised his muzzle to test the air, but perhaps he had run afoul of a heron's beak before, for he left it alone.

Clarissa said, 'There are people at the water's edge.'

She pointed to a group of around thirty near the breakers, mostly dressed in black, with a dozen or so conspicuous in long white robes. They were gathered around a man who stood apart and was preaching to them, though his words were carried off by the wind. Even at a distance I could tell it was Mr Darby. I looked at

71

the Brethren all standing together. Could Emilie's seducer be there, huddled among them on this windy beach?

'Let's get closer.'

Clarissa pulled at my sleeve. 'No, Abby. Let's just leave them.'

'But I want to hear what Mr Darby is saying.'

She relented, and we picked our way towards the crowd. All the men wore identical black coats with bent metal hooks instead of buttons, including Darby. He spoke quite naturally, without the heavy tones of other preachers, but I only caught snatches of what he said before the ceremony began. As we got near, those in white robes were brought to the edge of the water, including an old man who was carried on a chair. Two men in dark coats waded out to the level of their waists, one holding a Bible aloft.

I said to Clarissa, 'Does Mr Darby not perform the rites?'

'In the Brethren, any member can preach and administer the sacraments without ordination.' She glanced at me. 'Though I'd say Darby just doesn't want to get his feet wet.'

I laughed quietly, enough for a woman to look towards us. It was Mrs Nesham, dressed in black like the others, her dark hair tightly pinned beneath a white cap. She held my eye for a moment, before turning away.

The first woman to be baptized walked into the sea. Her white gown became soaked and clung to her, and I shivered at the thought of how cold the water must be. She stood between the two men, then knelt down facing the shore.

One of them began speaking while the other held a white cloth draped over an opened palm. At the last moment he covered the woman's face, and both men pushed her head beneath the water. The force of the action surprised me. They held her submerged for several seconds before allowing her up. She gasped and clawed at the hair plastered over her face. Those on the beach muttered a prayer unprompted, sounding almost like a collective sigh.

Mrs Nesham had gone to stand next to Darby. She spoke into his ear, and he glanced over his shoulder towards me.

The newly baptized woman emerged on to the beach, sodden and trembling like the last survivor of a shipwreck. She was bundled up in blankets by waiting Brethren members. The old man was next, and he was borne into the sea, chair and all.

Clarissa said, 'Let's go. This is unnerving.'

One of the women awaiting her turn carried a small boy. He also wore a white gown, which made his skin seem all the more pale. His low sobbing was interrupted by racking coughs, and his head rested weakly on his mother's shoulder.

I told Clarissa to wait, and began walking towards him. The young mother had dark hair and tired, staring eyes. I touched her shoulder.

'Perhaps you should wait until the weather is warmer.'

A few of the members around me began to mutter, but none spoke up. The woman looked at me, held her child closer and said, 'He can't wait.'

73

'Summer will return soon, and the water won't be as cold.'

She narrowed her eyes. 'How do you know?'

'Because . . . it must.' I had no real way of knowing, of course, and it seemed wrong to tell her that I merely believed it.

I felt a hand on my elbow. 'This woman needs to prepare herself for what she's about to undertake.'

Mr Darby had spoken softly. He was taller than me, and there was a slight upturn to his lips as if he were amused. His hazel eyes were very still.

'I am worried for him,' I said. 'That his sickness might worsen.'

Darby reached out to rub his thumb over the boy's forehead. The child scrunched his eyes shut.

'Do you really think that God would allow harm to befall him? Besides, Miss Abigail,' he said, glancing at me as he spoke my name, 'I know of a danger far greater.' He fixed the wide collar on the boy's gown, smoothing it over his thin shoulders. 'There is always such regret when a child must meet his maker unprepared. Do you not agree?'

'Like Miss Casey's son?'

His expression didn't change. He seemed ready to speak again, but then the young mother was called upon. Without hesitation she began walking into the sea. I said to Darby, 'She would stop if you told her.'

He cocked his head a little, as if confused. 'It is really not my decision to make.' With that, he

74

turned and moved through the crowd towards Mrs Nesham. Members of the Brethren parted way as I went back to Clarissa. I didn't look as the child was being baptized, but I heard the splash, followed by his weak, plaintive cry.

★　★　★

Francis Roberts and Annie Stamp lay together beneath a sheet in my father's workrooms, completely covered except for Annie's yellow hair, which streamed on to the table-top. They'd never met in life. He had been a middle-aged labourer from Mayo, whose most recent abode was the House of Industry in Grangegorman, and she was a beggar and prostitute who'd come from the female penitentiary at Newgate. The only thing that they held in common was their date of death — a curious shared destiny. No one had come to claim them, for Francis was too far removed from his family in the west, and Annie was disowned. They had died from a combination of the damp in their respective cells, and diseases from their respective trades, and my father had no need to examine them. All that was required was sanction from his office for their transfer to the anatomists.

I sat alone beside them awaiting Ewan's arrival. The wall-clock above the table whirred into action. Years ago, Father grew weary of the distraction from its peal and had the chime removed. Still, the hammer diligently struck the air eight times.

There were steps on the pathway outside.

75

Ewan came up to the workroom carrying an inkpot and pen, with some printed forms clasped beneath the same arm. He failed to notice me in the corner, and went towards his own desk, snuffling while reaching into a pocket for his handkerchief. He'd returned to work a few days ago, though I hadn't seen him since the night Father sent him from the house.

I said, 'May I speak with you?'

Even the most stoic can be unnerved by an unexpected voice in a room containing dead people, and Ewan dropped his inkpot on to the table. It bounced and rolled, but he recovered his poise before it could fall to the floorboards.

'Miss Lawless, I am not sure we should — '

'I didn't get the chance to apologize,' I said. 'I never intended for things to happen as they did, and I'm sorry. I feel terrible that you were punished because of me.'

He looked at me for a moment. I thought he was about to claim responsibility for the incident once again, but then he nodded and began shuffling the forms on his desk.

In the silence, I rose to push Miss Stamp's tresses beneath the cover. Her hair was clean, and I smoothed down the sheet as if fussing over an unmade bed. 'Were you able to study at home during the last week?'

He said he'd used his unexpected leisure to explore the city, which he'd never had the chance to do before.

'That must have been nice,' I said. 'Did you hear what happened to Emilie Casey?'

'Yes, your father sent word.'

'I've been thinking about it quite often.'

'You shouldn't blame yourself, Miss Lawless. Miss Casey wasn't of sound mind.'

'I meant, I was wondering how she managed it.'

'Your father didn't tell you?'

'Yes, I heard all about the broken glass. It is just . . . we saw her being strapped to the bed, Ewan.'

He looked to the side as if trying to recall, then pulled one of the forms from his sheaf to set on the leather inlay of his desk. 'Those restraints may have been temporary.'

'Perhaps,' I said. 'She was brought here for examination, during your absence.'

'I don't doubt it.'

'Father's notes on the case will be in the ledger.'

'Yes.' He glanced across to Francis Roberts hidden beneath the sheet, and took up his pen. 'How do you spell Ballyhaunis?'

'I don't have a key to the cabinet.'

'If you want to see your father's notes, then I suggest you ask him.'

'He'd refuse me.'

'Then why would I go against his wishes?'

I was about to argue, but instead I spelled out the name of the Mayo town.

As he wrote, I said, 'I'll leave now, and won't ask again. But only if you can tell me honestly that you don't intend to look at these notes in my absence.'

His pen stilled, and he raised the nib before the ink could blot. He finished filling in the form, seeming to take special care with each letter. Then he rose and took a small key from his pocket, with which he unlocked a shuttered cabinet in the corner. It contained a series of cloth-bound ledgers: Father's notes of his examinations in chronological order. Ewan pulled out the most recent book and flipped it open to its final entry.

When I didn't move, he looked across at me, gesturing at the page. 'Don't you want to see?'

I rounded the desk to stand beside him, and we both leaned down to read. The form was a mixture of printed words and my father's own handwriting.

Michael Lawless examined the body and investigated the circumstances of this death, and certify that death occurred on *8th July 1816* between the hours of *12 and 6 in the* a.m. and that in my opinion resulted from . . .

Several options were printed in parentheses: natural causes; accident; homicide; undetermined; but all were crossed out by neat double-strokes except for the word 'suicide'. The form continued:

The causes of death were: *Two lacerations to the ulnar artery above the radiocarpal joint of the right hand by means of a piece of broken glass.*

Ewan distractedly ran a thumb over his own wrist. He said, 'A shard from the jug must have lodged in her bedclothes.'

Beneath the printed section, there was space on the page for notes and observations. Ewan pointed to question-marks dotted throughout, saying they were my father's way of noting oddities or unanticipated elements. The first one said, *Absence of tentative wounds?*

'What does that mean?'

'Miss Casey did not make any initial shallow cuts, as people usually do because they misjudge the effectiveness of the blade.' He frowned and said, 'Really, cutting one's wrist is a poor method for suicide, unless submerged in water, because of — '

'The coagulation of blood.'

He glanced at me. 'Quite.'

Beside that, Father had written, *Both cuts severed the ulnar artery . . . beginner's luck?*

Ewan traced his hand down the page. The nail of his index finger was blackened with ink so he used his middle finger instead. *Gathering of pulmonary fluids and congestion in the brain.* But Father had written by way of explanation: *See Labatt's notes: patient sedated throughout her stay because of persistent hysteria.*

'When I spoke with Emilie,' I said, 'her lethargy was no more than could be expected of one bed-bound for a number of days. In fact, she seemed alert and guarded.'

Ewan finished reading through the notes. 'I think your father had doubts about this case. I am surprised that he would recommend a verdict without being completely certain.'

I thought of the men who had come to visit the night before the inquest. It could not have been a coincidence that Mr Nesham and Dr Labatt were among them. 'Perhaps it is because of us,' I said. 'He knew that if the matter was investigated further, we would have to be questioned.'

'But so be it, if there is a possibility that Miss Casey did not take her own life.'

Downstairs, we heard Father call out to Liam in the stables, and then his footsteps sounded on the staircase.

Ewan glanced at me. He closed the ledger and hurriedly placed it back in the cabinet, while I moved away from his desk to stand in the middle of the room. He pulled the shutter down with a clatter just as Father came into the office.

He paused on the threshold when he saw me, and then looked at Ewan who had lingered beside the cabinet.

Before he could speak, I said, '*There* you are. I've been searching the house all over.'

Father frowned. 'I was in my chambers, as usual, attending to correspondence.'

'You mustn't have heard me knock. Never mind.' I turned to Ewan. 'I am sorry for the intrusion, Mr Weir.'

'Not at all.' He nodded towards my father and said, 'Good morning, sir.'

As I slipped towards the top of the stairs, Father stopped me and said, 'Why did you wish to see me?'

'Oh. It can keep.'

'If you turned the house upside-down then it must be important.'

My mind went blank. Ewan used the moment

to move back to his own desk and take his seat. Still I was at a loss. It could be anything: some announcement, or concern, or favour.

'My piano lesson,' I said. 'Mrs Meekins is expecting me again this morning.'

'I haven't forgotten.'

'And I was wondering if I could walk there myself instead of taking the carriage — it's only a few minutes after all — and then go into Henry Street to buy a new bonnet?'

I thought the question served its purpose rather well: as a request it was plausible enough, and it would give me the opportunity to leave in an apparent huff when he refused. But instead he looked at me and said, 'You may. Just wrap up against the cold and be home before lunch hour.'

He seemed to note my surprise, for he smiled. Perhaps he was glad that his daughter was eager to do something that his wife at one stage couldn't countenance. All I could say was, 'Thank you,' while feeling sorry for having deceived him.

4

Tentative notes from Mozart's 'Turkish March' drifted from the salon of Mrs Meekins. An elderly servant brought me to an adjoining parlour, and she told me that her mistress would not finish the lesson with her current appointment until that day's piece was played without fault. Given the amount of times the music was interrupted by the whack of a cane and the tuneless hum of piano strings, that seemed likely to be a while yet.

The maid knelt before the hearth, placing individual lumps of coal on the fire with brass tongs as if their use was carefully rationed — a thriftiness that seemed at odds with the general décor. Little in the room was understated: the blue-and-white-striped wallpaper, the gilded frames of portraits and mirrors, the flecked marble chimney piece. A book lay on the table beside my chair: *The Mirror of the Graces* — *Hints on Female Accomplishments and Manners* by 'A Lady of Distinction'. I turned to a random page in the first chapter.

> Fine taste in apparel I have ever seen the companion of pure morals; while a licentious style of dress is as certainly the token of laxity in manners and conduct. To correct this dangerous fashion ought to be the study and attempt of every mother, of every daughter, of every woman.

I closed the book and tossed it back on to the table, where it landed with a thud and slid on the polished surface. The noise made the housemaid start. She replaced the guard before the fire, rose with discomfort and took her leave.

A bookcase stood in the corner, but the titles it contained were no more agreeable: *On the Moral Influence of Etiquette; The Polite Letter Writer; The Young Wife: Duties of Woman in Marriage*. There were several volumes of *Debrett's Peerage*, and the most up-to-date edition of *The Dublin Directory*. I took it down and opened it. Father was noted among the city officers in the first few pages: *Coroner for Dublin North — Michael Lawless, 4 Rutland Sq*. How easy it would be for anyone to find our address. I was about to replace the book when another name entered my head: Longsworth.

That was the woman who shared Emilie Casey's ward; her name had been written out in Mr Gray's ledger. If anyone could have been witness to what occurred that night, it was her.

In the alphabetical roll under 'Nobility and Gentry', three Longsworths were listed: two barristers and a silk-mercer, living in well-to-do streets south of the river. I thought again of the surgical ward in the Rotunda. It was unlikely that those men would allow their wives to be treated in such a place.

In the directory headed 'Merchants and Traders', only one Longsworth was mentioned, and she was a woman: *Longsworth, Maria. Button and Trimmings merchant, Pill-lane*. The address wasn't far, just tucked in behind the

Four Courts. I looked again at the door of Mrs Meekins' salon. Inside, the latest attempt to complete the Mozart piece faltered in its opening bars.

The skies darkened as I walked through the city, threatening a downpour that never arrived. Beyond Sackville Street, paths became narrow and choked, with side-alleys offering glimpses of listing masts and snapping sails and the new iron bridge arching over the Liffey. Seagulls wheeled in wide circles over the dome of the Four Courts, just visible between the eaves of the tenements on Pill Lane. On the street, women gathered outside their houses in twos and threes, chatting together with shawls gathered against the cold. A street-trader stood on a corner, stoking the fire of a portable stove. She was an old woman, one hand propped against her back as if nursing an ailment. A round pan contained a pile of assorted nuts with their edges blackened, though it was hard to tell if that was the result of roasting or decay.

When I got near she called out to me, 'Nuts for a farthing.'

'No, thank you.' I was about to pass, but then I paused and said, 'I am looking for a shop along this road, a haberdashers called Longsworth.'

The woman waved her spoon about to dispel the smoke. 'Shop's closed. Maria hasn't been well.'

'Do you know if her baby lived?'

She glanced at me, and seemed to take note of my clothing for the first time. 'Yes, though I heard it was a close-run thing. She's only back from the hospital these past few days.' The woman pointed towards the end of the street. 'Her shop is down there a ways, across the road.'

A hanging sign over the door of a narrow two-storey house bore the Longsworth name. A man was peering through the darkened windows between cupped hands, the brim of his hat pushed back by the cane he was still holding. He was looking beyond the boxes of buckram and button-moulds that were visible in the window display.

I said, 'Is the shop still closed?'

He lifted his head to look at me, and his thin lips stretched as he smiled.

'I was just wondering that myself.' Then he rapped the window with the top of his cane, so hard that I was surprised the glass didn't crack. 'Do you hear that, Mrs Longsworth? You have a customer. And here the doors are shut.'

'No, I didn't want to buy anything.'

This time he thumped the front door with his fist, and shouted, 'It's little wonder that no money passes the tills.' He peered through the glass again, then stood on his tiptoes. 'Do you think I can't spot you skulking behind the counter?'

I was about to back away, for this quarrel was not my concern, and at least I had found where she lived. But the man's manner was so brutish.

'Perhaps she has no wish to see you.'

'Oh, no one wants to see me. No one likes it when old Fitch comes to call. They know I won't leave without what's due, isn't that right, Maria?'

Across the street, women had come to their

doors to watch. I told the man that Mrs Longsworth had not been well.

He felt along the edges of the window frame, brushing away flakes of green paint, then stood back to look at the upper floor. 'There's hardly been sight of the sun for six months,' he said. 'And noxious vapours fill the air. If every invalid was forgiven their arrears, then Mr Purser would be severely out of pocket.'

'Mr Purser of Mountjoy Square?'

He frowned at me, and seemed to realize that he should not have mentioned his employer's name. I didn't know the man, but the Purser family had a pew in St George's.

'I doubt that he would approve of his debts being collected in this manner.'

'You'd be surprised.'

'Well then I doubt his wife would like it known that a new mother, one barely out of hospital, was being hounded. Lady Purser has such a reputation for charity. It would be a shame if her friends were to find out.'

He gripped the top of his cane to hammer on the door again, but then paused. His gloves were too big for him, and the brown leather at the tips of his fingers folded back. He placed the cane on the ground, twisting the tip slightly in the dirt, and pulled his brim lower.

'This day week, Mrs Longsworth.'

Mr Fitch brushed my shoulder as he walked past. He didn't glance back, even when he turned into a side street towards the river.

I heard the scrape of bolts being undone, and the door was pulled ajar. Mrs Longsworth leaned out to ensure that the man had gone. She looked at me and said, 'Thank you.'

'Not at all.'

'We really are closed, though, unless it's something simple . . .'

'I wanted to ask you about the girl who was in your ward in the Rotunda,' I said. 'The girl who killed herself.'

The sound of an infant's cry came from upstairs. Mrs Longsworth held the latch and seemed ready to make an excuse, but then took a step back and said, 'Come up.'

She led the way through the stalls of her shop, past the raised flap of a wooden counter and up a cramped stairway. The room above was low, with a fire burning in the hearth. Clothes hung from a line that spanned the walls. There was a crib beside the kitchen table, and another child sat on a hearthrug: a young girl in a simple dress who combed the hair of her doll. Her mother leaned over to kiss her forehead, saying, 'He's gone, love.' Then she went to the crib to soothe the baby.

The little girl came to stand before me and asked me what my name was. When I told her, she said, 'I'm Maggie.'

She didn't say anything more, but neither did she move away.

'Do you like having a new sister?'

She thought about it, her eyes focused on the middle distance. 'She cries a lot. And she made Mammy sick.'

'That wasn't her fault. You are very lucky. I wish I had a sister.'

'You can have her if you like.'

Her mother said, 'Maggie,' while placing the baby back in its cot. I took a pin from my hair, which had a yellow buttercup made from tortoise-shell, and gave it to the girl. She smiled as she took it, brought it back to the fireplace, and fixed it in the hair of her doll.

The baby's eyes were still scrunched and her lips pursed, but all of a sudden she settled, and her face became placid. I wondered if a child that age was able to dream, and if so what images did she see. 'She looks beautiful and healthy,' I said.

Her mother nodded. 'The midwife had given up hope.' She pulled a chair from the table and sat down, and I could tell by the stiff way she held her side, and her wan complexion, that she was sore and wearied. She didn't offer me anything, or invite me to sit, which was understandable seeing as I'd arrived at her doorstep unannounced.

'Is your husband here?'

She shook her head.

'You manage the shop by yourself?'

'When I'm able.'

There was a silence then, except for Maggie softly talking to her doll in a sing-song voice.

Mrs Longsworth said, 'I'd expected someone to ask me about it before now.'

'About Miss Casey?'

'I didn't know her name.' She leaned across the table for a cup of water, which was just out of reach. I handed it to her while sitting down. 'But you remember she was in the room with you?'

'Angela was only a few days old. And I wasn't

well, trying to sleep as much as possible because of the pain. Nobody told me what that girl had done, but I could guess.'

'Did she talk to you?'

'No. I could hear her often enough, weeping.' She swirled the water in her cup. 'On the day it happened, a young lady came to the ward to speak with her.'

'That was me. I came to see her.'

She frowned. 'It was you?'

'Emilie got upset, and the doctors restrained her.'

'Yes, her shouting woke me.'

A gust outside sent a puff of smoke into the room. Mrs Longsworth got up to check on Angela, even though the baby hadn't stirred. When she sat back down, she said, 'Later on, I don't know the time, it was pitch black, a man came in carrying a candle. Perhaps he was one of the porters . . . ' She glanced at Maggie. 'But I'd been told to watch out for men like that.'

'Did he go to Emilie?'

She nodded. 'He stood over her for a minute, then one by one he unbuckled her restraints and laid them on the floor. She was barely conscious. He came to me and said that the doctors had to give everyone some new medicine, to help us rest, to take away the pain, and he offered me a vial. He even helped me sit up so I could drink it.' She closed her eyes, and I could see her knuckles whiten over her mug. 'I didn't think that I would be so yielding.'

'Could you see his face?'

'Not very well. When he was near the candle I

could see one of his eyelids drooped halfway down. It seemed he couldn't help it.' She lightly dragged at her own eyelid with the tip of her middle finger.

'He had ptosis?'

'What's that?'

'The lazy eye.'

'Yes, that is what he had.'

'What did he do then?'

'I could feel myself drifting to sleep, but I saw him leaning over the girl's bed. He laced his fingers through her hair, and cradled her head while he brought the vial to her lips. Her eyes were open, but she didn't try to stop him. After that, I don't know. I woke up in a new ward. I didn't even know the girl had died until a few days ago.'

'You didn't tell anybody?'

'I just wanted to take Angela home. Besides, nobody asked, until you arrived.'

She rubbed both hands over her eyes and down her face, leaving white finger marks on her red cheeks. 'Maybe it was nothing,' she said. 'Maybe he did work there.'

'Did you see him in the hospital again afterwards?'

She looked into the fire and shook her head. Maggie came over and showed her mother the doll with the buttercup in its hair.

'Look, Mammy.'

'It's very nice. Now give it back to the lady.'

'No,' I said. 'It is a gift.' A church bell began to toll for midday. I said that I had to go, and thanked her for speaking with me. As she walked

90

me to the door I mentioned that a friend and I were going to need material for some ball-gowns. Perhaps I could leave an order with her.

★ ★ ★

Mrs Meekins had not been pleased to find me missing from her drawing room, but I arrived back soon after, full of apologies, and the lesson went ahead. Afterwards, I returned home to find a carriage waiting outside the house. It had delicate scrollwork around the door frames and a gig lantern of polished brass. There was no sign of a driver, and it was odd to see such a fine vehicle unattended. When I went inside, Mrs Perrin was coming out of the dining room, bearing a tray with a few china plates. She said, 'We have visitors.'

'I saw.'

'They're having lunch with your father. He wants you to join them.'

I asked who it was while draping my coat and bonnet on the banister, but she hadn't caught their names. She looked at me and put her tray down. 'Abigail, what happened to your hair?'

'I . . . may have lost a clip.'

She took one of her own hairpins and held it between her lips, then smoothed a tress over my ear and set it in place. She stepped back and regarded me critically, brushing a thread from my shoulder.

'Don't keep them waiting.'

When I entered the dining room, Father and his two guests stood up from the table. I recognized the younger man: James Caulfeild, the son of Lord Charlemont, who would host the ball next month. Clarissa had always admired James, and I could see why. He had an open countenance and light-blue eyes. The other man was older, his mouth straight and stern, though it relaxed into an engaging smile when Father introduced me. He was Professor Reeves, the Royal Astronomer, who lived on an estate in the foothills of Dublin. I had read some of his papers, and knew that his house had a famous observatory built years before.

'I have just finished showing the gentlemen around my workrooms and library,' Father told me.

I sat next to James and opposite the professor, a tureen of vegetable broth between us. 'He was kind to do so,' Reeves said, 'since our arrival was unannounced. I was impressed by the tools of your profession, Mr Lawless, and the precision behind your work.'

Father picked up a periodical that lay beside his plate and handed it to me. 'But in truth, the professor came because of this.'

It was the latest edition of the Royal Society journal, opened at its letters page. My observations of the sunspots — signed off with Father's name — was the most prominent, and even though all three men were looking at me, I couldn't help but scan through it to ensure that it had not been edited.

'I had intended to congratulate your father on his contribution,' Professor Reeves said, 'when lo and behold . . .'

Father looked at me. 'I tried to keep up the pretence, but my knowledge was sorely lacking.'

'It is wonderful to find a young lady with such interest, and such insight.'

James had been polishing his soup spoon with a napkin. He peered at its concave side for a moment as if checking his own reflection. 'And what did you write about, Miss Lawless?'

The professor turned to him. 'Have you not read it?'

'I didn't get the chance.'

'Well,' I said, feeling my face become warm, 'ever since the sunspots became visible, it has been common, even for men of learning, to blame them for the peculiar weather.'

'At least they do not call them a harbinger of the world's end, as some in the city have been quick to do.' A slight scowl settled over the professor's features, but it left almost at once, and he bowed his head. 'Forgive me.'

'Not at all,' I said. 'It is just that 1761 and 1783 were well known for the number of sunspots, without any noticeable fall in temperature. Today they have captured the imagination simply because they are visible in the dimming effects of the haze.'

'I very much liked your theory on what has caused the fog.'

'Yes,' I said, slightly more at ease. 'I had read accounts of similar weather thirty years ago: the sun turning blood red, a mist that closed the ports in England, then spread to Paris and Prague. People at the time blamed volcanoes in Iceland, which had erupted the previous year. So

93

I looked for reports of recent eruptions.'

I was directing my answer to James, who already seemed to be losing interest. He took a sip of broth and raised one eye-brow, possibly not in appreciation.

The professor nodded his encouragement. 'And?'

'Tambora in the Dutch East Indies. They said its explosion was heard a thousand miles away, and a huge area around the summit was plunged into darkness for several days.'

Reeves looked out at a portion of sky visible above the roof of the coach house. 'To think that we may be seeing the remnants of that event.' He remained still, as if lost in thought, though his eyes were focused on something in the distance. 'I have heard of more unusual notions,' he said, returning his attention to the table. 'That the haze was created by gunpowder from the European wars, or the result of forest fires in America.'

'Perhaps they were close to the truth.'

'That is generous of you. Your idea, I think, has more validity. But we can at least discount sunspots as the source of our miserable summer.' He took up the journal once more. 'I enjoyed your final line, rebuking those who are so alarmed. 'When real evils are numerous, we ought not to create imaginary evils.''

It was embarrassing to have it read back to me. 'I thought there was more chance of being noticed if it ended with some rhetorical flourish.'

'And you were right.'

'Have you ever studied the sunspots, professor? Do you know why they appear?'

'Who can say? Opaque bodies swimming on the liquid matter of the sun, perhaps, or the impact craters of comets. I mentioned that to a lady of my acquaintance, who could not tolerate the idea that God would construct a solar system with such little precision that celestial bodies were forever colliding with one another. She found the whole notion repugnant.'

James looked up. 'Who was this?'

'Lady Ogilvie in Lucan.'

He shook his head. 'A tedious family. Her son a doctor of divinity, and three daughters indistinguishable behind their white caps and prayer books.'

I said to the professor, 'Did you ever direct Lady Ogilvie's attention to the surface of the moon?'

He smiled and said, 'I doubt that it would do any good. The minds of the devout are not for turning.'

Mrs Perrin came in to clear the soup bowls, taking care with Mr Caulfeild's as it was still nearly full. Kathy followed with plates of cold meat and cheese, and another decanter of wine. A silence had settled over the table, so I turned to James and said, 'I am very much looking forward to the ball in Charlemont House next month, Mr Caulfeild. Will you still be in Dublin?'

'I believe so. My studies have finished in London, and I have taken up a position at the observatory. I shall be here for quite some time.'

'Oh, good,' I said, knowing that Clarissa would be pleased. I could almost feel her pinching me to mention her name, so that he might remember. 'Miss Egan and I shall both be in attendance.'

He frowned slightly, and I said, 'Reverend Egan's daughter, Clarissa.'

'Ah, yes. Is she not a friend of Miss Gould in Fitzwilliam Square? I seem to remember they were inseparable when I visited last year.'

I had been there also, at a levée to mark Edith's coming out. That was before Mr Darby's church had become prominent, and already it seemed a more colourful, carefree time.

'All three of us were friends,' I said. 'Though Edith has been keeping different company of late.'

'Yes,' James said, flatly. 'So I believe.'

Father asked him what his duties would entail in the observatory, and he replied, 'As yet, I do not know. Whatever the professor demands.'

Reeves folded his napkin on the table. 'It has been some time since my last assistant moved on, so I can scarcely think of tasks to assign, but I am sure we shall have a productive summer.'

As the lunch passed, the professor asked Father about his work as coroner, posing his questions with a frank curiosity that made him appear more youthful. Father was happy to answer, expounding on the use of the skull-chisel while deftly slicing the white flesh of a chicken breast. Eventually, James took a pocket watch from his waistcoat and said that it was time they were leaving. 'We are expected in the Royal Academy shortly.'

'I have been asked to give a lecture,' Reeves

said. "On perturbations in the orbit of the Georgian Planet'. Very dull, I fear, but you would both be welcome if you wish to come.'

I knew Father preferred to avoid the Academy and the interminable intrigues of its members, and I saw him straighten his mouth, the way he did when he was about to refuse something, so I interjected.

'We'd be delighted.'

'Well,' Father said, 'it is very kind, professor. But would Abigail be allowed to attend?'

'Oh, yes. There is no official bar on females. It is just a habit they have fallen into. There is even talk of electing Caroline Herschel as an honorary member.'

I thought that unlikely considering the Academy's history with regard to women. When it was founded, one of its most prominent antiquarians was Charlotte Brooke, who translated Gaelic poetry into English. She fell on hard times, and members of the Academy wondered what they could do to improve her situation. They decided to appoint her housekeeper of the Academy premises.

'It is settled then,' I said.

Father looked at me. 'Yes, it would appear so. We shall follow you there, gentlemen.'

As we crossed the city in the carriage, I wondered if I should tell Father of my visit to Mrs Longsworth and the things she'd said. I knew that he considered the inquest into Emilie's death closed, the verdict delivered, and he would be upset with me for continuing to interfere. I would keep the information to myself for now, at least until I could find something more.

Liam let us off by the steps of the Academy building on Grafton Street, and we hurried through a dark-oak door into a hallway lit by candelabra. Several gentlemen were ambling up a staircase towards a room on the second floor. A porter greeted my father and gave me an enquiring look, as if I had wandered from the street in error. He took our coats to a cloakroom, where I saw him hang my felt cap among the black tricornes and toppers.

The room upstairs was lofty enough to have a mezzanine level, each wall covered in books with gold-leaf lettering. Stained-glass windows were decorated with images of science and industry: hammers and tongs, clockworks and escapements, the burners and glassware of a chemist's laboratory. Rows of chairs had been set out before a raised stage and lectern. Father was waylaid by someone, so I went to claim two seats next to a grey-haired gentleman with a protruding lip like that of a scolded child.

A doorway near the stage opened, and Reeves and Caulfeild made their way to the lectern. They watched the crowd assemble, and seemed to take note of certain individuals.

The gentleman beside me leaned towards my shoulder. 'I must say, I'm rather vexed to see you here,' he said, though there was humour in his eyes.

'Oh?'

'I have to write a report for the *Transactions*, and I already had my first line prepared: 'A very respectable association of gentlemen were pleased to attend the Royal Astronomer on such and such date . . . '' He glanced at me. 'Saying 'an association of gentlemen and one lady' is rather more clumsy.'

'Perhaps another woman will come.'

'I doubt it,' he said, folding his arms. 'In any case, it is not a trend to be encouraged. I remember in London years ago, attendance at lectures in the Royal Institute became a fashionable pursuit in some circles. Ladies would scramble for seats as though they were boxes at the theatre, which was all very well, but if you could only hear the clamour of their tongues!' He closed his eyes briefly, as if the noise still assailed him. 'The eloquence and learning of the speakers was often lost in the din.'

He looked at me as though he expected sympathy for this ordeal.

'I have become adept at holding my tongue,' I said.

'I am glad to hear it.' He introduced himself as Mr Brinkley, and when I told him my name, he asked, 'Is your father the Doctor of Physic in Cork University?'

'No, he is the coroner here in Dublin.'

'I am thinking of someone else entirely.'

The porter was just about to close the main doors to the hall when four men entered, dressed much alike in dark coats and white cravats. They took seats near the back, underneath the mezzanine.

Brinkley was regarding the stage. 'I wonder why Lord Charlemont's son is up there with Reeves.'

'Mr Caulfeild is his new assistant at the observatory.'

'How do you know?'

'The professor told me himself.'

Brinkley's mouth turned down on both sides, as if he were impressed by this first-hand knowledge.

'A surprising choice,' he said.

'Why is that?'

'Well, only in comparison to his previous assistant. It was years ago now, Reeves took in a young man, a Trinity student who had shown great promise but who had fallen on hard times after expulsion from the college. If not for Reeves, he would have found himself on the streets.'

'What had he done to be expelled?'

'An ill-advised experiment with electrical currents. He constructed a Voltaic pile of such power that when it discharged he managed to maim himself and several others, and burn down a lecture theatre, as well as an extensive collection of pinned moths from New South Wales.'

'Goodness.'

'Indeed.'

'And Professor Reeves was willing to employ him?'

'He took the view that one cannot make breakfast without addling eggs, that it was only fair to give the young man a second chance. And when Reeves is convinced that an action is justified, he will not be dissuaded from carrying it out. A rather admirable trait.'

Everyone in the room had settled in their seats, including Father, who had come to join me. James left the professor on stage, and took a chair in the front row. The Academy president, Earl Bury, stood up and introduced the lecture, welcoming old friends and new faces, and inviting the professor to begin.

Reeves took a moment to straighten his notes on the lectern. He spoke in the same manner as he had done at the dining table, his voice only loud enough to fill the room. He described how Descartes had proposed that the world and all the planets were carried around the sun in vortices of ethereal fluid, just as chips of wood are carried in a whirlpool. 'By this system, the moon and every secondary planet has its vortex, every falling body has its current to urge it towards the earth, requiring such a clash and interference of forces as must produce universal confusion. Even Newton could not untangle the multitude of influences that heavenly bodies should exert on each other. 'It is not to be conceived,' he said, 'that mere mechanical causes could give birth to so many regular motions. This most beautiful system of the sun, planets and comets could only proceed from the counsel and dominion of an intelligent and powerful being.''

He surveyed the audience for a moment. 'If you ever read the *Principia*, you may notice that the only time Newton invokes God is when he has reached the limits of his own understanding. I am pleased to say that the mechanics of these subtle influences, these perturbations, are no longer a mystery. With new theories, and new mathematics, we can explain the discrepancies in the orbit of the Georgian planet, and God need not form part of our hypothesis.'

Brinkley glanced around the room. He whispered to me, 'I'll have to remember that quote for my report.'

One of the men at the back of the hall stood up. 'Professor Reeves,' he said, 'may I ask you a question?'

The professor began to say that he would prefer to take queries at the end of the lecture, but the man spoke over him. 'You wrote recently that in your view the age of the earth was not four thousand years before the birth of Christ, but that it could be several hundred thousand, or millions of years old.'

'Yes. What of it?'

'Do you not feel that it is an insult to this body that you falsify and misrepresent the word of God to such a degree? You can only inspire horror at the blasphemy of your utterances.'

James Caulfeild turned in his seat to glare at the speaker. Reeves remained impassive. He leaned his forearm on the lectern for a moment, and seemed to be composing some response, but then he smiled to himself and shook his head.

'I shall continue with my remarks.'

Another voice yelled, 'Do not ignore the question,' and several others followed suit, not just from the back of the room, but from rows close to where Father and I were sitting. Earl Bury got to his feet. He turned with his arms outstretched. 'Gentlemen,' he said, waiting for the voices to subside. 'This is not how we conduct our business.'

'I thought this was a debating chamber,' someone said. Each voice came from a different person, but they sounded alike, high in volume and tinged with unmerited outrage.

Bury said, 'Professor Reeves can debate any point he wishes. But first he must be allowed to deliver his lecture without interruption.'

'If we allow him to go unchallenged now, if we give him this platform, we may as well say that the Academy endorses every one of his vile beliefs.'

Reeves leafed through some of his papers. He dabbed a forefinger with his tongue and removed one page from the sheaf to place at the back.

'I need not remind you,' Bury said, 'that the Academy, as a body, is not answerable for any opinion, or representation of facts, or train of reasoning that may be uttered here. The speakers alone are responsible for the content of their lectures.'

Now James was on his feet. 'How can you suggest that the professor must answer for anything? You take the side of these zealots by entertaining their absurd demands.'

'I only wish to provide an opportunity for Professor Reeves to finish his remarks. Then anyone may challenge him if they wish.'

'But this lecture has nothing to do with the age of the earth. Their only wish is to be disruptive.'

The original speaker said, 'No one should be allowed to occupy that stage if he intends to utter falsehood, no matter the subject. It is harmful to the reputation of the Academy, harmful to the religious life of the city.'

I elbowed Father in the arm. 'Say something.'

He glanced down at me, 'What would you have me say?'

'Defend the professor from these attacks.'

'He is well capable of defending himself.'

The man came out from beneath the mezzanine and stood in the weak light from the stained-glass windows. 'I say it again, you cannot wilfully and contemptuously falsify the word of God. We shall not allow it.'

'I believe that I know the word of God better than you,' Reeves said.

'You cannot possibly.'

'I fear it is true, and not just in the way you imagine. I was bid to read the Bible over and again when I was a child, and much to my sorrow, I can summon any verse. If I had read in any other book, 'Happy is he that dasheth thy little ones against the rock,' I would have set it aside with revulsion.'

'You are distorting scripture again,' the man said, and others began to speak, but Reeves would not be silent, and he raised his voice to speak over them.

'What kind of society would counsel that a slave submit himself to his master, or that a woman learn in silence and subjugation, as your book commands?' He folded his papers on the lectern and set them aside. 'You see, I do know the *true* word of God, written for all to see in the workings of nature, in a language that you cannot corrupt or falsify or suppress,' he said, extending an index finger towards his critics. 'It speaks to all nations and to all people equally, and reveals everything that we need to know the mind of our creator.'

Several others in the room rose in protest, their chairs scraping over the floor, but Reeves ignored them.

'I have no wish to argue with you, gentlemen. If all you want to do is listen to a preacher, then I suggest you go to church.'

He nodded to James, and they both walked through the crowd towards the door. James seemed ready to answer every catcall and gesticulation, but the professor remained impassive. Even after they had left, the arguments continued, and Father suggested that we depart as well. In the hallway, I looked out for Reeves, and again on the street, but he must have slipped away quickly. Liam was parked on College Green, and we climbed into the quiet of the carriage to make our way home.

Father settled in his seat and drew the window down slightly. 'I remember now why I stopped attending the Academy.'

'How awful for Professor Reeves to be attacked like that,' I said.

'It was unfortunate.'

'It was maddening, for a man of science to be shouted down. You were correct when you said that he could fend for himself. I thought he answered them so well.'

Father had been observing the passing streetscape, but he turned to look at me for a moment. 'His rhetoric was indeed forceful.'

'Did you not agree with all he said?'

'I don't recall a point with which I disagreed. But Abigail, there is a way to put forward ideas without upsetting the beliefs of others.'

'It was their fault for confronting him.'

'That may be. But some would look upon what the professor said as heresy and treat him accordingly.'

'All the more reason to stand by him. We should not be cowed by those who claim ownership of the truth.'

'Nor should we seek to provoke them.'

'Why not?'

'Because they might hurt you.' I glanced at him, but he shook his head at his own choice of words. 'I mean sully your name, damage your reputation. I hope that Professor Reeves does not come to regret that.'

It seemed to me that the professor could not be daunted, but I let the matter rest and we continued the journey in silence. Outside, there was a gleam on the surface of puddles and pavements, and in the distance I could see the steeple of St George's over the rooftops. It seemed the fog was beginning to lift.

5

We had a room in the loft next to Kathy's bedchamber that contained a jumble of odds and ends. My old rocking-horse sat in one corner, tilted forward. It had scuffed paintwork and chipped nostrils, and a black mane of real horsehair combed over one eye. There were boxes filled with my mother's old dresses and correspondence. Jimmy picked his way between the clutter to open a small sash window. Outside, there was a ledge, sheltered by eaves and gutters extending from the roof overhead.

Three devices sat on the sill exposed to the late-morning air. Jimmy leaned forward to examine the first: a Swedish thermometer, the temperature marked in centigrade after Anders Celsius. It had been a gift from my father on my fifteenth birthday, but though I loved the scrolled redwood surround, the slender glass tube and vein of quicksilver, I thought the Fahrenheit scale better suited to the Irish climate; for how could one consider a day's temperature to be less than zero?

A breeze made Jimmy's eyes water, and he blinked once.

'What does it say?'

'Sixteen,' he said, the highest we'd seen it since we began taking measurements in the spring. The sun's warmth had finally penetrated, and, for the first time that summer, hearths remained cold and winter cloaks were set aside.

The barometer was Jimmy's favourite device, since he'd made it himself: an empty glass jar sealed with a thin piece of pig's bladder stretched over the top. When air pressure was high, the membrane had a depression in the centre, and when low, it ballooned upwards. He bent lower so his eye was level with the top of the jar.

'What do you think?'

'Flat as a flounder,' he said.

Church bells chimed over the city, and I said we had to hurry. The third instrument was a brass frame in which a small weight hung suspended from a single strand of my own hair. When we first set it up, I'd spent a finicky afternoon tying one end to the frame and the other to the weight; several had snapped before I got it right. Human hair was considered the best fibre for the task, expanding in the presence of moisture, and contracting when dry. And since my hair was completely unmanageable in muggy weather, I told Jimmy we had the most sensitive instrument in the city.

As the weight rose and fell it caused a long needle to oscillate within a half-moon scale. Fine lines had been etched in the metal denoting percentages, with the words '*humidité extrème*' and '*sécheresse extrème*' at the top and bottom of the arc. On the day we set it up, a fog rolled in over Dublin. The weight descended and the pointer crept upwards, and I'd told Jimmy to imagine how slight the droplets must be that they could permeate the filament. He had found it pleasing, that something so imperceptible could still be detected.

Jimmy peered at the scale and said the humidity today was forty-two per cent, declaring that to be relatively dry. He opened a notebook on the sill. Each page was filled with lists of measurements arranged by date, tracking not only changes in weather, but the progression of Jimmy's handwriting. He leafed to the final page, uncorked the inkpot and took up a quill.

'Sixteen and forty-two,' I said. 'The year that Galileo died.'

Jimmy wrote out each figure with care, though his 2 had an exaggerated loop making it look like a lower-case a. Down below, my father and Ewan emerged from their workrooms. Father was speaking with expansive gestures, probably expounding on some medical phenomenon, and Ewan walked beside him with his head bent and hands held behind his back. They paused next to a wall where coils of sweet pea were just beginning to flower. In the sunlight, Ewan's hair appeared more blond than auburn. He swept a forelock over his left ear with his thumb, a habit that I had begun to notice.

Jimmy was saying my name.

'Hmm?'

'I said should I close the window?'

'No, I'll do it. You go and get ready.'

He nodded and hurried from the room. While reaching up, a breeze ruffled the lace on my cuff, and I noticed that the temperature outside had dipped by a degree. The membrane atop the barometer swelled upwards. I gazed at the horizon over the terraced rooftops, but all I could see was a hazy blue.

★ ★ ★

St George's Church faced on to a wide crescent of houses in Hardwicke Place, where parishioners were congregating from the surrounding streets. I walked with Jimmy and Mrs Perrin, while my father and Ewan went a few strides ahead. We turned a corner, and the elegant spire of the church came into view. A large group of Brethren stood on either side of the railed entrance. There were close to fifty of them, of all ages, their black cloaks billowing against the white façade.

Mr Darby was to the forefront, and once again Mrs Nesham stood near; it seemed she rarely left his side. It was still odd to see her dressed in black like the others. Whenever I'd met her before — in crowded salons, or even walking in Rutland Gardens — she'd worn refined gowns befitting the young wife of an established barrister. If her place within the Brethren had been affected by the scandal in her household, it didn't show; indeed, she seemed to be the first among them. There was no sign of Mr Nesham; but there towards the back of the group stood the maid Martha, with young Lucia in her arms. Martha noticed me, and our eyes met for a moment before she lowered her gaze.

Two of the Brethren held a sign between them, a long black board with letters painted white, saying 'Hosea 2:4'. My father and Ewan

110

passed them without turning their heads. I had intended to do the same, but then I stopped, for I recognized the girl holding one side of the board. It was Edith Gould.

It had been months since I'd seen her last. She was paler than I remembered. The dark cloak didn't suit her.

I said, 'Hello, Edith.'

She searched my face for a moment, before lifting the sign higher, as if she hadn't recognized me.

'It's Abigail. Abigail Lawless.'

Her father was standing to one side, wearing the black coat and metal hooks like all the Brethren men. Judge Gould turned his head when he heard my name, and he said something in his daughter's ear. She still didn't speak, and focused her attention on people coming in behind me. In the silence I moved past her into the church.

St George's was filled with the smells of varnished wood and candle smoke. I went towards our pew, where Ewan was already seated. Usually my father would be next to him, then Mrs Perrin, myself and Jimmy. But Father was speaking to Dr Barry, whose family occupied the pew in front, and Mrs Perrin and Jimmy were nowhere to be seen. Rather than wait for them, I stepped in and sidled towards Ewan, who straightened in his seat.

We remained silent for a while amidst the sounds of neighbours greeting one another. In the pew in front, a woman held a baby girl against her shoulder, and the child gazed back at us both. Pudgy arms emerged from folds of frilly white linen. The baby held a soft woollen mouse — with pointed ears, stringy whiskers, and a bootlace for a tail. She gnawed happily on its head until it slipped from her grasp and fell at Ewan's feet. He picked up the sodden toy and handed it back. The girl accepted it with a smile and promptly threw it down again.

Bibles sat on the ledge of the pew. I picked one up and flicked through the books of the Old Testament until I reached Hosea, the first of the twelve minor prophets.

Ewan once more handed the toy to the baby, but this time he kept hold of its tail. When she tried to release it again, he said, 'No,' with a soft voice, the vowel made long by his accent.

I traced my finger to the second chapter and the fourth verse. *And I shall not have mercy upon her children, for they be the children of whoredoms.*

Mrs Perrin sat down beside me, saying, 'Dr Barry has relations visiting, so he's asked us to make room.'

I looked towards the aisle where Father was speaking to an elderly couple.

'But we're over as far — '

The housekeeper shifted in her seat, pushing me against Ewan to the point that our shoulders and hips touched. Mrs Perrin noticed the Bible in my hands. 'Good,' she said. 'You two can share that.' She passed out the others, and said in a loud voice, 'Here you are, Dr Barry.' The old man reached over and took one, saying that he could hear perfectly well.

The congregation quietened as Clarissa's father entered the pulpit. Rev Egan placed some notes on a lectern and then looked for his spectacles, first by patting his silver locks, before locating them in a front pocket. 'I thought I might have been able to start by thanking God for the break in the weather,' he said, just as strong gusts began to make the front doors creak, and rain pattered against the roof. 'But I fear it has reverted to form.' He looked up over the rim of his spectacles. 'Also, I believe you all had to run the gauntlet this morning.' An amused murmur spread throughout the church. Rev Egan said, 'I just pray those dark cloaks of theirs are watertight.'

The vicar read the parish announcements, raising his voice when the wind grew stronger. An organist in the balcony played a prelude, while rain continued to fall against the stained-glass windows behind the altar. The panes showed scenes from the gospels, as well as the apostles standing with bare feet and mournful eyes. Of the twelve, St Thomas was my favourite: Doubting Thomas, who would not believe that Christ was resurrected until he'd examined the wounds from the nails and spear, showing a healthy respect for forensic medicine that I'd always liked.

I was only thirteen when the stained-glass windows were installed. Back then, Rev Egan had encouraged the children of the congregation to look upon the images, to think about the stories and people portrayed. I could remember staring dutifully for several minutes, but then I whispered to my father, asking how could the light from the sun be blocked by the wood and metal of the window frames, yet pass through the glass that was just as solid. The colours had projected on to the nave floor in ruby red and cobalt blue, and I wondered why the designs hadn't cast a plain shadow of black or grey. How had the light known the colour of the glass through which it passed? He said that he would explain it all after the service, but later he was called away — for me, people were forever dying at inconvenient moments. That evening as I readied for bed, I discovered a copy of Newton's *Opticks* left on my nightstand.

Rev Egan continued to recite from first Corinthians, and we all looked down at our Bibles as if testing his reading. I held one open between myself and Ewan. He shifted in his seat, causing that side of the bench to creak. When he settled, his elbow rested against my arm, but not uncomfortably, so I decided not to move. Sheet lightning flashed behind the windows, and a few seconds later a low rumble echoed in the roof. Mrs Perrin tut-tutted, and said that she was glad she'd taken the laundry in. A brighter flash was followed by a loud peal. The baby girl in front of us began to cry, and Rev Egan had to raise his voice.

The side of my leg rested against Ewan's, and I was reluctant to shift about, despite a stiffness from the awkward way I held the Bible. Eventually I allowed myself to relax. The pressure between us increased, and I wondered if he would feel it and pull away; or perhaps even press back.

Ewan reached over to turn the page, for I had failed to notice that Rev Egan was already reading several verses overleaf.

The lightning grew in frequency, and people started at the claps of thunder. A hinged window near the ceiling was forced open; the sash tilted and strained against the stile as rain swirled about, and then it was sucked closed again with a bang. Rev Egan faltered in his reading. He removed his spectacles and looked towards the church doors, saying, 'Our friends would not have maintained their vigil, surely?' He came down from the pulpit and marched through the church. All heads followed his progress. He grasped the door handle to pull it open, but had to brace himself as it was blown inwards. Rev Egan bent his head to peer outside, his wispy hair flying about. He began calling out, but his words couldn't be heard above the wind. Gusts resonated in the pipes of the organ, adding a tuneless keen to the racket of the storm, and the sheet music of the organist was whipped into the nave.

Members of the Brethren began to enter in ones and twos. Their cloaks and hats were drenched, their faces reddened; it was incredible that they'd not sought shelter when the weather had turned. I looked out for Martha, concerned that Lucia might have been soaked, but when the maid came in she held her charge close beneath the cover of her cloak. Mrs Nesham and Darby were the last to enter. Though several pews near the entrance were empty, the Brethren remained standing in the aisles, like mourners who had arrived late for a funeral, or penitents of old forbidden from passing the narthex.

Rev Egan returned to the pulpit to resume his sermon, though he had to cough before everyone in the congregation turned to face him. For some, the thought that their weekly observances were being judged must have felt like a prickle on the nape of the neck, and several couldn't resist glancing back towards the Brethren.

A flash of lightning and peal of thunder occurred simultaneously, its boom answered in the church by muttered prayers. Rev Egan suggested that we sing a hymn to lift our spirits, and invited Clarissa's mother to lead the congregation. He said, 'Number twenty-nine, I think.'

In our pew, Mrs Perrin sang in an ardent voice from the hymnal that she shared with her son. Ewan and I remained silent. Like me, it seemed he had no wish to join in.

> *'Amidst the storm Jehovah reigns,*
> *And guards his people's weal.*
> *He holds the lightning fast in chains,*
> *Though all creation reel.'*

I took up the Bible again, then turned to Hosea and pointed at the verse. Ewan frowned while reading. He whispered, 'The Brethren are keen to place all blame on the fallen servant.'

He seemed ready to speak again, but then he faced forward and remained quiet. My father was regarding us, one side of his hymnal drooping open and his glasses perched at the end of his nose.

116

There was movement at the side of our pew. Lucia Nesham, dressed like her mother in a black frock and white bonnet, stood in the aisle, one hand on Ewan's leg for balance. She and the baby in front of us stared at one another with wide-eyed captivation, their lips forming circles. The baby offered her woollen toy towards Lucia, who clasped her hands together, unsure if she should accept it.

Martha arrived and scooped Lucia up. The toddler creased her face and began to sob, then began to cry in earnest, despite Martha's attempts to shush her. The church was full of noise, with the storm outside and the congregation singing, but Martha seemed to know that Lucia could not be brought back to the Brethren in such a state. She brought her further up the aisle and out through a side door which was sheltered by a small portico.

I glanced back towards the Brethren. Darby and Mrs Nesham were hidden behind one of the columns. I closed my Bible and handed it to Mrs Perrin, who paused in her singing. 'I'm feeling slightly faint,' I said. 'It's so stifling. I might get some air.'

She looked at me with concern and asked if she should come with me.

'No, I'll be fine.'

Ewan leaned back as I brushed past his chest, and I hurried past the pews. The portico outside was in the lee of the church, and Martha and Lucia were well sheltered. The toddler had quietened, and she was watching hailstones skitter over the pavement.

Martha heard me come out. She regarded me for a moment, her gaze made dark by eyebrows that almost met at the bridge of her nose, and although she was a young woman, her back had already begun to hunch.

'Can I help you, Miss Lawless?'

I said that I just required some air, and she paid me no heed when I stood next to her. The hail continued to fall in sheets. Across the street, people had sought refuge beneath a shop awning.

'I am sorry about the loss of Miss Casey,' I said.

Martha's expression didn't change. She stared straight ahead, as if a winter shower in July were commonplace. A few hail-stones rolled close to my feet, became wet and translucent and then disappeared.

'The events of the past few weeks must have been very difficult for Mr and Mrs Nesham.'

Still no response. I wondered if she'd heard me above the din of the shower. Perhaps others would have been riled by her lack of deference; but I was rather impressed.

'It's been harder on the rest of the staff,' she said.

'Of course, I am sorry. Were you and Miss Casey close?'

'There's still the same amount of work to be done, but one less person to do it.'

'Oh.'

She passed Lucia from one arm to the other, and then glanced at me. 'Emilie was pleasant enough. She always did as asked, and believed

118

anything you told her.'

'Did you know she was with child?'

'Downstairs we knew. Though she hid it well. The mistress seemed to think she was just getting plump.'

A small barefoot boy ran out from beneath the shop awning, hunched his shoulders and held his hands up to catch the hail. His mother cursed and dragged him back beneath the shelter, and Lucia laughed.

'Emilie told me that you knew the child's father.'

Martha turned her head sharply. 'Some fisherman from a country town? How could I know him?'

'No, he was a member of the Brethren. Emilie would tell you that she was visiting her cousin in Clare Street, when really she was seeing him.'

Her eyes narrowed, but I didn't look away, and we remained silent as the hail turned into a cold rain. Eventually she said, 'She wasn't fooling anyone.'

'Even the Neshams?'

'Perhaps them.'

'What was his name, Martha?'

'I don't know.'

'You must.'

'Why are you so keen to know? Just because Emilie was ruined?'

'Because she was wronged. She was used and abandoned, and it's not fair that he should escape without blame.'

I expected Martha to look upon me with some derision, but instead her face was thoughtful.

'I must return to the others,' she said.

'Is he among them here today?'

She remained silent. The clouds had parted and weak sunshine made the black railings glisten. The sign carried by the Brethren had been left outside, and had been blown against the front gate so that it almost stood upright.

I pointed to it. 'Do you know what this verse says?'

'Yes.'

'They denigrate Emilie's memory completely.'

Martha shifted Lucia's weight again. We could hear the doors open at the front of the church, and members of the Brethren began to emerge on to the street, as if they'd only been waiting for a break in the weather. Inside, the congregation had finished their hymn, and in the silence a breeze echoed in the vaulted stone of the portico.

Martha began to walk towards them, but after a few steps she stopped and turned about. With her eyes still lowered she said, 'Gould.'

'The judge?'

She shook her head. 'His son.'

Someone called out, 'Martha.' Mrs Nesham stood by the railing at the front of the church, too far away to have overheard, but still Martha began to walk towards her without another word. Mrs Nesham kept her eyes on me until the maid passed her. She raised the hood of her black cloak and followed after the Brethren. I looked among them for Edith and saw her almost at once, for her head was uncovered. She walked beside her father and another young man, whom I recognized now as her brother, Robert. His dark hair was swept forward, and his starched shirt collar stood up against his chin. Edith caught me looking from the steps, and our eyes met for a moment. The Brethren continued to move along the street in dark procession. In the distance, the storm clouds had broken over the mountains, all their energy spent.

★ ★ ★

Mrs Perrin and I made our way through the back yard, past Father's workrooms and out into the stable lane behind Rutland Square. The housekeeper carried a basket in the crook of her elbow. We both lifted our skirts from the rutted surface — turned into a mire by the earlier rain — and picked our way to an establishment located on the corner. A curved wooden sign that hung from rusting chains said, 'Whistler — tailor and cordwainer'. Coils of smoke emerged from an opened half-door, but Mrs Perrin was undaunted. She leaned on the lower half and said, 'We're here, Mr Whistler.'

A grunt from within was encouragement enough for her to push the door open. It only moved a small distance before it scraped and jammed against an uneven floor, but we were able to squeeze by. The workshop was low and gloomy. Glowing coals shifted in a brazier in the corner, where a black terrier with milky eyes lifted his head to test the air, turning his head directly towards us. He lay by the legs of another dog, which had once been his mother, but all that remained was a tattered pelt, stuffed and badly stitched, with amber eyes that flashed red in the firelight.

Whistler stood by a bench surrounded by candles and a series of shoe moulds on slender metal stands, like upturned duck-bills. A mound of shoes lay beside him: leather riding-boots with their shafts drooping, silk slippers and dancing shoes, brocade ankle-boots, all in a great heap like the spoils of war. Whistler wore an apron over a grey shirt opened at the neck. He was skinny and stooped; his hair, which receded either side of a prominent widow's peak, was grown long and swept over one ear. A buckled shoe made of polished leather sat on a mould before him.

Mrs Perrin said, 'We've brought the — '

'Just a minute.' He reached into a bowl filled with small metal nails and took out about a dozen, which he promptly deposited in his mouth as if eating a handful of nuts. He took up a hammer, withdrew a nail from his lips and drove it into the sole of the shoe with one strike. Then with thumb and forefinger he extracted another and repeated the action. The point of the next nail was already protruding from his lips, and I thought of him rolling and flexing his tongue, separating one from the batch and manoeuvring it to the front, scraping over his scaly gums. His lips were blackened. Who knew what toxins were present in those tacks and hobnails? When younger, I would mention such things to people, hoping they would see the error of their ways. But Father had long since told me to stop. No one liked to receive advice from a young girl. 'And besides, Abigail,' he said, 'they already know.'

Whistler finished resoling the shoe and placed the hammer on the table. He spat into the brazier, sending a burst of sparks and puff of ash into the air. I leaned towards Mrs Perrin and whispered, 'I'm not sure this is the man for the job.'

Coming here had been a last resort. The levée in Charlemont House was only a week away, and every dressmaker and boutique in the city was inundated with orders. Only the most fashionable were receiving priority, which meant I was out of luck. I'd be forced to wear the old dress bought for my cousin's wedding a few years ago, which was terribly out of date and too small. We could have attempted to alter it ourselves, but sewing was never my strong suit, and, despite her many domestic talents, Mrs Perrin did not possess the finesse to create a ball-gown fit for Charlemont House. All had seemed lost, but Mrs Longsworth had assured me that she knew of a man.

'I believe you have a frock for me,' Whistler said.

The housekeeper stepped forward. 'That's right.' She placed her basket on the workbench and withdrew my cream muslin gown, and a length of the same material for adjustments.

The cobbler picked up the dress and examined it. I feared he would leave dark stains, but his hands and shirtsleeves were spotless.

'Tell Mr Whistler what you want done,' Mrs Perrin said.

I straightened my shoulders and opened the page of *Costume Parisien*, which had been bookmarked at the plate Clarissa had recommended. Whistler squinted at it.

'I'd very much like this design, Mr Whistler. With long sleeves as in the picture, the waistline raised and the neckline cut square, instead of the round one at present. Though I wouldn't want it to plunge any lower.'

Whistler looked me up and down and said, 'No.' He put the dress aside, took a rolled-up tape from the pocket of his apron, and held one end so it uncoiled like a snake. 'Well,' he said, 'let's get you measured up.'

Mrs Perrin cleared her throat and held out a sheet of paper. 'All the measurements are here, Mr Whistler. They're quite accurate — only taken yesterday.'

Whistler regarded the page for a moment, then took it from her. 'I won't be responsible if they're not.'

'Of course.'

'Day after tomorrow then,' he said.

'Thank you. Come along, Abigail.'

I left the magazine on the bench, retrieved the bookmark, and then replaced it, scared that he would look at the wrong picture. I was about to turn away, but stopped and said, 'Mr Whistler, I know you must think this a trifle, but it's important that the dress looks fitting. I beg of you to take care.'

The cobbler scowled at me for a moment, but then he blinked twice, as if some dim memory crossed his mind, and his expression softened. 'I know, girl. I know these things can seem important.'

'You'll make sure the stitches are neat?'

His scowl returned. 'Why wouldn't they be?'

I looked towards the poor example of taxidermy in the corner of the room and Whistler followed my gaze. 'That wasn't my work.'

'Oh, I'm sorry. I assumed she was yours.'

'She was mine, but someone else did the stuffing.' He held up the dress again by its shoulders, and then looked at me squarely. 'I couldn't bear to skin her.'

6

The genteel terraces of Fitzwilliam Square were broken up by houses still under construction. Men shimmied up ladders and disappeared behind hanging canvas — hod-bearers and brick-layers and stuccodores with their overalls daubed and starched by plaster. The south side was entirely unbuilt, giving the current residents a fine view towards the Dublin Mountains. In the haze, the hills seemed tantalizingly near, a patchwork of mauve and green, their peaks indistinct against a veil of cloud that spread towards the city. Though a stiff breeze caused the trees to rustle against the spiked railings, the sky was static, with spots of brightness here and there making the true position of the sun unclear.

Two labourers at ease regarded me from beneath peaked caps as I waited on the steps of number five. One leaned closer to his companion, murmured something and then spat, which drew a rasping laugh, just as a housemaid answered the door. She led me upwards through a dim staircase, and then rapped at the drawing-room door with a gloved knuckle. I listened for an answer, but only heard the sound of male voices coming from the floor above. Undeterred by the lack of response, the maid opened the door and announced me.

Edith Gould sat by the window, her writing desk positioned to catch the waning afternoon light. She was hunched over a wide sheet of cotton paper, with charcoal sticks scattered about. She didn't look up as I entered, just completed a stroke in her drawing, which she then smudged lightly with her fingertip. The room was sparsely furnished and tidy to the point of starkness. The only disorder was the clutter on Edith's desk, and a painting of an upturned bushel of apples on the fire-screen.

She sat up straight and regarded her picture, then stared intently through the window for several seconds, as if she'd caught a glimpse of some sinister and relentless pursuer, and finally back to her drawing with a tilt of her head. It seemed she was satisfied, for she placed her charcoal down, turned to me and set her face in a welcoming smile.

'Miss Lawless,' she said. 'How nice to see you.'

She looked more like herself in a blue cotton dress. Edith was considered beautiful by all, with smooth skin and dark eyes; though she had a slight pinch to her lip, which made it possible to imagine what she'd look like as an older woman.

'I am sorry to disturb your work,' I said, and she smiled again, without denying that I'd done so. 'May I take a look?'

The scene was the view from her window, particularly the terrace of houses on the far side of the square, the railed garden in the foreground, and a path to one side. Edith was a fine draughtswoman, with an eye for architectural detail, and the illusions she achieved of light and shadow gave the picture great depth. I complimented her on it, and she said it all came from practice. 'One has to while the hours away somehow.'

For a moment, I imagined her sitting there day after day, repeating the same drawing over and over.

Something struck me about the picture. 'You haven't included any people.' Despite the builders at work on the houses, the groundsman rolling the lawn, carriages that passed by and genteel residents who ambled with linked arms, the square in her picture was deserted. I feared she might have taken my comment as criticism, but she didn't appear put-out.

'No,' she said. 'No people. I never seem to get the perspective right.' She picked up the charcoal sticks and placed them upright in a grubby cup.

'It's been, what, six months since we last met?' I said. 'Clarissa Egan and I often speak of you.'

One of her dark eyebrows arched. 'Is that so?'

In truth, the things Clarissa said were rarely flattering, but at least I could honestly answer yes. I continued to make conversation as we took seats near the marble fireplace, asking if she still received instruction for her drawing, and telling of my few encounters with Mrs Meekins. A barking laugh sounded in the hallway, and Edith noticed when my eyes drifted towards the door.

Darker clouds had gathered outside, and an early gloaming drained the few bright colours in the room. Following another pause, I said, 'I'm sorry we couldn't speak for longer outside St George's on Sunday.'

'As am I. They expect us to maintain a certain . . . propriety.'

I said that I understood. 'Are your parents well?'

'Yes, quite well.'

'And your brother?'

A draught made the corner of her drawing waft upwards. She rose from the sofa and used a porcelain figurine as a paperweight, and then returned to her seat without making reply.

'Is your brother at home?'

The drawing-room door opened, and Edith's mother bustled in bearing a candlestick, with the housemaid in tow. Mrs Gould was a thin woman, short of stature and temper. She said, 'Miss Lawless, Miss Lawless,' as she placed the candle on a side table and sat in a wood-backed chair next to her daughter. 'I am sorry to have been so long detained.' She arranged her black skirts over her knees with small precise actions that hardly moved the fabric at all, and then turned to Edith. 'Is it not kind of Miss Lawless to pay you a visit?'

Edith hadn't taken her eyes off me. 'Yes,' she said. 'Most kind.'

Mrs Gould asked after my own mother, and I told her that she had died the year before.

'Oh, I am sorry, I'm just remembering now. She had been ill for some time, wasn't that so? What exactly was it that ailed her?' she said, with a directness she no doubt considered a mark of candour rather than tactlessness.

I was unsure how to respond, or at least respond accurately, for no one could diagnose the multiple fixations and complexes that had bound my mother to her room.

'It was her nerves.'

Mrs Gould pressed her lips together, as if she found the idea of a weak will distasteful.

She trusted my father was well. 'Judge Gould often mentions Mr Lawless, and the number of new cases being sent to King's Bench.' She smiled — at least she drew her lips back and bared her teeth. 'He says it's wonderful to finally have a coroner willing to get his hands dirty,' as if my father belonged with the labourers clambering over the scaffolding in Fitzwilliam Square.

The male voices upstairs became audible for a moment; one in particular had been raised in anger. Mrs Gould met my gaze, the stillness of her eyes betraying an effort not to glance upwards. Raindrops pattered against the windows, then were lashed in a gust, and she seemed to welcome the noise and the distraction.

'Such wild weather we are having.'

'I was just saying to Edith that I saw you all taking shelter from the storm last Sunday.'

She thought for a moment. 'Of course, you are in St George's parish. We shall be at St Andrew's this week. Mr Darby is tireless when it comes to propagating our message.'

'I believe I saw him as well.'

'If only you could hear him speak, Miss Abigail. Such eloquence and command of scripture, don't you think, Edith?' Her daughter seemed to know that she wasn't expected to answer, for Mrs Gould continued without pause. 'The likes of Rev Egan are all very well, and I know your families are bound by old ties of friendship, but conventional preachers seem incapable of conveying the danger posed to the principles and power of true religion.' She spoke as if reciting from a pamphlet, saying that there had been a persistent decline in the morals and scruples of 'our own kind' in Dublin, while the Romish priesthood kept the great majority of the people in ignorance, superstition and idolatry. 'Why, a third of the country can understand discourse in no language but their own Gaelic tongue, in which, you can be sure, there is no Protestant instruction to temper their restless and intriguing spirits.'

I said that I was aware of that, and was tempted to ask Mrs Gould how many languages *she* could speak. 'Did Mr Darby preach in Dublin previously?'

'No, he had a small church in the Wicklow hills where he was able to contemplate and form his doctrine.' She seemed ready to elaborate on that further, but more noises came from the rooms above. Something fell and skittered across the floorboards, and the yelling swelled, this time with two distinct voices. Mrs Gould motioned for her maid.

'Sally, come here,' she said. 'I have been a very careless hostess. Would you like tea, Miss Lawless?'

The maid bent low and listened as her mistress whispered in her ear. Sally suffered from strabismus — a squint — and one of her eyes lingered on me, though I knew she couldn't help it. Mrs Perrin would have said that she'd been born in the middle of the week — looking both

131

ways for Sunday. Off she went on her supposed errand, no doubt dispatched to quieten the argument.

When the door clicked shut there was silence in the room once more. Edith had hardly said a word since her mother entered, though she'd not said much before that either. Rain continued to blur the windows, and the single candle did little to keep the gloom at bay.

'Mrs Nesham seems to be a prominent member of your congregation,' I said.

Edith became still, eyes cast down at her clasped hands, but her mother was unperturbed at the mention of the name.

'Naturally,' she said. 'Mr Darby is her brother.'

'Mrs Nesham's brother?'

'Well, brother-in-law. I believe her sister, Mrs Darby, died a winter or two ago in Wicklow. Some say complications in childbirth.' She pursed her lips. 'One doesn't like to pry.'

Once again, Mrs Gould began to arrange her skirts, pinching the fabric between her thumb and forefinger as if she plucked at loose threads, but after a moment she glanced up at my lack of response.

'How very sad,' I said.

A door banged shut in the floor above, and heavy footsteps sounded on the stairs. The drawing-room door was thrust open, causing the candle-flame to gutter. Robert Gould strode in and said, 'Mother, I — '

He stopped himself when he saw me, and tried to straighten the angry curl in his lip, but couldn't manage it. The buttons of his brocade waistcoat were undone. He seemed ready to fasten them, but then he brought his hands behind his back and bowed his head. 'Forgive this intrusion.' He retreated from the room and shut the door again.

Edith looked to her mother, and then at me, an accusation in her glance, as if my arrival had heralded this quarrel. Mrs Gould sat open-mouthed for a moment, but then she adopted a lighter air. 'Do you have any brothers, Miss Lawless?'

'No, ma'am.'

'Then you must relish living in a house of peace and quiet.'

I said that perhaps this wasn't the best time for a visit.

'Not at all,' she said, but then we heard the heavy sound of the front door shaking in its latch. There had been no let-up in the rain. 'Where is Sally with the tea? And maybe we should light a second candle to better see the first.'

'Really,' I said. 'My father will be expecting me, and I'm loath to leave Liam in weather like this.' I stood up. 'It was very pleasant seeing you, Edith. Feel free to call on me in Rutland Square.' She rose alongside her mother, and I told them that I could see myself out.

Liam edged the horses forward when he saw me. He alighted from his seat, rain falling over his oilskin coat and hat in small rivulets, and he ushered me into the shelter of the carriage. I pulled my cloak about me, and looked up at number five. Edith had returned to her window, perhaps to continue her drawing, or perhaps to watch my departure. In the floor above, I caught a glimpse of Judge Gould in his study, closing over the shutters.

The labourers were taking shelter from the downpour, leaning on bars in the scaffolding or huddled beneath tattered awnings, looking out over the rain-swept square with glum, thoughtful faces, as if they'd been touched by the melancholy of the scene.

We turned the corner into Baggot Street and soon passed Robert Gould, who was striding towards St Stephen's Green. He walked with his head bent and hat tilted forward, hands folded beneath his arms, and he looked like a man sorry for the haste with which he'd left his house. He wore only a thin morning coat and flat leather shoes, and his grey trousers were already soaked through.

I knocked on the ceiling and called for Liam to stop, then opened the carriage door and waited for Robert to come abreast. 'Come into the carriage, Mr Gould, and Liam will take you where you wish to go.'

His head lifted, and he squinted at me for a moment as if trying to place me. The brim of his hat had started to droop to one side. He seemed ready to walk on without a response, but some gentlemanly instinct must have flickered, for he straightened and called above the noise of the rain, 'No, thank you. I've not far to go.'

'I cannot leave you like this.' I pushed the door open and shifted back in my seat, allowing room for him to enter. 'I insist, Mr Gould.'

He hesitated a moment longer, looked over his shoulder, and then climbed into the carriage. He sat opposite me and to the right, pulling the door closed and sliding the window shut. Once he'd settled, the only sound was the rain pattering on the roof. Robert picked at a sodden fold of fabric over his knee, in much the same way his mother had done, and then clasped his fingers together as if in prayer.

'Were you going somewhere in particular?'

Without glancing up, he said that he'd only been out for a stroll. 'Please continue on, and I'll depart once the rain eases.'

'Would you like us to bring you home?'

'Absolutely not.'

Perhaps he thought his emphasis imprudent, for he turned his face to look out of the window. I tapped against the roof, and the carriage jolted as we set off once more.

Robert's presence seemed to make the air feel cooler. At close quarters he appeared youthful: gangly legs took up much of the space between the seats, his forehead was smooth beneath a fringe of dark curls, and his attempted sideburns were thin and wispy. His wet clothes smelled musty, like an old cloth at the edge of a washbasin, and I became mindful of our proximity, and the tightness of the enclosure.

If Martha was correct, then here was Emilie's seducer, and though he may not have foreseen her crime, he still bore some responsibility. He had threatened to take away Emilie's livelihood, her reputation, and her child. She would have been cast out, her only prospects poverty and loneliness, while he could maintain his privileged life: an education and career, the possibility of a new family; and, half a century from now, while he looked upon his grandchildren playing in a walled garden, Emilie Casey would exist merely as a brief pang of his conscience.

'I came to your home today because I'd hoped to see you,' I said.

He turned to face me, and his eyes narrowed in what seemed like calculation. 'Yes?'

I reached into my coat pocket, withdrew a wrinkled page and handed it to him. He regarded it for a moment, then unfolded it, and saw his own inscription on the title page of Miss Casey's Bible — the one I'd found in her room — which read, *My Dearest Emilie, To light the way . . .*

The carriage turned a corner, and I had to brace myself against the armrest. Robert swayed as he held the flimsy paper open in both hands. He stared at it unblinking, his knuckles whitened, and I expected him to tear the sheet apart. Instead he folded it again, and gently smoothed the crease. He closed his eyes, squeezing them for a moment as if he were committing a passage to memory, and then took a long breath. 'May I keep this?'

He spoke quietly, and I'm sure that if I had refused, he would have handed it back without comment. I nodded, and he tested an inside coat pocket to see if it was dry, then placed it there.

'How did you get it?' His tone wasn't suspicious or accusing, merely curious.

I said that I'd spoken with Emilie the day

before she died. 'She told me . . . many things.'

His lips tightened in what may have been a smile. 'Then you must think very little of me.' Before I could respond, he said, 'Though you're not alone in that opinion.'

The carriage slowed to a halt, and Liam yelled at a costermonger whose cart was blocking the road. One of its wheels was submerged in a muddy pothole, its axle bent. The street-trader was attempting to cover his goods with a stiff tarpaulin.

Robert's forehead almost touched the window, but he seemed oblivious to the scene. 'She begged me not to tell them,' he said. 'She wanted us to run away, to some village on the coast; kept saying we could go at any time. But I was afraid of what I'd have to sacrifice.' One of the deep buttons in the seat was loose, and he twisted it back and forth. 'I think of it now; how I could have found a job as a scrivener or clerk, and a cottage that looked over the sea with a hearth where she could nurse our son.' He glanced up at me. 'How could a man willing to forgo such a life ever presume to find happiness again?'

'You told your parents?'

'My father. Perhaps Mother knows, but she pretends not to.' He said that his father took the news well. He was understanding and thoughtful, and maybe some resolution could have been found. 'But then he told Darby.'

The button snapped from its thread. Robert just left it in the groove without a word of apology. 'Father kept telling me that is what members of a church do: seek spiritual advice.'

'Emilie must have known Mr Darby, if he is Mrs Nesham's brother-in-law.'

Robert nodded. 'She hated him, said he prowled through the house in the small hours muttering to himself, that he treated everyone, except his sister, with utter disdain, even Mr Nesham.'

'Did they suggest that you send Emilie those letters?'

'They almost drafted them,' he said. 'Though I don't mean to shirk responsibility. I signed the letters, and posted them.'

'Did you not consider how painful they would be?'

'I thought of little else. But the tone had to be severe — to convince her that our life together would be impossible.'

'You threatened to put her baby with the foundlings.'

A colour entered his cheeks, and he lowered his eyes. Outside, the costermonger had managed to shift his cart, and Liam inched the carriage forwards.

'It wasn't meant as a threat,' Robert said. 'I wanted her to know that the child would be cared for, that she didn't have to raise him alone, with all the shame that would entail.' He pushed his fingers over his brow, causing the skin to furrow at his temple. 'She never replied. I didn't know that each new letter was adding to her torment.' He kept his palm over his eyes, and sat still for several seconds. The rain had eased, and a watery sunlight entered his side of the carriage, showing a gleam on a golden ring and a bald patch on the sleeve of his morning coat.

He lowered his arm. 'Do you know what happened to her?' His weary tone made the question sound rhetorical, as if he were ready to tell me.

'How do you mean?'

'After she died.'

'There was an inquest,' I said. 'They found it to be *felo de se*.'

'That's what your father decided?'

'That's what the jury decided.'

Robert held my gaze without blinking, but there was no malice in his eyes, or admonition, just a dulled sadness.

I said, 'Do you think they were mistaken in that finding?'

He shook his head. 'I meant after all that. Was she returned to her family?'

'No. The verdict . . . they would have been denied a Christian burial.'

'A small mercy.'

'In all likelihood, she was given to the surgeons.'

A comprehension came over him; he pursed his lips and swallowed, then turned his face to look at the passing streetscape, and I regretted my bluntness. I was too familiar with such procedures, not mindful enough of their ability to shock; especially someone like Robert — the thought that a girl with whom he'd been so intimate, so entwined in love and warmth, could be manhandled on a cold slab, unravelled and picked apart and quite literally eviscerated.

The carriage crossed the river. Our progress

became steady, and Robert remained silent until we neared the Pillar.

'So there is no grave?'

'None marked at least. I am sorry.'

'She has vanished completely.' He nodded to himself and looked skyward, as if only now noticing the improvement in the weather. 'Some will be pleased.' Robert removed his hat and shook drops from its brim, then donned it again. 'My thanks, Miss Lawless, for the refuge of your carriage, but I'd best make my way home.'

He raised his fist, ready to knock against the ceiling, but I said, 'Wait, Mr Gould. There is something that I can show you.'

* * *

The paths in St George's Cemetery had turned muddy from the downpour, and beads of water clung to the evergreens drooping over the red-brick wall. I could still see beyond the gates to where Liam sat huddled on the carriage, Newton and Boyle standing patiently in front, their heads bowed and muzzles steaming. Robert and I counted the paths and turned left, following directions given to us by an old gravedigger. The tombstones were smaller and less elaborate the further we went. At the end of the path, in the most remote corner of the graveyard, a plot contained several rows of small, simple crosses. The side of the plot that we entered was as yet unused and appeared like a well-kept lawn, but I lightened my step, conscious that I trod on the graves of infants not yet conceived. The crosses were mostly uniform, some adorned with pendants on string: withered flowers, a few rag dolls and toy soldiers. Among the newest burials stood a cross bearing the name Morgan Casey. There were no keepsakes.

Robert approached the marker slowly, then sat on his haunches and ran his fingers over the lettering.

'We didn't know to put your name,' I said.

'He's better off without it.'

I thought of the tiny body interred, and his various wounds: deep and ragged from his own mother's knife; clean and clinical from my father's scalpel.

Footsteps sounded as the gravedigger passed by, a pickaxe propped against his shoulder. He tugged at his cap without looking towards us. Behind him, high overhead, a flock of sparrows migrating south reeled momentarily in a twisting, shifting wave, as if spooked by a predator. Robert was clearing cobwebs from the cross, and powdery dirt that had settled in the etched letters.

I looked down at him and said, 'You don't believe that Emilie killed herself.'

He paused in his tidying, and the tail of his coat stirred in the breeze, but then he resumed as if he hadn't heard me, removing a weed where the cross was staked in the ground.

Robert rose and stepped backwards, tossed the weed into an adjacent gully, and brushed the dirt from his hands. 'On the day Morgan died, Father was the one who told me the news. He said that he was sorry, that no one could have foreseen what Emilie would do, but that perhaps it was all for the best.' He shook his head and glanced at me. 'Can you imagine? He spoke of his own grandson.'

A wagtail alighted nearby and flitted from one cross to the next, inspecting the ground with sharp tilts of its head for worms disturbed by the shower.

'He said that I would have to steel myself again. Emilie had been taken to hospital, but she would not endure long, and was lost to me as well. It was the way he said it — he didn't mean she was at risk from infection, or even that she might be tried and hanged, or perish during a long sentence. He seemed to know that she would be gone within days.' Robert noticed some earth stuck to the cuff of his shirt, and he flicked it off with his fingernail, leaving a dark smudge. 'When word finally came, let's just say I was not surprised.'

'But that would mean — '

'That my father knew of it in advance, and that your father failed to identify it in retrospect. I agree, it's easier to believe such things impossible.'

I remembered speaking with Mrs Longsworth, and what she had seen on the night that Emilie died. 'Have you ever come across a man with a lazy eye or drooping eyelid? Is there a member of the Brethren like that?'

He thought for a moment. 'Not that I've ever met. Why?'

I was about to answer, but there were more steps on the path, and I turned to see Liam approaching, lantern held aloft against the gathering dusk. He stopped at the edge of the plot, looked between Robert and me, and said, 'Getting on, miss.'

'Yes, of course. But we'll have to bring Mr Gould back to Fitzwilliam Square.'

'No,' Robert said. 'No, thank you. I'd prefer to stay a while longer.' Before I could speak again, he said, 'You cannot know how much I appreciate your taking me here, Miss Lawless,' and he bowed stiffly from the waist, bringing the conversation to a close.

I bid him good evening, and Liam led me towards the cemetery gates. Before we turned on the path, I glanced back to where Robert stood over Morgan's grave. He had retrieved the page he had inscribed for Emilie from his pocket once more, and bent down towards the cross.

7

When I got home, I found Father in his study, reading a newspaper in the red glow of the fireplace and sipping from a glass of claret. A small pile of letters lay opened on his desk.

'Responses to your piece in the Society journal about the weather,' he said, looking at me over the rim of his glasses. 'You have a knack for provoking the ire of the ill-informed.'

There was a range of theories espoused, the most far-fetched delivered with unwarranted confidence. A schoolmaster from Sligo was convinced that the proliferation of lightning rods had served to stir up storm-fronts rather than protect against them. Another gentleman thought that seismic tremors had interrupted 'the flow of electrical fluids' circulating beneath the earth. One response at least was noteworthy. A retired admiral from Cobh said that for years the polar seas had been melting, with ice floes observed far to the south, so that a search for the Northwest Passage was likely to begin again. He said the thaw had led to 'exhalations of vapour', which had deflected the heat of the sun.

At the bottom of the pile, there was a short note from Professor Reeves. He thanked my father again for his hospitality, and apologized for the abruptness of his departure from the Royal Academy. He invited us both to a gathering at his observatory the following month. I folded the letter so the two sides of its broken seal aligned. Its design showed a callipers, the points opened out like the Greek letter lambda.

Father said, 'Did you see the one about the lightning rods?'

I nodded.

'You can write back and put him in his place if you like. I'll sign it off.'

'Perhaps tomorrow.'

His smile straightened. 'I thought you'd be amused.'

I said that I was just a little tired.

He regarded me with concern, gathered up the letters and set them aside. 'Why don't you fetch a book, and read with me here? I could do with the company.'

It would have been a pleasant way to pass an hour. The firelight in Father's study glinted on the spines of his books, but already it felt as if the shadows outside were encroaching.

'Father, have you ever disagreed with the verdict at one of your inquests?'

'From time to time. Very rarely.'

'Has it happened recently?'

'No. Not recently.' He began cleaning his spectacles with a handkerchief, holding the lens towards a candle-flame.

'What about Miss Casey?'

'Is that what has been troubling you, Abigail? I know I was severe when Labatt brought you back from the Rotunda. In truth, you had nothing to do with the death of Miss Casey.'

'I've known that for some time.'

His eyes narrowed a little as if he'd been

caught in a glare. 'The jury's verdict in that case was correct.'

'Did you speak with Mrs Longsworth?'

'I don't know who that is.'

'She was in the ward with Emilie. She saw a man remove her restraints on the night she died.'

'Most likely an orderly . . . When did you meet with this woman?'

'Do you really believe that Emilie could have made two incisions with her weaker hand, cut deep enough with a piece of glass, all while chained to a hospital bed?'

'Leaving aside how you've come to know those facts,' he said, 'the jurors saw the body, the glass fragment; they heard the testimony of Dr Labatt. There was only one decision they could make; only one I could direct.'

'That wasn't my question.'

'I could not ask a jury to doubt the word of the assistant master of the Rotunda.'

'Father, I'm asking whether *you* think that Emilie killed herself.'

He rose from his chair and went to the window with his arms folded. In the gloom, a light visible in the cupola of the Lying-In Hospital happened to go out.

'Abigail, I admire you for wanting to do right by Miss Casey, despite her own terrible crime, but this has gone far enough. I want you to stop making these enquiries, reading things you shouldn't, going to places you're not allowed. I'm loath to say it, but I fear it has become a fixation. It's not healthy.'

'Not healthy?'

'It is my own fault. I should have done more to keep my work separate; to not let details intrude into this house. And I'm sorry.' He was flustered, for it was rare that he had to reproach me. He held his thumb awkwardly in a buttonhole of his waistcoat.

'I only wish to find the truth, Father.'

'Promise me that you'll let the matter rest.'

'Would you wish me to make a promise that I know I cannot keep?'

His expression was pained. 'You can be so stubborn at times. Just like . . . ' He stopped speaking and bowed his head.

'Just like my mother?'

He didn't look at me as he sat back down. He placed the crystal stopper back into the decanter, and rotated his goblet on the side table without picking it up. He suddenly seemed quite old. There was more silver in his hair than black. Tiny blood vessels showed in his cheeks and nose. At first I'd felt annoyed by his rebuke, and the fact that he wouldn't listen, but now I was sorry for upsetting him. Perhaps I was just sorry that we were so at odds, sorry to be disappointed in him.

I stood up and placed my hand on his shoulder. 'If you want me to cease enquiring after Miss Casey, Father, then I will.'

He reached up and briefly held my hand. 'I am glad.' Then he cleared his throat and straightened in his seat. 'Would you still like to read with me?'

I looked towards the window. 'I might take some air in the gardens before it gets dark.' I bent down to kiss his cheek. 'I shall see you at supper.'

★ ★ ★

Two boys stood beneath a tree in the corner of Rutland Gardens, their kite stuck in the branches. Its line hung tantalizingly beyond their reach, swaying in the breeze. One boy cupped his hands and gave the other a boost, but to no avail. They glanced at me as I passed. If I stretched, I might have been able to grasp the line, but they didn't ask.

I thought of what Father had said. Was it so unusual to have taken such interest in Emilie Casey? If I'd merely heard about her while talking with Mrs Perrin, or from an article in the paper, would I have paid it any mind? I couldn't imagine Clarissa doing what I had done; but did that make it wrong? Perhaps my actions were enough to gain a reputation; nothing bad, just a certain peculiarity, and then people could say that the apple rarely falls far from the tree, and the minds of some would be set against me. Father may have been right to guard against that. Especially when many would have looked upon Emilie as nothing more than a fallen servant who had murdered her own child.

There were lights in the windows of the Neshams' house, where shadowy figures passed before the opened shutters. A Brethren meeting had broken up. The front door opened and people began emerging; men mostly, a few women, but none that I recognized. The group lingered on the steps, bidding each other farewell. Mrs Nesham came out, a man at her side, the metal hooks of his coat fastened up to his chin, and he was fixing a hat on his head. Even at a distance, I could see his left eyelid drooped halfway down, the skin pink and wrinkled. He leaned close to Mrs Nesham as if to kiss her cheek, but only spoke into her ear, and then turned away from the house. He crossed the road in the wake of a passing carriage, and entered the western gate of the gardens near the boys who stood beneath the tree. He paused and reached up to take the line, easing the kite from among the branches with deft tugs until it fell to the ground. He handed the string to the smallest boy, who looked up at him wide-eyed, before the other scooped up the kite and they both ran on to the lawns. The man watched them go, and turned slowly about until he faced me.

He didn't appear to recognize me, or seem surprised to see a girl unaccompanied on the path. The last of the evening light filtered through the canopy, and the gardens were dull and green, muffled by the wet leaves of an early autumn. The shouts of the children receded, and the people outside the house dispersed. Still the man's eyes wouldn't leave me, and I was conscious that we were alone on the darkening pathway.

Then, as if he'd committed my features to memory, he turned and walked towards the gate on Palace Row. My first instinct was to cut across the lawns for the safety of home, but I knew this must have been the man that Mrs Longsworth had seen. I followed him on to the street as if I'd intended to go that way. He was already several paces ahead, one hand in a chest-high pocket of his Brethren coat, his stove-pipe hat cocked forward and to the right.

I raised the hood of my cloak and kept my distance. The lamps were yet to be lit, though light spilled from the shop fronts on Dorset Street. The man's pace was steady. He crossed the road at right angles, and I wondered if this was a strange conscientiousness, or if his peripheral vision was poor. At one point he glanced about, and I stopped to look at the window display of a shop selling exotic foods: tins of tea and coffee, and jars of guava marmalade.

Carriages and carts slowed as they passed each other on Capel Street. The pathways were busy, and shop awnings fluttered overhead. The man walked through the crowd serenely, turning his shoulders this way and that so his progress hardly slowed. On the corner of Little Britain Street, a carriage tried to push its way into the traffic and almost collided with an oncoming cab. The drivers swore at each other, and for a moment my view was blocked.

The man had stopped to look at the commotion, one hand still in his coat pocket. I stayed hidden behind one of the horses as it shook its mane and stamped a hoof.

'He's not going to hurt you, you know.'

A middle-aged woman with pinned grey hair was waiting for me to move on.

'Pardon?'

'The horse. He won't bite.'

I smiled and nodded and told her to go ahead.

The man resumed walking, turning off at a narrow side street. By the time I got there, the alley was deserted, stretching away for a hundred yards with service entrances and padlocked gates. Only one door stood open, and I approached it slowly.

The mortar in the bricks had begun to wear away, so their edges were sharp against the gloom of the hallway. Arcs had been scraped over the tiled floor just inside the entrance, and weeds were growing against the doorsill. Right in the corner, a single buttercup grew, shivering on its stalk. No sound came from within, but it seemed as if the darkness could reach out and take me.

A narrow corridor led to a locked door — its brass knob wouldn't even twist — and beside that, a staircase to the basement. Though unlit, the passage was swept and clean. The faintest glimmer came from the bottom of the stairs; also a tapping sound, perhaps footsteps, but then I realized it was an arrhythmic ticking, as of several clocks running together.

A shadow passed over the stairwell, and I turned about. The door to the laneway was a grey rectangle in the darkness, and the man stood within its frame. Even in silhouette, I could imagine his crooked gaze upon me.

I felt backwards with my foot to the top of the steps, but I didn't know what kind of room might be below.

'I lost my way,' I said, speaking louder to stop

my voice from catching. 'My father and I were trying to find a certain shop.'

He made no reply, didn't move at all except for a slight bow of his head, as if disappointed.

'He's outside now, waiting for me.'

The man reached across to brush the wall, and then rubbed his fingers together like someone testing for damp.

'I should go back to him.'

'You should never have come,' he said, his voice soft and refined.

A small tinny chime sounded in the room downstairs. It was answered by several others, ringing in succession as if time seeped slowly through the room. 'But my father — '

'He isn't there.' He took a shuffling step towards me, his boot grazing the tiles.

If I called out, he would be upon me. The corridor was wide enough for two people to pass, but he'd catch me no matter how fast I tried to run.

'Father knows about you,' I said. 'He knows what you did to Miss Casey.'

He paused, close enough now that I could see his good eye move about. I expected him to deny any knowledge of Emilie.

'Your father inquired into that death. His verdict has already been reached.'

'Not every piece of evidence is presented at inquest.' My breathing had become shallow, and I could hear my voice taper off. 'He knows that you were in the Rotunda that night.'

The noise of a dog barking in the lane made his head turn slightly, but it jerked back to me when I took a step.

'Let me by.'

He stayed perfectly still without responding.

'I said, let — '

'What makes you think that I would stop you?'

A breeze blew through the door, ruffling my cloak, and a single leaf rolled along the crook of the wall. The man didn't move when I walked towards him, and only stepped aside at the last moment. His coat smelled of mothballs, and his bad eye fixed on me as I passed. Once beyond his grasp I began to run. I tripped and fell at the door, scraping my hand over the stone tiles. I expected to feel his fingers close about my ankle, but I scrambled up, and didn't look back until I reached Capel Street.

In the press of the traffic I felt cold all of a sudden. I couldn't seem to catch my breath. My palm stung. I looked down at the torn skin, and a woman cursed at me when I bumped into her. The best-lit road that would take me home was Great Britain Street, and I stayed close to a young governess and two small boys who happened to be walking in that direction. There were fewer people here, though many of the windows overhead were bright. I kept glancing back at the street. There was a man leaning against a lamppost, his arms folded and head bent, and I couldn't remember having passed him. The governess and her charges turned into one of the houses and shut the door, leaving me alone on the street.

Ewan lived along here; Father and I had collected him in the carriage more than once.

When I reached the house, there was no knocker, so I pushed the lid of the letter box several times. A skinny man in a grey dressing gown opened the door and peered at me.

'I am looking for Mr Weir,' I said.

'Who?'

'His name is Ewan.'

'Oh, the young Scot. He's on the first floor. Door on the left.' He stepped back and allowed me in, grinning as I passed. 'Expecting you, is he?'

Up on the landing, a child was crying in the room to the right, and a man's voice was raised. It took a few moments for Ewan to answer my knock. He was in his shirtsleeves, the top buttons open at the neck, and one brace off his shoulder.

'What is wrong?' he said.

I asked if I could come in.

He looked into the hallway, and I turned about, half expecting to see someone. Ewan seemed to note my worry, for he said, 'Of course.'

His room was about the size of our parlour, made bright by an oil-lamp and a glowing fire. A book lay open on an armchair, and a glass of wine sat perched on a wooden coal-box. The iron-sprung bed in the corner had a noticeable dip in the middle, but the covers on top were neatly folded. The room contained everything he needed: kitchen dresser and table, nightstand and washbasin. His shutters were open, and I went to a window to look down on the street. It was difficult to see anything in the darkness.

'Is everything all right? Has something

happened to your father?'

'I thought that someone was following me.'

'Following you?' He joined me at the window. 'Why aren't you at home?'

His presence was a comfort, and I had to stop myself from moving closer. My hand began to throb, and I blew into my palm.

'I saw a man come from a Brethren meeting, and I followed him for a while. But he spotted me.' I had never told Ewan about the man with the lazy eye, and I didn't want to say how close our encounter had been. Even now it seemed so foolish to have entered the house.

Ewan noticed my hand. 'Did he do that to you?'

'No, I fell.'

'Let me see.'

I placed my hand in his. He gently brushed a finger at the side of the cut, and I flinched.

'I'll have to clean it,' he said. 'Go and sit by the fire.'

Ewan opened his wardrobe and took down a leather satchel. He brought it to the table and removed a roll of cloth and stoppered bottle. I lifted his book from the armchair and sat down. It was a novel, *The Devil's Elixirs*.

'Can I have some wine?'

Ewan was cutting strips of cloth away with a scalpel. 'Yes, though I've only the one glass.'

'I don't mind,' I said, and took a long sip.

He fetched his washbasin and put it beside the hearth. Some water spilled over the edge and hissed when it touched the grate. He knelt beside me, cradled my hand once again, and dipped a folded piece of cloth in water.

Before he began, I said, 'Wait,' and took another sip of wine.

He looked at me. 'That won't dull the pain.'

'I know.'

He began to clean around the edges of the wound, removing pieces of grime with small precise strokes. Occasionally a sting would make me close my fingers against his. The cut ran up over my wrist, and he asked if he could lift my sleeve. I nodded. He undid the lace cuff of my dress, and twice folded it back.

He said, 'What possessed you to follow a stranger?'

'I cannot say.'

'You mean you don't know?'

'Will you accompany me when I return home?'

'Yes, but I shall have to speak to your father.'

'You mustn't.'

He picked up another cloth, soaked it in iodine and held it over my hand. 'This may sting,' he said.

'I promised him that I'd stop doing these things.'

'It has gone beyond getting in trouble. You are putting yourself in danger.'

I was going to say, 'Please don't,' but I could feel the stresses of the evening well in my voice, and I was loath to make some tearful plea. I pulled my hand away.

He leaned back and regarded me, the cloth still in his fingers. 'Abigail, why do you feel you must do everything alone?'

'Because no one offers help. They insist that I stay where I belong.'

He held my eye for a moment, then bowed his head and applied more iodine to the cloth. I thought of Ewan coming back to me in the Rotunda, showing me Father's files, even here now, tending my wound, and I realized that he had done more than most would be willing; probably more than he should.

I offered him my hand again, and said, 'I'm sorry, Ewan.'

The iodine left yellow streaks on my skin. He took a length of cloth and began wrapping it around my palm and the webbing of my thumb.

I said that he could inform my father if he wished, but first I wanted to tell him of all I'd found: meeting with Mrs Longsworth, and Martha and Robert Gould, and what had happened that evening. He listened as the darkness outside became complete, and the fire dwindled. The child across the hall in the lodging-house continued to cry.

8

It snowed on the first day of August, a light dry dusting that would sift from the leaves when disturbed by a wasp. Cart-wheel tracks criss-crossed the mired surface on George's Lane, and the costermongers were wrapped up in tattered layers, their wicker baskets tilted and mostly empty. When I entered Mr Whistler's shop, the milky eyes of the terrier sought me out. He got up to come towards me, hugging the wall at first, deftly sidestepping the leg of a table and the head of a broom, before crossing the shop floor. He sniffed at the hem of my skirt and wagged his tail.

Mr Whistler was in the next room, standing by a worktable with lengths of cloth, spools of thread and a box-iron, the coals inside still glowing. Whistler was flanked by two male dress-forms — limbless torsos on tripod stands. One was covered with a black coat, and when I came near I saw that he was sewing a hook to its front lapel, looking down his nose through half-moon spectacles. There was a rack against the wall, and several Brethren coats hung from its pole, my pale gown conspicuous among them.

'I won't be a moment,' he said, as he concentrated on the final stitches. He looped the needle several times to form a knot and snipped off the excess, then gave the hook a small tug to ensure it was secure.

'Now,' he said, placing his scissors back on the table. 'Your frock.'

On a tray beside him, a great jumble of the hooks were waiting to be used. I picked up one to look at it. 'Do you make these coats for all the Brethren members?'

'For the men at least,' he said, taking down my dress. 'I doubt the women would be seen dead in them.'

He showed me my gown draped over his forearm, and I had to say the job was neat, the alterations to the sleeves and neckline invisible. I thanked him, and he began folding the dress into a basket.

The Brethren coat drooped open, the canvas skin of the dress-form underneath scarred by Whistler's knife. I lifted one of the sleeves to feel the cuff, and then let it fall again.

'Who is this being made for?'

'I can't say.' I thought at first he was being discreet, but he added, 'They only send me the measurements, never the names.'

'Did you make the first one?'

'Oh, yes. Mr Darby was adamant about the particulars: the colour, the cloth, the hook and eyes. He told me then that he expected to order a few dozen.' He ensured the lid of the basket was snug. 'There were twelve new orders last week alone.'

I was about to ask him who took delivery of the coats, but he said, 'That'll be ten bob, miss,' looking at me over his glasses.

'Of course.' I counted the money from my purse, and he swept the coins from the table into

159

his hand. In the other room, the terrier began yapping, and Whistler went to deal with his new customer.

I brought the gown home, entering the kitchen from the back garden. Father had been busy that morning in his workrooms, and he was now raiding the pantry to break his fast, using a breadknife to cut a slice of cheddar. He greeted me over his shoulder, but then stopped me before I could leave the room.

He pointed to my wrist. 'What happened there?'

Father had yet to see the bandages from my fall. On the evening itself, I had said that I was feeling unwell and took to my room. We had missed each other at meals the following day, and, in general, I had kept my sleeve low over my wrist.

'I fell in the yard,' I said. 'It was only a small cut.'

He gestured for me to come closer, held my hand and ran his thumb over the wrapped cloth.

'Who dressed it?'

The truth was the most plausible answer. 'Mr Weir.'

Father frowned a little, and turned my hand over. After a moment, the corners of his mouth drooped down, and he nodded to himself. 'Mr Weir's bindings are getting much neater, I'm glad to say. Try to be more careful, Abigail.'

I said that I would try, and he returned his attention to his meal.

★ ★ ★

Half an hour to go before the ball in Charlemont House, and I was in Clarissa's room, helping to remove paper curlers from her hair. I was dressed and ready to leave; she was still in her stays and petticoats.

'I don't know why you must leave these things to the last minute,' I said.

She jutted her lower lip to blow a curl away from her eye. 'Last time I kept them in too briefly and my hair went flat after the first quadrille. I could see Edith Gould smirking at me.'

Mrs Egan paced the room, keeping one eye on the clock and the other on Maria — a maid who was sewing a ruffled silk blossom to the hem of Clarissa's ball-gown. Clarissa removed the two remaining curlers and examined herself in the mirror. She arranged the ringlets about her face, tilting her head this way and that to ensure they'd not go awry.

Perhaps she was more anxious than usual. She hadn't known that James Caulfeild was home from London until I'd mentioned in passing that he had called to my house. I knew that Clarissa admired him, even if she was an unlikely candidate for marriage. Though her father was relatively well-off, it was doubtful that Lord Charlemont would consent to his son marrying a clergyman's daughter.

Maria finished the repair, bit off the thread, and then assisted Clarissa in donning the gown. It was hitched at several points, allowing the hem to hang in drooping curves like the bottom of a theatre curtain, revealing the white skirt beneath.

161

When ready, Clarissa stood among discarded scraps of paper, her dressing table cluttered with scent bottles and brushes, tins of face powder and milk of roses, but she looked beautiful.

Mrs Egan said that she rather preferred my dress. 'So much more like the ones I used to wear.'

The entrance hall of Charlemont House was a lofty space with stone pillars and a chequered marble floor. A staircase swept up to the left, and we could already hear the hum of conversation in the rooms above. There was a queue near the top of the stairs waiting to greet our hosts. The ladies wore bold colours and extravagant trappings, with necklines so wide that it seemed the gowns might slip from their shoulders. I looked down at my dress, conscious of its plainness. Mr Whistler had done a fine job in letting it out, but it was of cream muslin with long sleeves and no train, and I felt demure and dull and immature.

The hardwood floor of the ballroom was already thronging with guests. Dozens of tall candelabra with fat, melting candles cast pools of light in the hall. The young and gaily dressed paraded in the brightness; the dowdy and decrepit kept to the shadows. A quartet played music on a raised dais opposite one fireplace, though the dances were yet to begin. Opened double doors at one end led to a smaller drawing room.

Mrs Egan began to speak with a neighbour from Mountjoy Square, leaving us to our own devices. Clarissa scanned the room, looking for

162

acquaintances. She nodded towards one corner, saying, 'There's Edith.'

Miss Gould was standing beside her mother. There was no sign of her brother Robert. In the same part of the room, James Caulfeild was in conversation with another young man. Lord Charlemont's son wore a blue dress-coat. His fair hair was swept back and cut longer than most of the other men present wore theirs, especially those in uniform, and I could see again why Clarissa was so enamoured.

She said that Edith had positioned herself so she could snare him for the opening dance. 'We'll have to get there first.'

'No, Clara. If he wants to engage with us he'll come over.'

'But he's already been to your house. It's perfectly proper for you to — ' She frowned and peered more intently over my shoulder. Then she said, 'My goodness.'

'What is it?'

'The man he speaks with is Mr Weir.'

I craned my neck to see. It was indeed Ewan, looking handsome in formal attire, though a lock of hair still threatened to slip over one eye.

'But this is ideal,' Clarissa said. 'You can greet *him* since you're almost related, and he'll make the introductions.'

I had seen Ewan several times in the week leading up to the ball, and he knew I meant to attend. Why wouldn't he have mentioned that he was going? And who had invited him? I offered my arm to Clarissa, and we made our way across the room. She whispered for me to keep my shoulders back, and to raise my chin a little. She tugged at my elbow. 'Not so fast. You're making us look eager.'

Ewan's back was turned so he couldn't see our approach. When I stood beside him I hesitated, unsure of what to say.

'Good evening, Mr Weir. I'm very surprised to see you here.' But at once I realized that I'd questioned his presence rather than welcomed it, so I added, 'Surprised and pleased.'

Ewan turned at the sound of my voice. He seemed taken aback himself, though I couldn't think why, and he bowed formally. I was so used to seeing him traipsing in and out of my father's workrooms, fetching water from the kitchen, or sitting across the dining-table, that I almost forgot to curtsy in return.

He said, 'Miss Lawless, Miss Egan,' and then fell silent.

I glanced at Caulfeild, who didn't seem put out by the intrusion; if anything he looked amused at the stilted exchange. Ewan realized that it was his duty to make conversation, and he said, 'May I introduce you both to Viscount Charlemont.'

'Please, say Mr Caulfeild. I wince at these titles that I've done nothing to earn. I'm already acquainted with Miss Lawless,' he said. 'How nice to see you again.'

'And Miss Egan is — '

'The daughter of the Reverend. Yes, I know your father well. I often pine for his services while I'm in London.' He smiled. 'The religious instruction there tends to be more severe.'

Clarissa said it was very kind of him to say, and took a step closer.

I said to Ewan, 'You never mentioned that you were coming.'

'I didn't think it would be of interest.' He looked at the others, as if aware that our exchange might seem familiar and unguarded.

Caulfeild said, 'Mr Weir speaks highly of your father, Miss Lawless. He says he has learned a great deal in the short time he has been here.'

'Oh, he would be glad to know that.'

'It is true. I was most fortunate to be placed in his household.'

I smiled at him and he glanced at the floor. Clarissa broke the silence by praising Caulfeild on the grandeur of the ballroom. Conversation turned for a time to discussing mutual acquaintances among the guests.

There was a slight hubbub near the door, and Mr Darby entered, followed by Mr and Mrs Nesham. Darby was dressed in an ordinary evening jacket and white cravat. Several people came forward to greet him, and I assumed they were members of the Brethren, though they were not so easy to distinguish without their religious attire. Darby responded to each of them without smiling; the most he offered was a brief nod of the head. He made his way over to Mrs Gould, who became animated in his presence. Darby spoke with Edith for a minute, and I was surprised when he reached over to brush a lock from her cheek with the tip of his finger. She didn't draw back from his touch; just bowed her head demurely.

Caulfeild had been looking at Darby all the while, and when he saw that I noticed, he smiled and said, 'If only we could choose our neighbours, Miss Lawless.'

I asked him if Professor Reeves was coming this evening.

'He was invited, though it's difficult to draw him away from Saggart at the best of times.'

Someone announced that the first dance was about to begin, and Darby offered his hand to Edith. She smiled, her cheeks turning pink, and he led her to the centre of the floor. Mrs Gould clasped her palms together as she watched them go.

Caulfeild placed his drink on a table and said that he'd been very lax in his duties as host. 'Why, I haven't even seen the dance card.' He turned to Clarissa. 'If you're not engaged, Miss Egan, perhaps you'd do me the honour of joining me for the first set.'

'No,' Clarissa said. 'I mean, no I'm not engaged. I'd be delighted.'

Couples paired off throughout the room, while Ewan and I stood next to each other. I became anxious that he might ask me to dance — perhaps he thought that etiquette required it. And if he did, I couldn't refuse. There would be no harm, of course, in an innocent dance at a private ball, but it would be awkward come morning, when we would see each other again in the humdrum surroundings of kitchens and cadavers.

'Miss Lawless?'

I turned to him, suddenly feeling warm. 'Yes, Mr Weir.'

'Will you excuse me?' And without waiting for a reply he moved to the other side of the room.

I stood alone for a moment, unsure of where to go. There were some chairs by the wall behind me, but they were empty, and it would be odd to sit there by myself; odder still to stand unaccompanied at the edge of a dance-floor. A woman bumped into my shoulder as she was being led by a soldier in a scarlet coat. She giggled and said that she was sorry, calling me 'My dear'. Another man approached with his face set in a half-smile. He was rather short. Jet black hair was slicked over a bald pate, and one side of his collar had come loose so it almost brushed a fleshy earlobe. I stood on my tiptoes and looked around the room, as if searching for a companion, and then made my way towards the drawing room before he could reach me.

It was less crowded there and cooler as a result. There was no music or dancing. Some of the older guests sat together playing whist. In a darkened corner, a magic lantern cast a vivid image on to a blank wall: galleons and ships of war at Trafalgar, plumes of smoke from cannon-fire, storm clouds and tattered flags. Each element of the picture had been painted on to a separate piece of glass, so they could move independently. The sea tilted to and fro, as if we saw it in reality, though the plumes of smoke remained station-ary, which rather spoiled the effect.

A crowd had gathered in another corner to catch a glimpse of a life-sized doll: an automaton of a young boy seated at a writing desk. He held a goose-quill over a sheet of paper, and was dressed in a suit of red silk and white ruffled shirtsleeves, like a wealthy child from the previous century.

Lord Charlemont was demonstrating it for his guests. The clockwork was already wound, for when he turned a small cabinet-key, the doll came to life with a whir and clack of shifting gears. His glass eyes rotated as if he were taking in his audience, and then he lifted the quill. He dipped the nib in an opened inkpot, and with a series of fluid movements began to draw a picture. The peculiar thing was the random order in which he formed the lines. He began with a stroke for the hem of a skirt, then the bend of an elbow, a tress of hair. Occasionally his head would rise, and his eyes sweep the crowd as if he were proud of our attention, before he dipped the quill again. Line by line, the picture emerged: a beautiful and simple drawing of a young woman in a flowing dress.

At the final stroke, the boy brought the quill to the side, holding the point in mid-air, and he bowed his head. The people around me began to applaud, their gloved hands creating a muted patter, like soft rain on a canvas tent. But then the automaton whirred into life once more. With his head still bowed, he scratched a line across the girl's face.

The applause stopped, and a few women murmured, 'Oh.'

His arm moved again. The second strike-through was vertical, the motion slower, and firm enough to slit the page, leaving the staff of a cross running through the girl's body. The quill lifted again, but Lord Charlemont turned the key before any more damage was done, and the boy drooped in his seat.

The earl cleared his throat. 'Perhaps a cogwheel has come loose.'

Despite the disappointing conclusion, many said to the earl that it was a splendid machine, and the crowd began to disperse. The boy remained with his gaze fixed on the page.

I returned to the ballroom, where a new set of dances had begun, and took a seat near the chimney piece between an older lady and two middle-aged men. The dancers had split into groups of four. They linked hands to form circles, rotating clockwise for two bars, and then anticlockwise, like wheels turning in a pocket watch. Clarissa was no longer with Mr Caulfeild. She was making do with another young man who seemed unable to maintain rhythm.

The woman beside me said, 'This reminds me of the balls that take place in the Castle. The room is very like St Patrick's Hall, is it not?'

I confessed that I had not yet been to Dublin Castle, and she regarded me more closely. 'I see,' she said with a thin smile. 'Perhaps one day.'

Mr Darby still danced with Edith. Every once in a while they would glance at each other, their hands held high and fingers linked, and Edith would smile.

The woman saw that I was watching them. 'Such a handsome pair,' she said. 'I believe Mr Darby has become a regular visitor to Fitz-william Square.'

I thought of what Robert had told me: how he

would meet with Darby and his father when his relationship with Emilie was uncovered. But this lady seemed to know of other gossip.

'He has been paying addresses to Edith?'

'Oh yes, for some time. Mrs Gould can hardly contain herself. She expects a proposal any day.'

Edith's mother stood on the far side of the hall, watching her daughter with hands clasped.

'Is he not a little old?'

'He is only a year beyond forty,' the woman said, offended on his behalf. 'It would be a most advantageous match.'

'For whom?'

'Why, for the Goulds.' She glanced at me as if I were being obtuse. 'Mr Darby's importance for the spiritual renewal of the city will soon be acknowledged by all.' She blinked, and her eyes regained focus as she turned away. She said that it was disagreeable to sit so close to the fire, and she rose to take her leave.

The music hadn't lessened in tempo, and the dance would last a while yet. The gentlemen to my right were speaking of the effects the weather was having on their country estates. One said that his tenants were struggling because crops had been destroyed in freak storms. 'It won't be long, Mr Graves, before I have to send in the bailiffs.'

The one called Graves responded with a vague grunt, saying that he left such matters in the hands of his steward. There was a wine stain on one of his silk stockings, which made it look as though he had cut himself while traipsing through brambles.

'Speaking of the weather,' he said, 'I saw a

theory advanced in the Royal Society journal that made me chuckle. Written by some amateur meteorologist who happens to be a sheriff, or coroner, or some such.'

His companion said, 'Mr Lawless?'

'Mr Witless more like! He said that the drop in temperature was due to vapours emitted by the eruption of Mount Tambora last year. Not Etna, mark you, nor Vesuvius, but a volcano in the East Indies.'

I listened to my idea being mocked with some indignation. 'Do you have your own theory, sir?'

He blinked at me, perhaps surprised by my forthrightness, but he'd drunk enough not to mind. 'There's no need for a theory, miss. It is just weather. Some men think that any unusual event in the short span of their own lifetime must be unique.' He went to take a sip from his glass, tilting it quite far before realizing that it was already empty. 'And the notion that an event in the South Pacific could affect us here is quite absurd. People confined to these islands have no proper sense of the extent of the globe. When you travel as much as I, you understand that its size is beyond imagination.'

'On a clear day one can see Snowdonia from Howth Head,' I said. 'That's eighty miles. Ten times that is eight hundred, and ten times that is a third of the world's circumference. It is not so hard to imagine.'

He frowned, as if checking the arithmetic in his head.

A voice came from over my shoulder. 'It is often said that the imagination can encircle the

171

world.' I turned to see Professor Reeves sitting in the chair that the woman had vacated, a crystal flute of water in his hand. 'You have provided a pleasing proof of that, Miss Lawless.'

'Professor,' I said. 'Mr Caulfeild wasn't sure that you could come.'

'Oh, for an event like this, I thought I should make the effort. The supper in Charlemont House is always excellent, even if the conversation can be less dependable.'

Mr Graves was squinting at Reeves, and seemed ready to make some comment, but his companion leaned towards him and whispered in his ear. They both regarded the professor with dark expressions, and then moved to another part of the room.

'Since my last engagement,' Reeves said, 'I have finally achieved some public recognition. My notoriety never leaves me in want of a seat. I never had a chance to apologize to you and your father for the scene at the Academy.'

'Really, there is no need.'

'I have not seen Mr Lawless this evening.'

'No, he could not come.'

'He remained at home?' Reeves said, his eyes drifting towards the drawing-room windows.

'He avoids these occasions, especially since my mother died.'

The set that included Edith and Darby swept close by, and they drew the professor's attention for a moment. I remembered Reeves say at the Academy that he studied the Bible as a child, and I asked if he grew up in a religious household.

'Oh, yes,' he said, almost wearily. 'You see, I was rather sickly as a boy, confined to my room for weeks on end. Unfortunately, my father, a dull and unimaginative man, believed that my ailments had been sent by God in chastisement for some fault. Every day I was commanded to recite the Bible. He would kneel by my bedside with members of his church, cut from the same cloth as the Brethren, and they prayed each night with such vehemence, stretching their hands above me in the candlelight.'

He took a sip of water, and paused for a second to study the shifting spectra on the crystal.

'God was inattentive to their prayers,' he said, 'or perhaps wearied by them. I wished only to be good and holy and well, but there was never a moment in which my heart responded to their words. It was my failing, and I was sure that I suffered because of it.'

'What of your mother?'

He looked at me for a moment. 'Mother brought comfort. Whenever they left the house, she would take the Bible from my hands, rub my forehead and hum a melody. Perhaps I only imagine it now, but in those moments my cough lessened, the aches in my joints disappeared, and only returned at the sound of Father's heavy footsteps clomping on the wooden stairs.'

The music slowed in tempo for a portion of the dance where the men stood still as their partners twirled about them. Edith did so gracefully, and Mr Darby followed her movements intently. People standing at the side of the room were watching the dancers, but some cast glances to where I sat with Reeves, whispering comments to each other, and I found that I was pleased to be spotted beside him.

'You overcame your illness.'

'Yes. Mother found a new physician in town, whose tonics proved to be far more effective. I was relieved of course, but it was a testing time as well.'

'How so?'

'It is a difficult thing to discover that one's father is fallible.'

I glanced at him, for I had come to learn that as well, but I remained silent.

'Once I began to question him, I found that I could not stop. The sermons at his church, or his favourite verses of scripture. I could not fathom why they were considered wholesome or desirable. They had left his spirit mean in every sense. When I was well enough, I left the house for boarding school, and my love for natural philosophy was awakened, much to Father's anger. Every time I saw him he would denounce my ungodly interests, and describe with relish the torments that awaited me. It was a relief when I departed for Dublin, for we never had to speak again.'

The last bars of the dance began to play, and Edith and Darby linked their hands once more. They bowed to each other as everyone dispersed to different parts of the room.

Reeves shifted in his seat and placed his empty glass on a side table. 'Forgive me, Miss Lawless, for dwelling on such unpleasant topics.'

I said there was no need. I only felt sorry for the sadness in his upbringing, and pleased that he was able to confide. The gong came for supper, and I wondered if Reeves was accompanied by anyone.

'I am going to sit with my friend for supper if you would care to join us.'

'That is kind of you, but I have promised to dine with Mr Caulfeild at the head table. Perhaps I shall see you at the next gathering in the observatory, Miss Lawless.'

'Father and I look forward to it.'

He rose and bowed and took his leave. In the dining room, I was glad of the chance to sit beside Clarissa once more. She was accompanied by her most recent partner, a pleasant if dreary young man called Mr Meredith, who was a fellow at Trinity College. He spoke at length with Clarissa, not at all put off by the veiled sarcasm of her responses. Just before the supper began, Ewan arrived at our table and asked if he could sit next to me.

I said that he could do as he wished, and reached for a soup spoon.

Ewan pulled his chair in. He picked up a napkin shaped like a swan, and dismembered it. 'Have you had a pleasant evening?'

'Somewhat pleasant.'

'I'm glad.'

We sat in silence for a while as the last guests took their seats. Professor Reeves made his way towards the hosts, his progress slowed by the throng of the crowd. He happened to walk alongside Mrs Nesham for a moment, but they didn't acknowledge each other, and soon parted as they headed to their respective tables.

I said, 'Did you ever attend balls in Edinburgh?'

'Of course.'

'You just never danced at them.'

He looked at me, and was about to reply, but a servant took my bowl to ladle in some soup.

'I thought it inappropriate to ask.'

'Because you work with my father?'

He said it was more than that.

'What then?'

'Your father requested that I come in his stead. How else do you think I was invited?'

'So you are here to keep an eye on me.'

'He was just concerned.'

At the head table, Lady Charlemont was leaning towards Professor Reeves, speaking in his ear while waving her hands about in expansive gestures. The anecdote must have come to an end, for he closed his eyes and laughed in appreciation. She picked up her knife and fork to resume her meal, pleased with herself. There was no sign of James Caulfeild at the table.

Ewan said, 'I am sorry. I left because I thought every other gentleman would think you were engaged. It was clumsy of me.'

He concentrated on spreading some soft butter on a piece of bread. Beneath my glove, I could feel the edge of the bandage against my palm, and I found that I was no longer annoyed with him. I told him that I didn't mind, that I was glad he was able to attend, and we said no more on the subject.

Clarissa took advantage of a pause by Mr Meredith to speak with me for several minutes. All the while I watched Edith Gould sitting with her parents, Mr Darby and the Neshams. She cut a piece of meat for several seconds, then left the morsel at the side of her plate. The others were engaged in conversation and, without a word, Edith placed her napkin on the table and withdrew. She kept close to the wall until she reached the door, and opened it just enough to slip out.

The supper wore on, and after several minutes I excused myself to go and find the bourdaloue. Clarissa offered to go with me, but I said that I did not wish to deprive Mr Meredith of her company, and she flashed me a dark glance.

The drawing room was empty except for some older men and women playing cards in the corner, and servants stoking fires and replenishing the punch bowl. They paid me no heed as I made my way to the mechanical boy, who still drooped over his spoiled portrait.

His pale blond hair was real, soft to the touch, and I briefly wondered if it came from a child living or dead. I looked more closely at the drawing, and the cross he had made over the picture of the girl, and I could not help but remember the marks on Emilie's wrist. There was a hatch concealed in the boy's back, clothed in the same red silk of his coat. I opened it to peer inside. The cavity of his torso was filled with a lattice of delicate rods and wire threads, all surrounding a column of discs tightly stacked like copper coins. A large cogwheel was inserted at the bottom, each of its teeth bearing glyphs inscribed in metal, with the needle of a stylus resting against one. There was a brass plate attached to the inside of the hatch. In fine cursive letters, it read: *David Elyan, Horologist of Abbey Street*.

Lord Charlemont's key remained in the device. It turned smoothly, without a hint of stiffness, but I was ready in case the boy continued to scratch at the portrait. Instead, he brought the quill to the bottom of the page and began to form letters. The ink on the quill had dried during the long interruption, and the point only left an occasional streak of black, but I waited for him to finish before removing the page from its frame.

I held the sheet against a candelabra so the light showed the stippled texture of the cotton paper, but the indents of the letters weren't clear enough to make out. One candle had gone out. I removed a glove to break off a piece of the wick, crumbling it between my finger and thumb, then lightly brushed the page until the letters began to emerge — white lines in the grey smudge spelling out *Hosea 2:4*.

That was the verse of the Bible that the Brethren had held outside St George's. Were they attempting to propagate their message in this grand setting? Would Lord Charlemont have allowed that? But, no; he had stopped the machine before it could write the text, alarmed that it had malfunctioned. The boy still sat at his desk, quill poised over the inkpot, his head bowed down with his eyes looking off to the right.

A woman's cry in the corner made me jump, but it was only a flighty lady complaining about the poor play of her whist partner. I looked at the portrait again, the black cross and the white impress of the verse. I folded the sheet and placed it in the long sleeve of my glove, which I donned once more.

I passed through the ballroom, and down a long gallery until I reached the top of the stairs. In a darkened corner of the wide hall below, two figures were standing next to each other, almost silhouetted like characters in a shadow play. It was Edith Gould and James Caulfeild, and I observed them from above.

James was speaking, his voice soft and earnest. Edith stayed still as she listened, but then she seemed to get upset and turned as if about to leave. James reached out and held her arm — not in a forceful way — and Edith remained beside him, her face looking off to the side. He curled his finger and gently pulled her chin towards him. They stayed like that for several seconds, and I thought that he would lean down to kiss her. But then a servant crossed the hall, shoes clicking on the marble floor, and they separated. Edith immediately began walking down another corridor, and James followed after her. I was about to return to the dining room, but I heard more soft footsteps down below. Mr Darby passed through the hallway and paused in a rectangle of moonlight. He looked down the corridor that James and Edith had taken and began to move towards it. After a few steps, he was lost in the shadows.

No one noticed when I re-entered the dining room to take my seat beside Clarissa. She invited me to speak quietly behind an opened fan. 'Where on earth have you been?'

I would have told her, but knew that she'd be disappointed about James. 'I just needed some air.'

'Mr Meredith will not stop talking: of his parish in Tyrone, his intention of returning there next year with a wife.' She paused to check that he could not overhear. 'He seems to think that because I'm the daughter of a clergyman I intend to marry one.'

Edith came back into the room, and Clarissa looked at her as she returned to her table, but didn't comment. She said, 'When will this wretched supper end?'

I leaned across and said, 'Excuse me, Mr Meredith?'

The Trinity fellow paused open-mouthed, a dollop of pink flummery on his silver spoon. 'Yes? Miss Lawless, isn't it?'

'Miss Egan tells me you are to be appointed a rector.'

He smiled at her. 'Did she indeed? It is true. I've been describing to her the delights of Ardtrea.'

Clarissa said, 'In some detail.'

'There is so much to note — the handsome simplicity of St Andrew's Chapel, the crooked coast of Lough Neagh, the — '

'Have you ever met Mr Darby?' I said.

He frowned, as if trying to place the name. 'Mr . . . ?'

'The leader of the Brethren.'

Mr Meredith placed the spoon on his plate with a clink. When he regarded me, his face was pleasant and carefully neutral. 'May I ask, are you a member of his congregation?'

I said that I was not; nor had I any intention of becoming one.

'I am glad,' he said, and seemed to relax. 'No, I don't know him very well. Only by reputation. He was a fellow in the college when I was an undergraduate, and he was very highly regarded, until he began his ministry in Wicklow.'

'With his new wife?'

'Yes, but she died soon after.' Meredith seemed to realize that Clarissa was regarding him with more interest than at any other time in the evening, and he took a sip of wine.

'I believe that she died in childbirth,' I said.

'Those were the rumours. Of course a tragedy like that is redoubled when it hardens the hearts of those left behind. He was a different man when he returned to Dublin. He saw evidence of God's punishment in everything, instead of his grace.'

Meredith said that Darby was clever when he founded his congregation. 'He knew from his time in Trinity that he needed to attract members that were . . . ' He stopped and gestured to the room. 'Well, people like this. Doctors and judges, the respectable and upright. And now his appeal will be broad because people are suffering. They look up at angry skies and ill omens, and in Darby they see a man not preying on their fears, but giving voice to them.'

He stopped speaking and looked over his shoulder, as if fearful of who might be within earshot. He left the remainder of his dessert untouched, and placed his napkin on the table. 'But as I said, I don't know him well at all.'

We sat for a while in silence, before Clarissa said, 'Lord and Lady Charlemont have risen. We must return to the ballroom.'

Ewan and I joined the other guests moving through the gallery, and when we entered the ballroom we stood by a large window that overlooked Rutland Square. Lord Charlemont had arranged for the central garden to be illuminated with coloured lanterns, and several carriages were parked in front of the railings. The coachmen had gathered together beside a burning brazier, their faces yellow in the firelight. Liam was among them, and I was glad that he had found company for the long evening.

I asked Ewan if this ball was very different from those he was used to.

'I'd say they are much the same all over,' he said. 'Though Lord Charlemont's interest in contraptions at least provided some novelty. I'll have to write to Hannah and tell her about them.'

'Hannah?'

'My younger sister back home. She's forever pestering me for news,' he said, but with affection in his voice. 'In fact, she's rather like you. Nose always in a book, clever, kind-hearted.' He stopped himself and glanced out of the window, as if he'd said more than intended.

'Perhaps one day I shall meet her.'

'Perhaps.' He smiled at me and said, 'You may finally meet your match.'

Somewhere in the hall, the closing dance — 'Le Boulanger' — was announced and, for the last time, gentlemen went in search of partners.

'Would you like to dance, Ewan?'

He held my eye for a moment, then said, 'Yes, I would.'

We stayed still until I whispered to him, 'Offer me your arm.' He did so, and we made our way to the dance-floor. I heard my name being called, and saw Clarissa waving us over. When I got near, she beamed at me and said, 'See? I knew you'd be asked.'

I told her to shush, just as James Caulfeild appeared at her side. He expressed delight that we could join them. Clarissa took charge, declaring that our set was complete with six couples. She urged everyone to take their places in a circle. We linked hands while we waited for the rest of the dancers to assemble. An older couple, whom I knew to be Mr and Mrs Lecky, stood to Ewan's left, and three other pairs completed the set. Mrs Lecky was a stout woman who compensated for her lack of height with a towering feathered headdress. Her husband was tall and awkward, and a slight swaying indicated that he'd been a frequent visitor to the punch bowl. He said loudly, 'Which dance is this?'

His wife tugged at his hand in reproach. ''Le Boulanger'.'

'And how does that go again?'

The gentlemen were standing with their feet crossed, waiting for the music to begin, but

Ewan had got his the wrong way round. I squeezed his fingers, and when he glanced at me I nodded to the floor.

He righted himself, and said, 'I fear I may be the weakest link.'

I moved closer. 'I daresay that honour will go to Mr Lecky.'

He hid a smile by pursing his lips, just as the band played the first long notes of the dance. Everyone in the room turned to bow and curtsy to their respective partners, and I could tell by Ewan's eyes that he was amused at the formality.

When the first bars struck up, we rotated in a circle with linked hands like a carousel. Everyone moved with a simple skip, though Mrs Lecky insisted on kicking her heels and was in danger of striking Ewan's shins. Her high steps caused her topaz necklace to jump and clack. I was surprised to see that Ewan moved elegantly, with an easy rhythm — his shoulders straight, but not in a stiff manner, and once or twice he glanced behind to see how I fared. When the rotation reversed, so that the ladies led, I concentrated on matching my steps to the music, counting the beats in my head, grateful that any slip would be hidden by my long gown. Clarissa and I had often practised these dances in our rooms; but I'd always played the part of the man. Other revolving sets of dancers skirted close by — a fast array of outfits and perfumes, and faces made red by the warmth of the crowd and the shifting light of the chandeliers.

The dance continued for several minutes and, as the music increased in tempo, the figures repeated again and again. Finally, the musicians played their coda. We halted to bow to each other once more, then applauded, and I felt pleased and relieved to be among the crowd, rather than watching from the sides. The dances were finished for the evening. The musicians continued playing more sedately, and the crowd lingered, for it would be bad form to leave with undue haste.

I was about to suggest to Ewan that we return to the window, but then I saw Liam at the door of the ballroom, incongruous in his plain livery. For a moment I couldn't think of why he'd be there, but then an alarm crept over me. I hurried towards him, Ewan following behind, and I asked what was wrong.

'Jimmy ran over to tell me,' he said. 'There's been a break-in at the house — well, your father's workrooms. He needs your help, Mr Weir.'

Liam said that he would fetch the horses, but our house was just around the corner, and he would need to bring Clarissa and Mrs Egan back home, so Ewan and I set off on foot. We hurried past the assembled coachmen, and must have looked for all the world like a couple eloping. The pavement felt cold beneath my dancing slippers, but it wasn't long before we reached number four.

Mrs Perrin answered the door, wearing her sleeping cap and dressing gown and holding an oil-lamp aloft. 'There you are,' she said. 'You needn't worry, everything is fine.' She clasped her nightgown closed beneath her chin. 'It was only the body-snatchers.'

9

I was just a girl when we had our first visit from the resurrection men. A noise woke me in the dead of night, and from my window I could see shadowy figures in the yard, one holding a lantern aloft, another forcing the door of the coach house with an iron bar. I ran to my father's room, and can still remember his sleep-scrunched face as I told him that there were men in the garden. He roused Ray Perrin, and their shouts and lamp-light were enough to scare off the intruders.

Only one of them was caught, a boy of no more than twelve or thirteen. He was brought to the kitchen, and I peeked at him from the doorway. I expected him to appear sinister and threatening, perhaps older and more haggard than his years would suggest, but he was youthful and timid, any fight in him long gone. He sat beside Mr Perrin, and they drank from mugs of milk like father and son while waiting for the constables to arrive. Mrs Perrin was pregnant with Jimmy, and when she caught me lurking behind the door, she ordered me to bed.

There were other incidents over the years, though very rare. Bodies unencumbered by tombstones, packed earth and coffin lids must have been alluring for men of that profession, but they risked much more by trying to steal from the coroner. A corpse in the graveyard was not considered the property of anyone. But to trespass against an officer of the crown, and interfere with an ongoing inquest, could mean transportation to the colonies, or worse.

When Ewan and I arrived up to the workrooms in our finery, Father was standing in the front office. The floor was a mess: drawers in desks had been emptied out, chairs toppled over, Father's tools strewn about. The door had been forced open, so the wood around the latch was splintered and the doorknob hung loose on its spindle. Father was replacing books that had been knocked from the shelves, but he had paused to read one opened in his palm, as if a certain passage had caught his interest.

He looked up as we entered, snapped the book closed and said that he was sorry for spoiling the evening. 'Really, there was no need for you both to return. The damage is only superficial.'

I said, 'No one was hurt?'

'We didn't even realize there were intruders until Jimmy spotted the stable door ajar.' He placed the book back on its shelf and bent to pick up another. 'They must have come searching for bodies, but when they found none they caused this damage from anger or spite.'

'What about the dissecting room?'

'They didn't even attempt to open it.'

Ewan went over and twisted the handle, but the door was still locked.

'Perhaps they didn't know it was there,' Father said. 'Or maybe they were disturbed by something and fled. Either way, it could have been much worse. A bit of tidying, a new lock, and we shall be back to normal.' He said that the police had been informed, but they thought it unlikely that anyone would be captured at this stage.

Father came over to me, his face set in a half-smile, and he told me not to worry. 'These are hard times,' he said. 'Some men will do desperate things.'

Ewan began placing the tools back on the workbench: a bone-saw and rib-cutter, and a small hammer with a hook on its handle used for removing skullcaps, all made from polished copper.

On top of the examination table in the middle of the room there was an axe with a rusted blade, its dark wooden haft polished smooth from years of use.

I picked it up. 'Where did this come from?'

'They must have forgotten it,' Father said. 'At least the evening cost them something.'

The axe was so worn that its edge had become jagged, and small flecks of corroded metal were left on my white gloves.

Father said that he would have to see about securing the stable doors, and he went down to look at them. Ewan continued to rummage beneath papers on the floor. He found a small forceps and placed it on the table with the other tools.

'Those instruments are worth more than any cadaver,' I said.

'Perhaps they didn't realize.'

In the corner, the lock on the cabinet had been broken and the shutter pulled upwards.

Ewan lifted it fully. The ledgers were still on their shelves, neatly arranged, though the most recent had been inserted upside-down.

I ran my fingers over the leather binding. 'Would you have left it in like this?'

He shook his head. 'Perhaps your father did,' he said, but we both knew that was unlikely.

He took the ledger down and opened it. I half expected to see the final pages torn out, but Father's notes on Emilie Casey were intact.

I looked at the room again, the upturned furniture and scattered pages, and the axe on the worktable. The ledgers containing Father's notes were the only items completely undamaged. That was what they had come for.

'Could it have been the man that I followed from the Neshams' house, the man with the lazy eye?'

Ewan closed the book and placed it back on the shelf. 'Why would it be?'

'I told him that Father knew about him, that he possessed information about Miss Casey's death not revealed at the inquest.'

'He would not break in here just to verify that.'

'He might if he thought that he was at risk. Who else would bring an axe to a burglary and leave a locked door untouched?'

'There is nothing to suggest that it was him. And even so, these notes would say that Mr Lawless knew nothing about him.'

I was about to speak again, but Father had returned, and he was regarding us from the doorway. 'Is everything all right?'

Ewan showed him the broken lock on the shutter, and gave it a loose rattle. 'They opened the cabinet,' he said. 'But obviously found nothing of value.'

Liam returned a little later. He fixed a new bolt to the stable door, but was still concerned that the workrooms were insecure, so Ewan volunteered to sleep there during the night. Mrs Perrin brought him some blankets and warm milk, and he propped himself between two wooden chairs. I pointed out that the coroner's table was still available, but he didn't think that would be conducive to pleasant dreams.

It took longer than expected to survey the damage, tidy the room and make an inventory of all the files, and the following night Father asked Mrs Perrin to make up one of the spare rooms so that Ewan could sleep more comfortably. A new lock was fitted, and a full report sent to the constables on Sackville Street, but there was little expectation of anyone being held responsible.

Father found me in the library the next morning, and pulled out a chair to sit beside me.

'What are you reading?'

'Just a novel.'

'Oh,' he said, a bit deflated. Kepler was lounging on the table, and Father scratched behind his ears. Kepler submitted for a few moments before arching his neck to bare his teeth.

'Mrs Perrin came to speak with me,' Father said. 'She is a bit concerned following the break-in. She frets about what might happen if the house were targeted, for I am getting a little old, and Jimmy is far too young.' He curled his little finger and swept some cat hair from the table-top. 'She thought perhaps that Mr Weir could lodge here for a while.'

I closed my book, and said, 'For how long?'

'Well, we could see. Perhaps until his term begins again in the autumn.'

'What does he think?'

'He seemed to be happy with the idea. His current rooms are not the most salubrious.'

'Yes, I know.' Father frowned, and I said that Mr Weir had once described them to me.

I was hesitant at first, even averse to the idea. I'd always considered the house to be my own domain. I could slip to the kitchen barefoot in my nightdress for a cup of water, or lie sprawled on the sofa with a book, or traipse in from the garden with mud on my petticoats and my hair undone. I disliked the idea of forever being wary of encounters, having to listen out for knocks on doors or throats being cleared. But perhaps these were the selfish vestiges of being an only child. I pictured having conversations with Ewan in the firelit parlour, and found the thought to be a pleasant one.

He arrived the following day with his trunk and satchel, and took possession of the spare room that was already prepared. It was on the same floor as mine, though on the other side of the house. Still, for those first nights I fancied I could hear him move about, a floorboard creaking, or the door of the wardrobe closing. I saw little of him. He studied in the morning, then took a quick breakfast before retreating to the workrooms for most of the day. He would join Father and me for supper, but he had often done that before, and so there was little novelty. Perhaps he was conscious of intruding, for even though Father would invite him to the parlour each evening, he would only stay a short while before retiring.

On the first Saturday, I saw Kathy and Jimmy take kettles of hot water to the iron tub on the third floor. I was in the landing when Ewan passed in his shirtsleeves and braces, a dry towel tucked under his arm. He bid me a good morning, and we agreed that the weather was very fine. I took a book to read in my room, but could still hear the slap and burble of water from the floor above, and perhaps, at the edge of hearing, a tuneful humming. It was rather distracting, so I decided to go down to the parlour instead.

At the end of the hall, the door to Ewan's room was ajar. The sheets on the bed were still in a tangle, and there was a faint musty smell, which reminded me of the times Clarissa and I would sneak into the rooms of her brothers, before they moved to London. A satchel hung from the back of a chair next to a desk, where a journal was laid out beside an inkpot and quill, its front cover lying open.

He must have been keeping it since he arrived in Dublin, for the first page was headed with the date from six months ago.

The crossing from Liverpool was brief, but one I won't soon forget. Our postal packet was tossed by a gale right against us, and I couldn't keep the lamp lit in my shifting cabin. All I could do was brace myself against the bunk and wait for us to limp into Dublin. First impressions of my new home were not at all favourable. It lacks the aspects of Edinburgh, and the grandeur of London, though its cabmen are just as surly and prone to overcharge. Mine dumped me at the door of my new employer, and was away in a clatter of hooves, leaving me to drag my trunk up the steps by myself. The door was answered by a willowy girl with dark eyes, pretty after a fashion, who I assumed to be a parlourmaid. It turned out she was the daughter of the house, and since our first meeting I've found her to be . . .

After a fashion? Here the page had ended, and I gripped the corner to turn the leaf, but then stopped myself. This was unfair to Ewan. He had every right to jot down his personal thoughts and expect them to remain private. Still, it was odd to see myself appear in a piece of writing like a character in a book. I could remember opening the door to Ewan — the brim of his hat was drooping, and he held the handle of his trunk so that it tilted against his legs. He'd appeared to me then to be rather brusque, but perhaps that was explained by his trying journey.

What was it about me that he was going to describe, though? A door banged shut in the hall below, and I hurriedly left the journal and stepped out of the room. Perhaps it was best not to know.

At first I almost missed it, the sign on Abbey Street for Elyan the horologist. It was just his name and an hourglass engraved on a brass plaque, which was attached to some rusting iron railings. His shop was on the basement level beneath a well-lit cutler's, down narrow granite steps where bits of litter and old newspaper had fallen from the street above. The front door was locked, so I tugged on the tassel of a bell-rope. A moment later, there was a clunk as the bolt was undone, and the door swung inwards silently. There was no one on the other side. When I entered, a lead weight beside the door began to descend, which caused a hinged metal arm to push the door closed again.

The bustle of the street was replaced by an incessant and arrhythmic ticking. There was no handle or latch on the inside, and if I wanted to leave, the same mechanism, whatever it was, would have to be used. The shop room was cramped. Bays of shelving and tall cabinets contained mantel clocks with casings of gilded metal and alabaster. Bracket clocks were affixed to the wall, and grandfathers stood in each corner, their faces adorned with numerals and astrological figures, slender lances and spades.

Behind the counter, a man sat at a table in a pool of candlelight, his back to the shop as if the contents were of no concern. He turned about to look at me, peering through spectacles with additional hinged lenses attached to the frame. He was younger than I expected, with a beard that was thick around the chin, more wispy the closer it came to his ears.

'Mr Elyan?'

He said that he would be with me in a moment, before returning his attention to a pocket watch, its intricate innards exposed and glinting.

I wandered about the shop floor, and stopped at a shelf with a tortoise-shell box. When I lifted the lid, pieces of metal rose from within like shapes in a fold-out book, forming a humming-bird in its nest. Its head tilted about, and a tiny bellows caused the bird to chirp and trill. At the bottom of the nest there was an egg, which began to tremble as if about to hatch. The hummingbird lowered its long beak towards it, but as the mechanism wound down, the egg became still. Its mother's song ended, and she stayed leaning over it as the lid closed by itself, folding everything back into the box.

Mr Elyan had come to stand by my shoulder. 'There are other designs, if you would like to see?'

'No, thank you, I was just browsing.' Before he could step away again, I said, 'How did you open the door?'

'There is a lever by my table. A simple mechanism of springs and pulleys.'

'There's no handle on the inside.'

'No.'

'So how does one leave?'

'I let you out.' He took up the tortoise-shell box and wound its key, then replaced it without lifting the lid. 'But were you not looking for something, a timepiece perhaps?'

'I happened to see one of your devices recently at Charlemont House.'

He smiled at the mention of the name. 'Ah, yes,' he said. 'The Draughtsman.'

I withdrew the spoiled portrait from my coat and showed it to him. He squinted at it for a moment, then took the sheet from me and held it up. The nails of his thumb and forefinger had been grown long and filed into points. He glanced at me over the edge of the page. 'What has happened to it?'

'The boy, I mean the machine, did that by itself.'

'No,' he said. 'Not by itself.' He brought the sheet back to the counter and placed it under a candle. He frowned while running his fingers along the scratched-out cross and the faint letters at the bottom of the page. 'Did many people see this happen?'

'A small crowd had been watching, though Lord Charlemont switched it off before the verse was written out. He seemed to think that it was malfunctioning.'

Elyan shook his head and tensed his fingers, as if he meant to crumple the sheet.

'I take it you didn't design it like this.'

'I was hoping to get commissions from being displayed in such surroundings. Who would want one now?' He held the page against the light to read the verse, but his expression remained unchanged. He didn't seem to recognize it, but neither was he surprised to see it there.

I said, 'Would it not require a special skill to

tamper with it like this?'

He remained silent as he took up a pencil and jotted something in an opened ledger, perhaps the verse itself.

'Mr Elyan?'

'It's relatively simple. The machine is designed to be altered and rearranged. Letters can be placed in any order to spell out whatever you like.' He pointed to the cross running through the girl's body. 'See, this line is the same as the hem of her dress; it's just moved up and repeated. The vertical line is the length of her leg.'

'But still, one would have to be familiar with such things to meddle with them?'

He held up a hand. 'I should not be speaking about it, except with Lord Charlemont if he so wishes. Are you a relative of his?'

For a moment I considered lying, but then answered no, and told him my name.

He seemed surprised, and a slight smile came to his lips. 'You are the daughter of the coroner?'

I nodded.

'Why, I know your father. I attended several of his demonstrations years ago.'

'In York Street?'

'Yes. We are fellow anatomists after all, even if my interests lie more in the mechanical, but the principles are the same. The lungs are like a bellows; the heart a pump; bone and tendons, rods and wires. Your father always told us: if you want to know how something works, first you must take it apart.' He held up a curtain that led to a back room, and said, 'Let me show you something.'

The workshop reminded me of Father's office: ordered clutter, with tables bearing callipers and gears, spring-wheels and pendulums. A life-sized figure sat in a chair. She was a young woman in a morning dress, her yellow hair uncovered and loose. She sat awkwardly with both hands held up to one side of her face. Elyan fetched a flute from his desk and inserted it between her fingers, placing the mouthpiece against her parted lips.

Her features were doll-like, but her hands looked almost real: very pale, with blemishes and creases. A fine suture ran like a seam along the insides of her fingers.

'I tried everything to make her cover the holes with the proper pressure and touch,' he said. 'The only thing that worked was when her hands were gloved in human skin.'

I saw him glance at me, perhaps to gauge my reaction. I reached out and touched the top of her knuckles. The skin was cold, and felt almost like wax, with the surface beneath hard and unyielding.

'How did you manage to preserve it?'

'Trial and error,' he said, narrowing his eyes as if remembering the less successful attempts. 'I settled upon a balm of liniment and alcohol mixed with zinc salts. I could give the recipe to Mr Lawless if he wishes.'

'Father has no need to preserve the dead.'

'No, I suppose not.' He removed the flute and cupped the girl's cheeks with both hands, pressing his fingers until there was a clicking sound. With great care, he took her face away.

Inside the head, two glass eyes were suspended on metal stalks. They were downcast as if to give her a demure expression. At the bottom, a silver tongue was fashioned and shaped to look real. Elyan laid the face on a worktable so that it tilted on her nose and chin.

'The biggest challenge has been to regulate the flow of breath,' he said. 'Her tongue moves back and forth to block the lips, coinciding with gaps in the notes.' Elyan licked the tip of his finger and dabbed a piece of lint from one of the eyeballs. 'Everything must work in perfect unison — the puff of the bellows, the movements of her fingers and tongue — for the tune to be played correctly.'

'Who are you making it for?'

'No one,' he said. 'I just want to see if it can be done.'

An odd noise came from the shop, like a glass marble rolling on a table, then the clicking of a ratchet, and finally the tinny chime of a clock. It was answered by another, which rang out a simple tune, then several more began to toll in succession. They were striking eleven, and so there was time for those lagging to catch up and synchronize. The noise swelled as they rang together, with peals of different pitch and resonance, before one by one they began to stop.

Mr Elyan turned his head sharply and frowned. Without a word he walked back into the shop, whipping the curtain aside as he passed through.

I had heard this sound before: when I followed the man with the lazy eye through the streets. We had faced each other in a darkened hallway, and the hour had struck. At the back of the workroom there was a stairwell leading upwards. Its upper reaches were lost in the dark, but I knew that it would take me to the alley behind Capel Street.

Mr Elyan returned through the curtain, a mantel clock in an ormolu mount clutched in his arm. He placed it on a table, and opened its casing to peer inside. 'I can never get this one to stay correct. Every day it lapses another few seconds.' With a thin pincer he began to grip the delicate gear shafts one after the other, the clockwork stopping and starting with each hold and release.

'Should not all the clocks have rung at the same moment?'

'I could make them do that, of course,' he said, reaching for a round magnifying glass with no handle. 'But there is no way of knowing which of them is actually correct. All that matters is that each stays true to itself.'

He unscrewed a cogwheel and extracted it, holding it up to his eye. Then he placed it in a vice, and began rasping one of its teeth with a metal file. He became engrossed, almost as if he'd forgotten about my presence.

I picked up the face of the girl and felt along the smooth inverse. If I'd been alone, I might have placed it over my own.

'Mr Elyan, I have seen someone visit your shop before. A man with ptosis. Could he have been the one who made the changes to Lord Charlemont's machine?'

Elyan paused in his work, but he didn't glance up. He blew the shavings away from the vice, and then resumed filing. 'I don't know who you mean.'

'He is hard to mistake. It was about a fortnight ago.'

Elyan turned and regarded me, his eyes slanting down in what may have been concern. He was about to speak, but then he stopped himself and gestured to the mask in my hand. 'Put that down.'

When I did so, he reached beneath his table and pulled a lever. I heard the bolt in the front door release, and a draught caused the curtain to sway.

Elyan returned his attention to the vice, and said, 'I am rather busy, Miss Lawless. Please give my regards to your father.'

I wanted to question him again, but it was clear that he would say no more. When I emerged on to the basement steps, the door closed fast behind me. I lifted my face to the narrow portion of sky above the railings, and felt a misty rain begin to fall.

★ ★ ★

The wind whipped up as the day wore on. By nightfall, thunder rumbled over Dublin Bay, bringing the odd flicker of lightning, and Kepler was unnerved enough to lie curled up beside me on the bed. He let out a plaintive mewl when I donned a dressing gown to fetch a book from downstairs. The house was dark and quiet. I could see through a crack in the door that the parlour was lit. Ewan was there, resting his head in the sofa and reading a book against the lamplight. I was about to retreat upstairs, but instead I tied my gown tighter, and pushed open the door with a gentle knock.

He turned when he heard me, and seemed ready to get up. 'I'm sorry, I thought everyone was asleep,' he said. 'Would you like to use the parlour?'

I waved for him to remain. 'Stay, I'll only be a minute.'

He nodded and resumed reading, leafing back a page as if he'd lost his place.

I went to the bookcase and scanned its titles. There was the copy of Lewis's *Romantic Tales* that I had come to get, but I felt conscious now of picking it out.

Ewan said, 'Has the noise of the thunder kept you from sleeping?'

'No, I am often awake at this hour.'

'I'm the same. It's easier to study in the smaller hours.'

'What are you reading?'

He turned the spine towards me. 'Very dull, I fear.'

I moved closer to see the gold-leaf lettering of Male's *Epitome of Forensics*.

'Your father likes to test me with hypothetical cases while we work, describing two or three signs of death and asking me to deduce the cause.' He pursed his lips and flicked through some pages of the tome. 'More often than not, I am stumped.'

'What a good idea.' I sat down on the couch, leaving a space between us, and held my hand out for the book. 'Let's see if you fare better now.'

He smiled at me, but then hesitated. 'Some of the descriptions are rather distressing.'

'Why, I have read it twice before.'

'Yes, of course, I keep forgetting.'

He passed me the book, and I leaned back to leaf through it.

'Don't give me one that is too obscure.'

'Then how will you ever learn?' I said, reading over an entry in the section marked 'Aerial Poisons'. I sat up straight and looked at him steadily. 'You are called to examine an unfortunate man who shows every appearance of strangulation, except there are no marks on his neck. His eyes are open and staring, tongue protruding, fists clenched and jaw locked.'

'You needn't say it so eagerly.'

'When you open him up, the ventricles of the brain contain a serum tinged with blood, the lungs are collapsed and the viscera are dark-coloured and turgid.' I closed the book in my lap. 'So, Mr Weir, how do you think this poor man met his death?'

He held my eye for a moment, an amused slant to his brow, and then he spoke his thoughts aloud. 'Well, there are no wounds or contusions, and you would not have given me a case so dull as a fit of apoplexy. Something was ingested or inhaled.' He drummed his fingers on the arm-rest.

'Do you give up?'

'No, no. I just need more details,' he said. 'In what kind of room was he found?'

'It doesn't say.'

'Well, imagine it.'

'A garret.'

'Above what?'

'A business on the dockside.'

Ewan thought some more. 'If he lived above a trade, his room may have been gathering vapours from below. Chemicals from a tanner perhaps, or carbonic gas from a lime-kiln.'

'Yes,' I said, opening the book to show him the entry in the *Epitome*. 'That's exactly it. Fumes from the burning of lime.'

Our shoulders drew close as he leaned over to see. 'Really? In truth, it was a guess.'

He asked if he could have the book back.

'What for?'

'Because it is your turn.'

'But I have not read Male in several months.'

'Oh, don't make excuses.'

Like me, he flicked through the pages to pick out a case, glancing at me suspiciously once or twice as if I might spy the chapter. When ready, he told a tale of three sisters at a masquerade, chatting by the punch bowl. As the night wore on, one was seen to be flighty and unsteady in her dancing, another retired early feeling unwell, and at midnight, when everyone was unmasked, the third was found dead in her seat, her young, fair face contorted in seizure. 'During autopsy, you find no other symptom or sign of death.'

'But there must be.'

'I am afraid not,' he said, pleased with himself.

Outside, a gust made the window shutters creak, and the clock on the mantel continued to tick.

I tried to recall some of the more exotic poisons and their symptoms, but I could think of none that would touch three people so differently. Ewan was humming a strain from a Scottish folk-song, and I told him to hush. Years ago, when I ate the petals of a buttercup, Father had shown me all the flowers in the park that were toxic: wolfsbane and nightshade and laurel. He said one of the most common of all presented the greatest danger. Its odour caused giddiness and headache, while those who consumed it suffered convulsions and death.

It was all I could think of, so I said, 'The punch was laced with water-hemlock.'

Ewan let out an exasperated sigh, and opened the book again.

'Am I correct?'

'That was far too easy,' he said. 'I'll have to give you another.'

'Oh, no,' I reached over to grip the top of the book, 'the next question is for you.'

'I knew I should have asked the one about copper sulphate.'

I shifted closer to take the book back, but he kept his hold, and we were smiling together at our small tug-o-war when a voice by the door said, 'Miss Abigail, what on earth are you doing up at this hour?'

Mrs Perrin stood on the threshold, a small conical flame-snuffer in her hand.

Ewan let me have the book. He straightened his mouth and got up.

'I was just helping Mr Weir with his studies,' I said.

'I am sure Mr Weir is well capable of studying on his own.'

He bowed his head and said that she was quite correct. 'I am sorry for keeping you so late, Miss Lawless. It is time that I got to bed, so I shall bid you both good night.'

He left the room, Mrs Perrin keeping her eye on him as he went, and she waited for his door to shut up above.

'Look at you, Abigail. Talking to a young gentleman late at night half dressed.'

'I would hardly say that,' I said, getting up.

'You should not be encouraging him any further.'

I looked at her. 'What do you mean, any further?'

She tutted and shook her head, and pointed at the lamp. 'Don't leave that on all night. I should have been abed an hour ago.' She closed her shawl, before bidding me good night and heading off to her room in the basement. The cushion where Ewan had been sitting was askew, so I set it straight. I did not think that I was encouraging him in anything, though when I considered it, I found the idea that there was a sentiment to encourage quite pleasing. I picked up the *Epitome* again and ran my finger over its spine. Flicking through the pages once more, I saw the entry for water-hemlock, placed the marker ribbon there, and slipped the book back into its gap on the shelf.

10

By the time we cleared the city limits the rain was falling in sheets, casting a gloom inside the carriage despite the early hour. Our progress was slow. We dipped and jolted through the countryside, the wheels sinking into potholes and splashing water on the windows. The roads became steep and narrow, and treetops crowded overhead.

Clarissa's hair was carefully pinned and didn't move as she glanced upwards. 'We'll be lucky if we make it back.'

'It is not far now,' I said. 'The professor's observatory is on a bluff so it is rather exposed to the weather.'

She braced herself against the armrest as the carriage turned a corner. 'How do you know?'

'Father told me.'

'Oh.'

Father had been called away at the last minute to chair a freeholders' election for clerk of the peace. He had not wanted me to go alone, and so I asked Clarissa to accompany me, promising that James Caulfeild would be in attendance.

We passed through a large iron gate and followed a winding drive through orchards and fields before the observatory came into view. It was a handsome house, with a wide turret rising over the rooftop crowned by a wooden dome like the cupola of a Greek church.

'It's a shame the weather is so foul,' I said. 'It would be nice to look through the telescope.'

'Hmm?' Clarissa's attention was drawn towards the carriages parked near the entrance. 'Oh, yes, I'm sure.'

The front door opened as we pulled up to the porch, revealing an elderly maid holding an oil-lamp as if she had been awaiting our arrival. Inside, the entrance hall was modest and dimly lit. Narrow corridors led away, suggesting a warren of passages. The maid set off through one. Her lamp cast a halo on the dark wooden panels and neat wallpaper. We could hear a murmur of voices ahead, and she entered a wide room with two tall windows overlooking the gardens. One wall was taken up by bookshelves that stretched all the way to the ceiling. In the corner, there appeared to be a large terrestrial globe hidden beneath green baize cloth. Armchairs and couches were arranged about the hearth, where men and women sat and talked. Another group were gathered around a table and seemed to be taking part in a parlour game. Professor Reeves and James Caulfeild stood by one of the windows, the professor speaking while James stared outside as if lost in thought, his hands clasped behind his back.

The professor noted our arrival. He came to greet us, and I introduced him to Clarissa.

'Your name is familiar to me, Miss Egan. Would I know your father?'

'You may. He is the rector of St George's.'

'Oh,' Reeves said flatly. 'Then perhaps not.' He signalled to a passing maid who carried a tray with glasses of a deep-red liqueur. 'Malaga wine,' the professor said, 'with a squeeze of lemon. We always serve it at these gatherings.'

I had a taste. It was rather cloying, but I sipped it to be polite.

Reeves brought us about the room, introducing us to some of the other guests. It was interesting to put faces to names that I had seen printed in scientific journals, and the men would smile if I quoted the title of one of their works. As we made our way between one small group and another, the professor said, 'You may be giving some the delusion that they are widely read.'

I smiled and said that I hadn't meant to.

'They may demand that you be invited to every gathering from now on.'

Clarissa kept an eye on James by the window. She asked the professor how often he hosted these events.

'Only once or twice in a season. You have seen yourself that the road is difficult, and the house remote. It was my grandfather's originally; my only addition has been the equatorial room up above. I remember coming here as a child, getting lost in the hallways, or exploring the loft.' He looked up into the high ceiling. 'Very little has changed; most of the furniture has been here longer than me.'

'And the globe?' I said, as we walked beside it.

He looked at me quizzically. 'Oh, that's not a globe.'

He placed his glass on a side table and removed the cloth to reveal an orrery, a mechanical model of the sun and planets. In the middle of a round table, a brass sphere about the size of a billiard ball sat upon a slender metal stem. The whole room and everyone in it was reflected in its polished surface. Six spindly arms radiated towards the edges, each holding smaller orbs of various sizes: glass marbles of red and blue and turquoise. The moons were attached to their planets with ever more delicate arms, and the table's rim was etched with days and months and the signs of the zodiac. Four metal bands arced over the surface, representing celestial meridians and ecliptics, and lending the whole table its spherical shape.

Reeves reached down to turn a handle, setting all in motion: the moons about their planets, and the planets about the sun, all with varying speeds of orbit, so that bodies would catch up with each other, or drift apart, or briefly align. After a few more cranks of the wheel, he let go, and it continued on its own. 'This was also here before I was born, but exactly how old it is I do not know.'

'It was built before 1781, anyway,' I said.

'Why do you think that?'

'Because that is when Herschel discovered the Georgian planet. And it is not represented here.'

'Most perceptive, Miss Lawless. Yes indeed, Uranus. It is what I am observing at the moment.'

Clarissa said, 'I had no idea that the planets were so close to each other.'

I felt a tinge of embarrassment at her misconception, but Reeves was kind when correcting her.

'Your intuition was correct, Miss Egan,' he said. 'If it were truly to scale, then the earth would be at the front of the house, and Jupiter somewhere near the front gate.'

'Which would make for an unwieldy mechanism,' I said, and he smiled.

He pointed to one of the planets. 'Something is not quite right, though. See how Mercury lags halfway through its orbit. One of the gears must have gone awry.'

I watched the machine turn slowly and allowed another year to elapse. 'There is a clockmaker on Abbey Street who perhaps could fix it.'

'Mr Elyan,' Reeves said. 'Yes, I know of his work. But I have grown used to its eccentric orbit. Besides, I have no real use for the device, when I am lucky enough to observe the planets in reality.'

'Abigail was hoping we could see the telescope,' Clarissa said.

'No,' I said. 'Well, perhaps. I mean I realize that it's not a plaything. Only if you thought it was appropriate.'

Reeves said, 'But of course. Why else would I have dragged you all the way here?' He checked his watch. 'We shall have supper, allow night to fall, and then we shall see what there is to see.'

I saw Clarissa stand a little straighter, and tilt her chin upwards. James Caulfeild approached. He greeted us with a brief bow, but immediately turned to Reeves.

'Professor, unfortunately I must depart, for I am expected in Dublin.'

Reeves frowned and said, 'I was expecting you to remain here, Mr Caulfeild. There are men from universities and academies that you should be conversing with, explaining yourself and the research that we are carrying out. This is not just a social gathering.'

'I believe I have already spoken with everyone of note.'

'All I saw you do was study the rain falling in the garden.'

'As I said, I have an appointment in the city.'

'With the card tables or the tavern?'

James took a breath through his nose. The planets in the orrery began to slow with a faint clacking, and then became still.

'You can do as you wish,' Reeves said. 'Though if you leave the gathering now, I shall be disappointed.'

'Mr Caulfeild,' I said. 'Clarissa and I would be pleased if you can remain. We have only just arrived, and were looking forward to your company.'

'Yes,' Clarissa said. 'I was hoping someone could explain to me the workings of this infernal machine.'

James held the professor's eye for a moment. He turned to Clarissa and said, 'Of course, Miss Egan. I would be delighted.'

The guests in the corner began to laugh together, and one called for Professor Reeves to join them. A group had gathered around a gentleman seated at a table. He wore a fur stole about his neck, which must have felt stifling, but he spoke with a Spanish accent and was no doubt used to warmer climes. The table was littered with scraps of paper bearing people's names, and an opened inkpot.

Reeves said to me, 'Dr Inez claims that he can discern any man or woman's character simply by the form of their signature.'

The doctor took a swig of Malaga wine. 'Would you like to see, miss?'

I was sceptical, but with smiles of encouragement from those around me, I took up the quill and dipped it in ink.

After a few letters, Inez gripped my hand quite firmly and turned the paper over. 'No, no, miss. Do not try to impress me. Write it quickly, without thinking, as you would if no one was watching.'

I did as he suggested, and placed the quill down. Inez picked up the sheet and held it close to his face. He spoke in that position, without looking up. 'There is grace and cultivation in the harmonious flow; self-assertion in the disproportionate loop of the g.' He tilted the sheet slightly. 'The sloping lines announce tenderness. The firm yet delicate cross of the A shows a sufficiently strong but not obstinate will. The dots of the i float far above and not in line with their letters, indicating the ardour and impatience of your Irish character.'

Reeves said, 'That sounds quite accurate.'

'I think the doctor is being generous.'

Someone said that the only person yet to submit to a reading was Professor Reeves himself. He held up his hands as if ready to yield, but then said, 'There is little about me that

213

Inez doesn't know, so I fear it would be cheating.'

Supper in the observatory was an informal affair, with people sitting down at different times and in no particular arrangement. The rain eased and the skies cleared as darkness fell, and I found myself in stilted conversation with a mathematician's wife who seemed used to passing her meals in silence. Afterwards, in the drawing room, I could not find Clarissa, so I stepped into the hall. There was a glow of light beyond a corner. Professor Reeves stood next to some opened shutters. An oil-lamp cast his shadow on a grandfather clock, and little could be seen in the window except the professor's own reflection.

He turned at the sound of my footstep, and I apologized for disturbing him. 'I was just looking for Clarissa.'

He smiled at me. 'You have caught me taking a quiet interlude.'

'Every host deserves that from time to time.'

'The last I saw, Miss Egan was talking to Mr Caulfeild in the conservatory. I am pleased that he found at least one reason to stay.'

'I might look for them there.'

'Actually, I was just about to seek you out. Would you like to see the equatorial room, Miss Lawless?'

'Very much so. What about your other guests?'

He picked up the oil-lamp, causing his shadow to shift along the wall. 'Most of those present have seen it before, or will be too comfortable by the fire if I'm any judge. Though perhaps you would like to ask Miss Egan?'

I thought of her speaking with James in the conservatory, and decided to leave her be.

'Very well,' the professor said, turning around. 'It is this way.'

He led me through another corridor to a spiral staircase that wound itself around a single column of stone. At the top he entered a circular chamber, the interior of the turret, with four tall windows looking out in each direction. A heavy oak desk sat beside cabinets and bookcases and a black fireplace with glowing embers. The ceiling was low and wooden, and a staircase led to an opening like a trapdoor. Reeves continued upwards.

We now stood beneath the dome, in a simple room with varnished floorboards and white-washed walls. In the centre, the telescope was set upon a granite plinth. It was about the length of a man, made from polished brass which tapered in segments to a narrow eyepiece. The vaulted roof overhead had a long aperture, which could be opened to reveal a section of the night sky. Reeves began to turn a handle attached to the wall, and the roof slid up like the shutter in a bureau. A chill breeze entered the room. The stars above seemed rather dim, and I asked the professor if the recent haze had affected his work.

'It hasn't helped, of course,' he said, placing his eye to the bottom of the telescope, which was set at a height so he could stand beside it comfortably. 'But the effects are mostly visible close to the horizon.' He made feather-light touches to the dials on the frame. 'We were observing the planet at this time last night, so it can't have gone far.'

'We?'

He moved back from the eyepiece to look at me. 'Mr Caulfeild and I.'

Reeves returned his attention to the telescope, and with one more adjustment to the focus, he said, 'Ah,' and invited me to look.

The professor was an inch or two taller than me, and I had to stand on my tiptoes. Loath to brush against the telescope in case I knocked it out of focus, I got as close as possible and closed one eye.

A pale-blue drop hung suspended in a dark circle. It seemed motionless and silent, indistinct at its edges, though I fancied I saw enough light and shadow to make out its spherical form. It was perfect, like a pearl on a black cushion, and I couldn't believe that I looked upon an object some two thousand million miles away. It felt as if I could reach out and roll it between my thumb and forefinger.

Reeves's voice came over my shoulder. 'You are seeing what Herschel looked upon thirty-five years ago, the first planet discovered since antiquity.'

I pulled back from the eyepiece and regarded him. 'It's beautiful.'

His mouth straightened a little. 'Yes, though our primary concern is not aesthetic.'

'No, of course — '

'There is something of a mystery, you see, one that I had intended to describe in the Academy some weeks ago. We thought that we had calculated the planet's trajectory perfectly, that we would know precisely the path it should take. But it turns out we have been wrong.'

I looked through the eyepiece again.

'The orbit has been perturbed,' he said. 'There is a body at work that we cannot perceive, yet we know it is there because of its influence on others.' He gazed at the portion of sky visible through the aperture. 'If we just keep looking, Miss Lawless. It cannot remain hidden for ever.'

'But what is it?'

'Another planet,' he said. 'As yet undiscovered. In a way, I am just like your father. Looking for evidence, and seeking out the truth.'

I smiled at him, followed his gaze, and said that it must be a thrill to forever peer into the unknown.

'Oh, there are many evenings of stiff joints and fruitless labours as well. It gets cold up here in the dead of night. But it is worth it, to work towards a greater purpose.'

'Which is what?'

'To understand everything,' Reeves said. 'To discover and know each of the threads that Nature uses to weave her patterns.'

A breeze began to whistle through the roof, and I gripped my elbows in the cold air. Reeves noticed and said that I should warm myself by the fire in his workroom while he closed the roof.

I went down the wooden stairs, and coaxed some flames from the embers, while the sounds of ratchets and gears echoed in the dome overhead. The fireplace was made from slabs of polished black limestone, dotted with white spirals and swirls, the relics of ancient sea-creatures and molluscs. Reeves came to stand beside me.

'It's a beautiful piece,' I said, tracing a finger over one of the fossil shells, tightly coiled like a ram's horn. 'I wonder if it could convince those who shouted you down in the Academy. That the world is older than they think.'

'They would only say it was evidence of the Flood. Or that God created the world with an appearance of great age to provide variety for the senses, or some such nonsense. It is a shame, when the truth may be far more fascinating. To think that these creatures lived in so remote a time, and toiled under the same sun as our own.'

I smiled at his choice of word. 'Toiled?'

He glanced at me. 'Perhaps that was a bit pessimistic.' He placed the guard before the fire. 'You know, Miss Lawless, at times I get discouraged when I see religious fervour hold sway in the city, but meeting people like you, and like your father, gives me some hope at least.'

I was about to thank him, but there were footsteps on the spiral staircase, and the faint approach of a candle-flame. An elderly servant entered and told the professor that Mr Caulfeild was returning to the city.

Reeves frowned and looked at a clock on the mantel. 'I must have a word with him before he leaves. Please excuse me, Miss Lawless.' He hurried from the room and down the stairs, and the servant followed after.

I warmed myself by the fire for another

moment or two, took the oil-lamp and went to find my way back to the drawing room. In the dark passages, nothing could be seen beyond the glow of the lamp, and I soon found myself in a corridor that we had not come down before. There was no wallpaper, just exposed stonework, and I thought perhaps it would lead to the kitchen or servants' quarters. An arched doorway stood at the end, with an opened callipers engraved in the keystone above. I knocked and, when there was no answer, I pushed the door open.

The room was narrow but long, with a workbench of wooden slats and cast-iron legs. Further on, there was an armchair beside a fireplace, and a small bed in the corner, its blankets neat and folded. The fireplace was clean, but there was less chill here than in the corridor, so perhaps it had been lit earlier.

I brought the lamp to the table. There was some order to the clutter of glass beakers and jugs, weighing scales and candlesticks, each in their own place. A polished rosewood b . with a hinged lid contained rows of stoppered bottles sitting snugly. Each was labelled with creased yellow paper and spidery handwriting. I picked up three at random: iodine, laudanum and potassium.

I heard a rustling in the corner and turned about. A tall bird-stand stood beside the shuttered window, its coop covered in a cloth so thin that the outline of the frame was visible like a ribcage. I raised a corner of the fabric to look inside. There was a canary, but instead of sitting on its perch, the bird clung to the side of the cage with its claws and beak, and remained motionless in the lamplight. Its bedraggled yellow feathers were tipped with white as if they'd begun to drain of colour. The bird twitched its head and I let the cloth drop.

This was clearly a workroom, but not for Reeves — he would have no need for a bed in his own house. Perhaps it was a space for James Caulfeild, a place to rest in the small hours, or to work if the weather turned against them.

A sheaf of papers lay on the workbench, the topmost page covered in mathematical equations and geometrical diagrams, all neat and precise. Beside that, a letter was indeed signed off by James. It was two months old, an inconsequential note to Professor Reeves describing correspondence with the observatory in Armagh. There was another sheet next to it, not a missive or thesis, but rather a single line repeated again and again: *In this Year of Our Lord, Eighteen Hundred and Froze to Death.* I could see slight variations in the handwriting. Some of the lines were slanted, some of the letters looped or exaggerated, others angular and unjoined. But each time, the style grew closer to James's, until the final line was undoubtedly his handwriting. Perhaps it had been another of Dr Inez's games.

I left the room as I found it, and retraced my steps, locating the correct passage that led back to the drawing room. Clarissa was sitting by the Spanish doctor, and I went to join them. When she looked at me I said, 'Mr Caulfeild had to leave?'

She nodded. 'He had business in the city.'

'At this hour?'

She shrugged her shoulders.

'That's a shame,' I said.

'Yes, but Dr Inez has been excellent company.'

The doctor nodded his head solemnly, as if he couldn't deny the truth of her statement. He topped up his glass with some Malaga wine. 'You ladies don't appear to have glasses.'

Clarissa said, 'Oh, that wine is far too sweet. I don't know how Professor Reeves could have developed a taste for it.'

Inez put his hand to his chest in mock indignation. 'It was I who gave him his first bottle some twenty years ago, when we were both undergraduates.'

'You studied together?' I asked.

'Well, we trained in different disciplines, but we shared dingy rooms overlooking Front Square — dark even in the middle of summer, cramped and draughty. You could not move without knocking over a pile of books or an empty bottle. I don't know how we managed,' he said, though I could tell from the warmth in his voice that he remembered it fondly. He held up his glass. 'My uncle sent us a case each term, and Reeves and I would have a glass or two in the evening to keep the cold at bay.'

I pictured myself and Clarissa in such a setting, and felt a brief pang that it would never be allowed.

'We were always there,' Inez said, 'even on feast days, or when term had finished. I was far from my family of course, but Reeves preferred to remain in the college. He considered it his true home.'

'He told me before that he was estranged from his family.'

'From his father most certainly. But he always had great affection for his mother. It was rather sad. I would see him write to her each week without fail, hunched over his small desk at the bottom of the bed. She never replied, but he was unconcerned. She had never been one for correspondence, he said. One morning he did receive a letter from home, from his father, attached to a bundle. In one brief message he told Reeves that his mother had taken ill several months before, and had finally succumbed, and he returned every letter that Reeves had sent her unopened. The old man had kept them from her. As far as she was aware, her son had left for an academic life and had forgotten her altogether.'

The professor had returned to the drawing room, and I watched him bid good night to some guests who were leaving, shaking hands and gripping shoulders. 'Such a cruel thing for his father to do, and so petty.'

'That was the measure of the man.' Inez reached for the bottle and topped up his glass. 'After that, Reeves had little inclination to leave the college walls. He also became conscious of young men like himself, those without family or means. He has shown kindness to many throughout his career, students in hardship, those who have fallen foul of the college authorities, often giving them positions right here at the observatory.'

Clarissa said, 'But that is not the case with Mr Caulfeild. James completed his degree without difficulty.'

'No,' Inez said. 'Mr Caulfeild is different. I confess that I do not know him well. But if Reeves has chosen him as his assistant, then I am sure he has a splendid character.'

The professor came to join us. He said that it looked as though the weather might turn again, so we had best make for home lest we become stranded. Clarissa and I bid him good night, and waited for Liam to come around with the carriage. As we pulled away down the long drive, I looked back at the house and the domed roof, and a glow of candlelight in the windows of the equatorial room.

★ ★ ★

Early the following morning, I saw Ewan make his way through the back garden towards the workrooms. Dewdrops had given the narrow lawn a silver sheen, and his footprints were visible in the grass.

Father once told me of a murder in County Clare. A big country house was surrounded on all sides by rolling lawns, and a retired colonel, who lived alone with his niece and a stable-hand, was found dead, bludgeoned in his own chamber. The girl told the constables that a burglar had broken in, killed her uncle and carried off some valuables, and she pointed to an opened window in his bedroom. But the police looked out upon a pristine carpet of dew,

223

undisturbed by trails or footprints, and they realized that the murderers had been in the house all along. The valuables were discovered in the niece's bedroom, her affair with the stable-boy was exposed, and both were tried and hanged at the next assizes.

Down below, the fire in the range had made the kitchen overly warm. Mrs Perrin stood by the counter, her hand wrist-deep in a plucked chicken.

'The dead arose,' she said when she saw me. 'You look a little peaky. Did you not have a pleasant evening?'

I said it was very enjoyable, though the Malaga wine may not have agreed with me.

'I'm sure.'

She withdrew the chicken's heart and placed it on a chopping block with some other entrails. When I was younger, Father gave me my first anatomy lesson with a butchered fowl. He showed me each organ in turn, told me to hold them, to test their texture and consistency. He tried to convey his wonder at how such pieces of offal could pump blood or filter waste or bellows air. Back then, I merely enjoyed the slimy feel. My chin barely cleared the table-top, and my fingernails were caked in gore.

Jimmy came in through the back door, a bundle of logs held beneath his chin. The cool air from outside was pleasant, and I was sorry when he kicked the door closed. He brought the wood to the hearth and began to use a small hatchet to split the thicker pieces in two.

His mother said, 'When you're done with that,

go and polish the dining table. And fetch some water for the drinking cask.'

'It's all right, Jimmy,' I said, taking the pail from beneath the sink. 'I'll get it.'

The surface of the tank at the front of the house felt cold in the morning air. The slanted lid had large scallop-shells in bas-relief, and I lifted it up fully so it leaned back against the wall. The tank was empty. The sides were wet and glistening with smears of green and deposits of limescale, but no water had collected at the bottom. The ballcock drooped down in the empty space, keeping the plug in the base of the tank open. I lifted the mechanism a few times to ensure it was still functioning, but there was no water being fed through the ducts.

I climbed the steps to see if the problem affected our neighbours. The road seemed busy for the time of day, with people walking hurriedly up the hill. A horse galloped by, a police constable riding low on its neck. I left the pail by the gate and followed the crowd. Several people had gathered by the gates of the Blessington Street Basin, and I pushed my way to the front. Two men knelt by the edge of the reservoir, reaching down into the water. The policeman that I'd seen had dismounted and stood behind them.

I asked a woman if someone had fallen in, but she remained silent. The men at the water's edge had become still, and seemed to confer with each other. A breeze caused the surface of the pool to shiver.

The policeman gave a command, and the two

men hauled the body of a young woman from out of the reservoir. Water cascaded from her dark skirts and long tresses on to the granite coping. The men held the girl beneath the crook of each arm, and they laid her down so she faced upwards, her unpinned hair plastered over her face. The constable stood for a moment, as if unsure what to do. He bent down to scoop her hair away, and laid it over her shoulder.

It was Edith Gould.

It felt as if the wind became chill, or the sun had passed behind a cloud. I bumped against a man who turned and muttered, just to get a better look, to be sure that it was her, but there could be no mistake. She looked so pale and cold, and I felt tears well as I pushed through the cluster of people.

The men by the reservoir turned at the sound of my footsteps on the gravel path. The policeman frowned, pointed towards me and said, 'Stay back, miss.'

'But I know that girl,' I said, and continued towards him without pausing.

Edith's eyes were open; a strand of hair still snaked over her nose and around her parted lips. I knelt down beside her, and the policeman said, 'You can't touch her.'

'I know, I just want to . . . ' But when I reached out I didn't know what to do — whether to remove the strand from her face, or close her eyes, or nudge her shoulder as if she still might wake up. I'd left the house without a coat, otherwise I'd have covered her with it, so she wouldn't have to stay beneath everyone's gaze. I could still see in her the girl from my childhood, quiet and reserved compared to Clarissa, but gentle and caring, and how pretty she was when her face would break into a shy smile. I covered my eyes, and the policeman remained silent as I cried for a moment.

Finally he said that he was sorry, and asked for her name. I told him that she was Edith Gould from Fitzwilliam Square.

His gaze swept south over the city. 'Then she's far from home,' he said. After a moment, he frowned. 'Is she the daughter of Judge Gould?'

'Yes.'

The crowd was continuing to gather at the basin's edge, and he moved towards them, his arms outstretched. 'Everyone must leave, get back beyond the gates.' Some complied immediately; others grumbled and then moved on. One pointed at me and said, 'What about her?'

I looked at Edith again, and remembered how she appeared at Charlemont's ball, the gown she wore, how it complemented the colour in her cheeks and the crystals in her hair. The dress she was in now was simple and unadorned, completely sodden. She wore leather walking shoes, the laces still tied in a double-knot. One shoe was missing a brown leather rosette over the toes.

Her right hand was lying away from her body, palm up, her fingers curled slightly, with thin blue veins visible in her pallid wrist. Her other hand was hidden beneath a fold of her dress, which I moved aside.

The hand was balled in a fist. I glanced over

my shoulder to where the policeman was still demanding that people leave. The men who had fished Edith from the water had gone to help him.

I reached towards her, but drew away from how cold she felt. I'd seen any number of bodies growing up, but this was different; never had I been so conscious of the absence of life. I whispered to her that I was sorry, took her hand again and gently eased her fingers back, just enough to peek inside. There was little or no stiffness. Edith gripped a dark metal hook with a fragment of black cloth still attached.

'Miss?'

I put the hand down and turned about.

The policeman said, 'I am sorry, but you will have to leave as well. The coroner will need to carry out an investigation.'

'I know,' I said, standing up and wiping tears from my cheek. 'I shall go and tell him.'

11

Father sent out a summons for twelve jurymen to assemble that afternoon. It meant that Edith was to remain at the reservoir, for the inquest had to inspect the body where it lay — where she lay — and although she was covered in a blanket, crowds still gathered at the gates on Blessington Street. I thought of her parents in Fitzwilliam Square, and her brother, Robert. Was it possible that they hadn't heard yet? I was glad to have been able to identify Edith, for at least then a messenger could be dispatched to her home — little or no comfort, but better than whispered rumours of a drowned girl on the far side of the city, when your own daughter was missing from the house.

In the afternoon, I watched as she was brought to the workrooms, hidden beneath a white sheet and borne on a stretcher by Liam and the constable. Ewan held the door open. The sheet caught on an exposed nail in the door frame and was about to be pulled away, but Ewan spotted the danger and unsnagged it. He noticed me at the window, and raised his hand in greeting. Before I could respond, he lowered his head and pulled the door closed.

I'm not sure how long I stayed watching the exterior of the coach house, and the shadowy movements visible through the opened shutters, before there was a knock on the front door. It was more like a banging, loud and persistent, and continued until I went to answer. Dr Labatt stood on the steps dressed in a frock coat, the head of his cane raised mid-rap. Three young men in Brethren coats stood on the pavement below, next to a horse-drawn cart and driver.

The doctor looked at me for a moment, expecting a greeting. Instead I ran my fingers over a panel of the door. His cane had left marks in the paint.

'I need to see your father at once.'

'I am afraid that Father is busy, and cannot be disturbed.'

'If he is at work, then it is all the more urgent that you fetch him.'

'You may not have heard, doctor, but there has been a tragedy.'

'Why do you think I have come? The Gould family are demanding to have their daughter returned to them.'

The three young men watched our exchange. One was quite young, and he regarded me with what seemed like hostility, though we had never met.

'She will be after the inquest,' I said.

'Tell your father that I have a court order allowing me to retrieve Miss Gould immediately.'

The doctor wasn't holding a document, nor were any of the others. 'May I see it?'

'It is not meant for you.'

'Did Judge Gould issue it?'

'Of course not.'

'But one of his colleagues did. I do not think that my father — '

'Miss Lawless,' he said, and waited for me to look at him, 'I have no desire to speak to you.' He came on to the top step, tall enough now to loom over me, and asked me to move aside.

'If you wait here,' I said, 'I shall tell Father that you wish to see him.'

Labatt pushed his way past my arm and shoulder, forcing me to take a step back. The three men followed on his heels, crowding into the hallway.

'Doctor, I said that I would — '

Labatt ignored me. He seemed to know the way to go: through the basement, past the shocked stares of Kathy and Mrs Perrin, and out into the yard towards the coach house. The horses in their stalls looked on impassively as the four men entered. Liam was cleaning the carriage. He raised his head to watch them climb the stairs. The doctor opened the door to Father's workrooms without knocking, and the others followed behind, their boots shuffling and scraping on the floorboards.

Father was writing at his desk. Ewan stood near the cabinets, looking through one of the ledgers. In the middle of the room, Edith was laid out on the examination table, still in the clothes she wore at the reservoir except that her shoes had been removed. The toes of her dark stockings were wet, but her skin had dried in the hours since her discovery. It was only the strangeness of her surroundings that made it seem as if she wasn't sleeping. Her hair had escaped its pins, and tumbled over the edge of the table in a tangled mess. The youngest of the

231

Brethren craned his neck to look at her.

Before my father could speak, Labatt took a folded document from inside his frock coat and handed it to him. Father held the opened page next to an oil-lamp. His eyes scanned over the text, and everyone stood quietly until he was finished.

'What nonsense is this?'

'We shall require a stretcher to transport Miss Gould to our cart.'

'No court can order a body taken from the coroner.'

'We can carry her without a stretcher of course, but I feel that would be less dignified.'

'You will not be taking her anywhere.'

Labatt turned to the young Brethren and said, 'Gentlemen.'

They approached the table, but before they could surround it, Ewan moved to one of the corners. My father stood beside him, and they faced the men across the table with Edith laid out between them.

Father looked at Labatt. 'The inquest has already begun, doctor. The body must remain in my custody until a verdict has been reached.'

'The Goulds have made their feelings clear. They cannot countenance the thought of their daughter being cut open. Surely their wish to commit Edith to the ground intact is not unreasonable.'

'I would have thought they would prefer to know the reason for their daughter's death.'

'She drowned,' Labatt said, an impatient edge to his voice. 'It is not uncommon. Come,

232

Lawless, the inquest can be open and shut: 'Casually Drowned' or 'Visitation from God'. Why must you search until you find evidence for suicide? Can you, of all people, not grant the family a Christian burial?'

Father didn't respond at once, though his eyes narrowed. I looked down at Edith's face in the grey light. Was that why the Goulds were so concerned? A belief that their daughter had taken her own life? On the table, Edith's hand lay open by her side, though the hook had been removed. Father would have understood its significance, of course, but he could hardly tell those present what such a piece of evidence indicated: that Edith had not been alone at the reservoir. I glanced at the jackets of the young Brethren. Their hooks were all accounted for.

'This court order will be rescinded,' Father said, handing it back to Labatt. 'In the meantime, Miss Gould will remain here.'

Ewan took a white sheet from a shelf beneath the examination table. It was folded in such a way that it could be unrolled in flat segments, and Labatt watched until Edith was covered completely.

'I tell you, we are taking her now.'

'You must know, doctor, that reports of a body stolen from the coroner's office will not reflect well on the people you represent, be they the Goulds or anyone else.'

Labatt placed the document on top of the white sheet, where it nestled against the peak of Edith's foot. Ewan was quick to pick it up, and he gave the doctor a dark look for using her body as a table-top. Labatt continued to regard my father. 'Let me talk to you in private.'

'No.'

'We arranged for the court order to be granted so that you could save face, Lawless.'

'Well, I do not require it.'

'Are you sure of that? This is not the first time we have had to speak with you.'

'I know, doctor, and I am weary of listening.' He turned and walked back to his desk, pulling the chair out to take his seat. He placed the nib of his pen on his finger to see if the ink had dried. 'You had no difficulty gaining entrance, gentlemen. I am sure you can find your way out.'

★ ★ ★

The black of Clarissa's mourning dress made her skin appear paler than usual and brought out the shadows beneath her eyes. We were silent as we made our way to Fitzwilliam Square. Had her mother not been with us, and had the tragedy befallen someone else, we might have discussed every rumour and speculation. But for Edith, that didn't seem right. I had wondered if I should go to the house at all after what had been said between Father and Labatt, but Edith had once been my friend, and I wished to pay my respects.

Several carriages had congregated near the front of number five, and we had to walk a short distance in the drizzle to reach the house. The door was off its latch, and opened immediately when we knocked. A young maid with dark hair

234

directed us into one of the front rooms. Several people were there, dressed all in black but for their white cuffs and handkerchiefs. They stood about the room in small groups, talking quietly to each other, their attention fixed on Mrs Gould. Edith's mother sat with one elbow on an armrest, and her hand over her brow. Two of her older sisters sat on either side, and were the principal responders to those who approached and offered condolences.

Judge Gould stood in a corner, speaking with another gentleman. There was no sign of Robert. Mrs Egan led us through the room towards the grieving mother, but Mrs Gould hardly lifted her head as we spoke with her sisters, offering platitudes that we knew to be inadequate. The oldest of the three knew Mrs Egan, and spoke with her politely. She also thanked Clarissa for coming, but when she turned to me she hesitated.

'I am sorry, but I don't believe we have met.'

'I am Miss Lawless.'

Mrs Gould looked up at the mention of my name. She didn't say anything, but her eyes lingered on me. Perhaps she was thinking of how her daughter was currently in my house instead of her own. Father's name may have been mentioned a lot before they dispatched Dr Labatt. Also, it hadn't been long since my last visit. A few weeks at most. In the depths of her mind, could she have forged some link between that event and this?

I told her again how sorry I was. She nodded, and covered her eyes once more.

We moved to one of the windows, where we

could see carriages splashing through the street outside Fitzwilliam Park. Clarissa and her mother began chatting to a neighbour of the Goulds, and a young maid came forward to offer tea. She was pretty and soft-spoken, with a mild Liverpool accent. Before she moved away, I said, 'Is Mr Gould here today?'

'Why yes, miss. That's him in the corner,' she said, nodding her head towards Judge Gould.

'I meant his son, Robert.'

For a brief moment she became still, and she looked at me more closely. But then her former meekness returned. 'I believe he's upstairs in the drawing room. I could bring him a message if you like.'

'There's no need. I may call on him to offer my sympathy.'

She hesitated, then looked down and said, 'As you wish.'

No one noticed as I slipped from the parlour to climb the stairs. The door to the drawing room was open, and I saw Robert at once, seated at the window where Edith used to draw her pictures of the square, her sketchbook still open on the table. Robert had his back to the door. He wore a dark waistcoat and white shirtsleeves, with his jacket hanging over the chair. He only turned when I said his name.

His eyes were red-rimmed, and he looked at me blankly.

'I am so very sorry for your loss, Mr Gould.'

His expression remained the same. He hadn't shaved for a few days, probably since Edith had died.

'I hope, Miss Lawless, that I can meet you one day when there is no tragedy to mourn. First Emilie, and now . . . '

He ran his fingers through his hair, pulled Edith's sketchbook towards him, and began flicking through the drawings, page after page of the streetscape before the window. Another carriage pulled up below and Mr Darby alighted, followed by Mrs Nesham. Several others on the street came forward to shake his hand as he made his way to the house. After a moment, we heard the front door open and an increase in the hum of conversation.

Robert's jawline had become set, and his breathing shallow. He said, 'I shall be expected to greet Mr Darby with my family. Will you excuse me?'

He left the room and descended the stairs, leaving his jacket draped over the back of the chair. I waited for his footsteps to recede, then lifted the coat up and examined the hook-and-eye fastenings. They were black and uniform, and undoubtedly the same design as the one Edith had held. None was missing from this jacket, though. Each hook was attached to the coat by an inch of fabric. I took a hold of one and gave a sharp tug. The double stitching of the hem held fast, though the slightest ripping noise of a thread or two made me think that a forceful pull could remove one. Even with my tame effort, the point had dug into my palm, leaving a small indent without breaking the skin.

I had seen these jackets being made, and searched the inner lining beneath the collar. The small label was black and the lettering grey, but when I held it to the light of the window I could see the name, *Whistler, Rutland Lane.*

Someone coughed in the door behind me. I turned to see the maid with dark hair regarding me coldly. She waited for a few seconds, then said, 'Mr Gould forgot his coat.'

I held it up and folded it at the shoulders. 'I was just about to bring it to him.'

She approached me with her hand held out. 'He asked me to do it.'

'Yes, of course,' I said, and gave it to her. As she was about to depart, I said, 'The events of the last few days must have been a shock for the entire household.'

The maid was caught between completing her errand and replying politely. 'It has been very difficult, but we do our best.'

'Can I ask you, had Edith been well on the day she disappeared? Was she anxious or preoccupied at all?'

'No, miss. She had supper with her family and went to bed as usual.'

'Nothing occurred that was out of the ordinary?'

'Mr Darby called on her earlier in the day, but that was not unusual.'

'He came to visit her specifically?'

'Well, yes. Though Mrs Gould was here of course.'

'Of course. Did he wear a coat like this?' I asked, indicating Robert's.

'They only wear those when they meet together. He was dressed in a normal frock coat.

But I'm sorry, miss, I must bring this to Mr Gould.'

I told her to go ahead, and thanked her for speaking with me. She hurried from the room with the coat draped over her arm. Rain continued to patter against the window, blurring the view outside. I reached out to close Edith's sketchbook, then rejoined the others downstairs. Robert had taken up a position at the top of the room near his father. He was still buttoning his coat. One of the elder sisters had given up her seat for Mr Darby, and he sat beside Mrs Gould, leaning forward with his elbows on his knees while holding one of her hands between both of his, a gesture that seemed oddly intimate. Mrs Gould was sitting straighter, nodding occasionally to the things he said.

All focus in the room was upon them. The conversations became hushed, and I had the uncomfortable feeling that this had become a Brethren meeting, especially when Darby stood up to address us. He waited with his head bowed until the room became completely silent, and when he spoke his voice was barely loud enough to reach the back of the room.

'Some things in life are beyond our understanding,' he said. 'Edith should be here, safe beneath this roof in the company of her family, whom she loved, and her community. Nothing I can say would bring meaning to what has happened, nor would I even wish to try. No words can express the ruin in our hearts.' His eyes slowly swept the room, as if he tried to look at each person in turn. But then he became still and stopped speaking. One by one, we all turned to follow his gaze. A police constable stood in the doorway, a sealed document in his hand.

'Which one of you gentlemen is Mr Darby?'

Even if the constable didn't know him, it was quite obvious that Darby was the preacher. Perhaps he was obliged to make certain.

Mr Darby remained silent, unwilling, it seemed, to identify himself, and no one else in the room spoke up. Judge Gould began to walk towards the officer, as if he intended to escort him from his house. Then Robert pointed at Darby and said, 'That's him.'

Mrs Gould turned her head sharply towards her son. The policeman began to make his way through the room, squeezing past people, bumping their shoulders without offering apology. When he stood before Darby, they looked at each other squarely.

The officer proffered him the letter. 'Mr Darby, you are summoned to appear at St Thomas's Hall, Marlborough Street, for an inquest into the death of Edith Gould.'

Darby didn't move, and for several seconds the letter was held up between them.

'You have to take it,' the officer said.

Darby slowly reached out and accepted the writ. He ran his finger over the wax seal, then sought me out again in the crowd.

There was an edge to his voice: 'Perhaps it would have been quicker if your father had asked you to deliver it, Miss Lawless.'

Everyone in the room turned to look at me, and there was malice in the eyes of many of the

Brethren. Some of them could not have known who I was, nor why Mr Darby had spoken to me. But they were hostile none the less.

Clarissa whispered to me, 'Did you know that was going to happen?'

'I had no idea.'

'Well, perhaps it's time we left.'

I nodded, and Clarissa, Mrs Egan and I left the Goulds' home in the company of the constable.

* * *

Overnight, the wind turned and came from the east. Cold air drifted through the flue, and I rose at dawn to place a fire-screen before the hearth. It had snowed again, another dusting that collected in patches on the lawn. As the sun rose behind a bank of cloud, the snow appeared discoloured, with patterns of mauve and tan swirling on its surface, as if powdered dye had been scattered from a bag. I was tempted to go down and look closer, but in the chill room the warmth of my covers was more inviting.

It remained cold all morning, and when I went downstairs the snow had not yet melted. Kathy was at work in the kitchen, wearing a thick woollen cardigan while cleaning out the fireplace. I fetched my own morning coat and stepped out into the yard. Ewan was there, standing beneath the eaves, hands tucked beneath his arms. He smiled when he saw me, and gestured towards the tinted snowfall. 'Pretty, isn't it?'

I stood beside him, pulling the lapels of my coat against my chin, and said that I'd never seen anything like it. It began to sleet again, tiny flakes emerging from the grey sky in eddies, but we were sheltered in the lee of the house.

'Your father has gone to the Chancery Court today to have the Gould petition overturned,' Ewan said.

'Do you think he will succeed?'

'I'm sure of it. The laws under which your father operates are ancient, and cannot be set aside.'

Ewan took a step forward to glance at the sky, as if checking the weather, then returned next to me, a little closer than before.

'The lawyers will delay him as much as they can,' I said. 'They have always been antagonistic towards my father.'

'Something to be proud of.'

I bent down to scoop up some of the coloured snow. Seen close up, it appeared normal. The tint was subtle, and could only be perceived in swathes.

'What do you think it is?' Ewan asked.

'I presume it is the same dust that has been dimming the sun, carried to the earth by the snowflakes.'

'Taste it.'

I looked up at him. 'You taste it.'

'No, thank you. I have been poisoned enough by these Dublin vapours.'

'As if Glasgow would be any better.'

'I come from Edinburgh.'

I tutted, shook the snow from my hand and

blew into my fingers.

'You'll get chilblains,' he said. 'Let me see.'

I looked at him, and then held out my hand, as if we were being introduced. He gripped it lightly, pretending to gasp at how cold it felt. 'You're perishing,' he said. He covered my knuckles with his palm, and we stood quietly for a moment. The wind shifted. Small flakes collected in the creases of his cravat, and either melted or were blown away.

A voice behind me said, 'Abby.'

I withdrew my hand, and turned to see Jimmy in the kitchen doorway, the day's papers draped over his forearm.

'I'm back from the market,' he said, giving Ewan a mistrustful glance.

'Oh, very well,' I said. I looked at Ewan again. 'Will you tell me if you hear word from my father?'

'Of course.'

I took the newspapers from Jimmy, thanked him and tousled his hair, and brought them to read in my mother's room as usual. It was still cold, so I kept my coat on while perched on her bed, looking through each of the papers for news on Edith's death. Only the *Gazette* mentioned anything about it, though they didn't name her. They called it 'a tragedy in Blessington Street', and referred to a young lady in fine clothing who had been found drowned.

There was nothing in the *Morning Post*, but an article on the editorial page was headed: 'God's Vengeance Against Hypocrisy.'

Hypocrisy is pretending to feel what we do not feel, to believe what we do not believe; it is pretending to practise what we do not practise. By assuming the garb of virtue, it is a disgrace upon virtue itself.

Hypocrisy in public office is an even more odious vice. It is founded in evil design, because it proceeds from cool deliberation, and through lying and fraud, is intended to produce injury to our neighbours. Numerous are God's denunciations against it.

The hypocrite endeavours to excite in others a high opinion of his own purity and integrity. He next proceeds to slander those by whom he is thwarted. Is it no wonder, then, that to attain the fruits of his malicious schemes, he will, without the least remorse, dip his hands in the blood of the innocent?

It is our duty to report that one of the officers of His Majesty's government in Ireland, with jurisdiction over the north wards of Dublin, Mr L —, by use of unnatural and invasive techniques, presumes to pass judgement on the demise of our dearly departed, when he has gone to great lengths to conceal the true and wicked nature of the death of his wife.

My eyes kept skipping lines to read ahead. I forced myself to note each word, though I could feel my fear and anger rising.

It has come to our knowledge that Mrs R —L —, a suicide, terminated her own existence, in defiance of God's will, by ingesting a vial of laudanum. It is also known that Mrs L —, a suicide, had been confined to her chamber in the months and years before her death, and so the poison could only have been provided by her own husband. However, if you search through the records of the Court, you will find no mention of this case. Mr L —could not have been expected to carry out an inquiry into the death of his own wife. But he lied to the authorities, claimed that she had died of natural causes, abused his position and good standing to quash any investigation, any attempt to discover the truth.

The result was that Mrs L —, a suicide, was interred in the grounds of St George's chapel, to lie among the devout and righteous, infesting that hallowed ground with her mortal sin.

Her husband has continued his work, impervious to criticism, to censure. One can only wonder, how many men have been sent to trial, and then the gallows, on the strength of his word alone? How many innocents have been buried at crossroads with their hearts impaled?

Our consolation, as usual, is found in the Bible. Job 8:13 declares that 'the hypocrite's hope shall perish', and in 20:5, 'the triumphing of the wicked is short, and the joy of the hypocrite but for a moment'. What can we do to carry out God's will? I say nothing more than this: to strip Mr L

—of any power and position, and to uproot his wife from the consecrated earth.

I started reading the article again, but stopped after the first paragraph. How could they be allowed to print such a thing? It was sickening, the crude masking of my father's name, the cruelty shown to my mother. I thought of Father reading the *Post* in the Law Courts, or being told about it; the sidelong glances and whispered slights. Its timing was no coincidence, after his refusal to return Edith to her family, and then the summons on Mr Darby.

Worst of all, I knew that it wasn't true. Mother had died of typhoid during an outbreak that swept through Rutland Square just before my seventeenth birthday. A Dublin dairy had delivered tainted milk to several households, and many of our neighbours succumbed to the fever.

Those who were able packed their children off to the country. Jimmy and I went to my father's cousin, a kindly spinster who lived in a rambling, ivy-covered cottage on the outskirts of Trim. I remember bidding Mother farewell. She was propped up in the bed, a hanky peeking from the sleeve of her nightgown, and the strings of her sleeping-cap untied. If anything, she was more alert and cheerful than usual, and said that she looked forward to my return. I kissed her cheek, and her cold fingers gripped my hand before I slipped away.

Less than a week had passed before the first letter came from home. Mother was ill, a sore throat and raised temperature, but Father told me not to worry. The postman in Trim was always accompanied by a small Jack Russell who heralded each delivery by scrabbling against the door, and I would hurry to greet them each morning. Several days passed before the next message arrived. I recognized the cream envelope and Father's neat hand at once, and I broke the seal to read the letter on the cottage threshold.

Jimmy and I made our way back to Dublin that evening, and he held my hand whenever I began to weep. It was dark by the time we reached home, the windows in Rutland Square glowing with lamplight. Father greeted us in the hallway, and held me for some time. Mother was laid out on the bed, dressed in a long-sleeved morning gown, her auburn hair visible beneath a sheer gauze cap. I had not seen her dressed like that in months. Her fingers were linked together as if in prayer, resting on her tummy. In the light of a single candle, there was a bluish hue to her lips.

The front door creaked open and banged shut. Father was back already. He hurried up the stairs, and when he entered Mother's room I was still perched on the bed, the paper laid out before me. By the way he looked at me, there was no need to ask if he had read it.

'You will have to find out who has written this,' I said.

He held my eye before closing the door quietly. 'I am not sure that would be possible.'

'Well, then the newspaper must be held to account.'

He took a chair still covered in a dust sheet, brought it closer to the bed and sat down. 'It may be wise to let the matter rest, Abigail.'

'But the things they said about Mother. Are you not angry?'

'Of course I am.'

'Then why not answer them?'

He shifted in his seat, and the dust sheet was dragged from the back of the chair. 'I know who would testify on their behalf.'

'Who?'

He got up and opened the shutters on the window in the corner. The weak sun had broken through the clouds, and cast a shadow of wavering branches on the white bedclothes.

'Do you remember the weeks before your mother died?' Father said, his eyes focused on the park outside. 'She stopped sleeping. I am surprised it hadn't happened before, cooped up in this room. She was tormented by lack of rest, and asked me to get something from the apothecary. A tincture of opium, a few drops each evening.' He came back towards the bed, and pulled open the top drawer of a small chest. It was empty, but he looked inside it anyway. 'It seemed to provide some relief.'

'Did Mother fall sick at all while I was in Trim?'

'Yes,' he said. 'She had symptoms when I first wrote to you. More than likely just a cold. One evening, Mrs Perrin found her here unconscious. The vial lay empty on the floor, but the carpet was dry. Laudanum is so bitter, Abigail, she could only have swallowed it all through a great force of will.'

I stared at him, but he wouldn't meet my eye.

'Why did you not tell me?'

'I tried everything that night, salt-water purges, sulphate of zinc, a stomach pump. When I asked Liam to fetch help, he went to the Rotunda and returned with Dr Labatt.'

Father sat on the bed beside me, but he just looked down at his hands.

'Nothing could be done at that stage. The doctor knew what had happened. He said that if anyone asked, he would swear that she had succumbed to fever, and I never once doubted him. I thought that he was an honourable man. At least back then.'

His shoulders were slumped, and his head bowed a little. He began rubbing his fingers together, as if feeling the cold in the room, then he turned to look at me.

'I should have told you at the time, but I thought that it would be less painful.'

I was upset with him, though I knew the secret would have caused him nothing but heartache. Most of all I felt sorrow for my mother, for what she had gone through. The words we had used to describe her illness — her fixations, and phobias, and manias — they were so inadequate. How frightened she must have been, how deeply unhappy. When I sat with her each morning, speaking lightly of the day ahead, did she smile despite the darkness that surrounded her; or did it really ebb for those few moments? And if so, could I have stayed longer, lain beside her, told her that I would not leave until she felt safe and happy and well? I had convinced myself that she was content to be alone. When she would quail at the front door, reject my father's attempts to bring her outside, and sometimes lash out at him, I was frustrated with her. She wasn't trying hard enough. She didn't want to be well. When attending salons with Clarissa, I became tired of answering questions about her health. There were only so many times I could say that she was indisposed, or visiting relatives, and I was relieved when people stopped asking. It all seemed so selfish now, so petty.

I moved closer to Father, and leaned against his arm.

'I didn't want you to worry,' he said. 'About her reputation, or what people would say. I didn't want you to fear what may have happened to her soul.'

'I do not believe God would have her suffer any more.' The shadow of the treetops continued to play against the bedcovers, fading with a passing cloud. 'I refuse to believe that.'

We stayed still for some time. The sun took the chill from the room, bathing the dust sheets in white light, and revealing a slow drift of motes against the window frame. Eventually, Father said that he would have to return to court. His petition had not yet been heard.

'Do you think it will be granted?'

'I am certain of it. The inquest will resume tomorrow.'

I remained lying on my mother's bed for some time, then roused myself and went back down to the garden. The light snow had melted at this stage, except for some patches on the north-facing steps. I walked among the shrubbery, picked a nosegay of pale yellow primroses, and then made my way towards St George's. A small graveyard was situated behind the church, bounded by brick walls that ran at odd angles because of the surrounding houses. The gate in the black iron railing was unlocked, and I wandered along the short paths to the corner where Mother was buried.

When I leaned down to place the flowers by the headstone, I saw a round stump of wood barely peeking above the level of the earth. A thick stake, like those used to mark plot outlines, had been driven into my mother's grave, the fibres of wood at the top flattened from the hammer blows. I began scooping the dirt from around its edge, but I couldn't get a grip in the cold, wet mud. I knelt down and began digging further, dragging earth over the hem of my dress, and scratching my finger on a rock. About six inches of the pole was now exposed, but it wouldn't budge, no matter how I grasped it. The earth sucked at the wood, and I feared it had been driven deep enough to achieve its purpose. I would have to fetch help, but I couldn't bear leaving if Mother's coffin was broken, and her body pierced. With a final heave there was move-ment, a tiny release more felt than seen. It was enough for me to keep working, and bit by bit the pole inched upwards. My coat was ruined, but I continued regardless. I could feel it give way, and the rest came free in one go. It was only three or four feet long, too short to have caused any damage, but I knew what it symbolized: the pierced hearts of suicides buried at crossroads. I had left an untidy mess on the bed of the grave, and I knelt down beside the headstone, exhausted. On the path beside me the primroses lay strewn. One rolled over in the breeze.

Several people glanced at me as I made my way home, my hands and clothes covered in mud. When I turned the corner for home, I could see them, a group of Brethren, four men and a woman, standing at the bottom of our steps, handing out newspapers to the passers-by. The woman saw my approach. She looked me up and down, and a smile came to her lips.

I stood before them, and said, 'Get away from my home,' forcing myself to be quiet.

The men ignored me, and continued to hand out papers.

'We do not want you here,' I said. 'Leave us be.'

The woman still looked at me. Her serene smile never wavered.

'Why do you smirk like that?'

She leaned closer, as if to tell me a secret, and held my eye. 'Because I know that your mother abides in agony.'

I reached for the newspapers draped over her arm and ripped them away so that they fell and scattered in the gutter. The woman took a step back, but she did not appear to be alarmed. Her smile became an ugly leer, and she yelled out, 'We are being assaulted.' People in the street turned to view the commotion. I heard the front door open, and Mrs Perrin called out, 'Abigail!' She hurried down the steps, and put her arm about me to take me back to the house.

One of the men said, 'The girl is wild. She cannot control herself,' but Mrs Perrin hissed at him to be gone. She led me up the steps, and I leaned my head against her shoulder as she closed the door behind us.

12

It was getting too late to read. The house had fallen dark and silent, and the air in my chamber was so still that the candle-flame hardly wavered. Everyone else was asleep, and the only noise came from outside: the clip-clop of a passing horseman on some midnight errand, and the tuneless singing of a drunk. I recognized his song: 'Bonny Farday', about a man who killed two women because they spurned him, before he realized they were his lost sisters. The drunk sang, 'He asked one sister would she wife, He robbed her of her own sweet life.'

The singing faltered when the high-pitched laugh of a woman rang out. I opened one shutter by a crack to look down. Lamps on the gates of Rutland Gardens cast a dim light, but otherwise the roadway was dark. I thought of girls my age and younger abroad in the night, huddled on cold corners, subject to the whims of coarse and dangerous men. But perhaps they'd look upon my concern with scorn, while I peeked from behind lace curtains.

The fire had dwindled some hours before, and the room was cold again. I held my hands cupped over the small candle-flame. The lines between my fingers glowed red, and I wondered at how the light was able to burrow through my skin. I took the candle into the hallway and towards the landing on the stairs, where a window looked down over the back yard. No lights shone from my father's workrooms.

In the kitchen, I lifted the lantern off its hook above the sink, and removed a loose brick at the side of the chimney stack where Father kept his keys hidden. Before I picked them up, I noted how they lay, so I could put them back as I found them. I crept through the basement, past Mrs Perrin's quarters and the small room adjacent to the pantry where Jimmy slept.

The garden was long and narrow, with high walls on both sides, and a straight path that skirted past shrubbery and vegetable patches towards the mews. I held the lantern aloft by its wire handle, though the light only fell a short distance, which made the darkness beyond seem all the deeper. The breeze picked up, causing the leaves to whisper overhead, but once I reached the coach house everything had fallen silent.

Inside, the ground was bare except for the usual clutter by the wall: buckets, forks and sweeping brushes, and the hulking form of the carriage unhitched at the back. I could hear the horses shuffle in their stalls as I went towards the stairs. The new lock to the workrooms was heavy and stiff, and only turned after much effort, and with a loud clunk.

Strange shadows fell on Ewan's desk from the pen-holder, paper-stamp and stacked files. I ensured the window shutters were closed tight, so no glimmer of light could betray me, then I unlocked the dissection room. The doorknob squeaked as I turned it, but the hinges were oiled, and the door swung inwards with a gentle nudge.

Even from the doorway, I could make out Edith on the examination table, the white sheet pulled up to her shoulders, and her long tresses hanging towards the floor. The room was stark, with dark floorboards and whitewashed walls, and a hearth with no mantelpiece. Cabinets and benches lined the walls, and wooden shelves held large glass jars, all clean and empty. A white porcelain sink sat in the corner, the space beneath filled with metal pails, folded white sheets and towels. All was spotless, despite the work that Father and Ewan had done in the last few days.

The lantern-light fell on Edith's face with a yellow hue. Her head rested on the raised lip that went around the table, causing her chin to dip slightly. Her shoulders were white and bare, which made the black threads of the slanting suture scars running beneath her collarbones all the more vivid. They met at her sternum, and another line going beneath the sheet would have formed a Y over her abdomen.

She had been pulled apart and put together again, and despite the smell of potash-soap clinging to the surfaces, there was still a tang in the air, like the inside of a victualler's shop.

I placed the lantern on a small side table and stared at Edith's face. She didn't look like herself, and not just because of her pallor. A sagging and waning of the skin had begun, straightening her lips and eyelids, and making her cheeks gaunt and sunken. When was the last time I'd seen her? It was in Charlemont House beside one of the fireplaces. Mr Darby had asked her to dance, and her face, already flushed from the warmth of the room, became pinker still. Heads had turned to watch him lead her to the centre of the ballroom.

I lifted the sheet at the side enough to bring Edith's hand out. Her flesh was as cold as the table. I let go and rubbed my palm against my dress. How did Father and Ewan bear it? Did one ever become accustomed to handling the dead? Her fingers were pliable, and I opened them to look closer. Father once told me that external examinations had to be carried out in daylight, since some wounds would not show up in artificial light, but I had to make do. There was no sign of washerwoman's hand — the wrinkled, sodden appearance in flesh that came from submersion in water. She may have been in the water for less than a few hours before they found her; or perhaps that appearance only lasted in drowning victims for a certain amount of time. I'd have to look it up, or ask Ewan.

I thought back to how she lay in the reservoir, to ensure this was the hand that had clasped the hook. It was no longer there of course, but I remembered testing the strength of the hook on Robert Gould's coat. Even my half-hearted effort had hurt my hand and left a small indentation in my palm. Edith would have been frantic, grasping at anything that came within reach, struggling in the dark. I drew the lamp closer and held her palm towards it like a fortune-teller. But for the normal lines and bumps of her hand, there were no other marks, no signs of injury. Maybe she managed to grasp it flat. Or perhaps the hook was loose and came off easily.

A noise came from the office outside, a knock on a desk like someone putting down a cup. I let go of Edith's hand, which fell flat on to the table. There was another sound: a swish of paper, perhaps the opening of a folder. No light came from the door. Whoever was out there must have seen the glow from my lantern; perhaps they assumed it had been left behind by accident.

My light showed the space between the worktables and the surface of Ewan's desk, but the corners of the room were cast in shadow. I listened for any movement downstairs. The horses hadn't been disturbed.

On Ewan's desk, an inkpot lay on its side. I held the lantern higher; it swayed on its handle and cast shifting shadows on to the wall. Though the ink bottle was well fastened, I righted it in case it started to leak. I glanced back into the dissection room, and towards Edith on her table, one arm uncovered and exposed.

I said, 'Is anyone there?'

There was the slightest pattering of footsteps on the floorboards, and then Kepler leaped on to the desk. I had to grip the lamp so as not to drop it. If it had fallen and smashed and left me in the dark, I'm not sure what I'd have done, but after a moment I caught my breath and calmed myself.

Kepler stood amid Ewan's things. He regarded me for a moment, then mewed.

'You did that on purpose,' I said, and scooped him up to put him out.

I returned to Edith, replaced her hand beneath the sheet and smoothed the linen down. Whatever else my father and Ewan had learned would be presented at the inquest, and I would hear of it there. A cabinet beside the sink contained several items: the dress Edith had worn was hanging up, still stained with mud from the reservoir bed. The hook that was in her hand was sitting alone on a shelf, its small flap of fabric torn and ragged. There was a letter on the shelf below, folded and unsealed — no mark suggested it ever had been sealed. It was addressed to Mr Darby in forty-four Rutland Square:

My dear Sir,

I know that you asked me to think long about your offer before giving my answer, but from the first moment of its reception, I determined on which course to pursue.

You are aware that I have many reasons to feel grateful to you for the solace and counsel you have brought to my family. Do not therefore doubt my motives when I say that my answer to your proposal must be no. I feel convinced that mine is not the sort of disposition calculated to form the happiness of a man like you.

Believe me,
I am yours truly,
E Gould.

I read the letter twice, and then looked at Edith. Had her cheeks flushed at Charlemont House that night from discomfort rather than pleasure? Perhaps she had been loath to encourage the attentions of an unwanted suitor, and in so public a setting. In fact, the last time I'd seen Edith had not been with Mr Darby. She was with James Caulfeild, in hushed conversation in a deserted hallway, a conversation that Mr Darby had observed.

The letter was undated and unsent, unless hand-delivered by Edith herself or someone in whom she had the utmost confidence. Had Mr Darby even seen it? And if he had, how had it come to be in Father's possession? It could not have been on Edith's person when she drowned, for the paper was firm and intact, and the ink hadn't bled.

I returned the letter to the cabinet, then looked around the room to ensure that I'd left no item in the wrong position. I was ready to leave, but before doing so I paused at the table, placed my hand on Edith's over the sheet and stayed beside her for a moment. Then I locked the dissecting-room door and slipped back to the house.

★ ★ ★

I slept little for the rest of the night, and watched the grey dawn creep along a gap in the drapes. By the time morning came, the house was already busy. In the hallway, I saw Kathy bring coffee to my father's study. He was hunched over some documents, still making annotations, his spectacles perched on his head. In the back yard, Liam was preparing the cart to transport Edith to St Thomas's Hall, where the inquest would take place. The kitchen was its usual bustle of morning chores. Only the dining room was quiet. Ewan was alone at the table, a cup of tea and buttered roll before him. He stood and bid me good morning, then swept some crumbs from the tablecloth with his little finger and put them on his plate.

'Father will be late for breakfast,' I said, taking the seat opposite. It was my usual place, though it seemed oddly formal with just the two of us. 'You must have a busy day ahead.'

'Your father does, certainly. I assist only with the medical examinations, so have no part to play this morning.'

'But you'll attend the inquest?'

'Yes, I think so.'

'Then we can take the carriage together.'

Ewan placed a silver strainer in his cup and began to pour. 'Are you sure you wish to go? These proceedings are often lengthy and uneventful.'

I told him that I couldn't miss it. Besides, I'd been to several before, and knew what they involved. I was thirteen when I first accompanied Father to an inquest. He had been reluctant to allow it, but it had been a principle of his, as far as practicable, not to deny a request from his daughter that he would have granted to a son. Initially, he only brought me to cases where the details weren't overly distressing: a man killed by a carriage when the horses were spooked, or an old lady who had mistaken crystals of oxalic acid for Epsom salts. The first case that I heard declared 'wilful murder' was a strange one. A labourer had tossed a misshapen brick from the roof of a house on to the street below without calling a warning. The brick hit a young girl on the temple and she died in hospital a few days later. Though the man hadn't chosen his victim, the jury said his negligence had shown 'a malice against all mankind', as if he had coolly discharged a gun into a multitude. It was the first time I'd heard that expression, but it had stuck with me: that such a sentiment could exist in the world.

Ewan placed a lump of sugar in his tea, but he didn't stir it. Perhaps he liked the last mouthful to be the sweetest.

He said, 'Did you discover anything of interest in the dissection room?'

I felt a colour rise in my cheeks. 'What do you mean?'

'Someone was there during the night. When I laid out Miss Gould's body, I put her hand like this.' He placed his palm flat on the table, then after a moment turned it over so it faced upwards. 'Not like this.'

When disturbed by Kepler, I'd pushed Edith's arm under the sheet not minding how it lay. It seemed leaving a room without trace was more difficult than I supposed. I was annoyed with myself, but in a way the thought was encouraging.

'How did Father come across the letter that Edith wrote?'

Ewan didn't answer at once. He might have

262

scolded me that once again my actions were inappropriate, but there were only so many times you could say that to a person. If anything, he seemed relieved that I had not tried to deny it.

'Robert Gould came here a few days ago and gave it to him,' he said. 'He found it in her bedroom.'

'After she died?'

'Presumably, unless he made a habit of going through her belongings.'

'It's strange. He didn't mention it to me when I saw him.'

Ewan was chewing a mouthful of bread, and I pointed to a corner of my lip. 'You have butter here.'

He began to dab at his mouth with a napkin.

'The other side.'

Kathy came into the dining room with a plate of kippers and poached eggs. She placed it by Father's empty seat, and said that he was on his way.

When she left, I said, 'Robert knew that the letter would place suspicion on Mr Darby.'

'I should say so.'

'And he didn't trust to hand it to anyone else. Not even his father.'

'Perhaps Judge Gould told him to deliver it.'

I was about to say that Judge Gould had not been inclined to assist the inquest at all, but then Father came into the room. He seemed weary, the skin around his eyes was crinkled and his shoulders were stooped, but he adopted a light air and spoke of small things. He deftly removed the skin of his fried kipper with the point of his knife, and sliced through a flake of flesh. We spoke no more of Edith or Robert Gould or Mr Darby.

★ ★ ★

The exterior of St Thomas's Hall was like a church without a steeple, nooks of grey brick and weathered, sculpted figures. Inside the wooden hall, rows of seats had been set out. A square table sat in the middle of a raised dais with chairs for my father and a local justice of the peace. A longer table, borrowed from a local inn, had room enough for thirteen men. Only twelve were required for a jury; Father always picked one extra in case of a split decision.

When Ewan and I entered, the hall was nearly full. The people attending were well dressed and respectable for the most part, with several faces that I was more accustomed to seeing at church. There was an expectant chatter among the crowd, like the moments before a play began. The only concessions to the sober occasion were the muted colours of dress. Ewan and I found two empty seats next to the aisle.

There was no sign of Mr Darby or any of the Brethren, or members of Edith's family, though that wasn't unusual for an inquest, especially when distressing details might be aired. Edith was in a separate room where the jury could inspect her. Father would have to point out any features on her body visible from external examination, and I imagined the thirteen men gazing down on her, shuffling and crowding

264

about the table, their faces white in the meagre light.

I felt Ewan's shoulder press against mine. 'Isn't that Mr Gould over there?'

I looked to where he nodded. Robert sat hunched in a seat, his greatcoat buttoned up and the brim of his hat pulled down. His eyes were pressed closed as if in restless sleep, but then he opened them, his gaze fixed on the dais.

'Yes, it is. He must not have been willing to hear the evidence second-hand.'

The jurors emerged from a door at the top of the hall and took their seats at the long table. They were men from the locality, shopkeepers and apothecaries, chandlers and silversmiths, and except for the amount of grey in their hair, they could have been interchangeable. There were sheets of paper and pencils laid for each of them. I saw one man frown at the snapped nib of his own pencil. He swapped it with his neighbour's while the other was looking away. A constable administered their oath and told them to choose a foreman. After a brief huddle, a man with mutton-chop whiskers and a bald pate was put forward, who identified himself as Mr Heeney.

A hush fell over the crowd as my father and the justice entered and took their seats. The clock above the dais ticked towards the hour, and I knew that Father wouldn't begin until the appointed time.

The doors at the back of the auditorium opened and a draught stirred through the hall. Mr Darby walked in, flanked by several members

265

of the Brethren all dressed in their dark coats. There were a few seats left, but Darby and his followers gathered together in the shadows beneath a raised gallery, and seemed content to observe proceedings from there.

Many turned to look at them, including Robert Gould, who squinted slightly as if his vision was blurred. The chatter in the hall increased, and I thought Father would have to appeal for quiet, but I was proud of his composure. He addressed the jury members in a voice barely audible beyond the dais, which made the crowd go silent as they strained to pick up his words.

'Gentlemen,' he said, 'you are charged with inquiring when, how, and by what means Miss Edith Gould came by her death, if any person or persons were culpable, including the deceased, and, if her death took place away from her hearth and home, to follow the steps that brought her body to Blessington Street. If all oaths have been taken and everything is in order, I call upon Constable Matthews.'

The young policeman that I'd seen at the reservoir made his way to the dais, and repeated the oath administered by the JP. He placed his cap before him, but perhaps thought it looked conspicuous on the empty table, and put it by his feet instead. He addressed his answers to the jury, saying that on the morning in question, he had finished his night-watch in and around Sackville Street when he heard reports of a body in the basin. Shortly after he arrived, Miss Gould was retrieved, still dressed in a dark frock and leather half-boots.

My father interrupted him to say that those items could be shown to the jury. A helper brought the dress and shoes from the back room and placed them on the jury table, the black gown and its mud-encrusted fabric laid out fully, the shoes with their laces untied and tongues drooping. There was a leather rosette on the toe-cap of one, but it was missing from the other. I thought of Edith kicking them off beside her bed every evening, how she would have stepped over them, disregarded them, and here in front of a packed hall they had almost come to represent her. A jury member picked one up and inspected it close to his face, as if he were choosing a pair for his wife.

Father continued to question the constable. 'At the time, did you form any impression of what may have happened to her?'

'Well, there were no obvious signs of injury, so I thought the poor girl may have slipped into the water by accident. I was surprised though by the quality of her dress, and when she was identified as being so far from home I knew something was amiss.'

'Who identified her?'

'A young lady at the reservoir. I didn't get her name.'

I saw Father was about to enquire further, but then his head stilled and he turned a sheet in his folder. Ewan glanced at me. 'Perhaps you should be up on the dais.'

The woman next to us shushed him, and began removing bonbons from a paper bag with a persistent rustling.

Father said, 'Were any other items of Miss Gould's clothing present?'

'No, her head was uncovered and she had no cloak. If she did go to the basin alone, it would have been a long journey on foot with no coat on such a dirty night.'

There were no other questions, and the constable was excused. His boots echoed on the wooden floorboards as he descended the three steps of the dais.

Father next called Lisa Croft, and the maid with the Liverpool accent from the Gould household went to take her seat at the table. As she passed the jury, one of the sleeves of Edith's dress slipped over the table's edge and hung towards the floor. Miss Croft lifted it back and smoothed it down. I saw Robert Gould sit forward in his seat, one elbow resting on his knee.

The maid's voice was quiet and wavering as she swore her oath and answered Father's first questions. She took a sip of water, gripping the tumbler with both hands as if she might betray a trembling. But the glances she gave to the jury and the crowd were pointed and darting.

'You acted as a lady's maid for Miss Gould?'

'Yes, sir.'

'How long did you have that job?'

'Nearly four years, sir.'

'You must forgive me for prying, Miss Croft, but on the night she disappeared, did Miss Gould prepare for bed as normal?'

'As far as I know.'

'You mean you were not present?'

'Not that evening, sir, but that wasn't unusual for Miss Edith. As long as her things were laid out, she would often dress herself. If she didn't ring, then I knew I wasn't needed till morning.'

'So when was the last time you saw her?'

The maid looked to the side as if thinking, but she must have expected the question, and had her answer prepared. 'I saw her briefly outside her chamber just before she retired. But before that it would have been after supper. Miss Edith was drawing in her sketchbook in the front parlour, and asked me to bring hot water to her room at about nine o'clock. The usual time.'

'Did she seem agitated at all, or anxious?'

'No, sir. She was perfectly calm.'

'You fetched water and laid out her nightdress. How long did that take?'

'Fifteen minutes perhaps. I'm not sure.'

'And you say you passed her in the hallway just before she went to bed?'

'That's right, sir.'

'You bid her good night?'

'Well, yes.'

'Did you do so first, or did she?'

'I think I did.'

'Was that not presumptuous? Without knowing if Miss Gould required anything else?'

'Believe me, sir, if she needed anything she would have asked.'

Father wrote something out on a sheet, as if taking down her last answer verbatim, and the maid frowned.

Without looking up, Father gestured towards the jury table with his pen. 'Was that the dress she was wearing when you saw her last?'

'Yes, sir.'

'You're quite sure?'

'I had helped her to don it before supper.'

'And the shoes?'

'No, she was wearing her silk slippers, as she always did indoors.'

'So she entered her chamber at a quarter past nine, didn't change into the nightgown you laid out, but rather put on these shoes in which she was later found.' He paused for a moment, as if granting the maid a chance to correct or contradict him. 'Did you notice the rosette missing from the shoe before?'

'No, sir. They were as good as new.'

'What did you do then?'

'I went to my own room, directly above.'

'What time did you go to sleep?'

'Not long after.'

'Around nine?'

'No, sir, ten.'

'Yes, that's what I meant, ten. And Miss Gould never rang for you? You didn't hear anything strange in the room below? Even Edith moving about later than usual?'

'All was quiet throughout the house.'

Father removed his spectacles and closed over the temples. 'Let's go back earlier in the day, before supper. What had Miss Gould been doing?'

The maid glanced towards the galleries. 'She'd had a visit from a gentleman.'

'And who was that?'

'Mr Darby.'

A murmur spread throughout the hall, though

Darby's courtship of Edith was common knowledge.

'Mr Darby had been a frequent visitor in recent weeks?'

'It depends on what you consider frequent.' An edge had entered her voice, but my father wasn't perturbed.

'I'm willing to trust your judgement on that.'

Miss Croft paused and said, 'Yes, his visits were frequent.'

'They took a walk together around Fitzwilliam Square that afternoon?'

'That's right.'

'What did they talk about?'

'I wasn't there.'

'But your mistress must have spoken about it when she saw you later. When you helped her dress for supper.'

'Indeed she did not.'

'She wasn't in the habit of confiding things to you, despite the many years that you were her closest servant?'

The maid's face darkened.

'Did she seem pleased at the encounter, or angered, or indifferent?'

'Sir, she didn't discuss it at all.'

Father waited to see if she would add anything more, then rifled through some papers. He picked out a sheet and held it up for the jury. 'Gentlemen, I have here an affidavit from Mr William Hawkins, a cabman who plies his trade around Fitzwilliam Square. Allow me to read it.' He held his spectacles against the bridge of his nose without opening them. '*I was working on* the square that night, parked on the corner of Fitzwilliam Street, waiting for a dinner party to break up. It had gone midnight, and I was sitting in the cab to shelter from the rain. I could see another carriage, not a cabbie, parked outside the eastern gate of Fitzwilliam Square. It waited there for several minutes in the dark, the driver sitting out despite the weather. A door to one of the houses opened, which one I can't say for sure, but all the lights in the windows were out. Two women came down the steps, both wearing cloaks with the hoods pulled up. They hurried towards the carriage, and one spoke with the driver. He hardly seemed to acknowledge her at all, but the girl turned and opened the carriage door. I assumed both would get in, but instead they stopped and spoke on the street for several seconds, holding each other's hands. One girl lowered her hood. They embraced, and then the first woman entered the carriage and shut the door. It set off immediately. The other stayed in the street to watch until it turned a corner. She replaced her hood and returned to the house.'

Miss Croft stared at Father while he spoke, but as the narrative went on, her gaze lowered.

Father handed the sheet to a helper, so it could be passed among the jury members. He looked at the maid without speaking until she raised her eyes again.

'Is it necessary for us to summon Mr Hawkins so he can identify you in person?'

She shook her head.

'Very well. Who was Edith planning to meet that night?'

'I don't know.'

'Miss Croft, you may feel compelled to keep the confidences that you shared with your mistress, especially in so public a setting. But that will not do. These gentlemen must determine the truth of what happened to Miss Gould, and anyone who obstructs those efforts, anyone who is deliberately unforthcoming, or misleading, is open to criminal charges.'

'I swear she didn't tell me,' she said. 'I asked of course, again and again, but she wouldn't say.'

'Was she going to meet a gentleman? She knew there was a carriage waiting for her.'

Again, the maid hesitated.

'Did you recognize the driver at least?'

Still there was no response.

'Please answer.'

'I don't know. I can say no more than that. You may lay any charge against me you like.'

Father repeated his questions, but the maid remained silent. He told her that this wasn't the last she would hear of the matter, in a tone of voice I'd often heard, such as when I dropped a crystal glass on the kitchen floor one Christmas, or when he caught me reading an anatomical tome in his library several years ago. Miss Croft was dismissed.

When Mr Darby was called to the table, he walked up the central aisle instead of skirting around the side. His eyes swept over the jury, taking note of each member, and when the Bible was handed to him to swear his oath, he opened the cover as if checking the edition. He was undaunted by the rows of eyes gazing back at him, and he spoke in a clear, calm voice.

My father said, 'You heard the testimony of Miss Croft. Is there any part of it you would like to dispute?'

'Dispute?'

'You don't deny that you saw Miss Gould the day before she died, and that you were a frequent visitor to her house in the weeks before that?'

'Why would I deny such a thing?'

'Why did you call upon the Goulds so often?'

'They are members of my congregation. I had been offering them counsel in recent months, an issue involving their son.' Robert glanced up at this mention.

Father said, 'What was the issue?'

The corners of Darby's mouth turned upwards, for Father had held the inquest into the deaths of Miss Casey and her baby in these chambers only weeks before. Darby said, 'It was a private matter for the Gould family. Though when I called on them, I would often escort Miss Gould around the central garden.'

'Alone?'

'With the consent of her parents.'

'Naturally. You were courting the young lady?'

Darby regarded my father without blinking. 'I was.'

'Had you proposed marriage?'

'I had spoken to her of the possibility, and I had broached the subject with her father. Judge Gould was amenable.'

'Perhaps more amenable than she?'

Darby was stung into saying, 'Quite the contrary.'

'You believe that she was willing to marry you?'

'Yes.'

'So when she left her home that night, she was going to see you.'

'No.'

Father took down that short answer, then studied it on his page as if the ink had blotted.

'What happened to your first wife?'

For the first time, Darby was perplexed by a question. He stayed still for a moment, then shifted in his seat and crossed his legs.

'She was taken from me.'

Father said nothing, and waited for Darby to elaborate.

'My wife was with child. It was winter, and a fog covered the hills around St John's. I sent for help, for the doctor, the midwife. No one arrived in time.'

'What was the decision of the coroner?'

'There was no inquest.'

'Oh?'

'It was God's will.'

There was silence in the hall, enough for the fluttering of pigeon wings to be heard in the loft overhead.

'Did you ever speak to Miss Gould about your first wife?'

'Yes, quite often. We once visited my former parish.'

'What did you talk about in Fitzwilliam Square that day?'

'I forget. Nothing of consequence.'

'Nothing of your proposal?'

'I would have considered that consequential.'

'When did she tell you that she did not wish to marry you?'

Darby wanted to hold Father's eye, but he had already looked down to leaf through a sheaf of documents. With no answer forthcoming, Father handed him Edith's letter of rejection through a helper.

At first, Darby wouldn't take it, so the usher put it on the table before him. Darby looked down, placed one hand on the page then smoothed a dog-eared corner with his index finger. He picked up the letter. It wasn't long, but his eyes remained on the text for some time. His brow slanted and creased for just a moment, but then he became impassive once more. He turned it over to look at the blank reverse, then folded it, running the crease between his thumb and index finger.

Father asked for the letter to be handed to the jury members. The foreman, Mr Heeney, was the first to read it. After a moment, his neighbour impatiently reached over to take it, but Heeney turned his shoulder and flashed the man a dark look. Eventually, each juror had seen Edith's polite but firm refusal.

Father said, 'Where were you on the night Miss Gould died?'

'I never saw that letter.'

'Did you hear me?'

'She never gave any indication . . .'

'Mr Darby, would you like to have legal counsel before we continue? We can postpone this hearing until that is arranged,' Father said.

'That won't be required.'

'Then where were you?'

'I visited a member of the Brethren on Glasnevin Hill. I was there for much of the evening before returning to Rutland Square on horseback. It was late. The weather was so bad that night, the roads were treacherous.'

'Did you speak to anyone when you arrived?'

'My sister-in-law, Mrs Nesham.'

'No one else?'

'I asked a maid to ensure my clothes were dried.'

'They were soaked through?'

'Well, yes.'

Father pointed at the coat Mr Darby was wearing, with the black fabric and metal hooks. 'You were wearing the coat you have on at present?'

He shook his head. 'We only wear these coats when we gather.'

'Such as here today.' Father glanced at the Brethren who had advanced up the hall in order to better hear the proceedings. He rummaged in his pocket and lifted out the hook that was found with Edith, holding it up for the jury to see, the loose threads trailing.

'Miss Gould was clutching this in her right hand when she was found in the reservoir, most likely snatched from the coat of her attacker.'

Darby peered at the hook. 'I don't understand.'

'Mr Darby, may the jury examine your coat to ensure that no clasps are missing or re-attached.'

Darby looked down at his own coat, as if

277

someone had pointed out a stain. He began to undo the hooks, starting at the bottom and working his way up. There were six in all. He stood up, removed his coat and handed it to the usher, then remained standing in his white shirtsleeves and black waistcoat, defrocked and uncertain.

The jury members examined it, tugging at each of the hooks in turn. Mr Heeney said, 'They appear to be present and accounted for.'

Father told them that there was a gentleman who might be able to assist, and he called upon Mr Whistler. The tailor was sitting in the middle of a row, and there was much shifting of chairs and shuffling of feet to allow him out. Whistler smoothed his long silver hair over his brow, and marched directly to the table. He picked up the coat by the shoulders and held it at arm's length. After only a second, he curled his finger through one of the hooks and allowed the rest of the coat to fall, tails and arms sagging towards the floor.

'I didn't sew this,' he said.

Father said, 'How do you know?'

'I'm sure you can tell your own stitches as well, Mr Coroner.'

Father asked if Whistler might elaborate for the jury.

'I've cut dozens of coats for the Brethren, and the hooks are attached by tabs of fabric with twelve stitches each, no more, no less.' He examined the hook on Mr Darby's coat again. 'Though this is a relatively neat job, it has only ten. It was done recently as well, no fraying in the thread.' He laid the coat on the table once more, and invited Mr Heeney to look. Whistler walked past Darby without glancing at him, and took the torn hook from Father's side of the table. 'This one was mine,' he said, frowning at the loose threads for a moment. 'She must have been in quite a state to pull it off in one go.'

Darby had been looking at these proceedings with growing confusion. My father said to him, 'Mr Darby, despite your earlier protestations, I must recommend that you hire legal counsel before we continue. I should warn you that the constables present intend to escort you to the nearest magistrate's office, where you'll be charged with the murder of Edith Gould.'

Several members of the Brethren cried out, 'No,' as the policemen in the front row stood up. The crowd began to talk as well, but instead of calling for quiet, Father spoke over them. 'This inquest is adjourned until tomorrow morning. All jury members and witnesses are still under summons.'

The constables advanced on Darby. He still stood in his shirtsleeves, and they took hold of his forearms and shoulders.

Many people in the front had stood up to see the arrest, and the Brethren had moved further forward, almost to the edge of the dais. Robert Gould pushed his way to the central aisle, and began walking towards the front. He seemed focused and unhurried. The top buttons of his coat were open. He reached under his lapel and drew out a pistol.

Darby was the first to notice his approach, but with his arms pinioned he couldn't point or move. When he began to shout, the police just held him tighter. Robert held the gun straight in front of him for the last few steps. It fired with a flash and a loud bang.

Perhaps all the commotion had been enough to put Robert off, for the bullet only nicked the ear of Mr Darby before smashing through one of the stained-glass windows behind him. The constables released their hold. They jumped on Robert and tried to wrest the gun from his hands. Darby clutched the side of his head and fell backwards. Several women screamed out, and some of the jurymen crouched beneath the table. The Brethren swarmed on to the dais, overturning the witness chairs. I feared that they would attack my father, but their only concern was for Mr Darby. They surrounded him, gathered him to his feet and moved towards the front door in a huddle, his white shirt visible in flashes among their black coats. The constables had Robert subdued, though one was still struggling to prise his whitened fingers from the pistol. The dais was in disarray. Father's notes were scattered about and Edith's dress had been trampled on the ground. The Brethren reached the entrance and pushed the doors open. Sunlight and a cold draught entered the hall as they spirited Darby into one of their carriages, and he was away in a clatter of hooves.

13

We were gathered in the parlour in the hour before supper. Father sat by the fire reading his newspaper. Kepler lay on the windowsill, watching the evening rain with a mild air of displeasure. At a table in the corner, Ewan was teaching Jimmy the rules of vingt-et-un, with moderate success. Jimmy had accompanied his mother to the markets often enough to develop a good head for figures. He was only let down by a reckless optimism when asking for more cards, refusing to let a hand stand at anything less than nineteen. The latest round ended with another of his groans.

The logs in the hearth shifted, and a few sparks escaped up the flue like spirits. Father said, 'Did you see this?' He looked at me over the corner of his newspaper. 'Mr Darby has been spotted again.'

'Where now?'

'Down at the docks, boarding the post packet to Holyhead.' He took a sip from a glass of sherry. 'Probably just another stern-looking gentleman in a dark coat.'

In the days following the inquest, there had been several sightings of Mr Darby. A lady patron of Smock Alley had sworn that he was in one of the boxes during a production of *A New Way to Pay Old Debts*. Some said that he was briefly unmasked at Lady Ogilvie's annual masquerade; others that he was smoking a pipe in the clothes of a vagrant beneath Whitworth Bridge, in full view of the law courts.

Even his followers claimed not to know of his whereabouts. The homes of the most prominent Brethren were searched, including, of course, the Neshams'. From my mother's old room, I'd watched the constables enter the house across the square. Light from police lanterns had shifted about in every window, and I imagined them going from room to room, peeking under tablecloths and shaking all the drapes.

'If Darby escapes overseas,' I said, 'then he may never be found.'

'The police will catch up with him eventually.'

Father had paid little heed to the reports. As far as he was concerned his duties as coroner were fulfilled. He knew of no precedent for an inquest to be ended by gunfire, but it had not altered the verdict. Edith's body was returned to her parents, and she was buried soon after in a cemetery close to Coburg Gardens. Only her closest friends and family attended — though not her brother, whose bail hearing hadn't come in time. He had since been released under the recognizance of his father.

'Are you not anxious that Mr Darby will evade justice?'

'Of course I hope he stands trial. But I cannot take a personal interest in every death and every inquest. My work would never be done.'

'Would you not do so for Edith and her family?'

'I have great sympathy for Edith, and for the

plight of her parents.'

'And what of Robert?'

Father looked at me a moment longer. 'For Mr Gould as well. Though if he had not taken matters into his own hands, Mr Darby would now be in custody.' He opened his newspaper again and resumed reading.

In the corner, Jimmy lost another round of twenty-one and threw in his hand. I put down my book and went to observe. Perhaps Jimmy kept asking for more cards because there was nothing at stake. 'Something will have to be wagered,' I said.

Ewan began to shuffle. 'How about this? If I win the next hand, Jimmy must polish my riding boots before next Sunday, and if he wins, I'll buy him a cream cake from Mrs Benson's.'

'If Jimmy has to clean two boots then you should have to buy two cakes.'

Ewan narrowed his eyes and smiled. 'Very well.'

He dealt the cards. Jimmy received a nine and a three. Ewan kept one of his cards hidden; the other was the ace of clubs. He said, 'I must say, I'm pleased with that.'

Jimmy had no choice but to ask for another, and received a five.

'Now,' Ewan said, 'seventeen is a fine score. I'd advise you to stand.'

Jimmy regarded the cards with his head in his hands, hair spiking through fingers like tufts of grass. He looked up at me. 'What do you think, Abby?'

'I think Mr Weir may be right.'

'Of course I'm right. It's far too risky.'

He placed the deck on the table. There was a slight crease in the corner of the topmost card, barely visible in the paisley pattern. Not long ago, Kepler had nudged the cards over the edge of the cabinet. They had tumbled on to the floorboards, and one of them became dog-eared — but only one.

'Wait, Jimmy,' I said, placing my hand on his shoulder before he made his decision. 'Mr Weir is in a very strong position with his ace. In order to win, you may have to take a chance. Sometimes fortune favours the brave.'

He puffed his cheeks and nodded, then asked for another.

'On your head be it,' said Ewan, and he turned over the four of diamonds.

Jimmy let out a whoop, which made Father frown over the top of his paper. Ewan could still have drawn level, but his hidden card was an eight, and chasing twenty-one he ruined his hand with the queen of spades. He accepted defeat with good grace, and the game was broken up when Mrs Perrin came in asking her son to prepare the table for supper. Jimmy let her know that he had just won two cream cakes, and that he intended to give her half of one. Before he left, I stopped him by the door and said, 'Jimmy, I may need your help with a task tomorrow. At around midday.'

'Of course,' he said, more amenable than ever.

When I returned to the table, Ewan asked if I wanted to continue playing. 'Or some other game if you prefer.'

The only other card games I knew were Matrimony and Old Maid, and I wasn't inclined to suggest either. 'Vingt-et-un will be fine,' I said, and I held my hand towards him. 'I'll deal.'

★ ★ ★

The bells of St Stephen's were chiming just as the cabman reached Fitzwilliam Square. Jimmy and I got out at the corner of the enclosed garden. We could see the Goulds' house further along the terrace, where members of the Brethren had gathered outside. There weren't many: four men and three women with their dark cloaks gathered against the breeze. They didn't move or speak, just gazed at number five in silent vigil. The front door was closed, as were most of the shutters in the windows, as if the house had been abandoned.

Jimmy said, 'What are they doing?'

'I don't know, but we weren't going that way in any case. Come along.'

We walked around to the stable lane that ran behind the terrace. The paving stones and flat road surface gave way to muddy tracks, puddles and potholes. The narrow lane was bounded by high walls and mews buildings, and was busy with the servants of the townhouses: housekeepers with wicker baskets and coachmen in their livery. I counted the gates until we reached the home of the Goulds. Somewhere past the stables and the long back garden would be the servants' entrance to the house.

I turned to Jimmy. 'You know who to ask for?'

'I do.'

'And you know what to say?'

He tutted. 'Yes, Abby.'

'Off you go then. I'll be waiting here.'

He pulled his cap further over his brow, went through the gates, and returned a few minutes later with Miss Croft in tow. She paused when she saw me, but still stepped into the lane. I told Jimmy to wait at the corner and he hurried off. It looked as if Miss Croft had been disturbed mid-chore. Her cheeks were daubed with soot, and the sleeves of her dress were pulled up.

She was the first to speak, her eyes dark and sullen. 'Mr Gould is in discussion with his father, miss, and won't see any visitors.'

'I have not come to speak with Mr Gould. Why are there Brethren at the front of the house?'

'They've been here ever since his release. I don't know why. Perhaps you should ask them.'

'Perhaps I will.'

Miss Croft crossed her arms by holding both elbows, and she shivered slightly in the cold. 'I'll soon have to return to work.'

'I was at the inquest,' I said. 'I heard the evidence you gave.'

Her eyes narrowed. Father had told her at the time that there would be consequences for lying under oath. Perhaps she thought I'd come bearing some form of summons or censure.

'There's something I have been wondering about. You knew that Edith left the house willingly that night, you saw her into the carriage. But she could not have been intending to see Mr Darby, for she had already rejected him.'

A strand of hair came loose from the maid's cap, and she turned her face so it would blow behind her ear. She remained silent.

I remembered again Lord Charlemont's ball, spying Edith in a dim hallway on a chessboard marble floor, and the whispered intimacy of her conversation with the son of the house.

I waited for the maid to look at me again. 'She thought she was going to meet James Caulfeild.'

Her impassive face wavered for a second, and she looked over her shoulder towards the Goulds' coach house as if to check that no one could overhear.

I said, 'Was she willing to risk everything just to elope?'

'She was trapped here,' the maid said. 'She knew that her parents would make her marry Mr Darby.'

'But she was deceived that night. She never reached James.'

'Mr Darby must have found out.'

'Who arranged for the carriage?'

'I don't know. She just said that it would be there at midnight.'

'Then she must have received word. A letter or a note.'

'Miss Edith received correspondence all the time. There were always notes in the letter box.'

'Has her room been cleared?'

'No. Mrs Gould has asked for everything to be left as it was. She can't bring herself to go through her things.'

'Then the note might still be there. We could look for it.'

Miss Croft frowned and shook her head. 'No, miss.'

'Mr Darby could not have acted alone. The driver of the carriage was helping him, and could still be hiding him now.'

She looked at the ground, rubbed her forearms for a few seconds, and then looked at me directly. 'If Darby is found, could it be of any help to Robert?'

'Robert?'

'The authorities are angry because he allowed Darby to escape. If that's righted, perhaps Robert may face a more lenient judge.'

She held my eye, as if daring me to ask why that would be of more concern than the injustice to Edith. I said, 'I am certain that would be the case.'

She stayed still a moment longer, then turned and began walking towards the house. I hesitated, but when I followed after she said nothing to stop me. The windows on this side of the house were unshuttered, but as far as I could tell no one was watching. Miss Croft pushed open a door, peeked inside, and then brought me into a dim corridor next to the basement kitchen.

She whispered that I must remain quiet, and we began to ascend the stairs. The house felt deserted. No candles were lit, and doors stood open to cold empty rooms. On the third floor, there was a small hallway with two doors, one on either side. Miss Croft paused once more to

288

listen. She glanced over her shoulder, and then brought me into Edith's chamber.

The room was darkened by closed shutters. It felt as if the fire hadn't been lit for days, and there was a hint of dampness in the air. Edith's bed was made, though the white sheets were slightly furrowed. Perhaps people had been sitting there. A dressing table between the two windows had its oval mirror covered in a green baize sheet. Some families believed that the soul in reflection could be taken away by the spirit of the dead — not a superstition that I would have associated with the Brethren. Maybe Miss Croft had put it there, or the housekeeper. Or perhaps it was simply to protect the glass from dust.

I pulled at the cloth until it slipped from the frame and fell on the table. Miss Croft stood behind me, her face in shadow, one hand resting on a brass finial at the corner of the bed. The table was bare except for a scent bottle and tin of powder, and a hairbrush with loose strands woven in its bristles.

I looked at the maid in the mirror. 'We shall need a candle, or a lamp.'

'Someone might see the light.'

'Then I'll open a shutter.'

'No, miss. The people outside . . . '

'Just a crack.'

I undid the latch and opened one shutter enough to let a sliver of light fall upon the bedclothes. The Brethren were standing in a half-circle on the street below, speaking to one another. Edith's window looked down upon the square's central garden, and a lamp beside the eastern gate. Had she peered down from here on the night she died, to a carriage waiting in the rain, horses with their heads bent? Had the driver been looking up at the window, expecting her?

Miss Croft said that she would have to return to the basement, lest the housekeeper come searching for her. 'I'll fetch you when I can.'

She slipped out of the room and pulled the door closed with a click. There was a bureau in the corner with its lid opened, revealing closed drawers and letters aslant in cubbyholes. I pulled them out and began to go through them, glancing at the bottom of each page for the names of Darby, or Caulfeild, or for letters left unsigned. But for the most part they came from Edith's relatives in the country, the content cheery and trivial, and some of them years old. The drawers held even less. Blank stationery, some visiting cards — all from ladies in the locality — and old invitations to balls, kept no doubt as mementos. They were in chronological order, the final one coming from Lord and Lady Charlemont. But it was just like the one I had received, and nothing else was written upon it.

Rain had begun to patter against the window, and a gust of wind echoed in the fireplace. If Edith had received instructions to leave that night, or a letter from Caulfeild in secret, or from Darby in anger, she may have thrown it straight on the fire. I looked in the hearth, but the grey cinders lay undisturbed, and anything that may have been put there had burned away.

The drawers in the bedstand were empty

except for a copy of Mrs Tighe's *Psyche*, an edition that I'd read myself. I felt beneath the cold pillow, and then finally lifted the edge of the covers to check beneath the bed. A ledger, quite large and leather-bound, lay amid the dust and lint.

It was Edith's sketchbook. I remembered her sitting in the drawing room when I had come to visit, her fingers darkened with charcoal. The drawings were views that she could see from her window: terraces and doorcases, or trees overhanging the railing in the park, or the scaffolding of a house being built. I saw again how accomplished she was, her eye for architectural detail. Back then I had commented that there were no people portrayed. What was it she said? *I never seem to get the perspective right.*

One of the drawings was different. The view wasn't that of Fitzwilliam Square, but a run-down cottage in an overgrown garden. Ivy clung to the gable wall, and the crooked path was littered with loose stone. Dark clouds seemed to push upon the roof like a weight. Edith had written in the corner, 'St John's, Manor Kilbride', and it was dated from the start of the summer.

St John's was Darby's old parish in Wicklow, but Edith must have drawn the house from life. He had mentioned at the inquest that he had brought her there. Had her whole family visited, or had he taken her there alone? In the subsequent pages, the drawings of Fitzwilliam Square resumed, but towards the end the style

291

changed again. Perhaps she had taken my comments to heart, for the most recent sketches were of people, or rather studies of human features. The first was a hand resting on a table, and I assumed she'd drawn her own. Like her other sketches, it was striking for its sense of structure, the bones and sinews and folds of skin were so well rendered and shaded. The next drawing was part of a face, and I recognized her father, Judge Gould. She must have sketched him sleeping, for his cheek was slumped, with a double chin and whiskey nose. Page after page followed of these studies: the bottom of a neck and collarbone in a low-cut dress; a male arm extended and bent at the elbow; an ear partially covered with a lock of hair.

On the last page, Edith had drawn a set of eyes, with the bridge of a nose and a heavy brow, but no other feature of the face. One eye was perfect and round, its gaze strong and concentrated. The lid of the other drooped halfway under folds of crinkled skin. Its iris and pupil looked down and to the left, as of a person ashamed or browbeaten.

I stared at it for several seconds. Raindrops running down the window cast grey trickling shadows on the sheet.

I remembered the man with the lazy eye in Rutland Gardens, when he emerged from the Neshams' house following a Brethren meeting. If he was a member, it was natural that Edith would have seen him. But the other drawings were of people she'd known personally, people with whom she'd interacted.

The doorknob squeaked and turned, and Robert Gould entered the room. I closed the book and rose from the bed, but before I could speak he placed a finger against his lips, and beckoned me to follow him out.

His chamber across the hall was warm and bright compared to Edith's. A fire burned in the hearth, and two oil-lamps were lit: one on a writing desk, and another beside the unmade bed. The room was in disarray: piles of clothes on the floor, stacked books and sheaves of paper. A brass-bound trunk lay open on the hearthrug, and a kneeling Miss Croft was placing items into it.

Robert spoke in a hushed voice. 'Miss Lawless, you cannot remain.'

'I just wished — '

'I know why you are here.'

He opened a drawer in his desk and began to rummage for something.

I said, 'Are you going somewhere?'

'Soon enough. Possibly to gaol, though I think my father has enough influence to ensure that doesn't happen.'

'You are fortunate.'

Robert paused, but only to listen for sounds of movement in the hall. He said, 'Perhaps in that regard. But don't think he makes the effort for my benefit. Having a son imprisoned for attempted murder would be a hindrance to his own career. Whatever the outcome, I shall be leaving this house.'

'Is that your choice, or that of your mother and father?'

'The decision is mutual.' He grew exasperated and said, 'Lisa, where's the . . . ?'

Miss Croft rose and went to the desk. She said, 'Try the other drawer,' her voice soft and familiar. I looked at her standing close to him, and wondered if she knew about Emilie — about Robert's previous dalliance with a domestic servant. He had seemed so genuine in his grief for Miss Casey and Morgan. But his willingness to use his position to gain the affections of less privileged women was not becoming.

He found what he was looking for: a letter, which he offered to me. The grey paper was folded and stained. Only Robert's name was written on the outside, so someone must have hand-delivered it. The broken seal was made with drops of white wax, as if whoever had penned the letter had dripped a candle over the back.

Robert said, 'Mr Darby has written to me.'

There were noises downstairs. The front door closed with a bang, and there were raised voices, perhaps from the people waiting outside. Robert went to his window to look down on the street.

The note from Darby was short, the writing small and spidery. There was no date, no signature, and no address. In the first few lines, Darby assured Robert that he forgave him for what had happened at the inquest. The only mention of Edith came at the end. He wrote, *It is such a shame, for I am sure she would have been happy here. She could have sketched the scene from the parlour every day and never drawn the same picture twice.*

There was nothing else. From the window, Robert said, 'You will have to leave, Miss Lawless. You cannot be found here.'

'Do you know where Darby is?'

'Not for certain, but he had promised Edith that when they were married, he would take her back to his old parish.'

'Have you told anyone?'

'Who can I tell? I'm confined here.'

'Surely your parents would — '

'Did you know that they attended Edith's funeral dressed in full Brethren attire?' He shook his head. 'They are the last people I would tell.'

He came close to me, and when I handed him the letter, he refused to take it.

'Show it to your father.'

'I doubt he'd accept it as evidence of anything.'

He stayed looking at me, his brow creased at the bridge of his nose in a way that reminded me of his sister. Somewhere downstairs, a man called out his name, most likely Judge Gould.

'Keep it anyway,' Robert said. 'I must go before my father comes searching. Lisa will bring you back to the street.'

He moved to the door, opened it enough to peer into the hall, and then stepped out. He glanced back at me, but didn't say anything. I folded the letter to put it in my coat pocket. A piece of white candlewax broke off and skittered on the floor.

★ ★ ★

295

Liam had brought the horses and carriage to the front of the house, and was busy attaching a trunk to the roof. He stood when he saw us approach, his feet wide apart for balance. A dog on the pavement ran out beneath Newton's legs, and the horse shied, causing the carriage to rock. Liam shifted his weight to retain balance, and clucked his tongue until Newton settled.

I called up to him, 'Is Father going somewhere?'

He removed his cap and ran a forearm over his brow. 'Yes, miss. To the north of the county, I believe.'

Father was in the library, standing on some folding steps and running his finger along the spines on a high shelf. Ewan sat at the table, taking notes from a volume that lay open before him.

'Have you been called away?'

Father looked at me over his shoulder. 'The constabulary in Howth sent word. A young man was discovered in a field after he went walking in bad weather. They think he may have been struck by lightning.'

He found the book he wanted, took it down, and descended the three rickety steps. He opened the book to a certain plate, and showed it to me. It was the torso of a man with strange markings on his skin: lines branching and forking into ever more delicate strokes, running over his chest.

Father said, 'They're Lichtenberg figures. Ruptured blood vessels beneath the skin, caused by the shock of the bolt. I have always wanted to observe them . . . in the flesh, so to speak.'

The lines even looked like forked lightning; or the roots of a tree; or streams in a riverbed; and I thought it could not be a coincidence that such disparate elements of nature should adopt the same pattern.

Father closed the book and said to Ewan, 'We shall take both these volumes with us, Mr Weir. We had best leave soon so we can arrive before dark.'

Ewan stacked his books and notes and placed his pen back in the holder.

I said to Father, 'How long will you be gone?'

'No more than a day.' He smiled at me. 'You will have the whole house to yourself.'

Ewan rose from his seat and they both began walking towards the door. I was about to let them go, but then said, 'Robert Gould has given me something.' I took the sheet from my coat and held it out. 'A letter from Mr Darby.'

Father frowned while he came towards me, taking his spectacles from his front pocket. He read the short note, and then turned the leaf over to look at the reverse.

'This says nothing.'

'Mr Gould believes Darby was in his old parish of St John's when he wrote it.'

'When were you speaking with him?'

'Today.'

'Abigail — '

'If he's correct then Darby might still be found.'

'It is wholly inappropriate for Mr Gould to speak with you about these things.'

'He wished for me to show it to you, Father.'

'Then why would he not send it to me directly?'

I couldn't answer, and remained silent. Ewan came to stand beside us, and he asked to read the letter.

'Can you not send it to someone, Father?' I said. 'To the constabulary in Wicklow?'

'Abigail, you know that there are sightings of Mr Darby every day, here and in England. The police do not need another phantom to chase.'

'They would believe it if it came from you.'

'Precisely why I have no wish to send it.'

Before I could speak again, he held up his hand. 'If we have come to learn anything, it is that Mr Gould is not to be trusted. I thought that you would be able to see that.'

'I believe I know the character of Mr Gould very well,' I said, feeling an edge in my voice.

Father removed his glasses, and bent his head while folding the temples. Ewan read the letter again. He held my eye for a moment. 'Perhaps it would do no harm, sir, if you were to send this to Wicklow. You could simply say that you received the information in secret, and that you will leave it to the discretion of the police in that county to judge its veracity.'

My father remained still. He looked from Ewan to me, nodded his head, and took the sheet. 'When we have settled in our rooms in Howth later this evening, I shall compose a letter and send it from there.' He opened the cover of his book and placed the letter inside.

They left the library to make their final

preparations. Ewan fetched a travelling bag from his room, and Father went to the study. Liam came in to say that the horses were ready, and Mrs Perrin joined us in the hallway to see the men off. Father kissed my forehead. He ruffled Jimmy's hair, and said that until their return he would be the man of the house.

I remained in the doorway as they climbed into the carriage, and Liam edged the horses out on to the road. As they set off, Ewan turned in his seat and looked at me through the window.

I closed the door. Mrs Perrin said, 'Peace at last,' and she asked if I wanted anything to eat, but I only wished to rest a while in my room. On my way upstairs I passed my father's study. The door stood open, and a lamp was lit on his desk. I went to put it out, and noticed one of the drawers ajar. It was stiff, and the wood squeaked against the edges as I pulled it open. Mr Darby's letter was sitting there on top of a sheaf of papers.

14

Muddy water splashed against the windows of the stagecoach as it forded a narrow stream. The carriage lurched and swayed over the far bank, and I steadied myself against the side armrest. Two middle-aged sisters sat beside me. They clasped threadbare fur stoles beneath their chins, and spoke little except to complain about the cold. In the seat opposite, a thin man with wispy locks and a priestly bearing sat next to his young daughter. Seeing them made me think of long trips I had taken with my father, particularly when I was small and could fall asleep in his lap. The little girl glanced at me shyly once or twice before complimenting me on my travelling cloak. I smiled at her, and was about to ask her name when her father took a Bible from his satchel and told her to attend to her studies.

The journey passed in silence, which suited me well enough. We cleared Dublin in less than an hour, and made good progress through the villages south of the city. The clouds were the colour of wood-smoke, and seemed to shift about just as much. Strong winds began to whip leaves about the carriage. Before we entered the foothills of Wicklow, Professor Reeves's observatory was briefly visible on a bluff in the distance. The young girl spotted its domed roof between the trees, and asked her father was it a type of church. He peered at it for a moment, and simply answered, 'No.'

At one point I caught him staring at me. He may have wondered why I was travelling unaccompanied, but his gaze was so blatant and unashamed. He didn't look away even when I held his eye. Eventually, I leaned towards him. 'Did you say something?'

All heads in the carriage turned. The girl glanced up at her father. He frowned and shifted in his seat, then wiped some condensation from the glass with a balled fist and watched the passing scenery.

The dark, tree-covered slopes began to close about us. Our pace slowed as the horses struggled uphill. Occasionally, the road ahead was visible winding through the mountains, seemingly unending.

The journey was only twenty miles from Nelson's Pillar, but we were well into the fourth hour when the carriage shuddered to a stop. The road appeared no different to what had gone before, slanting fields bounded by hedges and thickets of trees. There wasn't a building in sight, but still the driver yelled out, 'Manor Kilbride.'

I bid the girl goodbye and opened the door. The heel of my walking shoe sank into the earth as I alighted. There was a side road leading further up the hill, and I assumed the village lay in that direction. The stagecoach was to continue on to Blessington.

The driver was looping his lash against its handle. 'Did you have a bag?'

I shook my head and pulled up my hood, but it was immediately blown down again. I asked what time he was returning this way to Dublin, and he said four, all going well.

He glanced up at the sky, then turned abruptly in his seat to look back at the road. I followed his gaze, but the path was empty.

'Is there no one here to meet you?' he said.

'I'm sure they'll be along in a moment. Besides, I know the way.'

'These hills aren't safe, miss. I'd best wait till you're collected.'

The breeze grew stronger and the trees swayed overhead. 'Really, it's fine,' I said, and before he could answer, I began walking up the narrow side road. After a few steps, I heard the harness shake and the wheels creak, and I knew he was on his way. I watched them go. The little girl had taken my seat, and she was looking at me, her face pale behind the glass.

I pushed on. Black hills loomed over me to my left, and I kept expecting to see the village after each bend. The sky continued to threaten rain, which would have made for a truly miserable trek. I began to wonder if this was the right road. Surely the coachman would have corrected me if I set off in the wrong direction — though I had been adamant that I knew the way. Even the sign of a farm or an outhouse would have been welcome, a spiral of smoke or a scarecrow. There was a rustling in the ditch beside me and I stopped to listen. A pigeon burst out of the undergrowth, beating its wings together as it flew past my head.

Finally, I came to an entrance in the hedgerow, barely visible through unkempt briars and nettles. There was a gate lodge, also run down, but a lamp was lit in the fanlight above the door. A path wound its way towards a big house. All I could make out of it was a slanting slate roof with moss in the joins and a granite chimney stack. It must have been the manor of Kilbride. After that, more houses were visible dotted in the fields and clustered around the crossroads of the village itself. There was an inn with a ship's wheel attached to the gable wall — an emblem that seemed at odds with the setting — also a well with a rusting pump, and a flour mill. There were only a few people on what passed for the street, and they were gathered around a building under construction, surrounded by scaffolding and pulleys and piles of grey bricks. It was a church, though only the lowest portions of the walls were complete.

A man bearing a hod of bricks over his shoulder paused at my approach. He pushed the brim of his cap back with his thumb. 'Can I help, miss?'

I pointed at the weight on his shoulder. 'Would you like to put that down?'

'Easier to carry it now than try to pick it up again.'

'Oh. Is this St John's?'

He shook his head. 'St Brigid's, miss. The Protestant church is further up the road, about a half-mile.'

I thanked him, and continued on, leaving the small bustle of the village behind me. Once again, the road became deserted. The higher it climbed, the worse the surface seemed to be: a mixture of soft ground and rough stones, with trails of cart-wheels criss-crossing. I thought of Darby's young wife, what she must have made of the isolation and seclusion. The road bent sharply around the contour of a hill, and a stone bridge arched over the young River Liffey. It was running quick and clear, unlike in Dublin, where it was thick with the silt of the country and waste of the city. I felt drops on my cheek, and thought it might have been spray from the rocks below, but it was the first hint of rain. The clouds seemed to press against the peaks of the surrounding hills, and though it was mid-afternoon, a gloom had already descended.

I hurried on and came to St John's chapel. It was small and neat with a square tower. A sloping graveyard ran towards the river. Across the road there was a two-storey house, the walls white-washed and the windowsills covered in flower boxes: the vicarage, I assumed. Was that where Darby and his young wife once lived? It didn't look at all like the house in Edith's drawing.

The hinges squeaked as I opened the gate to the church yard. Wind rustled in the long grasses between the headstones. The vaulted oak doorway was closed, and there was no sign of a handle, only a brass keyhole. I pushed the door but it didn't budge. A raven perched atop the tower looked down at me, its head cocked to one side. It opened its wings as if about to take flight, then closed them again and settled.

I walked among the headstones. The most prominent were those of the former pastors, tall marble columns with etched letters painted gold. A small tomb had a carving on top in bas-relief: two infants asleep beneath a thin sheet, their arms entwined. Away from the chapel, in the shadow of a copse of sycamore, there were smaller, humbler gravestones, littered with the twirling seeds from the trees above. Right in the corner, a granite stone bore the name Darby.

Noises came from the road. A horse and trap rattled past. Its driver wore the clothes of a labourer, and a straw hat with a wide brim. He saw me in the graveyard, and slowly reached up to tug the front of his hat, just as he and the cart moved out of sight.

The gravestone said, *Here lies Catherine Darby, wife of Joseph, daughter of William Shaw of Dublin. Died 24th February 1814 aged 20. And her child, a day old.*

I had only vaguely heard of the Shaws, a banking family who lived in Merrion Square. There were three daughters: Mrs Nesham was the eldest. Catherine must have come next. It was said the youngest was simple, and confined somewhere in an asylum.

The door of the church opened and a young man backed out. Turning around, he pulled it shut behind him, catching the tail of his coat in the jamb so he had to open and close the door again. He locked it with an iron key. When he turned about, he studied me for a moment before offering a loud 'Good afternoon.'

He wore a white cravat, a dark coat and round spectacles, and introduced himself as Reverend Coogan. 'Are you visiting the village?' he asked.

'I am just passing through.'

He looked down at the grave. 'You were a relative of Mrs Darby?'

'No.'

'Oh. You bear a resemblance.'

'You knew her?'

'Actually, no. But I have heard people here describe her. Tall, dark hair, pale skin.'

'Did you replace Mr Darby in the vicarage?'

'Yes. After he left for . . . pastures new.'

'Have you heard the news from Dublin?'

'News travels slowly in these hills.' I didn't say anything, just waited until he continued. 'Though we have heard rumours.'

The grave seemed tidier than the others, with fewer weeds and sycamore seedlings.

'Has there been any sign of him here?'

'Goodness, no.' The vicar smiled. Perhaps he thought I was concerned, for he said, 'You need not worry on that account, Miss . . . ?'

'Lawless.' I pointed to the house across the road. 'Was that where he lived?'

'That house was built for me last year. It is most handsome, don't you think?'

'Where did Darby live?'

'A cottage further up the hill, but it has fallen to ruin. Lord knows how it is still upright.'

We stood for a moment in silence. Coogan looked about. 'How are you returning to the village? If you would like me to — '

'When is your next service, Reverend?'

'Tomorrow morning.'

'I might see you then.'

'Ah, excellent,' he said. He waited a moment

longer, and turned away, nodding to himself as if he'd just remembered a task. I waited for him to enter his own house, and a bit longer in case he was watching from behind his curtains, then set off along the road once more.

The cottage was perched near the summit of the hill facing south. It was quite large, one storey, with a lofty roof that made it imposing. The windows were closed up. One shutter hung askew, giving a glimpse of the dark interior. The shrubbery that arched over the iron gate was so overgrown that twigs clung to my cloak as I squeezed by. The front door was in a small porch with its own pointed roof. Several slates had fallen and smashed to pieces in the threshold. At first glance the house seemed forlorn and abandoned, but I realized it had probably once been quite handsome. A gap in the trees gave a view into the valley below, and of the Liffey tumbling over a small waterfall. If the garden had been kept and the walls white-washed, it would have been idyllic.

It was difficult to approach the door without scraping and crunching shards of tile underfoot. The knocker was so tarnished and rusted that it seemed fused into one piece of metal. I gave the door a nudge and it shifted inwards. I pushed further. A bevelled glass lampshade behind the door toppled over and rolled along the stone floor until it bumped against the skirting. I paused on the threshold, looked into the dark hallway, and then stepped inside.

An entrance to the left opened to what was once the parlour. The floorboards were warped and bare except for some broken furniture. Large gaps in the ceiling revealed thick rafters. There were cold cinders in the hearth, but it was difficult to know how long they'd been left undisturbed. Loose planks from a crate and a length of cargo rope made one corner of the room untidy.

The shutters in the kitchen were half open and the room was brighter. Another door led to the back yard, but it was locked, as was the window over the sink. In the crook of the sill, some initials had been inscribed: JD and CD, the letters flowing and cursive, and also the year, 1813. Blankets lay bundled in the corner. This room wasn't as cold as the others. When I placed my hand on the hatch of the stove cooker, the metal had the faintest hint of warmth. I went to the corner and picked up the blankets. A copy of the Bible was hidden underneath.

'Come out, Miss Lawless.'

Darby was standing in the middle of the parlour, dressed in the clothes he wore at the inquest, except for a borrowed coat that was too big. The beginning of a scraggly beard covered his chin. He held a fire-iron by his side, the tip resting on the floorboards.

There was no other way to leave the kitchen, and to try to barricade the door would be futile. I placed the blankets back in the corner, and went into the parlour, staying close to the wall.

'Who else is with you?'

'My father, and two constables.'

He looked towards the front door. A burble from the river could be heard outside.

'You are lying.'

'Do you think he would allow me to come alone?'

'I don't think he would allow you to come here at all.'

Still, he was unsure, and he went to the window to peek from the shutters. I moved farther into the room, but only made it to the hearth before he pointed the poker towards me. 'Stay where you are.' He pressed his nose against the glass, then moved his head to look through a different pane.

How had I left the front door? Off its latch, but I'd still have to pause to pull it open. Then the garden path, the gate. What if my dress caught in the brambles again? I could run in these shoes, and in a straight race I could outpace him. He looked weak and haggard from lack of sleep. But the road was uneven and my skirts would be a hindrance. Any tumble and he could catch up.

He ran his hand over his forehead and down his cheek, then drew back his arm and struck the wall with the fire-iron, leaving a crack in the plaster. He turned on me.

'What now, Miss Lawless? You cannot leave, you know that?' He kicked about the loose slats in the corner, then picked out the rope, shaking it to remove dirt and flakes of plaster. He came towards me, and I stepped back, tripping on the hearthstone.

'I'm not the only one who knows you're here,' I said.

'Hold out your hands.'

There was nothing in the room I could use as a weapon, no candlestick holder, or coal shovel. 'Do you think I just guessed? Somebody told me.'

'I won't ask again.'

He took a step to the side to block off the door.

'If they told me, they could tell others.'

'Only my sister-in-law knows I'm here. And you'd be the last person she would tell.'

A gust of wind whistled through the loft, and dust sifted from the exposed rafters.

'But I cannot stay now, and I can't let you go until I am away.' He placed the tip of the poker on the ground and it toppled over with a clatter. 'When darkness falls I shall make arrangements to leave, and only then will I let others know that you are here. Most likely you will be found tomorrow.'

'Who in the village will help you?'

He held the rope with both hands now, pulling a short section of it taut. 'It gets cold at night, but I shall light a fire and leave the blankets.'

'Will you not go back and answer for what you've done?'

He slid one end of the rope out further, and looped it over his hand. 'Show me your wrists.'

'No.'

'This is your own fault, Abigail.'

'Was it Edith's fault for refusing you?'

He held my eye without blinking, his face shadowed in the waning afternoon light.

The gate outside creaked for a long moment as if it had blown open in the wind, but then it was closed again, deliberately.

Darby went to the window. He let the rope slip from his hands. I was about to call out, but backed into the kitchen instead. I tried to shut the door. It jammed against the uneven floor and remained open a crack.

Darby waited in the middle of the room as the sound of shoes crunching on the broken tiles drifted in from outside. Footsteps echoed on the flagstones in the hallway, and then there was silence.

The man with the lazy eye entered the parlour. His coat was wet, and he removed his hat to shake water from its brim. Without even glancing at Darby, he placed it on the mantelpiece, and then turned to survey the room.

'You're alone?'

He spoke with such familiarity that I knew they must be acquainted. Perhaps this was their plan, to meet here with me already trapped. But Darby didn't betray my presence.

'Who sent you, Devlin?'

'It's not so easy to find this place. Especially a day like today with the wind right against you.' He began rubbing his bad eye. 'Do you mind?'

He arched his neck back, pulled the loose eyelid upwards and pushed the tips of his fingers underneath. After a moment the eyeball emerged, white and solid and untethered. He held it up to his face, as if he were regarding himself, then draped it in a handkerchief and began to rub vigorously. When finished, he placed it on the mantel next to his hat with a glassy click.

'That's better.' He looked about the room. The inside of his socket was smooth and red like an exposed gum. 'Not much in the way of furniture,' he said. A Windsor chair lay on its side beside the window. He righted it, but a leg was missing, and the chair collapsed again.

Darby took a step closer to the poker. 'I am not going back to Dublin,' he said.

'Yes, I know that.'

'You didn't answer my question.'

The man took a pocket watch from his coat. He checked the time and then peered through the window as if surprised at how dark it was getting.

'I said, who sent — '

'Catherine.' He closed the lid of his watch, squeezing it until a tiny catch clicked shut like a knuckle cracking. 'Catherine Shaw sent me. And Emilie, and Edith.'

Darby had become still at the mention of his wife's name. As the list continued, he bent down to pick up the poker without further pretence. The man smiled. He was about to replace his watch, but put it on the mantel instead, as if he feared it might be damaged.

He began walking towards Darby, who backed towards the wall much as I had done minutes before. Darby swung the poker in a wide arc, but Devlin caught his elbow and forced his arm upwards, squeezing until Darby lost his grip and the poker tumbled between them. Darby was a few inches shorter, and slight in comparison. He grimaced in pain as Devlin turned him about, wrapped his left arm around Darby's neck and clamped his other hand on his forehead.

Darby thrust his elbows backwards, but it made no difference. Devlin slowly arched his back, lifting Darby off his toes as if he were just a child. Darby continued to kick, and I could hear him trying to yell, but his mouth was covered. Devlin remained still, bringing his head back to look at the ceiling, pressing his good eye closed as if in prayer.

I didn't see any sudden or exaggerated movement, but I heard the break. There was no more struggle. Darby slumped down, his knees bending beneath him so at first he remained half-upright before toppling forward, his forehead striking the floor.

I backed away from the crack in the door, hand over my mouth, bumping against the corner of a sideboard. I felt my arms weaken, and wanted to take a gasping breath but feared the noise I would make. Every movement now seemed loud in my ears: the rustle of my skirt, the scrape of my shoes. I leaned over the sink and tried the window-latch again, knowing it wouldn't move, and praying the pane wouldn't creak. I felt along the top of the back door for a key that might be hidden, but there was nothing. What could I do if he came in? The kitchen was bare: no pans hanging from hooks, or kettles, or flattening irons.

In the parlour, Devlin was moving about again. I peeked through the crack. Darby remained where he was, his head tilted a little towards me so I could see his opened eyes. His killer was at the window, breathing heavily and holding his ribs. He looked out at the scenery for a minute as if lost in contemplation, then bent down to pick up the rope, unravelling it to its full length. He came back into the middle of the room, and tossed the rope over one of the exposed beams in the ceiling. The dangling ends were tied into a sailor's knot, and he pulled it so the rope closed tight against the beam, leaving a hanging length of four or five feet.

He tested its strength. The beam began to creak and the rope stretched, but it didn't break, despite him lifting himself off the ground at one point. Then he retrieved the broken chair and placed it underneath, nudging it so that it fell over. He stood back and surveyed the scene critically.

Finally, he fashioned the end of the rope into a wide noose about a foot above his own head. He did so expertly, as if that might have been his profession. He puffed out his cheeks and looked at Darby on the floor, glancing between him and the rope a few times as if figuring out the best way to approach his task. He leaned down, put both his arms beneath Darby's shoulders and began to lift him up. It was a struggle, and the first time Darby fell from his grip, crumpling to the floor again.

There was a dust pan in the kitchen next to the stove, half filled with grime and grit. I emptied it into my palm, then placed the pan down again as quietly as I could. Devlin had got Darby almost upright, arms around his chest. He was looking again at the wide noose, preparing for the final heave.

I pulled open the kitchen door, and walked towards him. His head turned and his good eye opened wide. As he dropped Darby's body, I flung the grit into his face. He brought his hands up and stumbled backwards, tripping over the chair and falling to the floor. He was blinded, but still he reached towards me, grasping the air where he thought I stood. I circled around him, staying close to the hearth, and on impulse took the glass eye. It was already cold and felt clammy to the touch. Devlin was grunting, leaning over and holding his eyelids open with thumbs and forefingers, like someone trying to prevent himself from falling asleep. I looked once more at Darby's body and the swaying noose, and then rushed for the door.

It was raining heavily now. I skidded on the footpath with my second or third step, and forced myself to tread carefully. The iron gate wouldn't open at first. I tugged at it, glancing over my shoulder, expecting to see him there leaning on the doorjamb. But the path was clear. I took a breath to steady myself, lifted the iron latch on the gate and ran on to the road.

The wind was behind me. My skirts were blown out in front, always threatening to get in a tangle. I didn't remember the slope being so steep on the way up. Once or twice I felt like a child running downhill unable to stop; but if I fell and hurt myself now I'd be finished. I had to slow for a bend in the road, and halted to look back up the hill. The gate was almost hidden in its thicket of brambles. There was no sign of him. I opened my palm. His glass eye stared back at me, the iris green and gold flecked. I closed my fingers over and stuffed it in my pocket.

Water had begun to flow in small rivulets through the cart tracks. The trees swayed overhead, and the stones had become treacherous. The winding road meant I could only look back a short distance each time, and I imagined him behind each bend, gaining on me, determined and relentless. Through a gap in the ditch I saw the turret of St John's and ran all the harder. There were lights in the front room of the vicarage. Smoke from the chimney stack was scattered by the wind. I hurried through the front gate, up the short pathway, and hammered on the door.

The road was still empty. I knocked again, thumping the door with my fist. I was about to lift the letter box and call the Reverend's name, but finally I heard the key turn and the door was pulled open. I pushed through before Coogan had time to stand back, brushing against his chest. I moved his hand from the latch, and shut the door behind me, leaning over to catch my breath, then turning the key in the lock.

Coogan retreated a little, surprised by my abrupt entrance. 'Miss Lawless, are you all right?'

'Are there other doors to this house, Reverend? They must be locked.'

'They already are.' He frowned and held his hands towards me, as if he feared I might topple over. 'Have you caught a chill? Come and sit by the fire.' He began moving into the hall, but when I stayed by the front door, he paused.

'You know,' he said, 'a man came by here, enquiring after you.'

'Yes,' I said. 'He found me.'

'How do you mean? He is in the parlour now.' The door to the front room opened, spilling candlelight into the hall. Ewan stepped into the threshold, his face set in a stern expression. Before he could say anything, I threw my arms around his neck. I could feel his surprise, but after a moment he unhooked my hands and held them between us.

15

The fire in Coogan's hearth crackled as rain continued to drum against the window. He had given me a tartan blanket as well as a glass of whiskey with cloves and warm water, and though I wanted to peer through a gap in the shutters, Ewan and Coogan insisted that I remain by the fire. Ewan sat in a chair opposite, while the Reverend paced the green carpet, keeping an eye on the roadway outside.

Coogan had proved to be practical and willing to assist. If anything, he seemed to welcome the diversion: tales of murder and danger abroad, a strange couple embracing in his hallway. He was a young man in an isolated mountain parish, and his life may well have been bereft of incident. He paused again to survey the road.

I cupped the glass of whiskey to warm my fingers, and said to Ewan that we couldn't stay here. 'If the man goes towards the village, this will be the first house he comes to.'

'His only concern will be escape, Abigail. If he is disfigured, then he is easily identified, and he will avoid towns and villages.'

'All the more reason for us to go to one.'

From the window, the Reverend said, 'You are safe here, Miss Lawless. You can remain for the night if necessary.'

But I couldn't bear the thought of staying in a strange, darkened room. Devlin had crept through the Lying-In Hospital in the dead of night, and into my father's workrooms. There was no reason to think that Coogan's locks and window-latches could stop him.

I said, 'Is there a constable in the village, Reverend?'

'No, the nearest station is in Blessington.'

'Word must be sent.'

A dog's barking could be heard over the wind and the rain, and we became still. It stopped after a moment, and Coogan said, 'There are sheepdogs in the surrounding farmsteads. They bark to each other all the time.'

He glanced outside once more, and moved back into the room.

Ewan said, 'Miss Lawless is correct. We must get word to the village, and arrange for a group of men to retrieve Mr Darby's body. They may even be able to search for his attacker.'

Coogan offered to carry the message, but I said that it was unsafe for any one of us to travel alone. 'If we go, we should go together.'

'Very well,' he said. 'I have a trap in the shed.'

The back yard of the vicarage was enclosed by a high wall, but I was still wary stepping out into the open. It was like any other soft and muddy evening. Water dripped from the shrubs in the Reverend's small garden. A few hens sat hunched beneath the pointed roof of their coop, and in the corner a large black pig lay in the mire of an open-air pen. He raised his head as we hurried across the yard.

In the stables, Coogan hitched a horse to the two-seater trap while Ewan slid open the large iron bolt on the back gates. We squeezed beneath the shelter of the folded roof, and in short order were rolling down the hill towards Manor Kilbride. The roadway was deserted, protected from the worst of the rain by the trees overhead.

Earlier in the day, the trek uphill had seemed long and gruelling, but coming down we reached the village in minutes, and Coogan reined in the horse beside the local inn. Its common room was wide, with benches and beams blackened by grime and wood-smoke, the floor covered unevenly in stained sawdust. After stepping in from the bracing wind outside it felt oppressively warm, and was filled with the smells of sweat and sour ale.

Some of the workers at the church sat at a table by the fire playing cards, but there were few other patrons. All heads turned as we entered, and the eyes of the men lingered on me. Coogan approached the innkeeper, a stocky man with rolled-up shirtsleeves, and the alarm was raised.

Men gathered at the inn. The labourers volunteered to go immediately, and the local blacksmith offered his cart. Darby would have been known to many of them, and I saw some glance to the table where I sat with Ewan as Coogan gave instructions. They set off together. I thought they would have been silent and solemn, but there was an eager chatter among them.

Ewan and I remained by the fire, and sat in silence for a while. The innkeeper asked if we wanted anything, but I had no appetite, and Ewan made do with a mug of water. His fingers rested on the handle, and he absent-mindedly pushed it back and forth. He said nothing to admonish me, and when he spoke, it was only to check on my well-being.

I watched him as he stared into the fire, and said, 'How did you know to look for me here?'

'It was a guess,' he said, and smiled slightly. 'Perhaps an educated one. When your father and I reached Howth, there was nothing of real interest about the body found there, and so I returned home early. Mrs Perrin and Jimmy were frantic at your absence.'

I bowed my head. 'I had hoped to be home before dusk.'

'They sent word to your father, and I volunteered to search here. They shall be worried tonight, but will soon know that all is well.'

I was ashamed to be the cause of such distress, and Ewan seemed to note my sorrow. He said, 'At least your intuition proved correct.'

'That is little comfort. We are left with more questions than before.'

He leaned his elbows on the table. 'Thanks to Mr Devlin.'

'I am convinced now that he murdered Miss Casey, and that he drove the carriage that took Edith away, maybe drowned her as well. But I do not understand why. If he was killing at the behest of Mr Darby, why would he turn against his master?'

'Fear of being apprehended? With the defect to his eye, he could not remain at large if Darby denounced him.'

'Perhaps. What if he was working for someone else in the Brethren, a rival to Mr Darby?'

'You said that Miss Gould had plans to elope

with James Caulfeild. Could he have been involved? Maybe Mr Devlin was his man all along.'

I had seen James at the observatory on the night Edith died. He had left early, saying that he had business in the city. But if he planned all this, surely he would not have attended the gathering at all. 'What about Emilie?' I said. 'What possible motive could James have had for harming her?'

Ewan stared into the fire while he was thinking. 'The one person who is connected to them both is Robert Gould,' he said. He turned to look at me. 'He has already made one attempt on Darby's life, and he was the one who suggested that Darby had fled to Wicklow. He could have sent Devlin here to track you both.'

Robert had shown himself to be a man of weak character in his treatment of Emilie, and dalliance with Miss Croft. But he struck me as rather callow, his bungled attempt to kill Darby at the inquest showing the limits of his scheming. 'Even if he had a vendetta against Darby, what kind of man would sacrifice his own sister?'

Ewan shrugged. 'What kind of man would do any of this?'

The darkness outside had become complete, and the innkeeper shuffled from table to table lighting candles. A young boy pushed open the door.

'They are coming back,' he said, and we all went outside to see, standing beneath the eaves to avoid the rain. The cart rolled through the village, the head of the horse hung low. There was a body laid on the bed of the wagon, covered by a blanket. Several of the men were perched on the sides of the cart, and others walked behind, as if they were following a leader who had fallen in battle.

They took the body to a storeroom at the back of the inn. It was cool and dry, with haunches of salted meat suspended from hooks, and baskets of withered vegetables. The driver of the cart and one of the labourers laid the body on a table, and then went to stand by the door. Reverend Coogan asked us to come closer. He held up a lantern and drew the blanket aside.

Darby's head sagged to the left with his lips parted. There was a glisten from his teeth, and a wet sheen on his face like perspiration — most likely he had been carried through the rain. The noose was fixed around his neck, with only a short piece of rope still attached, the twisted braids unravelled and frayed.

Coogan looked at me. 'We found him in the parlour just like you said. There was no sign of anyone else. He was hanging, and we had to cut him down.'

I picked up the loose end of rope. 'So Devlin still went to the trouble of making it look like suicide?'

One of the men by the door exhaled sharply through his nose, as if amused, but when I looked back they were both impassive. The labourer scraped a muddy boot over the floorboards.

I said, 'Has word been sent to the constable in Blessington?'

'The feeling is that it's too treacherous to fetch him tonight,' Coogan said. 'It can wait until morning.'

'I cannot wait. I must return to Dublin.'

'We had a hard time of it taking the cart down the hill. No one will be leaving the village this evening.' He placed the lantern on the table and allowed the wire handle to fall against the glass with a clink. 'The coroner in Wicklow will have to be informed, and it may take days before a jury is assembled. This isn't the city. Things move a little slower.'

Ewan said, 'I must bring Miss Lawless home at the first opportunity. We can return to give evidence if required.'

Coogan used his thumb to close Darby's mouth fully, then wiped his hands with a handkerchief. 'We shall see what the constable has to say.'

'We know what he'll say.' Behind us, the driver of the cart was scratching the side of his beard. His pale fingernails stood out against the grime of his fingers. 'He'll wonder why has he been dragged twelve miles through the muck to see a man that's hanged himself.'

The Reverend said, 'Mr Burke, please.'

The driver looked at Coogan from beneath his brow, glanced at me once more, then turned and left the room with the young labourer in tow.

'What did he mean by that?'

'Among the men, there was a . . . consensus that Mr Darby had taken his own life.'

'Did you not tell them — '

'They only believed what their own eyes told them.' Coogan folded his handkerchief and placed it in his front pocket. 'Miss, anyone would be shocked if they came upon a person hanging from the rafters. Are you sure you saw another man there?'

'Of course I am.'

Before I could say anything more, Ewan leaned forward. 'This assailant was not some stranger, Reverend. He is known to us.'

'Have you ever seen him, Mr Weir?'

'Well, no.'

Coogan nodded to himself. 'I believe the mind can play tricks when one is so alarmed.'

I took Devlin's eye from my pocket and placed it flat on the table. The lantern-light flickered in the iris. 'This is no trick.'

Coogan reached over as if he were about to pick it up, but then just nudged it with his thumb. He didn't say anything, but I knew that if the men here didn't believe me, they would not be swayed by a glass bauble.

Ewan stepped between us. He unbuttoned his coat, and laid it on a corner of the table. Then he took the lantern, placed it next to Darby's head, and leaned over to examine his features at close quarters. Beneath the right ear, Ewan found the knot of Darby's cravat. He moved the noose aside, and carefully unwound the grubby scarf from Darby's neck, leaving his throat and prominent Adam's apple exposed.

Ewan pulled at the noose to see if there was any give, revealing a deep groove running beneath Darby's jaw and curling up towards his ears. He slipped his fingers beneath the rope and pressed firmly into the skin, like a parent feeling a child for glandular fever. He opened the mouth and peered inside. Finally he lifted both eyelids, pinching the skin with a firm, sure touch that made Reverend Coogan wince.

Ewan held the lantern over Darby's face, and he turned to Coogan. 'Mr Darby was dead before the rope touched his neck.'

'How do you know?'

Ewan began to point out features on Darby's body inconsistent with hanging. The face wasn't swollen, nor the hands clenched shut. The eyes had not projected or turned red, and the tongue was unscathed by any convulsion of the jaw.

Ewan glanced at Coogan to see if he wished to comment, but the Reverend was silent, his face coming ever closer to the corpse.

'The rope wasn't even used for manual strangulation,' Ewan said. 'The noose is relatively loose, and a garrotter will always use his entire strength to pull it tight. The hangman is content to let gravity do the work.'

Coogan lifted the rope and rotated it slightly to see for himself. Ewan took it from him and placed it back on the table, and Coogan mumbled an apology.

'Mr Darby died of a broken neck. At least one of the vertebrae is disconnected. It is possible that the damage was done by the impact of the drop, but at so short a height, that seems unlikely.'

Coogan remained silent as he looked over the body.

Ewan said, 'Would you like me to repeat what I said?'

The Reverend frowned. 'Why?'

'Because tomorrow, you will have to report

these observations to the constable. Miss Lawless and I cannot wait while a messenger is dispatched to Blessington. We depart as soon as there is a break in the weather. I am sure you understand that she must be reunited with her father.'

Coogan glanced at me and said, 'Yes, of course.'

'If the Wicklow coroner has need to contact us, then he can correspond with myself or Mr Lawless.'

'You are both welcome to stay in the vicarage, of course.'

I said, 'I do not wish to return up the hill.'

Coogan tried to reassure me that the man would have been long gone by now, but I was adamant.

'Very well,' he said. 'I shall arrange some rooms for you here.'

Ewan and I were the only guests in the inn that night, though the labourers and some other villagers remained in the common room, growing ever more raucous. The innkeeper showed us up the stairs to two rooms facing each other across a narrow hallway. He opened one door, and said, 'For the young lady.'

The room was cramped, low enough that I could brush the ceiling with my fingertips, though I wouldn't wish to. Everything was coloured in a light earthen hue: floor, walls and bedcovers. Bits of straw emerged from a tear in the mattress, and the chamber-pot held a shining residue. There was only one window, the glass scratched and cloudy, and the cast-iron fireplace was cold to the touch.

Ewan said, 'Surely there is better than this.'

The innkeeper seemed to take affront. 'There is not.'

'The fire isn't even lit.'

The man handed Ewan the candle, pointed to some kindling by the hearth, and said that he had to return downstairs before all the kegs were emptied.

I told Ewan that it would be fine, and he set about making the fire, building a lattice of tinder in the hearth. He attempted to light a slender stick to use as a kind of taper, but though the wood blackened and smoked, it didn't take. I watched his efforts for a while, stopping myself from asking to try. I withdrew a small clump of straw from the mattress. It was dry and crinkly, with sharp edges. Some manner of black weevil scurried over the bed frame, disturbed from his lair.

I knelt beside Ewan and showed him the straw. 'Here.'

He took it from me, placed it in the firebox and soon the wood was burning. He watched it for a while, leaning over to blow on the flames, and I stayed beside him, our knees almost touching.

The fire began to blaze, and a pleasant smell of wood-smoke replaced the room's stale air. I held my palms towards it, glad that Ewan remained where he was, for I had no wish to be left in the room on my own. I undid the string of my bonnet, and laid it near the hearth to dry. Ewan picked up a larger piece of wood and placed it on the fire, dislodging some sparks that brushed up and over his hand.

We heard the braying of laughter from the common room below, and Ewan seemed to break from his reverie. Before he could get up, I said, 'The men in this village think me deluded.'

'Perhaps the Reverend will convince them. But it doesn't matter.'

There was a scar on the heel of my hand from where I'd fallen some weeks before at Elyan the clockmaker's. It was almost healed, just a white seam that traced the shape of the cut. Ewan saw the blemish and asked to look closer. He cradled my hand in his, then brushed his little finger over the line. He said, 'There may always be a slight mark.'

He looked at me without releasing my hand.

I said, 'It will be a reminder.'

He smiled for a second, then his lips straightened again. His eyes seemed to flit over my face, as if he were searching it. I closed my fingers over his hand, and leaned closer.

An ember in the fire burst. Several sparks swept over the hearth, and a few landed on my dress. We both looked down and began to brush them off. The fabric was still slightly damp so there was no real danger, but the startle made us bow our heads, and Ewan laughed slightly. He shifted backwards and stood up in one movement, and said that he had intruded for too long.

'I'll call on you in the morning, and we can start for home.'

I got up as well. Ewan was about to offer help

but then thought better of it. I wanted to thank him for coming, but he immediately nodded his head and turned to leave, not looking back as he closed the door. I couldn't hear his footsteps in the hall so it seemed as though he'd paused for a moment outside. Then I heard the door opposite open and click shut.

I stayed sitting by the fire for a while, and picked out more straw from the bed to clean my shoes. I would have preferred to stay seated all night rather than join whatever creatures inhabited my bed, but the chair was slight and wooden, and the stresses of the day meant I was weary and aching. I donned my bonnet again so as not to have to lay my head bare on the pillow, wrapped my coat about me and lay down over the covers.

Sleep was a long time coming. I watched the fire dwindle, and heard the sounds in the common room get lower and lower as revellers drifted away. Soon all was dark and silent. Whenever I felt that I was about to drift off, some image would pass before my eyes: Devlin lifting Darby from behind, his arms tightening around his neck; or Darby in the back of the cart, the rain falling on his pallid face and the ravelled ends of the noose.

The stillness in the room was broken by the muffled sound of horse's hooves on the earthen street outside. They seemed to slow as they neared the inn and come to a brief halt, then continued on again.

I slipped from the bed and went to the window. The only light from the room was the last glow of the fire, and I was sure to remain unseen from below. The street was just as dark. The rain had let up, and a pale moon was visible behind hazy clouds, but there were no lamps. Across the street, outside a low house, a man was standing on his own. His arms hung by his side, and he wore a stovepipe hat. I couldn't see his face, but his head was inclined towards the upper floors of the inn. I watched him for a full minute, and all the time he hardly moved. Then his head jerked to the left. Two other men approached. They all greeted each other with cheerful voices and slapped backs, and the first man led them both into the house.

I moved away from the window, and went to check again that my door was locked. There was a slight creaking in the hall outside, but when I listened again, silence. I opened the door a crack. Ewan had taken the chair from his room and was seated outside his door, legs straight out in front and crossed at the ankles, arms folded across his stomach and his chin resting on his chest in slumber. A candle guttered on the floor beside him, almost spent. I looked at him for a while, and thought of covering him with a blanket, but he'd surely wake up. I closed the door again as gently as I could, lay down on the bed, and was soon asleep.

★   ★   ★

Coogan's two-seater was light and quick, but it was open at the front, and I laid the blanket that he had given me over my lap. Ewan kept his eyes on the road and a tight grip on the reins. We spoke little for the first hour of the journey, and we both avoided mention of the clouds gathering again, even darker than they were the day before. With the next gust of wind, I felt the first drops on my face. The horse kept a steady pace, his mane shaking with each step, and his head beginning to bow, and soon the rain was falling in earnest.

One of the wheels dipped into a pothole hidden by a puddle and we lurched to the left. I fell against Ewan and gripped his arm, but once he regained control we continued without slowing. The dark skies seemed to press against the treetops. Thunder rumbled in the distance, and though it was early in the afternoon it was as if we travelled at dusk.

At the foot of a hill, a wide stream swollen by the rain crossed over the road. The horse splashed into it at first, seemingly undeterred, but then his step became hesitant. Before reaching the other side he stopped and stood stock still. He wouldn't budge, despite Ewan flicking the reins and urging him on. The rain fell harder, and little could be heard above the burble of water and the heavy patter on the roof.

Ewan handed me the reins and climbed down from his seat. The stream reached his shins. He rubbed the horse's head for a few seconds, then took hold of the bridle and coaxed him forward. Once out of the water, Ewan looked back along the road for a few seconds. He fumbled to light the gig lantern, before climbing back under the hood.

I said, 'You're soaked.'

'I was wet already.'

I unfolded my blanket so his legs were covered as well.

We set off again, and the wheels skidded beneath us on the first sharp bend. The thinning of the trees made us more exposed to the headwind. It felt as though the hood could be folded back on its pleats, but there was nothing else for it. We had to push on.

A copse of trees provided some shelter and Ewan pulled in for a moment. He lifted the edge of the blanket to dry his face, and reached into his coat for a pocket watch, which he held up to the light.

'The stagecoach may be passing in an hour or two. Perhaps it would be best if we waited. You would be dry at least and I could follow.'

'I won't leave you alone.'

'If the rain continues the road will become impassable for us, but not for a stagecoach.'

'We can't just sit here, Ewan,' I said, looking beyond the trees to where the ground fell into a gorge. 'The nearest village cannot be more than a few miles away. We'll find an inn and shelter there.'

He considered this, then nodded and we set off again. Either the road veered slightly, or the wind did, for we were buffeted from the side. A gust lifted one of the wheels from the surface, and I thought we might topple over. The horse was covered in mud up to his flanks, and the lantern tossed and swayed about, knocking against the frame of the roof. It became harder to see the potholes and bends, but then Ewan slowed and pointed between the trees. There were lights about half a mile in the distance.

The road narrowed as we followed the contour of a hillside, and then straightened for a gentle decline, with hedges crowding on both sides. Something lay on the road up ahead. At first I thought it was a person stretched out, clothes all in a tangle. As we got closer we could see it was the bough of a tree, covered in gnarled shoots and dead leaves, its bark blackened but for a strip of pale wood where it had ripped from its bole. I looked up. None of the surrounding trees had lost such a hefty limb.

It lay slantwise across the path, too big to skirt or drive over. Ewan reined in the horse and clambered down again. I offered to help but he said that it didn't look heavy. He lifted the broken end with both hands and carried it to the verge, leaving a muddy trail of twigs and leaves in the road. As he let the branch fall, a man walked from behind the carriage and past the horse. He wore an oilskin hat and greatcoat, and carried a pistol by his side. I yelled Ewan's name, but only in time for him to turn and receive a blow from the butt of the gun. He fell to his hands and knees, his head bowed, and his hat rolled in the mire.

The man pointed the muzzle at the nape of Ewan's neck, and I cried out for him to stop. He didn't fire. Instead, he raised his hand and struck again. Ewan collapsed on the road, face down and unmoving. I took the reins from the seat beside me and lashed them, hoping the horse would spring forward, but he barely took a step. I slipped on to the road, behind the carriage and into the trees. The trunks were thin enough that I could move between them, but thorns in the undergrowth clawed at the hem of my skirts. I came upon a low stone wall and tried to climb over. My shoe slipped on a mossy rock. All I could hear was the rain and wind in the trees overhead. When I looked back he was almost upon me, the skin of his useless eyelid drooping enough to cover the socket, water dribbling from the slick brim of his hat, and the pistol raised against the grey, shifting sky.

★ ★ ★

Cold was seeping against my elbow and shoulder, and the side of my face. Everything felt heavy, even my eyelids as I tried to open them. The chill spread about me like a cloak. I tried to lift my hand to wipe my face, but it wouldn't move. My wrists were bound, wrapped several times in a cord no thicker than a bootlace, and my fingers were gripped together, the knuckles of one hand resting in the muck. When I concentrated, I could open my fingers, but they were stiff and unfeeling, and after a moment I had to close my eyes again because of dizziness.

There was a point on my head just behind my ear that stung when the rain fell on it, a pain that became sharper the more I thought of it. The sleeve of my dress had stains all over, brown dirt and red blood merging into one rusty colour. I could taste metal at the corner of my mouth, and felt caked droplets with the tip of my tongue.

The longer I kept my eyes closed, the warmer I became, so I forced them open, and stared at some buttercups wilting in the wet grass. I was on a verge, the trees looming overhead. The rutted surface of the roadway was only a few feet in front. Ewan lay in the middle of it, almost on his back, his knees bent and pointing upwards. His face was tilted towards me, eyes closed, a streak of blood running from beneath his temple and across his cheek. My vision blurred, and my chest hurt as I took a long breath, but I didn't say his name.

On the far side of the road, Devlin stood beside Coogan's horse and carriage. The horse's head almost rested on his shoulder, and he was caressing it, speaking into its ear. This wasn't the place where the branch had blocked our path. We were further up the hill, where the road had bent sharply. Devlin stood back, still rubbing the horse's nose, and he took hold of the reins just beneath the bridle. He coaxed the horse forward by a step, then another, and began leading it towards the far verge, where the ground fell into the gorge below. The drop wasn't steep, and without the carriage the horse might have been able to walk down, but the left wheel crossed over the lip and began to list. Still he brought the horse further over the side. Its step became hesitant, and Devlin had to pull on the bridle to keep the horse moving.

After a few more paces, it would go no further. I could still see the top of its back over the lip of the road. Both wheels of the carriage were over the edge. The horse was stuck. It refused to go forward, and couldn't back up. If it tried to turn about the carriage would topple over. It would have to be unhitched before it could be moved.

Ewan was unconscious. His features didn't flicker as the rain fell on his face. Blood seeped from his wound, which meant that his heart was still beating. I lifted my hands again, and tried to move my wrists beneath the cord. They were held fast. I picked at the top of the rope with my fingertips, but couldn't get a grip, and my head swam from the effort.

Devlin took the pistol from beneath his coat. He blew into the muzzle, cocked the gun, and then placed it close to the horse's eye. At the last second, he raised it slightly and fired. The bang and muzzle-flash caused the horse to lurch forward, only a step or two, but it lost its footing in the soft ground, and the carriage behind tilted and began to fall down the slope. The car remained balanced with one wheel raised aloft for a few seconds, then collapsed downwards, dragging at the horse until all disappeared from view. I could hear its screams, and the crashing as the carriage rolled in the undergrowth. Devlin stood on the lip of the slope looking down. He remained still until the horse's weak cries ceased and all else became silent.

Devlin placed the pistol inside the lapel of his coat. He moved back to the road, hoisted Ewan beneath both armpits, and began dragging him towards the edge of the drop. After a moment he stopped, and examined the furrows that Ewan's heels were leaving in the surface. He began sweeping them with his own boots, and seemed content that he would be able to conceal them, for he lifted Ewan again.

I pushed myself up on my elbows, and managed to shout for him to stop. Devlin cocked his head, as if to look at me squarely with his good eye. Once he saw that I was still bound, he continued with his task.

I brought my wrists to my mouth and began biting on the cord. It was stiff and wiry, and tasted of oil, and I could hardly get a purchase. The feeling of sickness came over me again, and I had to lower my head. I thought of Father alone in the house, and Jimmy and Mrs Perrin. When would they get word? In a day or two? Would Father come and collect me himself? How many times had he gone on such trips to view the dead, always someone else's child or loved one, someone else's tragedy?

In the gully below, the horse let out another scream, and Devlin once more let Ewan down to go and look.

He had planned everything well. What would people say? That Darby had hanged himself in his old parish; that the coroner's daughter and assistant were killed in a carriage accident on a stormy evening. Perhaps Coogan could convince them of what we had told him, unless Devlin had plans for him as well.

Once more he took up Ewan and dragged him to the verge. I rolled on to my side so I wouldn't have to see. I tried to push myself up, but still wasn't strong enough, and the effort made my stomach heave. Something dug into my hip. A stone perhaps. No, it was in my pocket: Devlin's glass eye. Did he know that it was with me? If they found that later, would it be enough to raise suspicion?

Father would come out here, even in his grief. He would not examine me himself, but he would insist that someone do it — the Wicklow coroner perhaps. I had to show them something: bite my palm, or rip my clothes, or chafe my wrists. The cord was tight, but I did my best to rub my hands back and forth. I could feel little effect, and besides, how could they be sure that any injury was not caused by the fall?

The buttercups dotted in the verge continued to quiver in the wind. I reached both my hands out to pluck one, placed it in my mouth, and tried to swallow it whole. It stuck in my throat, but, though I coughed several times, I was able to get it down. I picked another and swallowed that as well. Then reached out for a third.

A hand gripped my shoulder. Devlin pulled me over and sat me up, and I could see that he had left Ewan on the verge of the road. He cupped my chin and squinted at me. 'What are you doing?'

I tried to lift my bound wrists to push him away, but hadn't the strength.

He shook my face. 'I said, what are you doing?'

I looked at him in his good eye, and spoke in a voice I could barely hear myself. 'I am leaving him something.'

He frowned, and looked down at my mouth. 'What do you mean?'

'It is a message for my father.'

He dragged me to my knees and pushed an index finger into my mouth, hooking his thumb under my jaw. His jagged fingernail scraped over my tongue and the roof of my mouth, and I could taste salt on his skin. I bit down, felt the bone twist beneath his finger, the warmth of his blood, and he wrenched his hand away with an angry cry.

Devlin grabbed the front of my dress. He had raised his fist and was ready to strike when a shot rang out. He turned his head sharply as if startled. His grip loosened, and when he looked back at me his drooping eyelid was just a tattered piece of skin, hanging torn and ragged. The hair above his temple was matted in blood, which began to flow over his cheek in a stream. His good eye swivelled, as if trying to observe what had happened, and then he toppled over, without lifting his arms to break his fall.

16

Professor Reeves and his coachman laid Ewan on one of the seats, wrapped me in coats and placed me on the other. The professor knelt in the space between, a cloth pressed against the wound on Ewan's head, which was still seeping. Two pistols lay on the carriage floor amid the grit and muddy shoe prints — the professor's, and the one retrieved from Devlin's body. Ewan was so pale, except for streaks of red on his face from where the blood had been wiped away. For a moment his eyes opened. He frowned and tried to raise his head. The professor told him to settle, but Ewan looked about until his eyes met with mine. He quietened, let a breath out through his mouth, and closed his eyes again.

I couldn't get warm, and may have drifted off once or twice during the short, swaying journey. The wheels crunched through a winding gravel driveway, and I saw the domed roof of the observatory through the trees, the windows of its equatorial room lit in the grey afternoon. I was able to walk, so the elderly housekeeper, Miss Pike, assisted me into the house, while Ewan was carried to another room. She took my dress, said that she would wash it, and gave me a nightgown to wear — rather old-fashioned, but clean and dry.

I sat huddled by the fire in a tartan blanket that smelled of tobacco while she washed the

341

blood from my hair with a bowl of warm water. She tutted every now and again, though I didn't ask if that was from the sight of the wound or just the tangles.

I sipped from a glass of water containing drops of laudanum, and after a while the aches drained from my body. 'I don't think I was able to properly thank the professor.'

'You can do so later,' the housekeeper said. 'He has gone to Saggart to see the magistrate.'

'Is Mr Caulfeild here?'

She said no, which didn't surprise me. The weather had not lent itself to astral study. But she added, 'That young man never stays a minute more than he has to.'

'I thought that he roomed here while assisting the professor.'

'Oh, no. His carriage is always ready to take him back to the city at a moment's notice.'

The hairbrush caught in a knot, and I winced as she tugged at my wound. I felt a soreness in my throat, which I assumed came from the sap of the flowers. Perhaps they would make me ill, but so far there were no other symptoms. The rain on the window and warmth from the fire were soothing, and after I had nearly nodded to sleep twice, Miss Pike said, 'Would you like to rest in the bed, my dear?'

'I must find out if Ewan is recovering.'

She told me that she would check on him, and took my wet clothes from the room. I gathered my knees beneath the blanket, and gingerly felt the back of my head. There was a bump, not too big but very tender. My hair felt damp and clean, and when I looked at the tips of my fingers there was no sign of blood. The housekeeper returned with another candle and a glass of warm milk. She said that Ewan had recovered his senses for a time, and had been able to speak with the professor. He was dry, warm and resting.

'I would like to see him.'

'Not now. Not dressed like this,' she said. 'Sleep for a few hours, and we'll see then if you're both well enough for some supper.'

The sheets in the bed were stiff and cold, as though they'd been unused for quite a while. I fell asleep quickly, but would wake whenever I rolled on to the sore part of my head. The flames ebbed and the embers lost their glow. At one point, I heard the rattle of carriage wheels, but when I went to the window I couldn't see anything. It must have been early evening, though it was difficult to tell in the heavy rain. I placed another log on the fire, and went back to bed.

When I woke again, the room was gloomy. My dress and stockings had been left hanging over a chair, and the fire had been stoked. I rose, feeling light-headed and hungry, and changed back into my own clothes, which still bore some stains in the folds of the cotton. I realized that I had eaten nothing since leaving Dublin the day before. Rev Coogan had only offered me a whiskey when I arrived at the vicarage, and the fare at the inn had not been tempting. There was no bell cord to summon the housekeeper, so I went looking for her. She hadn't returned my muddy shoes, and I slipped noiselessly through the house in stockinged feet. Our rooms were located in a large and disused wing. Some of the doors stood open, revealing chambers with closed windows and bare floorboards, all silent and still. One of the doors was ajar, with a glimmer of firelight in the gap.

Ewan lay in a bed much like mine, the covers pulled up to his chest, and his arms resting on top. He wore a white shirt that wasn't his own, opened at the neck. His face tilted towards the hearth. A gust rattled the window frame, and a draught crept through the room, so I closed the shutters, slipping the brass hook into place. I stood by Ewan's bedside, and placed my fingers on his. Some colour had returned to his cheeks. The bruising had spread from his temple to his jaw. He shifted slightly. His eyes scrunched in pain, and I leaned over to kiss his forehead. His skin felt cool and clammy beneath a flat curl of hair, but when I drew away his features settled and his breathing was steady.

Downstairs, there was no sign of the housekeeper or any other maid. I recognized some of the passages, and found my way to the drawing room, which seemed smaller than I remembered. On the night of the reception it had been filled with guests and conversation; now most of the armchairs were covered in dust sheets. A small side table held an opened bottle of Malaga wine and a glass tumbler, smudged thumb-prints visible in the firelight. The orrery in the corner had been set in motion, all the planets silently orbiting the brass sphere. I watched them twirl for a few moments, and

344

something struck me. The path of Mercury was smooth and constant, when before it had lagged every half-rotation. I reached in and placed my finger against Jupiter, and the whole mechanism stopped. Time stood still, until I withdrew my hand and the planets resumed their courses. In the curved reflection of the sun, I saw a figure standing in the doorway behind me.

Miss Pike had my shoes in her hand, the leather polished and gleaming. 'I went to your room to look for you,' she said.

I thanked her, took the shoes and sat by the fire to put them on. She said that the professor had returned from Saggart, and was about to have some supper. 'He asked for you to join him.'

In the dining room, two places had been set on the corner of a long table, lit by silver candelabra and a warm fire. Thick red drapes covered the windows, and the rain outside continued to patter. Reeves rose from his seat when I entered. He said, 'Miss Lawless, I am so pleased to see you up and abroad.' He held a chair for me to sit down. The fare on the table was simple: soda bread and slices of cheese, and a bowl of red apples, the poor summer shown in their pale wrinkled skins.

Miss Pike brought in a tureen of broth, and served us both before withdrawing. The soup was rich and steaming, and with the first sip I began to feel better.

'I never had a chance to thank you for what you did on the road,' I said. 'Mr Weir and I were so fortunate.'

'There is no need for thanks.' He took a slice of soda bread from a plate, and broke it into his soup. 'I was able to speak with Mr Weir about what happened. What a harrowing time you have had.'

I was about to demur, but really it could not be denied. 'And for you as well,' I said.

He paused and frowned. 'How so?'

'To shoot a man. In any circumstances, it must be distressing.'

He considered this, and said, 'If I had delayed at all he would have hurt you. It was an easy decision to make.'

'Well, I am very grateful.' A gust of wind caused some smoke to billow from the fireplace, and all the candles wavered. 'How did you come to be on the road?'

'We were on our way back from town when my driver heard the gunshot. These hills have always been a hideaway for bandits and ribbon-men. It is why I keep a pistol hidden in the armrest.'

'Did you ever have cause to use it before?'

Reeves blew on a spoonful of soup. He placed it in his mouth and swallowed before speaking. 'No. To be honest, I was surprised that the shot found its target.'

'What happened to the body?'

He looked at me for a moment, and smiled. 'You are always enquiring.'

I bowed my head. 'I cannot seem to help it.'

He said that once Ewan and I had been brought back to the observatory, he and his coachman had retrieved Devlin and brought him

346

to Saggart. They sought out the magistrate, but he was not at home, so they left the body at a nearby inn with instructions for the innkeeper.

'Mr Weir told me that you had come to Wicklow without your father's knowledge.'

I was embarrassed to hear my own actions described, to think again of the terrible worry I must have caused him.

But Reeves continued without admonishment. 'So I arranged for a messenger to go to Dublin, to let him know that you are safe and well.'

'Oh, thank you.'

'The weather is still too treacherous for you to make the journey tonight. If Mr Weir is recovered in the morning, my coachman will take you back to Rutland Square.'

The thought of seeing Father was so comforting, just to rest my head beneath his chin. He would probably confine me to the house for a year, but I didn't mind.

'What of the magistrate?' I said. 'He will wish to speak with us. And the local coroner will demand an inquest.'

'All that matters at the moment is your recuperation. The best place for that is at home. If the inquiries of the magistrate or coroner are delayed, so be it.'

'Father would be the first to say that the proper procedures should be followed.'

'I suspect that in this case, he will see reason.'

Reeves poured himself some more claret, and offered me a glass, but I could still feel a soreness in my head, and I persevered with water. The professor only sipped at his wine, but did so frequently enough that he soon had to fill his glass again. Perhaps the stresses of the day had affected him more than he cared to admit.

'Miss Lawless, I have been considering something.'

He remained silent for a moment, and I placed my spoon on the plate.

'I would not wish for your name to be associated with the events of the past few days,' he said.

'How do you mean?'

'You know the nature of the Brethren: their malice, the cruelty they showed to the memory of your mother. If you are connected at all with the death of their leader, they may turn their spiteful eyes towards you.'

'Perhaps,' I said. 'Unfortunately, it is too late to change that.'

He smoothed a ruffle in the tablecloth beside his glass. 'But is it? What if you were to go home rest and recover and withdraw from public gaze? I can tell the magistrate that my driver was attacked on the roadway by a crazed man. We shall not mention you or Mr Weir. Let the coroner in Manor Kilbride declare that Mr Darby hanged himself. What difference would it make? Two wicked men have met their just ends; you are home and safe with your father, and no more is said of the affair.'

The tablecloth was smooth, but he continued to press it with the tips of his fingers.

'I couldn't possibly ask you to do that,' I said.

'I am the one proposing it.'

'Reverend Coogan saw me in the village, as did many others.'

'I shall write to the Reverend. I am sure that he would be discreet if he knew that your well-being was at stake.'

'But whatever Mr Darby has done, it is only fair that people know the circumstances of his death. The truth is the most important thing.'

'We shall know the truth. You and I, and Mr Weir, and your father. That is enough.' Reeves saw that I was about to speak again, and he held up his hand. 'I know that this may go against your principles, Miss Lawless, but it will keep you and your family safe. Please consider it.' He smiled again, though his eyes didn't change shape. I told him that I would, and he poured himself another glass of wine.

'It is very admirable that you are guided by what is true,' he said. A drop ran down the outside of the glass. He smeared it with his little finger and dabbed his tongue. 'An irony, perhaps, that Mr Darby should benefit.'

'Why is that?'

'All he ever did was peddle falsehood.'

Before, I would have agreed, but I felt some compunction not to speak ill of the murdered.

'Perhaps he believed that what he preached was the truth.'

'Nonsense.' Reeves frowned slightly, and glanced at me. Perhaps he had placed more emphasis than intended. 'Even if that were so, on what did he base this truth? Divine revelation. Archaic texts. Scriptural secrets of such importance that only the elect can escape perpetual torment.' Reeves had looked away from me, his eyes fixed on the hearth. 'Imagine what it must be to think like that,' he said. 'To look upon people strolling in a park, young men and women with their arms linked, children chasing each other through the pathways, and see nothing but lost souls; not only that, to relish the prospect of their torture.' He made a face as if he had tasted something rotten, and took another sip of wine. 'Imagine the arrogance to believe that a god would grant salvation to his wretched sect alone — a tiny number on a small island, on a solitary globe in the vast heavens.'

I said that every religion was guilty of that conceit, but Reeves wasn't listening.

'They contribute nothing,' he said. 'They are like a canker. The spirit that Mr Darby fostered was one of ignorance and censure, where enquiry and creativity and joy could only wither. What do you see when you picture his followers, Miss Lawless?'

I guessed that the question was rhetorical, and he soon provided his own answer.

'I see an old man on his death bed, racked by despair, convinced that some petty lapse has condemned him to the fire. Or a young woman berating and scourging herself for a yearning that is perfectly natural and pure. I see only suffering because of Mr Darby's delusions.'

'Professor, there are still good people in the city who will not be swayed.'

'That is exactly the complacency I fear. Men of the Brethren are sitting on King's Bench, on hospital boards and in science academies. Do you not find it disheartening, Miss Lawless? All of Europe basking in enlightenment, and Dublin facing another dark age.'

I had not taken a sip of broth for some time, and found that it had grown cold. Despite sleeping a few hours, I felt weary and sore, and wished to return to the room.

Reeves had finished his soup as well, but he still drank the wine. 'If news reaches the city that Darby was murdered, I see him being lauded as some hounded martyr.' He was silent for a moment, and only continued when I met his eye. 'But imagine if his death is ruled a suicide. His followers would have to admit that they had been deceived. Only a man who had lost his faith, or had none to begin with, a man who had no fear of God's punishment, could take his own life. He would be called a hypocrite, and we could say that their supposed fraternity was founded on a lie.'

Reeves may have forgotten his reference to my own mother's death minutes before, and also, it seemed, his primary concern for my welfare.

'Professor, I do not intend to draw a veil over what has happened.'

'Why not?'

'There are still too many questions. I wish to know why Devlin tracked down Mr Darby, and why he killed him. If he was acting on behalf of someone in the Brethren, or if he had a motive of his own.'

'What does that matter now?'

'I have encountered Devlin before,' I said. 'Prowling in the wards of the Rotunda on the night that Emilie Casey died. And he was known to Edith Gould, for she had drawn his lazy eye in her sketchbook. I am sure that the murder of Mr Darby was not his first crime.'

'He can no longer trouble anyone. Whatever he has done, surely you can say that he has received his punishment.'

I folded my napkin on the table. 'Perhaps. But I still want to know why. As I said, I cannot seem to help myself.'

The professor's chair creaked as he leaned back, one elbow on the armrest, his other hand stretched out to twirl the stem of his wineglass. The door opened, and Miss Pike came in to clear away the tureen and our soup bowls. I used her interruption to say, 'I shall think about what you have said, Professor. We can discuss it again in the morning. Now I am rather tired.'

We rose together, and he said, 'Miss Pike will show you back to your room.'

'I know the way. I very much enjoyed our supper, and thank you again for all that you did today.'

He answered with a small bow, and took his seat without waiting for me to leave. Candles were lit in the hallways, and I found my way back to the guest wing. I opened Ewan's door by a crack. The fire burned brightly. He still lay beneath the covers, his face to one side, and I began to pull the door closed again.

'Abigail?'

'Yes,' I said, walking in to stand by the bed. He squinted up at me with his hair tousled, as if I had woken him from a deep slumber.

'You are not hurt?' he said.

I told him that I was fine. 'A few aches and

bruises. What about you?'

He rubbed his fingers over his eyes. 'My head feels as if it is in two halves, but better than it was.'

'Do you know of all that happened?'

'Yes,' he said. Reeves had told him.

He reached for a tumbler of water on a side table, and I helped him take a drink. The only chair in the room was a large armchair by the fire, so I sat on the edge of his bed.

I said, 'Are you warm enough?'

'Too warm if anything. I may be getting a fever.'

I placed my palm on his forehead. He didn't have a temperature, and I began to take my hand away, but he said, 'Don't. Your fingers are cool.'

He closed his eyes, and I remained leaning over him until his breathing became steady. My thumb rested against his temple, and I began to rub it gently.

I told him that Professor Reeves would take us home in the morning, and described our conversation over supper. 'When you spoke to Reeves earlier,' I said, 'did he suggest to you that we conceal the truth about Darby's hanging?'

I felt his brow stir beneath my hand, and he opened one eye. 'He did not mention the hanging at all. I don't believe that I brought it up.'

'You must have.'

'The professor only asked about Devlin. Whether he had spoken to us on the road; if anyone else had seen him. We did not discuss Mr Darby.'

'You were half unconscious. You must not remember.'

His eyes closed again, 'Perhaps. What was it that Reeves suggested?'

I told him, and after a moment Ewan said, 'I cannot see your father agreeing to that.'

'Nor can I.'

We stayed together in silence as the fire crackled and the wind whistled in the chimney stack. Ewan fell asleep. I considered fetching a blanket to curl up in the armchair, but enough scandal would dog me without spending the night in the room of a young man.

The fire in my own chamber had dwindled. I could tell that Miss Pike had been in again. She had folded the nightgown on my bed. I didn't want to change clothes, and lay on the bedcovers, watching the clock tick past ten. My weariness came from aches in my muscles. Sleep was still a long way off. I rose to close the window shutters. The dome of the observatory jutted from the front of the house, and I could just about see it looming to my right. Candlelight flickered in the windows of the turret, and I wondered at Reeves working on such a foul night. I thought back to our conversation over supper. I was sure that the professor had been first to mention Darby's hanging. *Let the coroner in Manor Kilbride declare that Mr Darby hanged himself*, he had said. *What difference would it make?*

I lit a candle from the embers, and left the room. Down below, there were no lights in the dining room, no sign of Miss Pike. She had

354

probably retired for the evening. I followed the narrow passages that led to the equatorial room. The light from my candle was lost in the curve of the spiral staircase, and I could only see a few steps at a time. At the top, the door to Professor Reeves's workroom stood open. I knocked but there was no answer. A low fire burned in the hearth, but there was no other light, and all I could hear was the rain resounding in the dome overhead. Through the four compass-point windows I could see the lines of the landscape in the last of the gloaming. From here, the professor could look down upon the foothills of Dublin and the roads leading to Saggart, and on the other side the dark Wicklow mountains huddled beneath the clouds. On a desk near the fireplace, a wooden box sat on the leather inlay. I brought the candle close and saw a brass plaque on the lid: 'Givens Gunsmiths'. Inside, the box was empty. From the size and contours of the red baize mounts, it had held two pistols. Both were missing. Reeves had said that he kept one in the armrest of his coach, but I remembered the two pistols lying on the muddy carriage floor: one of them Reeves's, the other retrieved from Devlin's body. Both looked exactly the same.

I went downstairs again, and turned into the passage that led away from the living quarters, to the arched door with the callipers engraved in the capstone. At the gathering, I had thought the room belonged to James Caulfeild, but I believed Miss Pike when she said that he never stayed at the observatory. No hint of light came from the keyhole, so I pushed the door open without knocking.

Cold cinders lay in the hearth, and a fire-iron leaned against the black metal hood. The cloth that had covered the birdcage lay in a heap on the floor, and the canary sat on its perch, barely moving. In the corner, the bed was unmade, its sheets in a tangle, and the pillowcase stained yellow. Someone had stayed here recently. Not the housekeeper or any other maid. It was a man's room, perhaps the professor's coachman, but the bookcases by the wall and paraphernalia on the desk made me doubt that. I looked in one of the wardrobes. A few jackets were hanging from a pole, their fabrics faded and rumpled and a few years out of date — clothes that James would never wear.

I opened a drawer in the desk: just a pile of papers and a magnifying glass. Near the top, I saw the sheet with the odd message repeated: *In this Year of Our Lord, Eighteen Hundred and Froze to Death*. It was not Mr Caulfeild's handwriting as I had assumed before, but rather an attempt to mimic it. The drawer beneath held the trappings of a clockmaker: tiny screws and gears that rattled in their cubbies, fine tools and tweezers. In the third drawer, I could see little except the head of a flower. It was thick and solid, and I held it against the light. Folds of brown leather had been sewn together to make a rosette, exactly like the one that had been missing from Edith's shoe. I looked at the bed again. This was where her killer lived.

The canary opened its wings and flitted about

the cage, and I turned around. Professor Reeves was standing in the doorway. How long he had been there I couldn't tell. The light from my candle barely reached him, and his face looked pale against his dark suit. I backed further into the room. It was narrow and cluttered, and my leg touched the corner of the bed. His eyes drifted across the fireplace, the wardrobe and desk, and finally he fixed on the rosette in my hand.

He didn't say a word as he stepped into the room, a pistol held low by his side. At first he moved towards me, but he stopped at the desk, brushing the top with his fingertips as if checking for dust.

'You knew, professor,' I said. 'You knew that he was here all along.' Others had been speaking to me about Devlin, I just hadn't realized: the protégé, the reckless young man expelled from Trinity and taken in at the observatory. 'Your former assistant never left you.'

He glanced at me briefly, and then nudged some of the papers with the muzzle of his gun. The hammer was already drawn back, and the metal sounded heavy as it scraped over the wood.

'What about James Caulfeild?'

Reeves found a sheet of scrawled mathematical equations, and he scrutinized it for a few seconds before setting it aside. He spoke quietly, as if to himself. 'That idler and dilettante? He was only here as a favour to his father. Though we found a use for him in the end.'

I looked at the rosette in my palm. Edith

thought she was meeting James that night, I was sure of it. She had rejected Darby, and would not have risked all to leave her house for anyone else. But why did she think that James was waiting? 'Devlin was the one that brought her messages, wasn't he? Enough that Edith could sketch his eye from memory so perfectly. That was why he practised James's handwriting. You tricked her, and on the night, she stepped into Mr Devlin's carriage without a backward glance.'

The professor smiled. Lines of shadow shifted about his face. 'I had a feeling that you would comprehend.'

I pictured Edith on that midnight journey, her face flushed with excitement and perhaps a little anxiety, her fingers clasped together, her hood raised. How her heart must have dropped when she realized that Devlin had deceived her, the fear and confusion, the terror when he turned on her, covered her mouth and brought her to the reservoir. She must have felt so helpless and degraded, so utterly alone.

I did not speak, but as Professor Reeves regarded me, his smile faded. He said, 'It was not an easy decision. We knew that for the most part Miss Gould was innocent.'

'She was entirely innocent.'

'She was a member of the Brethren.'

'Only because of her parents.'

'Come, Miss Lawless. She was free to choose her path in life, just as you have chosen yours.'

'That is not the case.' Perhaps a young man had leeway to defy his parents; a young woman had none. Edith believed that she was forsaking

358

all she had ever known by stepping into that carriage. 'And what of Miss Casey? She did not choose to be deserted and cast out.'

'I agree entirely,' Reeves said. 'I only wished to expose her mistreatment.'

'By having her killed?'

His brow creased in irritation. 'She was due to hang anyway. Why not make her death count for something? I was naive enough to think the scandal might splinter their congregation.' He passed the pistol from one hand to the other, as if bothered by its weight, and he pointed it at me briefly. 'It was your father who helped conceal her murder, under some duress perhaps. And yet you claimed that we had no need to fear the Brethren's influence.'

He inserted a finger in his fob pocket, and rummaged about as if scratching an itch. He withdrew Devlin's glass eye and tossed it on the table. It landed with a clack, and rolled on to its flat side so the iris stared at the ceiling. I patted my own empty pocket. Miss Pike must have found it when cleaning my dress.

'He arrived back here last night, drenched and angry. It was the one thing he said about you, Miss Lawless: you could always be found in places that you were not supposed to be.' Reeves opened his arms to gesture at the room, as if to say the same was true again. 'Something had to be done, he said. You could not be reasoned with. He kept pushing the idea of the carriage accident again and again. But I told him. I said your contempt for Darby and the Brethren might rival our own, that you could be convinced to remain silent for the sake of the city, for the sake of progress.'

'It appears that he was not persuaded.'

'When Devlin set his mind on something, I could do little to stop him. But I knew this time he was wrong. Why had we gone to all this trouble to rid ourselves of the Brethren if not for people like you, Miss Lawless?'

He looked at the gun in his hand, and reached towards the hammer, I thought at first to ease it down, but all he did was ensure that it was cocked fully.

'I could not rest,' he said. 'I went out hoping that it wasn't too late. I found the branch on the roadside, the muddy carriage tracks. Then the gunshot rang out, and there you were, struggling at the edge of the gorge. I had to choose. Devlin had been loyal and ever willing, but with Darby dead, he had served his purpose.' He regarded me critically. 'I hope that I shall not regret my decision.'

Wax dripped down the side of my candle and ran over my thumb. I felt a slight sting before it cooled and congealed. The candle was the only light in the room, and Reeves would only have one shot. If he missed, the pistol would be an encumbrance more than anything. He would have to miss, though.

'What do you wish from me? A promise that I will remain silent?'

'More than that. You can promise anything now; but what about when you and Mr Weir are home and safe in the parlour with your father? You cannot merely humour me. You must believe that what I did was right.'

I held his eye. He did not waver or look away, and seemed entirely in earnest.

'And how would you test my faith?'

'I suppose that is the dilemma.'

A gust rattled in the chimney-box, and some of the cinders shifted. The canary took flight in its cage once more, its wings fluttering against the wire. I gripped the rosette from Edith's shoe, squeezing it in my hand.

He said, 'Well?'

'You are not rational, Professor Reeves.'

He blinked once. 'Pardon me?'

'You are wicked. Your reasoning has made you callous and deceitful. You are worse than any Brethren member, certainly more dangerous. Did you really expect me to remain silent about what you have done? Whatever happens here, you will be found out. You will be captured and punished. It would have been better for you to leave me on the road, for I will not help you now.'

The professor stood still as he listened. He didn't sigh or twitch his hands. When I was finished, he began to nod.

'Do you know the most important difference between men and women of science, Miss Lawless, and men and women of faith?'

He raised the pistol, and levelled it at my head.

'A man of science can admit when he has blundered.'

I crouched down and threw the candle. The flame dragged and guttered in the air, and Reeves used his pistol to bat it against the wall.

The candle was extinguished, except for the red glow of the wick, and the room was plunged into darkness. Reeves didn't fire, and I was reluctant to barge past, for he couldn't fail to hit me at such close quarters. I could not discern his outline, and since he had been watching me hold the candle, I hoped his vision was even worse. There was no sound of footsteps. He was not marching through the room to seek me out, so I stayed perfectly still, afraid that any noise might draw his fire. A pillow jutted over the edge of the bed. I picked it up and tossed it against the opposite wall. It landed and tumbled with soft thuds, but Reeves did not react.

'Do you think that you have left the world a better place than you found it, Miss Lawless?' he said. 'In the end, is that all one can hope for?'

His voice had not come from where I expected. It seemed closer to the door, as if he planned to cut off any escape.

'Do you remember when we spoke of the age of the earth? Those aeons of time that existed before you were born? You are certain they were real, aren't you? Even though you have no sense of them, no memory or experience.' I heard the floorboards creak, and I slid towards the bottom of the bed. 'What is there to fear, then, if that oblivion is all that awaits you?'

I felt beneath the bed for anything. A slat of wood, even a chamber pot.

'I can see the outline of the window,' he said. 'And the corner of the bed. But do not worry about the darkness, Abigail. I cannot miss from here.'

The muzzle flash lit the room for a quarter-second, and a pale image hung in the blackness like the projection of a *camera obscura*. The professor was closer than I imagined. He loomed above me with his elbow bent and his eyes scrunched shut, the gun pointed at his own temple. I covered my face and turned my head, but still saw his white grimace against my eyelids. The sound of the gunshot was followed by his collapse, and the clatter of the pistol on the floorboards.

17

The workman in Rutland Park let down the handles of his barrow, wiped his brow, and lifted his face towards the sun. He went from tree to tree, picking out lamps made of hooped wood and coloured paper, and hanging them from the lowest branches. Above him, the dry, lingering mist had been scattered into twirling trails of pink and lilac, as if dispersed by a great wind, and people basked in the first days of an Indian summer. Clarissa entered by the eastern gate, and came to join me on the bench. She wore a muslin gown of light yellow, the sleeves rather short, and the neck low cut.

When she sat beside me, I said, 'Are you not a little chilly?' Though the day was bright, it was mid-September, and still quite cool.

'I have been waiting to wear this dress since the start of summer, and may not get another chance,' she said. 'I am determined to be warm.'

She suggested that we stroll around the park, and held my arm a little tighter than usual.

'Where is Mr Weir today?' she said.

'He is at home packing. His ship leaves for Liverpool this afternoon.'

'Oh dear. Shall you miss him terribly?'

'Hush,' I said, pushing my elbow against hers.

An elderly couple passed us by. We skirted the shrubbery to make room on the path. The gentleman doffed his hat to us with a smile, but his wife fixed on me with narrow eyes and pulled on his arm in reproach. He replaced his hat, unsure of his transgression, and they carried on. Clarissa made certain to meet the woman's gaze with her shoulders straight and chin held high. Once they had gone a few steps, she leaned towards me, and said, 'You have scandalized the whole city, Abby. It is quite delicious.'

Weeks had passed since Ewan and I returned from the observatory. We had recovered fully, and Father and I had moved through stages of relief and recrimination, tears and contrition, embraces and assurances. On the night that Reeves died, I had stayed with Ewan until morning, waiting for the magistrate to arrive. We had feared that Miss Pike or the coachman might have turned against us, but they were both in shock, and we had travelled back to Dublin the following day. The Wicklow coroner and I became well acquainted. I was summoned to three inquests in quick succession, with much of my testimony printed in the Dublin papers, and at home Clarissa had pestered me for every grisly detail.

We turned through a copse of trees and out into the central lawns. Children played in the sun, boys in their shirtsleeves and girls making the hems of their petticoats grubby. More workmen could be seen here and there painting railings, or festooning branches. The Sunday Evening Promenade had been reinstated, and everyone was anxious to take advantage of the change in weather. Clarissa in particular. It was pleasant to hear her talk of small things, of dressmakers and hairdressers and the intrigues of her companions. As we walked, a toddler crossed the path before us, the strings of her bonnet undone, and some gravel clutched in her hands. It was young Lucia Nesham, and I watched her move towards a bench where the maid Martha was sitting with her mistress. Darby's sister-in-law was no longer dressed in the garb of the Brethren. She wore an olive green walking-gown, the cuffs and neckline trimmed with white lace. Lucia dropped the gravel into a small pile that she was making, and turned about to fetch some more.

I asked Clarissa to wait, and I went to stand before them. Martha saw my approach, but Mrs Nesham only lifted her head when my shadow fell across the bench. She looked up at me, raising her hand to shield her eyes.

I said, 'May I speak with you?'

She told Martha to check on Lucia, and I took the maid's seat. I had forgotten how young Mrs Nesham was, only a few years older than Clarissa and me. The austere cloaks had made her appear older.

'I am sorry for what happened to Mr Darby,' I said.

She didn't reply.

'How have his followers taken the news?'

She ran her finger along the wrought-iron armrest. 'They no longer meet in my house, so I am not sure what they intend to do. Mr Nesham and I may return to Reverend Egan's congregation.'

'I am sure he would be glad.'

She noticed Clarissa standing on the path and watched her for a moment. A young boy had offered her a flower, and Clarissa bent down to cup his cheek.

'I never saw the house in which my sister lived,' Mrs Nesham said.

That was all, but I assumed she wanted to know my impressions of it.

'It was rather remote and run-down,' I said.

She pursed her lips and looked away.

'But only when I saw it. I am sure that it was once a cosy home.'

'Was there a garden?'

'Yes. Quite wild now. It overlooked a valley in the mountains. Actually, it was rather beautiful.'

A lock of dark hair came loose beneath her bonnet, and fell across her eyes. It fluttered gently in the breeze.

'How did you know Mr Devlin?' I said.

Her head remained still, and she slowly blinked. 'Only as an imposter in the church.'

'When Mr Darby asked Devlin who had sent him to Manor Kilbride, he said an odd thing. He said, 'Catherine Shaw sent me, and Emilie, and Edith.' Why do you think that he would mention your sister's name?'

'I do not know.'

'Then Darby wanted to know how I had tracked him down. He said, 'Only my sister-in-law knows I'm here. And you would be the last person she would tell.''

She pushed the strand of hair beneath her bonnet. 'Yes, he told me where he intended to hide. What of it?'

'Did you tell Devlin?'

She took a long breath, as if about to speak, but then remained silent.

'But what I wonder most of all,' I said, 'is how Devlin got hold of the hook that he placed in Edith's hand? How was it removed from Mr Darby's coat, and another sewn in its place without his knowledge? Only someone in your household could have arranged that.'

Mrs Nesham turned her dark eyes upon me. 'Do you wish to accuse me of something, Miss Lawless?'

'No,' I said. 'That evidence amounts to little. I just wanted to tell you what I know.'

Across the paths, Lucia waved and called out to her mother from behind some shrubs.

'You do not have a sister, Miss Lawless?'

'I do not.'

She nodded. 'All my life, I could not recall a time that she was not at my side. We shared a room, we shared clothes and books. She was my only and constant companion, yet she was all I ever needed.' Mrs Nesham picked a leaf from the slats and let it fall to the ground. 'Mr Darby took her away to the mountains and she died.'

She rose and departed without another word. Martha noticed her mistress walking in the direction of their home. The maid took Lucia by the hand, and they followed in her wake.

I rejoined Clarissa on the path, and we continued on.

She said, 'What did you say to her?'

'I just gave her my condolences.'

As we passed in front of Charlemont House, a

footman hurried from the door. He entered the park, bowed to us both, and then turned to Clarissa. 'From Mr Caulfeild,' he said, handing her a note.

She glanced at me, broke the seal and began to read. I surveyed the windows of the townhouse. Was James up there, looking down on us? After a moment, Clarissa showed me the note. It was an invitation to a gathering at Marino House the next weekend, addressed to Clarissa alone. How she would have longed for such an invitation a few weeks ago. Perhaps she still did.

She returned the note to the messenger. 'Please give my apologies to Mr Caulfeild,' she said, taking my arm. 'Tell him that I shall be engaged in needlework with Miss Lawless.'

After another circuit of the park, Clarissa said that she would have to run home for a shawl. She kissed my cheek, and we agreed to meet again tomorrow. I hurried between the carriages on the street, and saw a cabbie parked outside our house. Jimmy was in the parlour, cleaning out the fireplace, a streak of soot on his chin.

'Has the cab been here long?' I asked.

He said only a short while. 'I shall be helping Mr Weir with his trunk in a minute.'

Upstairs, Mrs Perrin stood on the threshold of Ewan's room, giving him a parcel of hard cheese and sliced meat for his journey. It was rather large, and he was having trouble fitting it into his trunk.

I continued to my room, fetched a new edition of Maria Edgeworth's latest that I had tied in a ribbon, and returned to the hallway.

From the door to his room, I said, 'I almost forgot, Mr Weir. A gift for Hannah.'

He smiled at me as he took it, ran his finger over the letters on the binding, then placed it on top of his clothes in the trunk.

'I don't know how I shall close it now.'

Mrs Perrin said, 'Well, I must check on the supper, so I shall leave you to it.'

Ewan shut the lid and pushed down upon it, but the catches were still inches from their clasps.

'Why are you bringing so much? You will be back for the new term in a month or two.'

'I am just taking what I need.'

'Are you sure you need those shoes?'

'I like those shoes.'

He sat on the lid, which improved matters, but still not quite enough.

'Make room,' I said, and I sat beside him. Our combined weight did the trick, and we each worked on a clasp, clicking them into place, and smiling together at our small triumph.

I did not want him to go. Even if it was only for a short time. I would miss his presence in the house, the company he gave to my father, his playful manner with Jimmy. I would miss seeing him at the breakfast table, or traipsing through the yard towards the workrooms, or reading by the fire in the parlour. Many times he had risked his well-being and reputation for me, and I knew in that moment that whatever might happen, I would not forget.

Our shoulders were touching, and I leaned

over to kiss the corner of his mouth. He remained still at first, then pressed his face closer. His fingers moved over mine, and we remained sitting like that with our lips touching for several seconds.

Jimmy's footsteps sounded on the landing. 'Ewan,' he called. 'The cabbie says if you don't come now he's going without you.'

We parted and stood up and stepped away from the trunk just as Jimmy pushed open the door and stuck his head in.

'Did you hear me?'

'Yes, thank you.'

Jimmy came in and grabbed one handle.

Ewan had remained looking at me. He fixed a button on his waistcoat, and said, 'I shall write.'

I smiled and said, 'Yes, I know.'

He took the other side of the trunk, and I stayed in the room while they brought it downstairs, with many bumps and mild oaths. From the window, I watched them emerge on the front steps. The cabbie assisted with the trunk, and then climbed back up to his seat. Father came on to the steps. He shook Ewan's hand, and patted his shoulder, and they had a few words together. Before Ewan stepped into the cab, he looked up at the window. I raised my hand, and he smiled, then he disappeared beneath the roof, and pulled the door closed. The cabman set off at once. I stayed at the window and watched them rattle down the hill towards Sackville Street.

Father was still in the hallway leafing through some letters when I went downstairs. He looked at me over his spectacles. 'Now,' he said, 'you shall have the run of the house once again.'

'Yes, there is that.'

'Abigail, I shall be going to a demonstration in York Street on Sunday evening. You can accompany me if you like. 'On presentations of poison by nitrate of silver'. It should be quite stimulating.'

'I had hoped to attend the promenade this Sunday with Clarissa.'

'Ah,' he said, and he clasped his hands. 'That is even better.' He kissed my forehead as he passed me by, and then took the stairs to the basement.

I went to my room and shut the door. Kepler lay crouched on my bed, his tail swishing languidly back and forth. His eyes were fixed on the newcomer in the corner: the canary in its cage by the window. I sat beside Kepler and scratched beneath his chin. 'Leave poor Cavendish in peace,' I said. He closed his eyes and flattened his ears, but gently nipped at my finger when he'd had enough.

I opened a drawer in my dressing table, took out a pincushion, and removed each needle. I dug my thumb into its middle to leave an indentation, then went to my wardrobe to find the dress that I had worn in Wicklow weeks before. It was hanging at the back, still grimy with stains of blood and muck. I felt inside the pocket sewn behind the waistline, and took out Devlin's eye.

Flecks of gold in the dark green iris caught the sunlight. I breathed on the glass and polished it against my arm. It fitted neatly in the hollow of the pin-cushion. Newly mounted, I found space for it on the shelf above my desk, next to the skeletal hand in its glass jar. I stood up to admire them, and the eye stared back. They looked quite well together. The beginnings, perhaps, of an intriguing collection. Through the window I could see Father make his way along the garden path and past his workrooms. He unlatched the back gate and held it open, just as the cadaver cart trundled into the yard.

Acknowledgements

Thanks again to John Givens in the Gresham workshop for his careful reading and encouragement. Thanks also to fellow writers Serena Molloy, Caroline Madden, Joan Hayes, Antain McLoughlin, Oliver Murphy, Patrick O'Connor and Maura O'Brien for their input and ideas. Special thanks to Ian Flitcroft for sharing his expert and gory knowledge in eye surgery and anatomy.

Thanks to my agent Sam Copeland for his guidance, and to all at Doubleday Ireland and Transworld, in particular my editor Simon Taylor. Many thanks also to Vivien Thompson and Elizabeth Dobson for their fine-tuning of the text.

Finally, thanks to my family for their constant support.

We do hope that you have enjoyed reading this large print book.

Did you know that all of our titles are available for purchase?

We publish a wide range of high quality large print books including:
Romances, Mysteries, Classics
General Fiction
Non Fiction and Westerns

Special interest titles available in large print are:
The Little Oxford Dictionary
Music Book
Song Book
Hymn Book
Service Book

Also available from us courtesy of Oxford University Press:
Young Readers' Dictionary
(large print edition)
Young Readers' Thesaurus
(large print edition)

For further information or a free brochure, please contact us at:
Ulverscroft Large Print Books Ltd.,
The Green, Bradgate Road, Anstey,
Leicester, LE7 7FU, England.
Tel: (00 44) 0116 236 4325
Fax: (00 44) 0116 234 0205

Other titles published by Ulverscroft:

NEW BOY

Tracy Chevalier

Arriving at his fourth school in six years, diplomat's son Osei Kokote knows he needs an ally if he is to survive his first day — so he's lucky to hit it off with Dee, the most popular girl in school. But one student can't stand to witness this budding relationship: Ian decides to destroy the friendship between the black boy and the golden girl. By the end of the day, the school and its key players — teachers and pupils alike — will never be the same again ... The tragedy of *Othello* is transposed to a 1970s suburban Washington, D.C. schoolyard, where the kids practice a casual racism picked up from their parents and teachers. Watching over the shoulders of four eleven-year-olds, this is a story of friends torn apart by jealousy, bullying and betrayal.